MW01258029

ld be
that th
en
sts in the Sco
rliament a single
ian with the co
cency and gu
stand up to th
nse.
Our proud co
ot some Th
inpot dictato
ur elected
tives need
rememberin
the people,
ones they
mandate f
'We ne
the sect
from an
ment t
out fo

IN BRIEF

Protein Powder Pilferer Strikes

A spate of ram-raids at local sports shops steal thousands of pounds worth of body-building supplements:

Page 5

owies May Get otected Status

A baker in Torry has applied for PDO status for rowies and butteries, putting them on a par with Champagne:

Page 9

rdeen Examiner

ks with
vulnerable
just how
my father
r how we

SCRAPPED

sted.' Insiders say that the film
pulled because of cha

RE
says
ists
rs th
so
e b
ev
st

Stonehaven Drug Bust Nets £2m

A huge haul of cannabis,
fentanyl has

THIS
HOUSE
OF
BURNING
BONES

By Stuart MacBride

THE LOGAN McRAE NOVELS
Cold Granite
Dying Light
Broken Skin
Flesh House
Blind Eye
Dark Blood
Shatter the Bones
Close to the Bone
22 Dead Little Bodies
The Missing and the Dead
In the Cold Dark Ground
Now We Are Dead
The Blood Road
All That's Dead
This House of Burning Bones

THE OLDCASTLE NOVELS
Birthdays for the Dead
A Song for the Dying
A Dark So Deadly
The Coffinmaker's Garden
No Less the Devil
In a Place of Darkness

STANDALONE
The Dead of Winter

OTHER WORKS
Sawbones (a novella)
12 Days of Winter (a short-story collection)
Partners in Crime (two Logan and Steel short stories)
The 45% Hangover (a Logan and Steel novella)
The Completely Wholesome Adventures of Skeleton Bob (a picture book)

WRITING AS STUART B. MACBRIDE
Halfhead

Stuart MacBride

THIS HOUSE OF BURNING BONES

MACMILLAN

First published 2025 by Macmillan
an imprint of Pan Macmillan
The Smithson, 6 Briset Street, London EC1M 5NR
EU representative: Macmillan Publishers Ireland Ltd, 1st Floor,
The Liffey Trust Centre, 117–126 Sheriff Street Upper,
Dublin 1, D01 YC43
Associated companies throughout the world
www.panmacmillan.com

ISBN 978-1-0350-6485-4 HB
ISBN 978-1-0350-6486-1 TPB

In Chapter 33, Tufty paraphrases 'Jabberwocky' by Lewis Carroll, first published in
December 1871 – *Through the Looking-Glass, and What Alice Found There.* In Chapter 34,
Mrs McIntosh quotes from William Shakespeare's *Hamlet*, Act III, Scene I – first performed
at the Globe Theatre in either 1600 or 1601, depending on who you want to believe.

Pan Macmillan does not have any control over, or any responsibility for,
any author or third-party websites referred to in or on this book.

1 3 5 7 9 8 6 4 2

A CIP catalogue record for this book is available from the British Library.

Typeset by Palimpsest Book Production Ltd, Falkirk, Stirlingshire
Printed and bound by CPI Group (UK) Ltd, Croydon, CR0 4YY

Visit **www.panmacmillan.com** to read more about all our books
and to buy them. You will also find features, author interviews and
news of any author events, and you can sign up for e-newsletters
so that you're always first to hear about our new releases.

For Jane and Sarah
(who started Logan on his journey)

— in darkness, creeps —

One

Was there anything sexier than breaking into someone's house in the middle of the night? Moving from room to room in the darkness. Touching their special, secret, private things...

Course there wasn't.

Andrew paused on the top step, listening.

Because sometimes these rich wanks had very big, very angry dogs – and it didn't matter how carefully you scoped out their gaffs, you could always be surprised by a four-legged shredding machine with a taste for home invaders.

But the only sound was his breath, *whooshing* and *hissing* inside the ski-mask.

No sign of Fido.

Safe to step onto the landing.

A wee balcony overlooked the fancy double-height open hallway, with its fancy floor-to-ceiling windows, and fancy countryside view bathed in low, cold moonlight. There was even a fancy scroll-edged mirror at the top of the fancy stairs, and for a moment the world turned from a grainy green glow to a flare of bright white as the infrared LEDs on his night-vision goggles caught the shiny surface. Then the sensors adjusted, fading everything down again, revealing Andrew's reflection in all its horror-film glory.

A shark's-tooth grin beamed back at him, printed across the

ski-mask's mouth in jagged glow-in-the-dark fangs. Ready to party.

He paused for a quick flex, but the effect was kinda spoiled by the baggy black hoodie, black combat trousers, black boots, and little black rucksack – because everyone needed somewhere to keep their cable-ties, duct tape, and Rohypnol. Oh, and The Knife, of course. Can't forget *The Knife*.

Shame the goggles and mask hid his pretty face. What was the point of all that time in the gym, the Botox, plucking, manscaping, and moisturising if no one could see it? But lots of these places had nanny-cams and home surveillance things.

Which was a shame.

People should be more trusting.

Andrew ran his gloved fingertips along the handrail, like it was a woman's thigh and he's heading for the panty line. The black nitrile making a faint, *juddering* squeal. Keeping his voice nice and low: 'Come out, come out, wherever you are…'

The landing boasted half a dozen doors, but other than the mirror, there were no little personal touches. No pictures. No paintings. Kinda sad really.

He picked the nearest door and eased it open, peering into a family bathroom with lots of chrome and tiles. Tres swanky. Even if the medicine cabinet revealed nothing more exciting than a unicorn-themed electric toothbrush and a tube of 'RASPLE-BERRY TOOTHTASTIC TOOTHPASTE!' that looked like the Glitter Fairy puked on it.

The next door opened on an unfinished bedroom: metal bed frame and a bare mattress; no curtains; two flat-pack bedside cabinets, one of which was still in the box. Naked lightbulb dangling from the ceiling rose.

No fun there.

Next to that was another spare bedroom, but the lazy cow hadn't even finished assembling the bed frame. No mattress.

Instead, the place was packed with cardboard boxes, each stamped with 'BEARSDEN HOME RELOCATION SERVICES LTD' and a label to show which room it should've been left in. None of which were 'UNFINISHED BEDROOM' so either the movers couldn't be arsed putting them in the right place, or the woman of the house couldn't be arsed unpacking and dumped the lot through here instead. Still taped shut from the time she moved in.

Andrew slipped his rucksack off, pulled The Knife from its side pocket: six inches of blackened steel with a serrated edge, concealed inside a hard plastic sheath. Perfect for keeping the lucky ladies quiet while he gave them their little 'treat'.

He slid the blade free, and slit open the tape on a box marked 'STUDY'.

Books.

And really boring ones at that.

He had a wee rummage, but they were all called things like 'INFORMATION MANAGEMENT IN A DIGITAL ENVIRONMENT', 'MAKING THE GENERAL DATA PROTECTION REGULATIONS WORK FOR YOUR ORGANISATION', and 'NEWSTOPIA (SELECTIVE-DISSEMINATION STRATEGIES FOR "CONTROLLING THE NARRATIVE" & REDIRECTING PUBLIC DISCOURSE TOWARDS FAVOURABLE OUTCOMES)'.

Sod that.

He closed the box again, then dumped another one on top, so no one could see he'd been in here.

Popped The Knife in his hoodie pocket.

Shut the door behind him and tried somewhere else.

A sign hung outside the next room, about the size of an ashtray, with cartoon cats and rabbits on it, and 'PRINCESS BROOKLYN'S CASTLE!' in happy pink letters.

Unlike the last two bedrooms, this one looked lived in. Sort of. The bed was clarted in fuzzy unicorns and teddy bears and lions and tigers and penguins – their black, button eyes glittered in the night-vision glow. Rainbow-and-flowers wallpaper. Little birdies on the closed curtains. A dollhouse that looked way too posh to play with. And a large, stuffed Skeleton Bob sitting in a wicker chair in the corner. Grinning.

The place was spookily clean and ordered and tidy. No toys lying out. No clothes strewn willy-nilly. No pens and pencils. No Lego landmines waiting to be stepped on...

Like a shrine to a long dead kid.

Andrew shook his head.

Sighed.

Guess some people were just creepy.

But a woman with kids was *always* a juicier prospect.

He tiptoed back out into the corridor.

The last door on this side of the landing was unmarked, but when he opened it, Andrew's grin matched the one printed on his ski-mask. *Finally*: the master bedroom.

He slunk inside, leaving the door open behind him.

It was much larger than the other three, with framed photos on the walls, and a pair of doors leading off on either side of a king-sized bed – a big heavy wooden one, that looked like someone had sawn the top three foot off a four-poster. In fact, every bit of furniture in here was *way* swankier than the flat-pack crap in the other rooms. Three chests of drawers were arranged around the walls, along with a vanity unit festooned with bottles and jars and tubs and tubes. All of which probably cost a small fortune in their own right.

Much more like it.

Andrew helped himself to a few of the more expensive-looking ones. Then tried the door on the left side of the bed: a walk-in closet, bigger than Andrew's whole bedroom, stuffed full of stylish clothes and elegant shoes. Hanging on rails, displayed in racks, folded neatly on shelves.

Nah.

The other door opened on an en suite done up to look dark and opulent. The kind of place you could spend a few hours soaking in your claw-foot tub, drinking champagne, surrounded by bubbles. One of those sinks that were carved out of a big slab of solid rock.

He leaned on the cold granite surface and popped open the medicine cabinet. Grinning behind his mask's grin, because *this* one was full of goodies.

'Yummy, yummy. *Thank you*, Mummy.'

He picked through the boxes of prescription pills, pocketing anything that might come in handy later: Temazepam, Oxycodone, and a half-empty thing of Tramadol.

Because sharing was caring.

Andrew checked the time on his phone – 23:54 – she'd be home soon. Better get a move on.

Back in the bedroom, he opened the first chest of drawers. Top drawer: scarves and boxed jewellery.

Even though it was impossible to tell what colour everything was in the night-vision goggles' dark-green glow, it would all be stylish and expensive. And, OK, it went against the rules, but Mum's birthday was coming up and while the jewellery was too dangerous to risk, bet she'd love some cashmere.

He pocketed the most attractive scarf, then moved on to the next drawer down.

Bras: plain, T-shirt, sports.

And a handful of more exotic, lacy numbers.

Mmmmmm...

Andrew held them up for a good look, turning them in his gloved fingers, picking the skimpiest frilliest item and stuffing it into his hoodie pocket.

Drawer Number Three held a vast array of pants.

Andrew licked his lips and trembled out a little breath, then plunged his hands into their delicious softness. Working his fingers through them. Tugging at the elastic as that familiar warmth cupped itself around his cock. Stirring things up in anticipation of the big event.

Looked like the lady of the house favoured the big arse-hammocks, but there were a few saucy numbers that tickled his knob, so they went in the hoody pocket to join that bra.

Drawer Four was full of socks.

Fuck that.

A wicker laundry basket lurked in the corner, though.

Worth a dip.

If he was quick.

Andrew ripped the lid off and dug in, throwing dirty T-shirts and socks and leggings and big baggy knickers over his shoulder till something frilly appeared.

Snatching them from the basket, he pressed the pants against his mask's toothy grin. Took a lonnnnnnng deeeeeeeep sniff. Breathing in the musky sweet-and-salty scent of her pussy. Holding it deep inside him. Then hissing it out in a shuddering sigh, clutching his rock-hard groin. Squeezing.

But there would be time for that later.

So, Andrew pocketed the pants, then went back for another lucky dip. Coming out with a hold-up stocking. Black and sheer. Shiny in the night-vision glow.

He wrapped both ends around his hands, like a garotte...

Then froze.

Hold on.

A sound rattle-clacked out from somewhere downstairs. Keys in a lock.

Quick!

Andrew swept up the discarded washing and stuffed it back into the basket, then tiptoed over to the bedroom door. Adjusting himself through his trousers.

Soon be time to shine…

He poked his head out onto the landing.

Couldn't see much from here, but there was light outside. Probably a car, pulled up to the front of the house.

Then a *clunk* sounded, followed by the *whoomp* of an opening door.

Time to move.

Andrew crept out of the bedroom, ran on his tippie-toes across the landing, and flattened himself against the wall. Erection throbbing.

OK, so he couldn't see what was going on from here, but the important thing was being hidden from view.

When you gave the lady of the house a 'treat', it was always best to keep it a surprise till the very last moment.

Because tonight was going to be one of the *good* nights. When he didn't just slip away into the dark with his little trophies. When creeping turned to something *far* more satisfying.

But first:

He whipped off his night-vision goggles a second before the hall lights snapped on, bathing the cold, impersonal hallway in their harsh LED glow.

Which stung like poking wasps in his eyes, after the goggles' screen.

Down below, a man's voice shouldered its way into the house. A Central Belt accent, with an uncertain, grovelling edge to it. *'Excuse me? Excuse me, Miss Agapova? Natasha Agapova?'*

The answer came in the scraiky flat vowels of somewhere down under: Australia, or New Zealand. Sounding knackered and superior. *'Go away, I'm not in the mood.'*

Quite right. Bugger off, little man.

The lady has an appointment.

9

'*No. Sorry. Yes. But I'm with the police, see? Detective Sergeant Davis. Can I come in?*' You could almost smell the deference oozing from every pore. '*I'm afraid I have some bad news.*'

Oh, thank you *very* much.

A cop.

Just what the evening needed.

Bastard.

And Andrew's erection keeled over like a drunken tramp.

It was time for Plan B: find a nice dark, quiet corner to hide away and lurk there till the house was asleep, then sneak out the way he came in. And yeah, he could still give her a little 'treat' on his way out, but that hardly seemed fair. He wasn't a *monster*, after all.

But first: only human to want a little peek, right? See what he could've won.

Andrew peered around the corner, keeping the rest of him well out of sight.

The lady of the house, Natasha Agapova, might've been in her late forties, but she was still a total MILF. Mahogany-red hair framed a heart-shaped face with lips like cherries, high cheekbones, and deep dark eyes. And yeah, she'd probably had work done – given there wasn't a single wrinkle on her face – but there was nothing wrong with that.

Hadn't done Andrew any harm, had it?

Looked like she'd got a bit of the old nip-tuck done below the neck too, because she went in and out everywhere a proper woman should. The hourglass figure accentuated by a glittery black ballgown and jewellery that was way too showy to be real.

Got to wonder how she ended up having an Ozzy accent, with a name like 'Natasha Agapova'. Kinda think she'd sound Russian, or Ukrainian, or Eastern European...

Something else that didn't really make sense was the *massive* beige teddy bear, clutched under one arm. Thing had to be at least five feet tall, wearing a hard hat, rig boots, rigger gloves, and a 'PATHAK OIL SERVICES' T-shirt.

She, *Natasha*, turned her back on the doorway and ditched the bear in the middle of the hall. Kicking off her heels to pad across the deep oatmeal carpet to a long sideboard thing taste-fully decorated with expensive-looking ethnic vases, where she dumped her keys and took off her earrings. Then pulled a face. 'It's Adrian, isn't it. He's finally wrapped that *stupid* Aston Martin round a tree.'

'*It's probably best if I...?*' DS Davis stepped into the hall. Might as well not have bothered, though. He was an un-remarkable bloke with greying hair at his temples – the kind of guy you wouldn't look twice at if you passed him on the street – in a cheap-looking grey suit with a white shirt and blue tie. The only thing even *slightly* noticeable about him were the sandshoes on his feet. And even they were beige.

A sniff from Natasha. 'I take it someone's told that pudding-headed blonde tart of his? Well, she can whistle if she thinks I'm paying for the sodding funeral!'

Davis stared at her. 'Sorry?'

'The divorce settlement *clearly* states he's—'

'Pay for the *funeral*?' Davis threw his arms out. 'You just can't help yourself, can you? You've got to be a *bitch* about everything.'

Hang on a minute.

She stuck her hands on her hips, voice getting louder. 'I beg your *bloody* pardon?' Chin up. 'Who the hell do you think you're talking to?'

'Oh, I know *exactly* who you are. Bitch.'

'I want your name and badge number, right now!' Jabbing a finger at him. 'I happen to be *very* good friends with the Chief Constable and she—'

And that's when DS Davis punched her. Right in the mouth. Hard enough to send Natasha staggering backwards on her bare feet.

Hard enough to make Andrew flinch.

'Not so gobby now, are you, Bitch!'

Two

Natasha collapsed against the sideboard, one hand pressed over her mouth, blood dribbling down her chin to drip scarlet blossoms on the pale carpet.

Her small, muffled moan was cut short by another visit from DS Davis's fist.

Something shifted deep inside Andrew's stomach, fizzing as it headed south. Making his balls clench as he stood there and watched.

Oh, this wasn't good. This wasn't good *at all*!

Natasha crumpled to the floor, and Davis took a little run-up – slammed his foot into her stomach, like he was trying to score a goal from the halfway mark.

A short scream barked free, and his foot landed again. And again. Making her curl up, arms covering her head as his sand-shoes hammered into her legs and back.

Every blow came with a snarled word: 'I – know – who – you – are!'

Davis was going to kill her. He was going to kill her, right here, with Andrew in the house.

Oh God...

Then Andrew's eyes snapped wide, because what were the police going to think when they turned up at the crime scene? Dead woman downstairs and there's Andrew, hiding in the box room, with a rape kit in his rucksack and the murder-victim's underwear *in his bloody pocket.*

Think they'd believe he had nothing to do with it?

Think DS Davis would fess-up to killing her?

Course he sodding wouldn't – he'd point the finger right at Andrew. And his police bastard mates would believe him. And they'd plant whatever evidence they needed to make Andrew look guilty. And that would be it: prison for life, while their murderous colleague danced off into the sunrise.

Fuck that.

Because Andrew was getting the *hell* out of here.

He shuffled his feet on the bone-pale carpet.

But *how?* The only exits were downstairs, and no way was Andrew going anywhere near that mad bastard.

Oh God…

THINK!

There had to be a way out of here.

Just needed a couple of minutes to breathe and get his head together, that's all.

Andrew slunk away from the corner and opened the first door he came to – the kid's bedroom.

Not a lot of places to hole-up, but it would have to do.

Somewhere downstairs, a clock struck midnight – the twelve chimes echoing through the mausoleum house as Natasha cried and DS Davis huffed and puffed like a rutting bull. Kicking the living shit out of her.

Andrew eased the bedroom door closed so gently that the catch barely whispered into place. Then backed away.

With the curtains shut, it was dark as a crypt in here, not so much as a sliver of moonlight.

Shitting hell…

He kept going, putting some distance between him and the door. And whatever nightmare was going on downstairs.

Why did *everything* have to go wrong?

Hadn't he earned a little *fun* for a change?

Wasn't it *completely* unfair that—

The edge of the bed hit the back of his knee and that was it – both legs gave way.

No, no, no, no, no!

Andrew whirled his arms, arching his back, trying to get his balance back. Then gravity took over, thumping him down on the mattress hard enough to make the whole bed bounce. Not far. Just a fraction of an inch. But the bed's metal feet *clunked* against the carpet like a hammer.

An avalanche of stuffed toys tumbled to the floor.

The silence that followed was deadening.

Please no…

Oh Christing, buggering, no…

What if DS Davis heard that?

What if DS Davis decided to investigate?

What if DS Davis killed *him* too?

Andrew wrenched himself off the bed and scurried on his tiptoes back to the door. Making no sound at all. Not even *breathing*. And pressed his ear to the wood.

Silence.

Natasha wasn't crying any more. Might be unconscious? Or already dead.

Anrew bit his bottom lip.

Was that a creak?

Maybe it was a creak.

A footstep on the stairs?

And there was nowhere to hide.

The bed!

Hide under the bed…

Only the tiny gap wasn't big enough to take him and his rucksack and it was only a single bed and the metal frame wasn't going to conceal much and all DS Davis would have to do is bend down and look and see him cowering there and he'd be trapped and Davis would drag him out and kick him to death on a kid's bedroom floor surrounded by stupid stuffed fucking animals in this horrible lifeless house.

Andrew's throat tightened.

Jaw quivering as tears threatened to break free.

Please...

Should've hidden in the *other* bedroom – the one filled with boxes. But it was on the other side of the landing and how was he supposed to get there with all the lights on in the hall and DS Davis standing right there?

Oh God, oh God, oh God...

Andrew shifted his weight from one foot to the other, dithering, looking from the door to the curtains and back again.

Barricade the door?

No time.

And the noise. And Davis would *know* he was in here. And...

Wait.

He lurched into the middle of the room, thrust his hand up inside the tasselled lightshade, and twisted the bulb from its fitting. Cold and firm against his nitrile gloves. Then slunk back against the wall, on the leeward side of the door – so he'd be behind it when it opened. Hidden.

But maybe it *wouldn't* open?

Maybe DS Davis would come to his senses and realise what he'd done?

And maybe he'd run away like a sane person and not a total...

The door handle turned.

Andrew flattened himself against the wall, holding his breath, still as a corpse as the door swung open and light spilled in from the hallway.

It was faint, though. Like it was glowing up from the ground floor, instead of crashing in from the landing. Not bright enough to make much of a dent in the gloom. Leaving the kid's bedroom smothered in darkness.

Trembling so hard that his fingers barely worked, Andrew reached into his hoodie pocket and slipped The Knife free of its sheath again. Gripping it tight in his shaky hand, the other covering his mouth. Tears making the room shimmer.

A grunt from the doorway.

Then DS Davis must've reached for the light switch, because that distinctive *click* sounded. Only nothing happened – what with the bulb missing.

Davis tried a few more times.

Click, click, click...

Same result.

OK.

Very, *very* quietly, Andrew pulled the night-vision goggles down over his eyes again, and the whole room lit up like a bile-green Las Vegas. Just in time to catch DS Davis stepping into the middle of the darkened room.

Davis peered up into the empty lightshade.

On the goggles' screen, something ... *radiated* off him. Something sick and dangerous. Something desperate to slash and tear and destroy.

Partially hidden by the open door, Andrew tightened his grip on The Knife.

He could do this.

He *could*.

All he had to do was lunge forwards and slit this scary bastard's throat, then watch whatever the hell it was bleed right out of him.

Deep breath.

Do it.

Right now.

Before Davis turned around, saw him hiding behind the door, and battered him to death as well...

But Andrew couldn't even move.

DS Davis's head turned to the right: towards him.

Oh God, the bastard knows he's here.

Andrew's whole body clenched.

Across the room, Skeleton Bob grinned at them both, glassy black eyes sparkling – hungry and malevolent.

The Knife shook so much there was no way he could hold on. And if he dropped it, Davis would—

A *clunk* rang out.

But it wasn't The Knife – that was still clenched in Andrew's fist – and a breath later came the porcelain crash of something expensive shattering downstairs, followed by a wet, agonised sob.

Sounded like DS Davis hadn't killed Natasha after all.

A growl ripped out of the vicious bastard, then he snatched a stuffed penguin from the bed, and marched from the room. Not bothering to close the door.

Oh, thank Christ...

Andrew closed his eyes and shuddered out a silent breath. Sagging as his body unclenched. Then frowned down at the front of his black trousers. Damp and warm, followed by a yeasty smell.

Yeah.

Because things weren't horrible enough without that.

Outside: the sound of feet, thumping down the stairs.

Then Natasha's voice, wrenching between a loose-lipped mumble and a full-on scream. *'HELP ME! SOMEBODY HELP ME!'* Then a catch in her breath. *'No, please! I have money, I have—'*

A thud muffled out.

Silence.

Then a sort of *hissing* noise, like something was being dragged across the carpet.

A door opened.

More dragging.

And the final, coffin-lid *thunk* of the front door closing again.

Andrew folded in half, grabbing his quivering knees – the fabric of his cargo pants already starting to go cold and clammy through his nitrile gloves.

He stayed there as the room whooshed around him, breathing hard, like he'd just done a thousand reps on the bench press, blood pounding in his temples.

But what if it wasn't over?

What if Davis came back?

Stiff-legged, Andrew shuffled to the window and peered out between the curtains.

DS Davis was already halfway across the drive. He'd grabbed hold of Natasha's ballgown – between her shoulder blades – hauling her, one-handed, towards a car that was every bit as nondescript as he was. That stuffed penguin crushed in his other fist.

Please don't come back.

Please don't come back...

Andrew fiddled with the buttons on his night-vision goggles and the picture zoomed in to full magnification, giving him a perfect view of Davis bundling her limp body into the boot then hurling the penguin in after her.

The bastard looked left, then right, making sure no one was watching, before climbing in behind the wheel with a huge grin on his face. Far more terrifying than the one printed on Andrew's ski-mask.

Then the car's lights flared in the goggles' screen, washing out all details till the sensors caught up again. And by then the pale, anonymous Vauxhall was pulling away. Rolling down the drive and out onto the road. Heading left, back towards town.

Leaving Andrew alone in the house of horrors.

— we all scream… —

3

Logan stopped dead, squinting up at the hard blue sky, phone pressed to his sweaty ear. 'He's *dead*?'

A relentless sun baked the car park behind Tillydrone Library, making the sticky tarmac shimmer, the grass a thirsty shade of yellowy green. Trees drooping under the onslaught of an unholy Aberdonian summer. That peppery smell of roasting dust.

Detective Chief Superintendent Pine grunted down the phone at him. *'Given his injuries? Surprised he lasted this long. Lucky he never regained consciousness, to be honest.'*

Not much of a bright side...

It wasn't bad, as car parks went, with the wooden-clad rear of the library on one side, four-storey blocks of flats on another, and the arse-end of a McColl's on the third. A stand of tower blocks in the middle distance, their windows glowing like daggers in the punishing light.

Logan unhooked one side of his clip-on tie and undid his top button. Should've worn the pale-grey fighting suit, today. Too sodding hot for a dark-blue one.

The sound of a local radio station burbled through the lazy air, mingling with a bumblebee's buzz and the whine of a petrol strimmer. While off in the distance, the distinctive tinkly 'Greensleeves' of an ice-cream van beckoned.

And his phone was silent, so either they'd been cut off, or Pine was expecting him to say something.

'Yes, ma-am.'

That seemed to do the trick.

'I want this bastard caught, Logan. Operation Iowa is officially a murder investigation, as of fifteen minutes ago.'

'Yes, ma-am.'

'No cock-ups.'

'No, ma-am.'

A dozen or so cars were parked behind the library: hatchbacks mostly, with makeshift visors shading their interiors from the sun – cardboard boxes and old bed-sheets, giving them a boarded-up feel – but an unwashed police van sat off to one side, in the shade of a wilting tree, with its riot grille up, and every door and window wide open. Trying to lure in the non-existent breeze.

'The media are going full-on Bampot Junction. Let's give the buggers some good news for the evening bulletins, OK?'

'We'll do our best.'

'Good. Keep me informed.' And with that, she was gone.

Logan scuffed his way back to the grubby van, the radio getting louder with every step. So much for following orders.

And if *that* wasn't bad enough, his team of 'crack police officers' were sitting inside, in the full Method of Entry Gear: blue overalls; stabproof vests; hard plastic guards on their elbows, wrists, knees, and shins. Only they'd removed their riot helmets and gauntlets to enjoy a variety of ice lollies.

Ice lollies.

The song on the radio clattered to a halt, and a broad Doric DJ boomed out instead:

'Richt, that wis "Twist and Wallop" by The Mighty Beetroot, and this next een's fer Alice Muchty, fae Rhynie, *fa says, "Aye, aye,*

Dougie, can ye dee us a favour and play oanything by the Rolling Stones for oor Cathy, who's sitting her driving *test the day—"'*

Logan clambered up into the passenger seat and switched the radio off – to an instant chorus of disapproval from the team.

Well, tough.

'No radio.' He dumped his phone on the dashboard. Which was like a sodding frying pan, so he snatched it up again, before the electronics cooked. 'Bloody hell...'

A voice from the back: *'Oh come on!'*

Logan turned around, scowling at the useless sweaty lumps masquerading as police officers.

Detective Sergeant Roberta Steel scowled back at him from the driver's seat, with her mad grey hair, chain-smoker's wrinkles, and strawberry Cornetto.

In the next row of seats sulked Detective Constable Veronica Lund – pageboy cut, cheeks starting to jowl a bit, little pink eyes, white chocolate Magnum – and DC David Barrett – a blond, rabbity-looking kind of guy, whose head brushed the van's ceiling. Sort of a pooka made flesh. Nobbly Bobbly.

The second row featured a pile of everyone's bowling-ball crash helmets and DC Owen Harmsworth – far too chubby to ever pass a bleep test – with a receding hairline, saggy face, and permanently disappointed look: Solero.

And at the back lurked the team's resident shortarse: DC Stewart 'Tufty' Quirrel – his thin pointy face beaming out beneath a buzz-cut – Lolly Gobble Choc Bomb.

Steel clicked the radio back on. 'Don't be a dick.' And 'Sympathy for the Devil' ripped out of the van's speakers for the whole three seconds it took Logan to switch it off again.

'No radio when we're on an op. You *know* that.' Pointing at the lot of them. 'Supposed to be paying attention.' Prompting assorted whinging and moaning from the back of the van.

'I don't care! And where did you get the lollies? You can't just send someone trotting off at the first sniff of an ice-cream van!' At least Barrett and Lund had the decency to blush at that one. Logan gestured out towards the sweltering afternoon. 'They could give us the "go" at any minute. You want to miss it, cos you're listening to *this* rubbish and scoffing ice cream? Everyone else is rushing to the dunt, and you're sat here like steamed farts while one of you's waiting in line for...' gritting his teeth, 'for a sodding *choc ice?*'

Harmsworth shuffled his bum in its seat. 'Yeah, but—'

'No radio! No more lollies! And that's *final.*'

Which was the cue for a lot of pouty posturing and folded arms.

Fine: *let* them stew in sweaty sulky silence. See if Logan cared.

Steel lowered her voice and leaned across from the driver's side. 'Thanks for motivating the team, *Inspector*. Really appreciate it.'

Logan stared back. 'One of our victims died fifteen minutes ago. It's murder now.'

She closed her eyes and sagged. 'Son of a...' A sigh. 'Great.'

'That enough motivation for you?'

Logan checked the dashboard clock. Four thirty-two, and still waiting for the shout.

At least the general funk of communal sulking had eased a bit. But that radio was staying *off*.

Pfff...

He huffed out a breath and slipped free of his fighting suit's jacket. It was like a sodding kiln in here. And the open van doors made no difference at all.

Didn't help he was on the sunny side of the vehicle.

Steel, on the other hand, had a wee battery-powered fan on the go, wafting her shiny face as she perused that morning's *Aberdeen Examiner*, holding it up as a kind of barrier between their seats. Because unlike the rest of her team, Roberta Steel sulked professionally.

The front page blared 'SICKO RACISTS TORCH MIGRANT HOTEL' above a photo of last night's blaze on Broomhill Road, with the subheading 'SLEEPING REFUGEES AWAKE TO FIND ROOMS ABLAZE IN MIDDLE OF NIGHT'. Because apparently people were sodding horrible now.

Steel looked up from page three – thankfully free of half-naked glamour models, or she'd be letching all over them – 'PROTEIN THIEF TAKES A POWDER' starring a sports shop's shattered front window and a man in a tight polo shirt miming disappointment at the empty shelves. 'What?'

'Nothing.'

A lone cat wandered across the library car park, tail in the air as a butterfly flittered by. The cat cocked its head for a moment, as if contemplating giving chase, before deciding it couldn't be arsed in this heat.

Steel turned the page: 'OPEN BORDERS "BRINGING NHS TO ITS KNEES" SAYS TORY PEER' next to a pinch-faced photograph of a baldy twat. A sniff. 'Wouldn't think it was thunder and lightning all last week.'

So, at least she was talking to him again.

Logan watched the cat wander off and flump down in the shade of a bush. 'That's climate change for you.'

'Rained so much, could've sworn I'd got mildew in my "intimate feminine areas".' She grinned as he gagged a little. 'And how am I supposed to get rid of my tan lines if I can't lounge about the garden in the nip? Airing out my fusty bits?'

'Urgh, *please*…'

'If it helps, you can imagine Susan smearing me all over with factor twenty?'

No. No, it did not help *at all*.

A wee brown bird landed on the van's bonnet, hopping up onto a windscreen wiper to peer in through the window as if the occupants were a bunch of dafties.

Maybe it had a point?

Stuck in here, wilting in the stifling warmth of a stuffy police van. Half the team were half asleep, and the other half were on their way to the full snooze. All except for one.

Tufty sat forward in his seat, eager as a spaniel. 'You know, there's *one* thing the Americans got right.'

At which, everyone woke up enough to groan.

A sigh from Barrett. 'Come on then.'

Steel pulled down the driver's sun visor and tapped the sign mounted on the back: 'DON'T ENCOURAGE HIM!' Scowling in the rear-view. 'You know the rules.'

Lund twisted around, so she was facing the daft wee spud. 'Tell us, oh Guru of the Tremulous Wingwang, what have Americans "got right"?'

'Oh, in the name of the hairy ... spudge.'

'Pants.' Tufty nodded, as if that was the most insightful thing anyone had ever said. 'They're right about pants.' Reaching into his overalls to ping his own elastic. 'I mean these are underpants, right? They go *under* pants. They're not under*trousers*, are they.'

'Thank you *very* much.' Steel massaged her forehead, re-arranging the wrinkles. 'What part of "don't encourage him" do you scrunkfudgers not get?'

Harmsworth shrugged. 'Don't look at me: I remember what happened last time.'

'Yeah,' Barrett turned around too, 'but maybe they're *pants* that go *under* your *trousers*. Ergo: underpants. Pants that go under.'

Tufty's eyebrows shot upwards. 'Ooh, good point!'

Logan hissed the words out the side of his mouth: 'Is it always like this?'

Steel just poked the sign, face creased in pain.

Harmsworth shrugged again. 'That's why we usually have the radio on.'

'*No* radio.' Logan checked the dashboard clock again – nearly quarter to five and still no shout. 'What the hell's the hold-up?'

'Aha! Now,' Lund wagged a finger, 'did you know "trousers" is Scottish? Comes from the Gaelic "*triubhas*", AKA: trews. Something else we invented.'

Steel banged the flat of her palm against the sign.

Barrett nodded. 'And it's a *pair* of trousers, cos you used to have one for each leg. Separate, like.'

There was a moment's silence, as everyone contemplated that. Then Tufty spread his hands, laying down the wisdom of the ancients: 'Like assless chaps, only without the built-in belt, and Y.M.C.A. disco vibes.'

Steel's face scrunched like a baby's fist. 'AAAAAAARGH!'

Yeah...

Maybe Harmsworth had a point.

Logan switched the radio back on.

A happy song burbled out of the van's speakers, as the six-person team sat and steamed in their four-wheeled microwave oven.

Barrett was slumped back in his seat, with his eyes closed and his gob open. Harmsworth had taken possession of Steel's newspaper, tongue poking out the corner of his mouth as he tackled the crossword with muttered curses and much rubbing out. Lund fiddled on her phone, playing some sort of game with the sound turned down, so only the occasional electronic *bing* and *wibble* escaped. While Tufty had his head right back, trying to balance a biro on the end of his pointy nose.

'They've lost him, haven't they.' Steel unzipped her overalls as far as the stabproof vest would allow and flapped the edges. 'We've been stuck here, sweating like sex offenders in a sausage factory, and the bugger's done a runner.'

Barrett kept his eyes closed. 'Pound in the swear jar.'

'Oh, go ... *crunk* yourself.'

Logan's thumbs ticked across his phone's screen, *tick, tick, tick-tick-tick...*

> Has ANYONE got eyes on this guy?!?

SEND.

The song crumpled to a halt, and the DJ's teuchter voice barrelled out: *'Fit wye's that no' been a massive hit?'*

Because it was rubbish?

'Yer listening till Dougie In The Aifterneen, *and time's fair bangin' oan, but we'll squeeze in* wan *mair tune afore the news, then it's "ta-ta" fae me, and "aye-aye" tae* Rush-Hour Records *wie Big Sandy Thomson!'*

Logan's phone dinged three times in quick succession. Incoming text messages:

BIOHAZARD BOB:
> Sod all here

DOREEN:
> Nothing doing on our end.

SPUDGUN:
> Think we've been sold a sack of shite?!?

'*So, oor last request fer the day is fae a loon cried "Stewart Quirrel"*—'

Tufty sat bolt upright, waving at the radio as the biro went flying. 'Turn it up! Turn it up!'

'*He's aifter a romantic, smoochie number, and he's gieed us a wee notey tae read oot.*' At which point a diabetically syrupy tune faded up under the DJ. '"*My dearest Kate," says the boy, "would you dae me the great honour of becoming my bidie-in?"*'

Tufty beamed.

Barrett gave a low whistle.

Lund: a celebratory round of applause.

Harmsworth harrumphed.

The background music swelled as a piano and guitar joined in.

'*Here's Custard and the Vegetarians, wie "Loveshine". Guid luck, Stewart, hope yer quine says "Aye"!*'

And saccharine vocals globbed out of the speakers, sticky as golden syrup:

'*I see your shadow everywhere,*
A scent that lingers on my heart,
Without your light the world's threadbare,
And all my dreams they fall apart…'

'Jesus.' Steel's nose curled. 'That sounds like turds smell…'

Lund poked her. 'Shut up. It's romantic.'

Yeah…

People were weird.

Logan's thumbs went ticking again:

How long do we give this before packing it in?

SEND.

31

'Cos your love shines brighter,
Your love shines brighter,
Your lo-o-o-ove shines brighter than—'

Everyone's Airwave handset blared out three bleeps, followed by DCI Rutherford's rasping voice:

'We're go! Repeat: go! Go! Go!'

4

The van's occupants scrambled to slam all the doors shut, windows buzzing into place as the Transit's engine roared.

'Let's catch us a murderer!' Steel clicked on her seatbelt with one hand, zipping herself up with the other as Harmsworth handed out the crash helmets.

Tyres squealing on the library tarmac, the van leapt forward, ripping out of the car park, turning right, then right again. Accelerating past the McColl's, lights flickering on. Siren: silent.

They wheeched past the library, where mothers with push-chairs stopped to watch them go by. Then a sharp left onto Gort Road, making the tyres screech again.

'Hoy!' Logan grabbed the handle above his door, holding tight as the seatbelt dug into his side. 'Like to get there in one piece!'

A grin. 'Don't be such a starchy gusset...'

They shot past the bookies, juddering over the traffic control bumps, going at least double the speed limit.

A patrol car whooshed past the playing fields, heading straight towards them, lights blazing as it scraiked around the corner onto Gort Lane, just in front of the Transit.

'Yeeehaw!' Steel hauled the wheel hard right, following it into a canyon between two terraced rows of three-storey flats, with big communal bins outside and alternating stairwells painted blue or orange.

Another patrol car howled in from the other end of the road, followed by a Dog Unit van. Because there was nothing like swarming in mob-handed.

The second patrol car performed a handbrake sideways slide, blocking that side of the road. The one Steel was following did the same.

Putting it broadside to their speeding van.

Which was definitely going to plough straight into it...

Logan tightened his grip on the handle and said a little prayer.

And as if in answer – Steel slammed on the brakes and jerked the steering wheel right, mounting the kerb, then bouncing onto the strip of grass outside the flats as the ABS juddered. Not coming to a halt until they'd crashed into a 'RESIDENTS PARKING ONLY' sign and bent it flat.

She unclipped her seatbelt. 'Everyone remember where we parked!' Then she was out of the van and into the blistering sun, pulling on her crash helmet as she ran for the entrance to Block Four.

The patrol cars' doors sprang open and the uniformed officers made for the same block, swiftly followed by the rest of Steel's team. Harmsworth huffing and puffing at the back of the pack, carrying the Big Red Door Key, struggling under the mini-battering-ram's weight.

Logan, on the other hand, took his time – strolling up the path to the stairwell door at a far more leisurely pace. After all, Steel's team had their riot gear on – if anything nasty happened, they were dressed for it. He wasn't.

The uniforms from the patrol car took up positions: two on either side of the door. Staying back as a saggy bloke in scruffy black cargo pants and a moth-eaten Police Scotland baseball cap appeared. PC MacLauchlan. Squint nose. Jagged little teeth. As if he'd recently crawled out from under a bridge to steal some children. And eat them.

He was being dragged towards the flats by a *massive* hairy Alsatian, straining at her leash, ears pricked, plumey tail wagging away as she bared every pointy tooth in her pointy head.

MacLauchlan grinned like a troll at the assembled officers. 'Don't worry, PD Branston doesn't bite. Do you, girl?'

Branston let out a short-sharp bark that made it clear she did *indeed* bite, enjoyed doing it, and was quite ready to demonstrate her skill in this department on anyone willing to volunteer. And possibly a few people who weren't.

Off in the middle distance, that ice-cream van tinkled its way through 'Greensleeves' again. Luring little kiddies for MacLauchlan and Branston to devour.

It sounded as if there were a bunch of them shrieking away behind the building, playing with something that went '*thud-adudadududa…*' over and over again. Unaware of the hairy scary stranger danger.

The intercom beside the door had seven buttons – one for each flat, and an extra one marked 'SERVICES'.

Barrett tapped the label for Flat E: 'MACGARIOCH'. 'This is us: Charles MacGarioch.' Pronouncing it 'Mac-Gar-eee-och' with a gritty coffee-machine hiss for the 'och' as in 'loch'.

Steel shook her head. 'It's "Mac-Geeee-reeee", you spudge-nugget.'

A frown. '"Mac-Gee-reee"? You sure? Because—'

'Ahem!' Logan pointed. 'Can we get on with this please? Before someone notices there's a dirty big police van parked on their lawn!'

'All right, all right. Keep your pants on.' Steel poked a finger onto every single button, except for 'FLAT E', and held them down, making the intercom growl.

Everyone stared at the speaker's dirty little grille.

Even Branston.

Then a woman's voice crackled out: *'What the buggering* hell *is it now?'*

Steel put on her broadest teuchter voice. 'Aye, aye. It's Ina fae the *cooncil*. Says here yer hivin' trouble wi some *rats*?'

'Rats? Ghhhaaaagh… We've got rats?'

The door buzzed, then clicked.

Steel shoved it open. 'Cheers, min!' Then let go of the buttons and waved Harmsworth through. 'You waiting for an engraved invitation?'

Harmsworth hefted the Big Red Door Key and lurched into the building, followed by Steel and her team, then PD Branston and PC MacLauchlan.

Good.

Logan thumbed the button on his Airwave. 'Entered main property.' Then nodded at the uniformed officers, and stepped into the manky stairwell.

Not *piddly* manky, but manky nonetheless.

The stairs doglegged around between each floor, and the first landing made a small cupboard-like space on the ground level, where residents had abandoned three knackered bicycles, a broken pushchair, and a doorless washing machine stuffed full of junk mail. That kind of manky.

The scrum bustled up the stairs, with Steel second from front – whipping Harmsworth before her. 'Come on, Lumps-And-Bumps, shift it!'

Logan jogged up the steps behind them, not stopping on the first floor with its pronounced sharp fug of uncleaned litter tray.

Rutherford's voice fizzed through the Airwave again. *'Eyes open, people – we want a result here.'*

Around the landing and on, up to the top floor, where

Harmsworth was already going a sweaty-beetroot shade of red. Meaning his complexion clashed with his mini-battering-ram.

'*And no heroics! We know this guy's dangerous.*'

The rest of the team crowded into the narrow balcony, leaving Logan loitering on the top step, contemplating a strange little shrine, erected in the corner, outside Flat F – complete with joss sticks and drippy candles. Only instead of a Buddha, Madonna, or statue of Shiva, there was a plastic Gary Lineker being worshipped by a semicircle of garden gnomes.

Steel smacked a hand down on Harmsworth's shoulder. 'Dunt it.'

Everyone else shuffled back a couple of feet, giving him enough room to swing the Big Red Door Key.

The first blow boomed into the door, setting the whole stairwell ringing like a bass drum. The second rattled it in its frame. And the third swing smashed the whole thing free, sending it tumbling into the flat with a crackle of splintering wood.

Job done, Harmsworth collapsed back against the wall, breathing like a leaky space hopper as the team rushed inside. Followed by a very excited PD Branston and her hobgoblin handler.

Logan stepped away from the shrine as shouts echoed out from the ruined doorway.

Steel: '*POLICE! NOBODY MOVE!*'

Barrett: '*YOU! ON THE FLOOR! ON THE FLOOR NOW! ... COME BACK HERE!*'

Followed by some enthusiastic barking.

Then an old lady's voice screeching obscenities, somewhere inside.

Tufty: '*LEFT! LEFT! LEFT!*'

Harmsworth wiped a heavy leather glove across his soggy strawberry face and grimaced at Logan. 'When ... when are ...

the sodding ... Operational Support ... Units ... coming back ... to work?'

'When they're feeling better. Now:' making shooing gestures, 'in you go.'

A groan, a droop, then Harmsworth dropped the Big Red Door Key, and staggered inside.

Tufty: *'SARGE! SARGE, HE'S IN HERE!'*

Logan followed Harmsworth into a short hallway that probably hadn't been redecorated since the Coronation. And not the latest one. Faded Union Jack bunting drooped in disappointed-grey strands, criss-crossing the ceiling, which gave the place a birthday-party-in-a-funeral-home kind of vibe, but really set off all the framed portraits of the late Queen on the walls. Some with Phil, some with other family members.

Not sure Her Majesty would've approved of the old-lady filth howling from the first room on the right, though.

Logan peered in through the open door, and there was Lund: standing in an *Antiques Roadshow* bedroom, complete with Union Flag duvet cover and a big photo of the King over the bed.

'OK: it's OK.' Lund had both hands out, doing her best to sound calming and authoritative while being subjected to a torrent of OAP-flavoured abuse. 'Everything's going to be OK. I need you to put the stick down, Victoria.'

Victoria had to be in her mid-eighties, but that didn't stop her swearing like a drunken soccer casual – swinging an NHS-issue walking stick about like Excalibur, trying to take Mordred's head off. And you could tell she was up for the fight, because she'd rolled up the sleeves of her brown cardigan, exposing the thin, pale, tattooed arms beneath.

Down at the end of the hall, Steel's voice was just audible between Victoria's bouts of profanity and anatomically impossible instructions: *'So get him out.'*

Tufty: *'Yeah, but the door's locked or something.'*

'Then break it down! HARMSWORTH! Where's that useless fat snudge?'

Well, it looked as if Lund had everything under control here – as the walking stick made another decapitatory attempt – so Logan left her to it.

He wandered past a small bathroom, and a galley kitchen, stepping into a living room even more old-fashioned than the hall, with antimacassars on the furniture and yet more royal portraits on the wall. A throw-covered armchair had pride of place in front of the telly, with a heaped ashtray balanced on one arm, next to a heavy, dark-wood sideboard that was home to a vast collection of china cat figurines. So the sweary Victoria couldn't be *all* bad.

It hadn't been a big room to start with, but cramming in four police officers wearing the full MOE kit; another in plain-clothes; a scruffy wee ogre, *and* his gargantuan Alsatian, made it seem positively minute.

Tufty was hauling at the doorknob through to what presumably was the flat's second bedroom, twisting and turning it, heaving away to no avail while PD Branston had a jolly good sniff at the gap beneath the door. Making excited doggy noises.

Meanwhile, Steel glared at a sheepish Harmsworth. 'What do you mean, you "left it on the landing"?'

A proper whine weaselled into Harmsworth's voice. 'Well, how was I supposed to know you wanted—'

'Go!' Jabbing a finger in his sweaty face. 'Go get it! *Now!*'

They all had to shift sideways so Harmsworth could lumber from the room.

Logan watched him go. 'Trouble?'

'Yes, Sarge.' Tufty hooked a thumb. 'Charles MacGarioch hoofed it inside; locked the door.'

'So kick it in. It's only an internal partition.'

That got him a grin. 'I does has being an action hero!'

Then Tufty took a couple of steps back and put some welly behind it – his boot slamming into the door, right beside the lock.

The whole thing boomed inwards, first go, and PD Branston surged inside, barking her furry-missile head off as Tufty scrambled after her. Then Steel. Then Logan.

Charles MacGarioch's bedroom was much more modern than the old lady's, with matt-black paint on the walls and lots and lots of posters: pop-star ladies in bikinis; Aberdeen Football Club; a bunch advertising video games like 'DiRT 6', 'ASSASSINS' CREED 5', and 'GTA: LONDON RAMPAGE'.

A trio of monitors hovered on arms above a small desk, with a PlayStation 4 and a complete steering-wheel~gearstick~pedals-under-the-desk setup. Single bed beneath the window. A little bookshelf stuffed with paperbacks. More on the windowsill.

And the almost *cloying* citrusy-woody fug of a young man who uses *far* too much deodorant.

The room also featured a man's backside, disappearing through the open window. Not a good idea on the top floor of a three-storey building.

Charles Mountbatten MacGarioch had clearly suffered a haircut since the photo in the briefing notes was taken, swapping a perfectly sensible short-back-and-sides for a number-two fade with a go-faster stripe above each ear. Leaving the spots polka-dotting the back of his neck on full display.

He turned to look back at the police officers and big barky dog that had just invaded his childhood bedroom, giving them a good look at his wispy sideburns and beginner's moustache-and-soul-patch kit. Which gave him the air of a cut-priced

Starlord from *Guardians of the Galaxy*. Ripped jeans; red-and-white leather jacket; black, 4 Mechanical Mice T-shirt. Tears in his eyes.

Oh shite. He was going to jump wasn't he.

Logan lunged forwards. 'NO!'

Charles MacGarioch faced outward again, snatched a deep breath, and jumped. Screaming, all the way down...

Logan clambered up onto the single bed, sticking his head out the window just in time to see Charles hit the ground.

Only instead of going *SPLAT!*, he bounced – almost as high as he'd jumped. Still screaming. Arms and legs pinwheeling as he soared away from the building, clearing a washing-festooned whirly by at least ten feet, before crashing into a tree.

Branches and twigs *snap-crackled* as he tumbled through it, then thumped to earth, facedown, in a shivering blanket of falling leaves.

Tufty's head appeared alongside Logan's, then PD Branston joined in – tongue lolling as she grinned.

'Wow...' Tufty pointed. 'Did you *see* that?'

Logan blinked. 'But...?'

How was that even possible?

He stared down the back of the building and there was the answer: a large children's trampoline, about twelve feet off to the right. That explained the '*thud-adudadududa...*' noise. And the shrieking kids.

The kids were silent now, though. All standing around on the communal back lawn, staring at the tree Charles MacGarioch had just crashed through. Then up at the flat, and at the heads of Logan, Tufty, and Branson poking out of the window.

Actually *hitting* the trampoline from this distance, instead of the ground, had to be a one-in-a-hundred shot. Charles was bloody lucky he didn't break his neck, and every other bone in his body.

Why did young men always think they were sodding invincible? Right up until the moment they got proved fatally wrong.

Tufty's eyes were wide as soup bowls. 'How cool was *that*?'

Charles MacGarioch wasn't moving, though. So maybe not so lucky after all...

No – wait a minute.

There was a bit of a struggle, then he rolled over onto his back and lay there, grimacing up at the blue sky.

'Boing!' Tufty bounced on the mattress, making the bed frame creak. 'From the *top floor*!'

Charles struggled to his knees, then his feet. Blinking and shaking his head – sending bits of tree tumbling out of his stupid haircut.

He'd landed just the other side of a shoulder-high fence that enclosed the back gardens, separating them from the path that ran behind a little shopping area and some small old-fashioned houses.

One hand against the chain link, he staggered off, breaking into a limping run.

'Bloody hell.' Logan scrambled off the bed and out of the room. 'He's getting away!'

5

Logan barged out of MacGarioch's bedroom into the lounge, not slowing down. 'GET THE VAN!'

Steel, MacLauchlan, and Barrett stared as he charged straight through into the hall.

'NOW!'

Harmsworth was on his way back with the Big Red Door Key – so presumably he'd taken the sodding long way round. He let out a little 'Eeek!' and flattened himself against the wall to let Logan hammer past. *'What? Where are we... Eeek!'*

Steel's voice bellowed as she sprinted after him. 'SECURE THE SCENE!'

The sound of a mini-battering-ram hitting carpet clattered out, followed by a 'Bumholes...'

And Logan wheeched around the balustrades and onto the stairs. Taking them two at a time. Then leaping whole flights in the rush to the ground floor, closely followed by PD Branston, who seemed to be having the Best Day At Work Ever!

Tufty scrambled along after her, then Steel, Barrett, and PC MacLauchlan – waving Branston's lead about as if that was going to curtail her enthusiasm. 'Wait up, wait up!'

Logan swung around the last flight and there were the uniformed PCs, milling about at the bottom, like wet farts.

He barrelled straight past them, making for the front door. 'You four: out the back! He's getting away!'

And off they jolly-well buggered.

The door boomed wide, and Logan exploded into the baking sun, slithering to a halt on the parched grass in front of the badly parked police van.

No keys.

Tufty burst from the building's door, hoofing around to the driver's side – plipping the locks and clambering inside. 'Which way?'

Good question.

Logan scrambled into the passenger seat, sweat popping between his shoulder blades, because the whole van was at gas-mark six. But before he could haul the door shut, PD Branston leapt over him and into the middle seat. Sitting there between the two of them, with her gob open, tongue lolling, *very* pleased with herself.

The engine roared.

'Sarge?'

Logan clicked his seatbelt on. Pointed left. 'Step on it!'

The police van *scrunk*ed backwards, off the 'RESIDENTS PARKING ONLY' sign and onto the tarmac, turning hard so it was facing down Gort Lane, as Steel, Barrett, and MacLauchlan stumbled out of Block Four.

They hauled open the side door and all three of them piled in.

Steel dove into a seat. 'Don't just *fudging* sit there: go!'

'We has a hot pursuit!' Tufty put his foot down, making the tyres squeal, sending blue smoke billowing into the hot afternoon air – then the van shot forward, clumping up onto the pavement to get around the patrol car blocking the road. Nearly losing a wing mirror to a communal recycling bin, then clumping back onto the tarmac again, soon as they'd passed the second roadblock vehicle.

At the bottom of the lane, Tufty gave the wheel a hard twist to the right, and the van's back end kicked out, leaving smears of burnt rubber on the sun-baked tarmac – curling in the wing mirror as they fishtailed onto Gordon's Mills Road. Narrowly missing a bluebottle-green Škoda.

Yeah…

Disco time.

Logan hit the dashboard button, and the van's siren wailed, blue lights flickering and swirling as they roared back towards town.

They'd just wheeched through the pedestrian crossing when Barrett banged on the roof. 'That's him!' turning to point through the back windows. 'That's him there!'

Tufty slammed on the brakes and the ABS kicked in, juddering the van to a halt as Charles MacGarioch hurple-jogged across the road in the rear-view mirror. 'Got it!'

He whacked the gearstick into reverse, and they were whining backwards, at speed. Past the bus stop, where a lone auld mannie ogled at them. Stopping halfway across the pedestrian crossing.

Logan threw the passenger door open and tumbled out. 'HOY!' Sprinting towards the tree-battered figure scrambling his way over the chest-high wall at the side of the road.

Barrett rumbled the side door back, leaping free of the van, handcuffs at the ready … but they were *both* too slow. Charles MacGarioch disappeared straight down. For the second time that day.

Logan peered over the wall. 'Sod.'

A twenty-foot drop, not quite vertical – the steep slope densely overgrown with elder and hawthorn and jaggedy-sharp brambles.

Down there, on the road below, a red Kia's hazards flashed, security system wailing as the driver blundered out into the hot afternoon to gawp at the large new dent in her car's roof. The windscreen all cracked and opaque.

The car alarm clashed with the more familiar jingly tinkle of 'Greensleeves' coming from the mysterious ice-cream van that had haunted the afternoon – it was parked outside a modern block of flats, with a line of kids gathered by the serving hatch. Others already munching on their purchase and staring at the accident. A bit of theatre to go with their Pokey Hats and Funny Feet.

A cavalcade of copyright-infringing cartoon characters frolicked all over the van, along with the words 'MR FREEZYWHIP'S ICEALICIOUS TREATS!' in bright cheerful letters. And perched on top: an eight-foot-long fibreglass 99 cone, complete with red sauce.

Charles MacGarioch limped into view, glancing over his shoulder at Logan and Barrett, his face covered in scrapes and scratches from the recent trampoline-tree trauma and down-hill bramble scramble.

Logan stood on his tiptoes, scanning the slope for an easier / less painful way down. The main road had a turn-off about four hundred feet further along, that doglegged around onto Papermill Gardens, where Charles MacGarioch was limping his way towards Mr FreezyWhip's ice-cream van.

OK.

'HOY!' Logan waved at Tufty, then pointed at the junction. 'That way! We'll cut him off!' He slapped Barrett on the shoulder and clambered over the wall, crackling and snapping and shoving and half-falling his way down the steep drop and out onto the road below, emerging next to the wailing Kia.

Up on Gordon's Mills Road, the police van Dopplered away.

MacGarioch yanked open Mr FreezyWhip's driver's door and clambered in behind the wheel.

'Gah...' Barrett staggered out of the undergrowth, looking as if he'd been pulled through several hedges sideways. Spitting out spiders' webs and bits of leaves. He curled a mocking lip at the ice-cream van. 'Well, he's not going to get very far in *that*, is he. Probably only does about ten miles an hour.'

Mr FreezyWhip's engine snarled into life and the chimes grew louder. Then the kids scattered as the van leapt forward, bouncing through a shrubbery border, and across another bit of the car park, slaloming between parked hatchbacks, onto the tarmac and hammering it off into the distance.

Sod...

Logan sprinted after it.

He'd barely gone half a dozen paces before the police van appeared at the far end of the road, roaring towards them as Mr FreezyWhip accelerated away. On a collision course.

The silly buggers were going to play chicken, weren't they.

Because young men were thick and invincible.

Till they fatally weren't.

Thankfully, someone more sensible than Tufty must've intervened, because the police van swerved at the last moment, stomping on its brakes to avoid wrapping itself around a lamp-post.

Unsurprisingly, Mr FreezyWhip didn't stop.

Logan and Barrett ran for the police van, scrambling inside just as Tufty completed his three-point turn.

PD Branston was still in the centre seat, beaming away as if this was the most fun she'd had in years.

Useless sod. What was the point of having a police dog if it didn't chase and bite the bad guy?

'Where the hell were you?'

Branston barked a happy bark, not in the least bit bothered.

Then everyone got shoved back into their seats as Tufty floored it again.

Up ahead, Mr FreeezyWhip performed an expert drift around from Papermill Gardens onto Papermill Drive, then opposite lock onto Gordon's Mills Road – smooth as a classic Magnum.

Tufty wasn't quite so slick, and the police van squealed and lurched through the two turns, wallowing like a speedboat, throwing the occupants against the van's walls, seatbelts, and each other.

It looked as if Charles MacGarioch hadn't been wasting his time, playing all those rally and driving games – weaving Mr FreezyWhip in and out of the traffic, both oncoming and outgoing, sometimes up onto the pavement, sometimes roaring into the empty gaps. But always absolutely *pelting* it as 'Greensleeves' tinkled out.

Tufty was having a tough job keeping up, and it was sodding boiling in here, so Logan buzzed the window down to let in a roar of air and sirens.

There was an appreciative *woof*, and PD Branston lumped her paws into Logan's lap so she could stick her head out of the window, partially blocking his view of the road with her big hairy back, tail wagging away inches from Tufty's face.

A much greyer head popped forwards from the back of the van: Steel, Airwave handset in her hand. Pressing the button as they raced past bungalows and a startled minibus full of boy scouts. 'Alpha Charlie Six to Control – we are in pursuit of an ice-cream van, heading north on Gordon's Mills Road. Request backup ASA-fiddling-P!'

There was a pause, then a distorted voice crackled from the little speaker, *'Hud oan: an* ice-cream *van?'*

'Backup! Get us some sodding backup before someone dies!' She let go of the button, and thumped Logan. 'This is what happens when we don't have a buggering helicopter.'

Barrett held up a hand. 'That's another two quid in the swear jar.'

She turned and gave him the middle-finger salute.

Up ahead, just visible through Branston's brown-and-black fur, an old lady with an ancient Labrador was three-quarters of the way across the pedestrian crossing by Tillydrone Play Park. Standing there, like a statue, eyes wide, clutching the dog's lead as Charles MacGarioch jinked Mr FreezyWhip into the oncoming traffic to avoid battering straight through her.

Tufty did the same, and the driver of a plumber's van had to jam on his brakes to avoid becoming a hood ornament.

The Labrador watched Branston whoosh by – tongue flapping like a soggy windsock – unperturbed by the whole near-death experience.

Looked as if a couple of wee boys on their bikes, slowly rolling across the entrance to Gordon Brae, weren't going to be so lucky.

Tufty thumped the horn and the siren *ponk-honk*ed, but instead of hurrying out of the way, the idiots rolled to a stop and stared at the ice-cream van barrelling towards them.

Jesus, this was going to be a complete blood—

At the last moment, Mr FreezyWhip screeched hard left, almost losing control as the van skewed up onto two wheels … then thudded down again – shimmying its way along the heat-rippled tarmac, following the river.

Tufty hauled the police van around the same corner, past grubby grey boxes and monolithic tower blocks on one side; trees, scrubland, and the ever-steepening slope down to the swollen River Don on the other.

Logan checked the rear-view mirror.

The kids just shrugged and cycled on, as if they hadn't been moments away from knowing what steak tartare felt like.

Now that they were on the straight, the police van's bigger engine was closing the gap.

Steel thumbed the Airwave's button again. 'Still on Gordon's Mills Road. Heading *west* now. Repeat: west!'

Down to the right, sunlight flared off the river, strobing through gaps between the trees and bushes. A slab of Communist-grey flats on the left.

Getting closer.

And closer.

Mr WhippyFreeze swung out, clipping the edge of a speed lump, sending up a shower of sparks from whatever part of its undercarriage clipped the raised patch on the way down again. Tyres shrieking as MacGarioch went hard left, leaving a scorched-rubber graffiti tag behind, into a quiet residential street – nice little semi-detached bungalows, with steeply pitched roofs and dormer windows. Neat wee gardens. Hatchback country.

Tufty barely made the turn, coming within a pube's width of ending the chase buried axle-deep in a VW Polo.

Steel grabbed the seatback, steadying herself as they raced after the ice-cream van. 'South on Donbank Terrace!'

A groan from Barrett. 'We're all going to die, aren't we.'

As the road climbed the hill, it narrowed, parked cars crowding in on both sides. Because, shockingly enough, it hadn't been designed with high-speed pursuits in mind.

Steel poked Logan's shoulder. 'Who're the useless tits in the bunnets?'

A Volvo's wing mirror burst in a shower of glass-and-plastic shrapnel as Mr FreezyWhip clipped it.

Logan flinched as the debris clattered against the police van's windscreen. 'Don't know – they're DS Marshall's.'

Up ahead, the ice-cream van performed a perfect drift around onto Don Street.

'Well, why aren't they...' Her eyes went wide.

And so did everyone else's.

Then screams rang out as Tufty rammed on the brakes to avoid whanging straight into an Amazon delivery truck. The police van shuddered and skidded, nose dipping.

Barrett was right: they were all going to die.

Logan grabbed Branston in a double-armed hug, cos the silly hairy sod wasn't wearing a seatbelt and this was going to be sudden, violent, and messy...

He closed his eyes, bracing for impact, only to be hurled against the passenger door as Tufty spun the wheel and accelerated after Mr FreezyWhip again.

How the hell did he pull that one off?

Logan peeled one eye open, and there was Branston, looking a little confused at the sudden bout of physical attention, but happy enough to go along with it.

Granite bungalows lined the right side of the road, but the ground disappeared on the left – down a steep embankment to the railway line, with more grey-and-beige houses beyond. A blue-and-yellow Scotrail train clattered along the track in a smoky diesel drone, heading for the city centre. The passengers staring out the windows as the police van rocketed past. Some even waved.

Steel swallowed, no doubt glad to still be alive, given she wasn't wearing a seatbelt either. 'North on Don Street.' She gave herself a little shake and poked a badge number into her Airwave's keypad, snarling into the microphone. 'Biohazard, you useless glob of titspunk! If I don't see your uniforms in their patrol cars *right now*, I'm jamming my boot so far up your arse I can use your nostrils for lace holes!'

Barrett sniffed. 'That's another—'

'I don't care!'

The road veered right, and so did Tufty, nearly clipping a green Clio. More bungalow semis on the right, terraced wee one-up-one-downs on the left, both reaching off down the hill, back towards the river.

Mr FreezyWhip had grown his lead again, while they were dicking about, almost dying in the fiery wreckage of a side-on collision with the Amazon van, and now MacGarioch was whizzing downhill, towards what looked suspiciously like a dead end and trees.

The default ringtone blared out of Logan's phone – Beethoven's 'Symphony No. 9' – and he let go of Branston long enough to check the caller display: 'CHIEF SUPT. PINE'.

Yeah. Maybe not.

The 'Ode To Joy' went on and on and on and on… Clashing with the siren.

Up ahead, Mr FreezyWhip's brake lights glowed, tyres leaving snaking lines of black behind as the ice-cream van slid sideways into a messy four-way junction, causing a taxi to swerve *bang* into a lamp-post.

It probably would've been easier going right, onto Gordon's Mills Road again and back the way they'd come, or first left and up onto Don Terrace, but instead Charles MacGarioch took the second left, roaring away down into the darkness between the trees.

'Ha!' Steel banged the back of Logan's seat. 'Got the bastard now! We—'

Screaming belted out from the back of the van, yells of terror from the front, as Tufty tried to make the same turn – passenger-side wheels bouncing over the weird sticky-out chunk of pavement that protruded beyond the end of Don Street.

The whole van parted company with the ground: going airborne, an Unintended Flying Object heading straight for a flimsy set of bright-orange, temporary, plastic barriers and a fifty/sixty-foot plummet into the river beyond.

6

Tufty held on tight to the steering wheel, knuckles white with the strain, eyes wide, eyebrows trying to clamber their way to safety. 'AAAAAAAAAAAAAAAAAAAAAAAARGH!'

Logan grabbed hold of Branston.

Barrett babbled away in the background, battering out the words as quickly as possible: 'Hail Mary, full of grace, the Lord is with thee, blessed art thou among women and blessed is the fruit of thy womb ... JESUS!'

Her womb-fruit must've been smiling on them, because at the *very* last moment the van's wheels thumped down on the teeny chunk of tarmac left, giving them a bit of grip before the granite setts began.

Hurling them down into darkness, past a cluster of signs: 'WEAK BRIDGE AHEAD ~ 3 TON G.V.W.', 'WARNING NO UNAUTHORISED ACCESS BEYOND THIS POINT ~ BARRIER CONTROL OPERATION 300 YDS ~ RESTRICTED TURNING FACILITIES' and a no-entry-to-cars-and-motorbikes 'EXCEPT FOR ACCESS'. Which wasn't exactly inviting...

The setts *burrrrr*ed and rumbled beneath the police van's tortured tyres, making everything vibrate.

Stone walls leapt up on the left, holding the embankment back as the road sank deeper and deeper to a tight right turn – rushing towards them at ever increasing pace.

Even though it hadn't rained for a week, the van still slithered on the little rectangular blocks, arse-end skittering out as they tried to make the corner, rear wing striking sparks against the granite wall.

But they'd made it to the bottom of the hill alive, and there was Mr FreezyWhip, just ahead.

Steel grabbed her Airwave handset. 'Grandholm Bridge: heading north!' A cruel grin snarled across her face as they clattered over the narrow bridge. 'There's bollards at the end here. He's *toast*.'

An almighty *BANG* sounded up ahead.

From the look of things, Mr FreezyWhip had rear-ended a bright-red hatchback, presumably as it was in the process of lowering the bollards that kept the vulgar public from accessing the residents-only areas.

The ice-cream van bulldozed across the barrier, while the bollards were down, but the things were already sprouting up from the ground again, ready to catch a poor unsuspecting police van unawares.

Tufty took one hand off the wheel to pull down the sun visor, but all he found there was the sign: 'DON'T ENCOURAGE HIM!' He flipped it up and down again, as if that would change anything. 'Oh noes!' Looking more and more panicked with every passing second. 'Where's the police pass? WHERE'S THE POLICE PASS?'

Too late.

The van's *front* wheels got past the barrier OK, but the rest of the vehicle wasn't so lucky. A rising bollard must've clipped the underside about two-thirds of the way back, because the back end jerked into the air in an agonised screech of metal-on-metal.

And everyone was screaming again.

The rear wheels thudded down against the setts and Tufty

hauled the wheel to the right, to avoid ploughing straight into that rear-ended hatchback, flinging everyone sideways. Then they raced along the mill road: parkland on one side; a line of trees on the other, with the River Don just beyond.

Only now an alarming grinding noise came from somewhere under the van, and the exhaust howled and roared like a werewolf locked in a train-station toilet.

They snarled along beneath the spreading branches, through the dappled pools of shimmering light.

Technically, they should've been gaining on Mr FreezyWhip, but whatever the bollards had done to the drive chain it wasn't good. The van was slowing down. And a quick glance in the rear-view mirror revealed clouds of greasy blue smoke filling the leafy lane.

But instead of making good his escape, Charles MacGarioch slammed on Mr FreezyWhip's brakes – the front end dipping as the tyres slithered on the setts.

The ice-cream van lurched right, leaving the road and crashing between the trees at the side of the river, through the bushes. Momentarily flying – like a big, fat, rectangular swan – before diving nose-down into the River Don in a huge whoosh of spray.

A wrinkly clutch of old ladies stood in the middle of the road, staring as the ice-cream van bobbed in the fast-flowing water. Most of them had ancient dogs on the leash, except for one who appeared to be walking her husband. And he was the only one who seemed oblivious to the fact that if MacGarioch hadn't swerved into the river, he would've ploughed through them like brittle meaty skittles.

Tufty whacked his brakes on too, and the police van shuddered to a stop – right next to the hole that Mr FreezyWhip punched through the undergrowth.

The doors flew open, and everyone piled out.

Logan scrambled over to the riverbank, the rest of the team hot on his heels.

The ice-cream van drifted downstream a dozen feet or so, sinking and turning as it went – that open serving hatch not helping with the buoyancy. Then it must've hit something below the surface, because there was a metallic *thunk* and the whole thing keeled over sideways in the swollen river until all four wheels were in the air. Followed by a muffled *bang* as it wedged against a rock and stayed there, with everything but the wheels and undercarriage fully submerged.

No sign of Charles MacGarioch. And no sign of whoever was selling ice cream to the kids, back in Tillydrone.

Crap.

That was all they needed – two dead, drowned bodies to round off a perfect sodding day.

Steel dragged her eyes from the van to Logan, mouth stretched out and down, like a worried frog.

'Stand back!' Tufty strode towards the water's edge. 'Tufty to the rescue!'

The silly wee sod was just about to leap in when Barrett grabbed him by the back of the stabproof – hauling him up short. 'Don't be a divot!'

'But the ice-cream man...?'

Logan stripped off his jacket and clip-on tie. 'You'll sink like an anvil, with all that gear on.' Then struggled his way out of his shoes, gave himself a nod, and jumped into the river.

Bloody hell...

The day might've been roasting, but the water wasn't – swollen by all of last week's rain, it was like an ice bath, only fast flowing, and with the occasional bit of tree being swept downstream.

Come on, you idiot: *swim*.

He struck out towards Mr FreezyWhip.

Branston trotted along the riverbank beside him for five or six feet, then leapt in with a hairy *sploosh*. Because as far as a huge police Alsatian was concerned, today just kept getting better and better!

Steel had her Airwave out again: 'Target vehicle has crashed into the river. Officer has gone in to rescue civilian. Now where's my *bastarding* backup?'

As she paced the riverbank, Tufty and Barrett stripped off their heavy stabproof vests and massive utility belts.

Good.

Why should Logan be the only one getting soaked?

He reached the overturned, sunken van – grabbing a tyre to stop being swept away. Which seemed to be the last straw for the vehicle, because everything left above the water sank with a *glooomp*.

Logan hauled in a deep breath and dived down after it.

Visibility wasn't great beneath the surface – silt, stirred up by the swollen river and caught in the blistering sunshine, turned everything milky, meaning most of the van faded into the glowing murk.

He pulled himself along to the upside-down serving hatch. Sod.

A figure floated inside, facedown and immobile, in green-and-white-striped dungarees. Heavyset with a combover that had floated free from his bald pate. He hung, suspended in the water, surrounded by bobbing wrapped lollies and disintegrating cones. Scarlet blooming out from a gash across his forehead.

Good job the River Don was relatively shark-free.

Logan grabbed a stripy-dungaree shoulder-strap and pulled, wrestling him out of his drowned vehicle and back to the surface.

Hauling the ice-cream man's head above the water, and keeping it there.

The fast-flowing river pinned them against one of Mr FreezyWhip's tyres. Stopping them from being swept off downstream.

Branston, on the other hand, seemed to have found some weird eddy current on top of the inverted ice-cream van. Doggy-paddling around in lazy circles. Happy as a toddler in a paddling pool.

Barrett swam up, treading water as he looked around. 'Where's Charles MacGarioch?'

'Give us a chance!'

Tufty wasn't far behind. 'I'll find him.' And under he went, Spider-Man socks flashing in the sunshine before the murky river swallowed him whole.

'Urgh...' Barrett grimaced. 'This is a *stupid* game.' Then followed Tufty into the depths.

Over on the bank, Steel hurried towards a bright-orange lifebuoy, mounted at the side of the road. Still giving someone a hard time on her Airwave. 'Yes, but *three* of them have gone in now, OK? SO DO SOMETHING!' She yanked and tugged at the ring, snarling and roaring till it popped out of its mount, then dragged it back to the rescue scene. Fiddling one end of the attached rope free and standing on it, before flinging the buoy, one-handed, upstream of Logan. 'Well, I don't know, do I? Coastguard, fire brigade...' She scooped up the spare end of rope. 'Any bugger with a boat would do!'

The ring was swept straight towards Logan, and he grabbed it – wrestling the thing over the unconscious man's head and shoulders.

Tufty popped up from the murky deep with a gasp. 'Nope!' Then disappeared underwater again.

A spluttering Barrett surfaced next, blinking and coughing. 'Sodding fudgemuggers...' He pulled his way along the sunken van. 'MacGarioch's gone.' Wiping the water from his face. 'Don't know if he's washed away, or what, but there's *zero* sign of him.'

Great.

Tufty resurfaced a second time. 'More nope.' He took a big breath and bobbed up, ready to have another go.

'Hoy!' Barrett waved at him. 'Stop, you daft...'

But Tufty was gone again.

'Seriously?'

'Oh, for God's sake.' Logan shoved the ice-cream man at Barrett. 'Get him back to shore.'

A confused look. 'Where are you—'

'To find the daft wee loon.' Logan ducked under the water, half-swimming, half-pulling himself along the side of Mr FreezyWhip, hunting idiots. Past the serving hatch and on to the passenger door.

At least the window was open.

The driver's one too – letting the current barge through the van's interior, making a pair of ice-cream-cone-shaped furry dice bob and twist above the inverted rear-view mirror.

The windscreen was cracked, but from the look of things it was because of the large boulder the van had wedged itself against, rather than Charles MacGarioch's head.

There was no sign of him, though. And no sign of Tufty either.

Logan turned, squinting into the milky water, but neither idiot was upstream of Mr FreezyWhip.

So he poked his head through the open passenger window.

The cab was *definitely* empty.

A gap between the front seats led through to the back of the van – sectioned off by a beaded curtain that undulated like a forest of multicoloured kelp.

Bracing himself against the wing mirror, Logan swung around to the leeward side of the van. Nothing but more rocks and the skeletal frame of a dead bicycle. Maybe MacGarioch had been thrown clear in the crash? If so, he was long gone – swept away downriver. Might even be halfway to the North Sea by now…

And *still* no sodding Tufty.

Lungs burning, Logan struggled back up, like a breaching whale, bringing a huge spray of water with him. Coughing and gasping, because this underwater-rescue stuff was a shit-load harder than they made it look on TV.

A hand grabbed his arm, hauling him up onto the underside of Mr FreezyWhip, where the water was only thigh deep. And Branston was still slowly twirling.

Tufty pounded Logan on the back a couple of times. 'You OK, Sarge?'

Over on the riverbank, most of the old ladies had their phones out – some filming Logan's attempts at deep-sea rescue, the others recording as Barrett and PC MacLauchlan performed CPR on the ice-cream man, while Steel looked on. Issuing instructions, as she paced back and forth in front of the knackered police van. Giving someone a bollocking on her Airwave at the same time.

The throat-shredding cough hacked its way to a halt, leaving Logan slumped and wheezing. But at least he had enough breath to give Tufty a good hard thump on the arm. 'Thought you'd drowned!'

'Nah. I does has an advanced swimming certificate. *And* a lifesaving badge.'

Logan thumped him again. 'You tried to jump in with the full kit on!'

'Yeah. But they made us rescue rubber bricks in our pyjamas, so I was kinda working on instinct. I is a *lifesaving* dude.'

Idiot.

So Logan thumped him one more time, for luck.

Extra hard, this time.

vii

Harsh sunlight streamed through the ratty venetian blinds as Colin Miller (56) – world-class journalist, snappy dresser, first-rate husband, brilliant father, and *total* legend, by the way – frowned at the printout in his leather gloved hands. 'HERO COP STOPS SICK "LIVESTOCK MARKET"' complete with photo of a burning cattle shed and some pretty bloody great writing.

Definitely good enough for the portfolio. So it got a quick visit to Mr Hole Punch, then snapped into Mr Ring Binder.

The *Aberdeen Examiner*'s bullpen was an anaemic photocopy of its former self. Aye, the big open-plan space still had loads of cubicles, with their tatty blood-red walls, but the wee personal touches had been stripped away, packed into cardboard boxes for that sad final trudge to the pub: goodbye speech, platter of supermarket sausage rolls, and empty promises to keep in touch. Leaving nothing but an empty desk behind, now covered in file boxes and dust.

Most of the chairs had gone too – pillaged by the handful of remaining staff to replace their own knackered ones.

Oh, the signs still hung from the ceiling, marking out the different sections: like 'PICTURE DESK' and 'OBITUARIES', but no one *worked* there any more.

Instead, the chair thieves sat at scattered desks, keeping

their heads down, poking away at laptops and phones, hoping they weren't going to be next...

But while everyone else had opted for the try to-no'-be-too-visible approach, Colin had built himself a wee fort out of file boxes and box files, walling off this corner of the bullpen.

He plucked another printout from the pile.

'BODIES FOUND IN CLIFFTOP-COTTAGE FREEZER' with the subheading, 'MISSING UNIONISTS "TORTURED TO DEATH" SAYS SHOCKED PARAMEDIC'.

Aye ... maybe no' his finest hour.

That one went in the bin.

'"CROOKED COP FRAMED ME" CLAIMS LOCAL BUSINESSMAN', subheading: 'OFFICER PLANTS CHILD PORNOGRAPHY ON SUSPECT'S COMPUTER AS—'

'Hoy, Grandad.' There was a knock on his file-box wall, and Tamsin Johnson (21) sauntered into his inner keep. She had a boy's haircut, Numbered Onions T-shirt, ripped jeans, and grubby Hi-Tops. Tattoos all down one arm. Spots. Enough piercings in both ears to pick up a decent FM signal.

'Who you calling "Grandad"?' Colin sat up a wee bitty straighter, so she could drink in the fitted, pink, Ralph Lauren shirt, top three buttons open to show off some tasty gold chains and manly chest hair. Even if it was going a little grey. And there was *slightly* more of it than there was on top of his head.

'Be still my beating.' Voice flat as her chest. She peered at the ring binder. 'Not done your homework for teacher, yet?'

Colin punched two holes in the printout and added it to the binder. 'Waste of bloody time.'

'And can you not do all this *digitally?*' Perching her wee flat bum on the edge of his desk. 'God, you're such a dinosaur.'

Cheeky sod.

'Haven't you got a listicle to write? "Top ten reasons cellulite is the new margarine!", or some shite.'

'Print's dead, Daddy-O.' Tamsin hooked a thumb at the door. 'Quitting time. We're hitting Dodgy Pete's for some scoofage: you want?'

He snatched another sheet from the pile – 'POLISH SHOPKEEPER BLINDED IN HORROR ATTACK' – scowling at the photo of Victoria Road in Torry. 'And who the hell does she think she is? You got any idea how many scoops I've written?' Waving his printout at the newsroom walls, and all the framed front pages hanging there. 'Seventy percent of these buggers are mine! Probably more like eighty.' But did that matter? Did it hell. 'Making me audition for my *own* spot on the bloody paper...'

Over in the opposite corner, the office printer squealed and clunked like someone was battering mice with a wooden mallet.

Tamsin shrugged. 'Yeah, it's a diabolical liberty, so it is.' She pointed at the door again. 'Now: Dodgy Pete's, yes or no?'

'Trouble is, most of this stuff's ancient.' He thumped his collection of scoops and exclusives. 'Could really do with a juicy *new* story to show off the old magic touch.'

'You'll be lucky. Nothing interesting's happened in this arsehole city for *years*.'

Colin stared at her. 'Someone just set fire to a migrant hostel with actual *people* in it!'

'Racists is as racists does.' She picked up the folder and flicked through his printouts. 'Your generation gets a stiffy for that kinda National Front crap, doesn't it? Assuming you can tear yourselves away from all the misogyny, ableism, and homophobia.'

'Aye, *thanks* for that.' He plucked the next potential front page from the pile. 'THE FACE OF EVIL' ~ 'SERIAL

Killer Strikes Again As Cannibal Terror Returns To Aberdeen'.

Now *that* was a story.

Tamsin handed his portfolio back, her voice losing the cynical-teenager edge for something a lot kinder. 'Don't sweat it, OK? I had my review yesterday and she was fine. You'll ace it.' Then nodded towards the exit. 'Last call for a pint?'

Aye, she was probably right.

He gave her a wee wince. 'Getting too old to go back on the dole...' He added the Flesher story to his folder and stood. 'If you're still there when I've finished with our new Lord and Mistress, I might pop in for a swift one.'

Colin did up his top three shirt buttons – not easy with black leather gloves on, and four prosthetic digits – flipped up his collar, and tied a Windsor knot in the burgundy tie from his drawer. Rolled down his sleeves. Pulled on the linen jacket that completed the suit. And gave his neck a wee stretch.

Cos if you were off to get fired, might as well look good while you did it.

He tucked the ring binder under his arm and sashayed across the bullpen to the double doors.

Paused to examine his reflection in one of the framed front pages. His byline of course, from 2011: 'TOE TERROR OF BRAVE JENNY – KIDNAPPERS PROVE IT'S NO HOAX' above a smiling photo of Jenny McGregor (6) with her curly red hair and freckles singing her little heart out during her last ever appearance on *Britain's Next Big Star*. Poor wee sod.

He straightened his tie.

Then frowned, running a finger through the furry layer of dust that'd built up on the frame. Making a wee hairy caterpillar.

Was a time when the cleaners would've dusted and polished

every single one of these, each morning. Now you were lucky if the office got hoovered once a quarter.

He shoved the door open and marched out into the corridor.

Which needed more than a quick once-over with a feather duster. The carpet tiles were festooned with coffee stains – like the floor was staging a dirty protest – the plastic pot plants drooped under the weight of furry grey grime, and the paintwork needed at least three coats to cover up the scrapes, scores, and greasy scuffs.

The only clean things out here, were the framed front pages. But unlike in the newsroom, these weren't from the *Aberdeen Examiner*, they were the worst kind of red-top tabloid: the *Scottish Daily Post*, with its lurid headlines and paparazzi photos. Female stars getting out of cars with their pants on show; unflattering beach bodies; posed underwear shots; cheesy smiles and Bisto tans. All displayed in brand-new frames – courtesy of their brand-new boss.

As if this shite was anything to aspire to.

Colin put a bit of swagger in his walk as he passed doors marked 'ADVERTISING / SALES' and 'ACCOUNTS' and 'DISTRIBUTION' and 'ARCHIVE', taking a right at the dogleg, pausing to gaze out over Altens Industrial Estate with its 'inspiring' collection of warehouses, lorry parks, fabrication yards, storage yards, offices, and yet more sodding warehouses. All in depressing shades of grey, grime, and blue.

And the paper's car park, of course. Where Tamsin and a couple of the other interns performed the loose-limbed amble, on their way to Dodgy Pete's for an after-work pint or three.

Lucky sods.

Anyway, this wasn't getting the monkey strangled, was it.

He sauntered past 'LEGAL' and the boardroom, to the corridor's end: the editor's lair.

The previous incumbent – Malcolm J Morrison (64), three

heart attacks, double bypass, dedicated gambler, and cigar fiend – had decorated the door with stickers and dynamo labels, proclaiming things like 'ABANDON HOPE ALL YE WHO ENTER', 'IDIOTS NEED NOT APPLY!', and 'I AM A CRUEL & VENGEFUL GOD!' Instead of 'EDITOR' the brass sign screwed to the wood said, 'THE MONSTER IS:' with a slidy bit for 'IN' and 'OUT', though it was jammed between the two options.

A lone, squeaky, plastic chair sat outside the door for those seeking an audience with The Monster. It was occupied by Louis Garfield (26): a bearded wee lad, with dark bags under his eyes and a black-and-white stripy top. Like a nervous burglar. Only instead of a stocking mask it was a pair of big round glasses, far too many tatty friendship bracelets, and a pair of American 'sneakers' – one of which bounced against the floor in time with his jiggling knee.

Louis was clutching a half-dozen sheets of black mount-board to his weedy chest. Because the Art Department loved sticking shite to bits of cardboard like that.

'Dear oh dear.' Colin leaned against the scuffed wall, opposite. 'You're no' telling me the great *Natasha Agapova*, forty-eight, editor to the stars, panderer to the great unwashed, is running late?'

'We're having a redesign. Need to get "stakeholder input".'

'Oh aye?' Crossing his stylishly trousered legs at the ankles, showing off the polished tan shoes. 'Come on then, I'm a stakeholder. See's a looky.'

'Right. Yes.' Louis turned the mock-ups, so they faced Colin, working his way through them one by one.

Bloody hell.

From the look of it, the *Aberdeen Examiner* was about to abandon all pretence of being a serious grown-up paper and embrace running about with a bucket on its head and trousers round its ankles instead. Each one of the four new designs were full-on tabloid tribute acts: complete with bikini-shots, crap about celebrity diets, garish banners, and big screechy headlines. 'OUR HEROES NEED YOUR SUPPORT!', 'MIGRANT CRIME RAMPAGE BLIGHTS BRITAIN!', 'LEFTY JUDGES PLOT TO CRIPPLE COUNTRY!', and 'LOONY PROBATION POLICY FREES PAEDO PERV!'

Colin whistled. 'Fuck me...'

'Really?' A small pout. 'I thought they were quite *good*.' Louis turned the mock-ups around again, staring at his own work. 'I was going for more of a *Scottish-Daily-Post* feel. You know, because she was editor there?'

Time to give the wee jobby a bit of advice.

'One: never, *ever* stick exclamation marks in a headline – it's called a "dog's cock" for a reason. Two: since when did we become a right-wing rag?' Leaning across the corridor to thump the mountboard. 'This really where we're going?'

Louis nodded. Then checked his watch. 'Do you think I could go for a pee? I want to go for a pee, but what if she calls me in and I'm off peeing?' Twisting one leg over the other, presumably to stop anything leaking out. 'Not a great first impression, is it?'

'God's sake.'

Kids these days...

Colin rapped his knuckles against the door. Gave it a count of five, then tried the handle.

Locked.

Aye, thought as much.

He gave the door a good thumping – just in case she was hiding in there.

Still nothing.

'She's no' in.' A sniff and a shrug. Then a wee sing-song

voice for: 'Ah well, what a pity, better luck next time.' Colin turned on his stylish heel and marched off. Pausing outside Legal, to have a squint back down the corridor.

The numpty hadn't moved, just sat there with his mock-ups, knees trembling like his bladder was about to pop.

'She's no' in, you idiot! Go pee. Go home. Go find a top that doesnae make you look like a zebra crossing.' Jabbing a finger in his direction. 'And stop it with the exclamation marks!'

Louis wrapped his sneakers around each other, upping the pressure. 'But what if she turns up and I'm not *here*?'

'She was at that SME charity-auction dinner bollocks last night. Probably still hungover, or got her legs wrapped around some poor prick from a downhole drilling company. Getting her "downhole" drilled. Honestly—'

Was as far as he got, before his phone launched into Green Day's 'American Idiot'. Which meant someone was calling the number they stuck on his columns for anonymous tip-offs. He answered it – one finger raised to silence Louis, just in case. 'Colin Miller.'

A woman's voice, bit teuchtery, calling from mobile: '*Aye: you the boy writes that stuff in the papers? Cos I got a story for you...*'

8

Logan shifted sideways, until his phone was shaded by the tree he'd hung his socks on, bare feet slapping against the warm setts. Shoes sitting on the riverbank. Trousers now uncomfortably damp, rather than sopping wet. Shirt no longer see-through. Which was just as well, because there were only so many Roberta Steel 'jokes' about your nipples one man could take.

The knackered police van had been joined by two patrol cars and an ambulance – lights swirling as a paramedic thunked the door shut. A *whoop* from the ambulance's siren, and off it went. Helped through the cordon of blue-and-white 'POLICE' tape by a moist Barrett.

The cordon stretched across the road, along the side of the parkland, and back to the river again – with its tail end tied to the metal pole where Steel had found the lifebuoy. Making a little rectangle of sanity in a world gone absolutely bonkers.

Take the group of old ladies who'd been out walking their assorted dogs and the token husband. For some unfathomable reason, they'd each been given one of those silvery 'marathon runner' blankets, even though it was hot enough out here to bake them like potatoes. Glinting away as a couple of uniforms took their statements.

Madness.

Logan moved around a bit further, till he could see the phone's screen properly.

TARA:

> Got our timeslot for parent/teachers tonight: 1850.

> I vote CHIPS for tea!

Excellent idea.
He thumbed out a reply:

> Motion carried – chips it is.

> I'm at a crime scene, but I think

Was as far as he got, because as the ambulance disappeared over the bridge, a short-arse wee hardman in a linen suit strolled into view, hands in his pockets. Like he was out for an early evening constitutional.

Colin Miller.

Logan groaned, put his phone away, then padded over, bare footed, to intercept him at the cordon.

'Aye, aye.' Colin gave a big Weegie grin. 'Hear you went for a wee swim.'

'How? It only happened *twenty minutes ago*. Who told you?'

'Gotta protect my sources, and all that.' He stood on his tiptoes, peering at the crime scene. 'So … you got something juicy for me?'

Logan returned the smile. 'No. Feel free to sod off.'

'That any way to talk to an old friend?' Digging into the suit jacket with a leather-gloved hand, he produced a much fancier phone than Logan's. Holding it out, so the screen was visible.

A sort of slideshow was playing, only instead of stills it was made up of short video files – shaky and a bit grainy, clearly taken on mobile phones – of Mr FreezyWhip being chased all over Tillydrone by the police van. Five bits of footage, none of which lasted more than a couple of seconds, on a loop.

Colin gave his phone a waggle. 'Thought it's doughnuts youse bastards are obsessed with?' Then put it away and had another peer at the collection of old folk. 'This wouldn't have anything to do with that fire last night, would it?'

'No comment.'

A tut. 'Hell of a thing. What kinda racist wanker torches a hotel for migrants? Lucky no one died, but.'

Logan kept his face completely still.

Colin blinked. 'Oh, you're *kidding* me!'

So much for styling it out. '*Strictly* off the record. Soban Yūsuf died of his injuries an hour and a half ago.'

'Christ.' Shaking his head. 'That who you were chasing: our xenophobic arsonist arsehole? You know, as we're "off the record", like.'

'Should you not be back at the office, currying favour with the new boss?' Logan pulled on his best American accent: 'Hold the front page! We got *eight new ways* to blast belly fat and you *ain't gonna believe* number six!'

'Aye, you think you're joking?' Colin pointed off towards Altens. 'See back in the good old days: that newsroom was thick with cigarette smoke, the smell of ink and cheap coffee, clattering with typewriters… Now it's just me, and a handful of sodding children.' Scowling out at the glittering water. 'Work experience and unpaid interns. Like it's sodding bob-a-job week!' Throwing his gloved hands in the air, because the wee sod could never resist a bit of melodrama. 'And these kids got *no* nose for a story. If you can't nick it off Twatter, ThickTok, or FacePuke it's too much work!'

Logan nodded. 'Yup.'

He puffed out his cheeks. Looked away. 'So come on, big man – dees a favour and support local journalism.'

Maybe he was right? Maybe the press could help for a change, instead of making everything worse? And it wouldn't hurt to have the *Aberdeen Examiner* owing them a favour. So maybe just a *tiny* bit of...

Sod.

A sleek black Mercedes appeared over the Grandholm bridge, then turned onto the riverside road. Making straight for the cordon.

Logan stood up a little straighter. 'Here we go...'

'Oh aye?'

Barrett snapped to attention, then raised the 'POLICE' tape to let the Merc through.

Colin lowered his voice. 'Won't be long till the numpties arrive with their outside broadcast vans and their camera crews.' He produced a packet of extra-strong mints, proffering the open end to Logan, as if that was going to be an effective bribe. 'Maybe you and me can do a deal? Back scratching, like.'

Logan tried not to grimace, he really did. 'Just... I'll think about it, OK? Now make yourself scarce – don't want the boss thinking I'm a fifth columnist for the fourth estate.' Then marched towards the Mercedes.

The driver's door opened and out climbed the Chief Super's sidekick, all done up in Police Scotland black. Sergeant Brookminster. Thin, and efficient-looking. The kind of man who could carry off a side parting and a David Niven moustache *without* looking like a sex offender. He jerked his rugged chin at Logan, then marched smartly around the car to open its rear passenger door.

There was a pause, then Chief Superintendent Pine climbed out – dressed all in black, like her sidekick, only with a lot more decoration on the epaulettes. Phone pressed to her ear as she pulled her peaked cap on, followed by a pair of sunglasses. 'Yes … I understand that … Look, I appreciate your concern, First Minister, but I assure you my officers are proceeding with the *utmost* professionalism.' She pressed the phone against her chest and grimaced at Logan – dropping her voice to a hard-edged whisper. 'What the buggering hell is going on here?'

'Sorry, ma-am.'

Back to the phone. 'I have to go: duty calls … Yes, First Minister … OK, love to Ellie and the kids … Bye.' She hung up, then sagged.

Logan stayed where he was and kept his mouth shut.

A drone sizzled through the air, with the Sky News logo on the side and a dirty-big gimbal camera mounted underneath. Performing a slow, panning pass of the crash scene for the viewers at home.

Nosey bastards.

Pine rubbed a hand across her forehead. 'Where's Detective Chief Inspector Rutherford?'

'Supervising the search of Charles MacGarioch's flat, ma-am. We're hoping there might be some clue about where he's—'

'*Why,*' squeezing the words out as if every one of them was physically painful, 'in the name of *all* that's holy, was there no one watching *the rear of the property*?'

'It's—'

'Did *no one* think he might do a runner?'

'*Don't be daft.*' – Steel's voice, right behind them.

Pine flinched. Logan winced.

Then they both turned and there she was, overalls unzipped to her waist, belly button on show where her 'SexWeasels!' T-shirt had ridden up. Pale and worrying. Like a zombie's eye… Steel gave it a scratch. 'The wee scrunk-bag lives on the top floor. What was he going to do, sprout wings and fly?'

'Sprout *wings*?' The Chief Super stared at her, then performed a slow three-sixty with her arms out, indicating the high degree of fuckupitude on display at this location and beyond. 'Well, he's doing a damned good impersonation of it!'

'Don't worry: we'll find him.' Stopping scratching for long enough to dig a vape out of her overalls. 'Roberta Steel always gets her man. Or woman.' A wink. 'And may I say you're looking *particularly* fetching today in that nice tight T-shirt? Really brings out the swell of your—'

'That's quite enough of that.' Pointing off towards the knackered van. 'Away and do something useful. Before I bust you down to the Friday Night Vomit Squad.'

That got her a lazy salute as Steel took a long drag on the vape and released a sticky-sweet cloud of strawberry short-cake. 'Ah, I love it when you're all take-chargey.' Another wink, then she sauntered off, puffing away. 'But if you change your mind...'

'And no vaping on duty!' Pine scowled at Logan. 'I swear to God that woman is *itching* for a constructive dismissal.'

'Her thirty's up next month. She'll be long gone by the time HR get the disciplinary paperwork sorted.' He shifted his feet on the warm setts. 'But she's right: we were on the top floor. The only reason Charles MacGarioch isn't on his way to the mortuary right now is he managed to hit a trampoline instead of the ground. Pure blind luck. By rights he should be splattered all over the dried-up grass in his nan's back garden.'

Pine grimaced out at the scene for a bit: from the silvered oldies and the ruined police van; to the lifesaving ring – currently bobbing in the river, because Logan had tied it to one of Mr FreezyWhip's tyres. Marking the site of the wreck.

'We haven't had a cock-up of this magnitude for ages.'

'Sorry, ma-am.' He shrugged. 'Everyone's doing their best.

Turns out: being an Operational Support Unit isn't as easy as Sergeant Mitchell and his thugs make it look.'

'Urgh...' She headed for the riverbank. 'Ice-cream van's owner?'

'Ian Rawlings. DC Barrett and PC MacLauchlan performed CPR till the ambulance got here. It was close, but they think he'll be OK.'

'That's something, at least.' She aimed a kick at a clump of weeds, clipping the puffy seedhead off a dandelion, making it explode. 'I take it we're working on the assumption that Charles MacGarioch survived the crash?'

'Unless his body washes up further downstream. Assuming he's not been swept out to sea, of course.'

She sagged some more. 'Oh you *do* know how to cheer a girl up, don't you.'

'We've circulated a lookout request.'

Mottled spots of sunlight swirled around them as a breeze caressed the leaves above. Out on the churning river, a confused-looking duck swept past. Someone coughed...

Pine stuck her chin out. 'I don't like racist, murdering, arsonous, wee bastards running around on my patch, Logan.' Then a sigh. 'I understand your desire to cover for DCI Rutherford, but planning the dunt was *his* responsibility. He should've had people positioned out back.'

'It was the *top floor*—'

'I appreciate the loyalty, but...' Another dandelion met the executioner's boot. 'I need to know if he's up to the job.'

Well, that didn't put Logan in a difficult position at all.

At the far end of the cordon, Colin Miller was making his way towards the OAPs in their baked-tattie tinfoil blankets. Ready to whip up a story.

That Sky News drone made another pass.

Chief Superintendent Pine grunted. 'Not that I can do

much about it. We're understaffed as it is: who am I going to replace him with?' Dandelion number three lost its head. 'Still waiting on an answer, by the way.'

'It's...' Deep breath. 'Everyone's just a bit stressed-out and frazzled right now. Having to pick up the slack from all the other departments.'

'Middle of a sodding heatwave and half the division's off with "Man Flu".' Victim number four died in a puff of teeny gossamer umbrellas. 'I want Charles MacGarioch in custody by close of play tomorrow *at the latest*. Custody or the mortuary – don't care which.' She held her hand up as Logan winced. '*If* he's drowned. Either way we're diffusing this issue before that stupid protest march. No point giving the mob something *else* to stick on their bloody placards.'

'Ma-am.'

Out of dandelions, her killing spree moved on to booting small stones into the river instead. 'Media briefing at seven. I want you there, prepped and ready to explain ...' waving her arms again, 'this.'

Ah.

'I can't. It's parent-teacher night at Lizzie's school, and we're—'

'Oh, you should've *said*.' All smiles. 'Right. Well, we'll just ask the assembled camera crews, TV broadcasters, news-papers, journalists, newsreaders, and podcasters not to talk about the story till you're free. How does Wednesday sound? Or is Thursday better for you?'

Heat prickled the skin on Logan's cheeks. 'Ma-am.'

'Good man.' The smile tightened as she patted him on the arm. 'Knew I could rely on you.' Then turned and marched back towards her waiting Merc. 'Press are going to crap in our stovies over this one, Logan. And I'm shit-out of brown sauce.'

Sergeant Brookminster opened the rear passenger door

for her, but she didn't even acknowledge him – already on another call.

'Nigel.' Slipping into her seat. 'No … Will you shut up for two minutes and listen? It's—'

Her sidekick clunked the door shut. Then gave Logan a sort of cross between a salute and a wave, then climbed in behind the wheel.

The Mercedes swung around in a scrunchy three-point turn. Slowing so Barrett could raise the cordon once more. And off they went.

A voice at Logan's shoulder: *'Nice arse.'*

'Arrgh!' He spun around, and there was Steel, letching as the Chief Super's car rumbled onto the bridge. 'Stop sneaking up on people!'

Steel produced another cloud of strawberry shortcake. 'Yeah, she's a bit stuck-up, but I like a challenge.' A good long puff. 'You got a crane sorted yet?'

A *what?*

He stared at her. 'Have you been drinking?'

'To get the ice-cream truck out the river. Or are you planning on leaving it there? Cos I can tell you for a fact: Scenes are gonna bitch and whinge if you make them take fingerprints underwater.'

Oh, for God's sake.

The horror had a point.

And what was worse: *he* should've thought of it.

Logan sagged, grimacing up at the swaying leaves and rippling light. 'Great.'

Steel patted his other arm. 'Don't worry about MacGarioch: the wanker won't get far. His days as a murderous arsoning wee shite are *over.*' A big sook on her vape, and she enveloped them both in another cloying fruity cloud. 'Till then: call a crane.'

9

Now that Charles MacGarioch's living room wasn't stuffed full of police officers and a happy barky dog it looked larger. But not much.

DCI Rutherford slumped on the sofa, in a suit so sharp you could shave with it. Which would probably help, because a heavy seven-o'clock shadow rampaged across his miserable face. Hair tussled at the front and fanned out at the back, where it pressed against a starched antimacassar. Bags under his eyes. Looking stretched, knackered, and defeated.

Logan turned to look out the window instead.

A handful of kids were out, playing on their scooters, pretending not to watch as a forensic tech from 'Scenes' lugged a blue plastic evidence crate to the grubby Transit.

They weren't the only ones keeping an eye on things – two photographers had their cameras out, snapping away, while a lone TV news crew filmed a bloke in a suit.

Had a perfect view of his bald spot from up here.

All shiny and strawberry-coloured in the baking sun.

'Just ...' Logan glanced back at Rutherford, 'forewarned, OK?'

The DCI slapped both hands over his face. 'Oh, for Christ's sake. We're on the top floor!'

'That's what *I* told her.'

A groan, followed by more slumping.

Rutherford didn't look as if he'd be surfacing anytime soon, so Logan pulled out his phone and checked his text messages instead. Scrolling back to where he was so rudely interrupted earlier.

TARA:

> Got our timeslot for parent/teachers tonight: 1850.
>
> I vote CHIPS for tea!

Followed by his unsent reply:

> Motion carried – chips it is.
>
> I'm at a crime scene, but I think

He deleted the whole thing and tried again – *tick-tick-tickticktick*:

> Sorry, change of plan – got to do a press conference (3-line whip).
>
> We're having 'a day'.
>
> I'll explain when I get home.

SEND.

That would go down well. Like a condom full of sick at a balloon-modelling party.

Rutherford still hadn't moved.

'You OK?'

There was a teeny whimpering sound, then a muffled, 'Do you have *any* idea how many cases I'm juggling right now?'

One of the many joys of climbing the greasy pole – higher up you got, the more crap they made you carry.

Logan leaned back against the windowsill. 'Assuming Charles MacGarioch made it out of the ice-cream van alive, and he swam ashore, what do we think: other side of Gordon

Brae bridge? Or would you tread water till Hillhead? Put a bit of distance between you and the crash?'

'First DI Vine comes down with the lurgie, so I get *his* cases. Then it's Evans. And McPherson. And Findlay. So I get *theirs* too!' Really pressing those hands into his face as a frustrated howl rang out. Followed by a little cough.

'I've called for a search team, but we'll be lucky if we get half a dozen bodies. Everyone's stretched thin.'

'Thin? I'm bloody anorexic here!' Rutherford's arms flopped sideways. 'Could sleep for a week.'

'Thought we were meant to get backup from other divisions?'

'Ha! They've all got the sodding plague too.' He levered himself forward, sagged, then smothered a couple more coughs. 'We'll just have to make do with what we've got.' Pointing at Charles MacGarioch's bedroom. 'They've got his computer in for analysis – I want you up their arseholes like a pineapple suppository till they *find* something. And we need to interview all known associates. And...' He frowned. 'What am I forgetting?'

'Chasing up the Fire Investigation Unit?'

Rutherford nodded. 'OK – consider yourself volunteered.'

Great.

That's what Logan got for being helpful.

'And there's the press conference at seven.' Logan checked his watch – 18:34. 'Better get moving.'

'Yeah...' Another groan as Rutherford levered himself out of the racist old lady's couch. 'Because apparently this crap isn't hard enough.'

Logan finished the last sentence from his prepared statement. '...a full recovery, thanks to the quick actions of officers on the scene.'

'No. No, no, no, no, no.' PC Nigel Sweeny bustled around the media liaison office, grabbing sheets of paper from the printer and whacking staples into them. '*Never* say some-one'll "make a full recovery". What if he comes down with MRSA, or something? Or has a stroke?' His mean little mouth crunched its way through yet another Gaviscon tablet as he gathered his papers into a six-inch-thick pile. The wee mouth didn't really go with the over-generous nose and enthusiastic chin, sort of *Mr Punch Joins the Police Force*. He grimaced. 'Way *my* luck's going, our ice-cream man will be dead just in time for Breakfast News.'

The office wasn't much bigger than MacGarioch's living room. Only instead of portraits of the King, shelves crowded in from every wall – making the room feel even smaller – jam-packed with folders and lever-arch files. Piles and piles of newspapers. There was barely room for the three desks, or the trio of flatscreen TVs. Each one tuned to a different twenty-four-hour rolling-news channel.

Two of them were covering a 'Vision For Britain' rally in Trafalgar Square – chinless wankers with beer guts and poorly spelled placards – while Sky News featured drone footage of the River Don as Steel's crane lifted a waterlogged Mr FreezyWhip from the depths.

Sweeny grabbed another antacid from the pack. 'Tell them he's "*doing well*" and doctors are "*pleased with his progress*". That way, if he snuffs it, it's their fault not ours.' Then rammed a peaked cap on his head, and stuck a manila folder on top of his stapled pile, pausing for a moment to check his own reflection in a little mirror mounted by the office door. 'Come on, Nige – only six more months and you're back in CID.' Popping one last Gaviscon, before hurrying out into the corridor, leaving Logan to catch up.

He scurried across the open-plan space, with its little

warren of cubicles and desks, checking his watch every thirty seconds on the way to the double doors at the end. 'Late, late, late, late, late…'

A handful of cubicles were populated by wilted officers and support staff, grinding their way through a back shift. Off in the distance, someone sneezed. Someone else coughed.

'Like a bloody ghost town in here, isn't it?' Sweeny fumbled with his folder. 'What was wrong with the old place? Lots of lovely hideyholes in Queen Street. Not like this … panopticon bollocks.'

They thumped out through the doors into a bland corridor, with a smoked-glass view of Broad Street and lots of cheery motivational posters about 'PROFESSIONALISM' and 'PUBLIC SERVICE'.

Sweeny checked his watch again, swore, and scurried faster. 'If any of the buggers ask about the protest march this weekend, don't engage, OK?' Battering into the stairwell. 'We're officially on lockdown till the Boss decides what the hell we're doing for bodies to police the bloody thing.'

Clattering down the steps, ignoring the posters demanding 'INTEGRITY' and 'HONESTY'.

Shoving through the doors at the bottom as his phone boomed out the *BBC News* theme tune. He juggled his papers and answered it as they strode across the short corridor, to the security-controlled entrance to the main lobby. 'Boss! How— … Yes, yes: I know it starts at seven.' A grimace as he poked the keycode into the lock. 'I know … Yes. … I've been working on DI McRae's—' Pink bloomed in his cheeks. 'Yes, Boss … Sorry.'

Logan followed him across the Police Scotland crest set into the lobby floor – the words 'SEMPER VIGILO' already getting a bit scuffed by all the foot traffic.

'We're on our way now … Yes, Boss … Just about to walk

through the door.' Sweeny performed a bit of human origami to pin the folder and papers to his chest and the phone to his ear as he fumbled with his lanyard – bending almost double to clack it against the automatic turnstile beside the reception desk. 'Honestly. We're like right there.'

The gate glowed green and beeped.

Sweeny shoved through, marching fast. 'I know I said— ... Yes, Boss ... Sorry, Boss. But it's—' Disappearing through the door marked 'CONFERENCE SUITES'.

Logan shared a nod with Big Gary – perched behind the desk, like an evil Buddha, with a sudoku book – and beeped himself through the turnstile.

The 'Conference Suites' door opened on yet another corridor, where a row of portraits displayed every Chief Constable from the old Grampian Police days, then every Chief Superintendent since Police Scotland came in and spoiled all the fun.

Down at the end, Sweeny was disappearing through into the main conference room. 'Yes, Boss ... No, Boss ... Honestly: I'm here, I'm here.'

Logan stopped outside the door. Straightened his suit jacket. Then his shoulders. Took a deep breath. And pushed into Bedlam.

A sea of journalists and cameras stared at the three of them, sat at the front of the conference room – the chatter falling silent as DCI Rutherford stood to address the mob.

He'd had a shave and combed his hair, put on a fresh shirt and tie, looking every bit the professional police officer. Almost unrecognisable from the wrung-out, despondent lump, drooping away on MacGarioch's sofa.

He was flanked by Sweeny on one side and Logan on the other, while Chief Superintendent Pine was nowhere to be seen. Having buggered off at the first available opportunity; putting a bit of distance between herself and whatever omnishambles was about to unfold. Because it wasn't going to be easy spinning this as anything less than a monumental cluster-wank.

Cameras *click-click-click-click*ed, flashguns flickering as Rutherford muffled a cough. Then pulled his chin up. 'Two days ago, nine people were injured, four of them seriously, when the Balmain House Hotel on Broomhill Road was deliberately set on fire. Earlier today, we learned that, sadly, Soban Yūsuf has died from his injuries.'

An outbreak of murmuring rippled through the press pack, accompanied by a fresh strobe of camera flashes.

'Our thoughts and sympathies are with his family at this terrible time.'

A bunch of hands went up, but Rutherford ignored them.

Had a wee cough instead, while the hubbub died down.

'Soban acted as a translator for British forces in Helmand Province, and then later in Kabul. He leaves behind a wife, Zahra, and two children: Kamnoosh, thirteen; and Shahmeer, eight. All of whom suffered from smoke inhalation during this *cowardly* and racially motivated attack.'

Another bout of coughing. As if in sympathy with the family.

'Excuse me.' Clearing his throat again. 'This afternoon – following information from a member of the public – we attended an address in the city's Tillydrone area. Officers attempted to serve a warrant on an individual suspected of being involved in the arson attack.'

More hands shot into the air.

But instead of taking questions, Rutherford turned to Logan instead. 'Detective Inspector McRae?'

'Thank you.' And it was Logan's turn to get up on his hind legs and face the hordes. He treated them to a long hard serious look – what Elizabeth called his 'Paddington Stare' – then a curt nod. 'Today, just after five p.m., I and a team of officers forced entry to the suspect's flat...'

Meeting Room Two was a lot less 'Out-Of-Town Convention Centre' than where they'd held the media briefing, but every bit as magnolia and impersonal. Windowless. With two white-board walls covered in marker-pen scribbles: lists and lists of officers' names with arrows and dates and various ongoing investigations. As if someone had been trying to brainstorm their way through the staffing crisis.

Good luck with that.

Now that the briefing was over, Rutherford was back to looking like squeezed crap again, grimacing at the cheap mug of cheap coffee in his hand, which came with an even cheaper biscuit on the side. Sweeny offered the tin to Pine, who demurred, and Logan. Who helped himself to a custard cream and gingersnap.

Maybe they'd make the coffee drinkable?

Biscuit duty over, Sweeny popped another antacid and crunched, face almost as miserable as Rutherford's. 'Could've been worse, I suppose.'

His partner in gloom grunted. 'And what's with all the *stupid* questions? "Are you *certain* this was a racist attack, Detective Chief Inspector?" Course we bloody are, you sodding halfwit! They firebombed a hotel full of asylum seekers – what the bloody hell did you think it was: *performance art*?' He turned to the Boss. 'Anything from the search team while we were in there?'

Pine sniffed at her coffee, as if it might be caustic. 'Not so much as a cocktail weeny. If MacGarioch clawed his way out of the Don, he didn't do it before Seaton Park.' She risked a sip. Shuddered. Put the mug down. 'And there's no point looking at me like a kicked puppy – we've got miles of river-bank to search and not enough people to search it.'

'Well ...' you could almost hear the gears in Sweeny's head, creaking, '*maybe* we could do an appeal for members of the public to help?'

Pine pursed her lips. Rutherford opted for a withering look. Sweeny crunched down another Gaviscon.

'Anyway,' the Boss turned towards the whiteboard wall with its lists of officers, 'D Division are lending us a drone operator, but not till tomorrow.'

'*Tomorrow?*' Rutherford's face soured a little more. 'MacGarioch will have scarpered halfway to Benidorm by then. That or been washed up on the Norwegian coastline.'

Time for Logan to inject a bit of cheer to the proceedings:

'Maybe we'll get lucky and he'll foul on an oil rig some-where along the way?' Not a single smile. 'OK... How about we get the TV news teams in and ask *them* to scan the river-banks? We know Sky's got a dirty-big drone, right? Saw it down at the crash site.'

Rutherford opened his mouth, looking ready to shoot that down, but Pine got there first:

'*Might* work ... if we give them an incentive. And make them sign an NDA.' A nod. 'Yes... Pretty sure I can sell that.' She tapped a finger on the table. 'Logan: I want all local hospitals, GP surgeries, chemists, and *vets* to keep an eye out. If MacGarioch survived, he's probably injured and looking for treatment.'

'Ma-am.'

'Ron: chase the search team. With a pointy stick, if you have to. We've got ...' glancing at the wall clock, 'two-and-a-bit more hours of daylight. I'll give you every warm body I can spare, but *find* him.'

Rutherford did a bit more coughing. One hand covering his

mouth, the other held up – till he could squeeze out a wheezy, 'Do our best.'

'And while you're at it, ride Forensics like a dirty bicycle.' Giving them all a much fiercer Paddington Stare than Logan ever managed. 'I need to see *progress*, people. Progress!'

And then she was off, pushing out through the door into the corridor, phone at the ready. Already dialling as she disappeared. *'Nigel: you're with me!'*

Sweeny grimaced, popped another antacid, then scarpered after her.

The door clunked shut and Rutherford wilted. Coughed. Sighed.

Which wasn't exactly encouraging.

Logan gave him a wee pat on the back. 'You sure you're OK?'

He waved that away, grimacing at the closed door. 'Why do I get the feeling there's an enormous tidal wave of shite coming our way?'

10

There wasn't much left of the Balmain House Hotel – not from the front, anyway. Just a flat-faced, mid-terrace, two-storey rectangle of smoke-blackened granite blocks, with a dormer layer on the top for those swanky penthouse-suite views of a baby-scanning centre, a newsagent's, and a dog-grooming place called 'Pup, Pup, & Away!'

All the windows were gone: blown out by the fire. The front door was missing too. And so was most of the roof, leaving only a handful of beams and a smattering of grey slates behind.

The front garden had been paved over, making a wee parking area for a pair of... Actually, it was difficult to tell *what* they'd been, because now there was nothing left but their blackened, flame-stripped carcasses. Even the wheelie bins were melted blobs.

But at least the wrought-iron railings had survived. Which gave people something to fix their floral tributes, football scarves, and teddy bears to. Votive offerings for the Gods Of Tragedy And Public Displays Of Grief.

The buildings on either side seemed OK, but the box-hedges between the three properties were screwed.

Logan parked behind the Mobile Command Unit – a very fancy title for a glorified Mercedes Sprinter van, kitted out as a half-arsed office – and climbed out into the sticky, oppressive air. Watching as a pair of little girls fixed a teddy bear to the iron railings with a cable-tie around its throat. Tightening the garotte taut enough to make Teddy's legs poke straight out.

Logan leaned back against his Audi and checked his phone, letting them finish their strangulated tribute.

Hmmm...

No reply from Tara.

That wasn't good.

The wee girls skipped away, and Logan wandered over to the gate. A double line of 'POLICE' tape was tied to the railings either side, to stop stupid members of the public climbing all over the crime scene. He untied one side, opened the gate, and walked between the burnt-out cars to the burnt-out hotel and its missing front door.

Putting his hands on either side of the doorway, Logan poked his head in through the gap.

Wow.

Complete devastation.

The building's supporting walls were granite, so they'd survived the blaze, but everything in between was reduced to a pile of charred debris. The upper floors had collapsed, offering a clear view out through the missing roof to an azure sky.

To be honest, the whole place was completely—

'HOY!' A hard Peterhead accent blared out behind him: 'GET OUT OF IT!'

Logan pulled his head back, and turned to find himself the target of an angry glower.

A uniformed PC stood between the roasted corpses of both cars, fists on her hips. Pointy of nose, with dishwater-blonde hair pulled back in a tight bun. A high-vis waistcoat on over her stabproof, and a deeply grumpy frown pulling at her heavy eyebrows. 'You heard me: out!' Jabbing a finger at the gate and its untied cordon. 'You see that tape? That means—'

'Where's Steevie?' Logan flashed his warrant card.

Her eyes narrowed. 'Oh no you don't. Let's see that properly.' She took the thing and gave it a good long stare. 'Ah. OK. Ahem.' Bit her top lip and handed it back again. 'Inspector. Guv. Sorry. Boss.'

'Guv is fine.'

'Only I'm usually based out of Peterhead...'

Which explained a lot. 'Bit of a bruiser, eh?' Smiling as she blushed. 'And do you have a name? Or is it a secret Bloo Tooner thing?'

'Hilary, Guv. Kent.'

'So, where's Steevie?'

'I'm just filling in, really. Because of all the ... you know: off on the sick...?'

'*Constable*: what have you done with Watch Commander Colins?'

She stood to attention. 'Sorry, Boss. Guv. It's... He's knocked off for the night. Says "twelve hours a day is enough for any man". Sorry.'

Logan hooked a thumb at the hotel doorway. 'This safe to go in?'

'*I* wouldn't. There's a basement, and the ground floor's a bit shagged, Guv. Sorry, Inspector. I mean, "its structural integrity has been compromised by the blaze". A chunk of the dining room caved in this morning.'

Sod that.

He took a step back, in case anything decided to collapse. 'Talk me through it.'

'Erm...' She checked her notebook. 'OK: At approximately zero-three-hundred hours on Monday the ninth of June, an accelerant was introduced to the premises via an aperture on the building's primary entrance—'

'Stop, stop, stop: you're not giving evidence in court. Just tell me what happened like a normal human being.'

'Oh.' Hilary drooped a little, as if she'd been looking forward to giving him the complete witness-box performance. 'Actually, I can show you if you like?' Digging out her phone.

Now that was more like it.

'We've got *CCTV*? How come no one mentioned—'

'Nah. I mean, the hotel *did* have cameras, but the recording stuff was all inside, so it's ... melted. Bunch of drunk teenagers staggered by, on their way home. Saw the flames and called nine-nine-nine. One of them videoed the whole thing.' Swiping and poking away at her phone's screen. 'Hold on, got it here somewhere...'

Well, that was something at least.

As she fiddled, Logan did a slow three-sixty: looking out over the roasted vehicles to the next-door building and the long line of grey granite stretching back up Broomhill Road towards the town centre; then the buildings opposite with their grim featureless grey facades. One of them had a drooping 'FOR SALE' sign in the tiny, gravelled front garden – good luck selling now, with a murder scene right across the street. Next up were more bland grey buildings as the road headed off to Kaimhill and the exotic delights of Garthdee, beyond. Then back up the granite terrace on this side, past a bus stop, and back to the incinerated shell of the Balmain House Hotel again.

And PC Kent was *still* fiddling.

The boy-racer's theme tune '*bmmm-tsh, bmmm-tsh, bmmm-tsh*' rattled out of a hatchback's windows as it drove by, followed by a florist's van.

A couple walked past on the other side of the street, arm in arm, fancy-dressed as pirates, swinging a carrier bag from the local off-licence.

Then a woman with a pushchair stopped to attach some sort of homemade banner to the hotel railings – her laminated

A4 sheets putting up a fight, while her toddler beamed at the brightly coloured display.

There was a young man lurking behind the bus shelter, clutching a heart-shaped mylar balloon and some petrol-station flowers. Watching as the mother fixed her banner into place. Awaiting his turn to perform at the Look At Me Mourning Theatre.

OK, this was getting silly now.

Logan stepped away from the hotel. 'If you can't find it, maybe—'

'Here we go.' PC Kent held her phone out.

Something was playing, but it was barely visible in the glaring sunshine.

He leaned in, cupping his hand around the screen to cast a bit of shadow. Cutting the glare. Then took the thing from her hand, turning his back on the sun. Finally, a fizzy mess of fuzzy-pixelled darkness appeared, with a couple of white trainers in the middle.

Then the footage wheeched upright, giving a wobbly view along Broomhill Road towards a smear of bright yellow and orange.

An *'Oh my God!'* shrieked out of the phone's speaker, the words tinny and brittle as the video lurched into a jiggling run sprinting towards the burning hotel.

Then a figure overtook whoever was doing the filming – a girl, thirteen, maybe fourteen years old, in cargo shorts and a leather jacket. *'Oh my God! Oh my God! Oh my God!'*

Another girl's voice, slurring the words. *'Call the cops! Call the … fire cops!'*

The wobbly footage came to a halt on the opposite side of the road to the Balmain House Hotel, watching it burn.

PC Kent nodded at the vacant front door. 'Whoever set it on fire, they stuffed one of those fleecy blanket things through the letter box, followed by about ten litres of unleaded. Blanket stops the petrol leaking away – acts like a big spongy candle. You drop a lit box of matches in after it, and: instant inferno.'

'Didn't screw the door or windows shut, did he?'

That got him a look of horror. '*What?* Why would anyone … I mean, even *think* of that?'

'You'd be surprised.'

A whooshing crash burst free of the phone as the hotel's upper windows exploded and flames shot out, curling and twisting as they grew.

It was bright enough to blow-out the camera's light levels, leaving the whole screen an angry shade of white that took a good five or six seconds to fade any detail back up again.

Logan whistled.

'Oh aye.' PC Kent leaned back against one of the burnt-out cars. 'Lucky the place was half empty, cos the header tank flooded the front four bedrooms.' Pointing at the empty windows. 'No way anyone would've got out of there alive.'

As the image came back, a blurred figure staggered into the middle of the road, phone to her ear. Another girl, barely in her teens, and more than a little wasted. '*Yeah, there's a fire. Like a* huge *fire … Yeah … Uh-huh … It's this hotel thing on Broomhill Road. Hurry, I can…*' She turned to the camera, eyes wide. '*Can you hear that? Jesus, someone's screaming!*'

The camera swung up, ran along the line of buildings, clearly looking for whoever it is.

'*Someone's screaming! You gotta get here now!*'

The footage went from portrait to landscape, shrinking right down till Logan turned PC Kent's phone sideways to catch up. But there was no sign of whoever was screaming, just gouts of black smoke billowing out, lit from below like a signpost to hell.

'*Oh my God! Oh my God! Oh my God!*'

'And that's that. They keep filming till the Fire Brigade get here. Then there's a break. Then there's more footage of them putting it out.'

Logan straightened up, handing the phone back. 'And they didn't go straight to the tabloids and sell the video?'

PC Kent winced. 'One of the girl's dad's a bit of an arsehole.' Her cheeks coloured again. 'I mean – sorry, Guv – he's a lay preacher with a history of domestic violence and they didn't want him finding out they'd been boozing it up and partying till three.'

Back here, in the real world, the mother with the pushchair finished wrestling with her DIY banner, took a selfie with it and the Totally Spontaneous And Not At All Cynical Public Outpouring Of Grief Diorama™ – duck pout, throwing a victory-V – then wheeled her toddler away. No doubt looking forward to all the comments about how kind and thoughtful she was.

Logan watched her go. 'Give me this lay preacher's name and I'll see he gets a little visit. *Without* mentioning the girls, of course.'

'Aye...' PC Kent bared her top teeth. 'No disrespect, Guv, but sometimes that just makes the bastards worse. Winds them up – then they go looking for an excuse to take it out on their wife. Or kid.' A shrug. 'Speaking from experience.'

Because no good deed ever went unpunished.

Logan sighed. Then nodded. 'OK. In that case, we probably better...'

Hang on a minute.

The young bloke with the mylar balloon was still lurking by the bus shelter. You'd think, now that the mother had gone, he'd be scuttling up here to take his turn, but he hadn't budged. Just stood there. Looking shifty. And disturbingly hairy. In blue jeans and a denim jacket.

Logan turned, so Mr Hairy was just visible in the corner of his eye. Keeping his voice down. 'You see what I see?'

PC Kent snuck a quick peek, then acted as if she was more interested in her phone. Matching Logan's whispery volume. 'Bloke like a half-shaved Sasquatch in a Torry Tuxedo? Yeah. Been hanging around off-and-on all day.' A wee smile. 'Think he's been working up the courage to ask me out?'

'Maybe I should play Cupid?' Heading for the gate. 'Give me two minutes, then go say hello.'

Logan stepped out onto the pavement, shutting the gate behind him. Which was when he finally saw the tribute of sympathy and support that Mummy Dearest had left.

The banner was made up of eight laminated A4 sheets, with a simple message printed across them in bright, bold, colourful letters: 'NO MORE MIGRANTS: SCOTLAND'S FULL!!!'

'Oh for...' He ripped the whole lot down, bundling it up – which wasn't easy with the stiff, plastic-coated paper. Then pulled out his phone and marched across the road. Kidding on he was actually talking to someone. 'Tara? ... Yeah ... No, it's me ... Did she?' Fake laugh. 'Yeah, yeah.'

Turning right, he strolled along the pavement, making for the junction those girls must've emerged from, going by where the burning hotel had been on the footage. 'I know. ... No!' Another laugh, camping it up a little. 'God, the woman's a *nightmare*, she really is...'

Mr Hairy barely glanced at Logan as he sauntered past, then went back to watching the hotel again.

Good.

Logan sped up a bit, dropping the fake-call routine now it was clear Mr Hairy wasn't interested.

Soon as he reached the junction, Logan turned to nip back

across the road. And stopped. *Staring* as a clown car puttered out from Balmoral Place.

A one hundred percent, genuine, bona fide, multicoloured, clown car – with big googly headlights and a polka-dot bowtie on the radiator grille. It even had one of those oversized manual honka-honka horns, and a man in the full make-up driving. Only instead of grinning and waving custard pies about, he was grim-faced, puffing away on a fag as his car 'backfired'. Producing a puff of bright-pink smoke that drifted away into the baby-blue sky.

Now there was something you didn't see every day.

The car crossed Broomhill Road and puttered away into the distance. Letting out another Barbie fart every hundred foot or so.

OK...

Logan gave himself a wee shake and hurried across the road, stuffing Mummy Dearest's shitty banner into the bin outside the corner newsagent's – 'M.C. GIBBONS Est. 1936' – almost falling over the A-frame headline board plonked outside it: 'PROTEST ORGANISERS CALL FOR "DAY OF DISRUPTION"'.

Well, they could sod right off.

He loped back along the pavement, heading for the bus stop. Like. A. Ninja.

Mr Hairy was still there, shifting from foot to foot, clutching his balloon and his flowers. Facing the burnt-out hotel as PC Kent stepped out of the gate.

She marched straight towards him.

He shuffled a bit faster. Clearly trying to figure out what to do next. Stay, or leg-it?

Leg-it must've won, but when he turned to make himself scarce, Logan was right behind him.

Mr Hairy flinched so hard his wee feet left the ground for

a second, his heart-shaped balloon escaping from his startled hand. He spun around, scrambling for the string, but the Mylar Gods must've been smiling on him today, because the balloon wafted in under the bus shelter's canopy. So instead of floating off into the great blue yonder, it was trapped beneath the Perspex roof. Bobbing there, as if it was beating.

PC Kent reached out and caught hold of the string.

Catastrophe averted.

Logan thumped a hand down on Mr Hairy's shoulder, making him flinch again. 'I think we need to talk.'

11

There was a fly, trapped somewhere inside the Mobile Command Unit, buzzing away. Banging its head against the van's walls.

Which pretty much summed up Logan's day so far.

A bulkhead separated the driver and passenger seats from the rest of the vehicle, meaning the only natural light in this bit came through a frosted skylight. Because 'no windows' meant the paparazzi couldn't stick their lenses against the glass, hoping for a juicy shot to sell to the tabloids. And even heavily tinted glazing was transparent if the buggers had a flash bright enough.

A fold-down table took up a big chunk of space, flanked by a pair of manky office chairs, beneath a triptych of wall-mounted whiteboards – bearing various diagrams of the crime scene in shonky marker pen. To add a touch of four-star luxury, someone had installed a teeny section of worktop, with a cupboard underneath, and a battered kettle the colour of smokers' teeth.

Mr Hairy sat at the table, hunched into himself, as if he was scared to touch anything. Fidgeting with his forecourt flowers as the sweat-bitter scents of beer and fruit oozed out of him.

Logan had the other chair, sitting directly across from Mr Hairy while PC Kent loomed. Mind you, she was still holding that heart-shaped mylar balloon, bobbing away on the end of its string, which rather undermined the sense of menace...

'I see.' Logan stretched back in his seat. 'And is there a reason you don't want to give us your name?'

Mr Hairy didn't look up from his flowers. 'Am I under arrest?'

'*Should* you be?'

The bouquet's lone chrysanthemum lost a petal to those jittery fingers. 'I don't have to give you my name or anything else unless you inform me why I'm being detained and questioned.'

'We're not *detaining* you, Mr...?'

Silence.

Apparently Mr Hairy wasn't falling for that one.

OK. Logan made a show of looking around the grubby, cramped, faux office. 'We invited you into our nice cool Mobile Command Unit for a chat. And you accepted our invitation.' Reassuring smile. 'My colleague was just a little concerned about your wellbeing. What with you hanging around a *murder scene*, in the blazing sun all day. Wanted to make sure you were OK.'

The fly buzzed.

The jolly red balloon swayed.

The chrysanthemum suffered: pluck, pluck, pluck.

Mr Hairy scrunched one shoulder. 'It's ... difficult, OK?'

Logan let the silence stretch, and grow, and fester into something truly uncomfortable.

Until Mr Hairy couldn't take it any longer. 'I mean, I read the papers, yeah? I stay *informed* about stuff.' He looked up from his tormented flower. 'We're such a small country, but they keep cramming more and more people in. Health service is fucked, transport's fucked, council's fucked... You try getting a dentist's appointment, or a decent job! *There's – no – more – room.*' He sat forward. 'I'm not saying it's OK to burn them out, but ... something, yeah?' Pointing towards the hotel. 'But not... I mean, there were *kids* in there. Kids!' Then went back to torturing that poor chrysanthemum. 'You don't *do* shit like that.'

'Do you know something about the fire? Or who set it?'

'I know they burned kids.' Mr Hairy poked the table. 'How can *anyone* do that and pretend they're not monsters? Should string them up.'

Logan tipped his head to one side, like a curious cat regarding a bird. 'So, why were you hanging about all day?'

'Wasn't. Came out to look. Went off to the pub for a bit. Came back. Had a bit of a think. Bought some flowers and a balloon...' Another couple of petals fluttered to the van's floor. 'They keep telling us we've got to take more and more people.' Pick. Pick. Pick. 'But they were *kids*...'

Time to try again: 'Sure you don't want to give us your name?'

'Darryl. Darryl Merickson. I stay with my nan in Headland Court. On account of Dad being a man with "strong opinions" and Mum being dead with cancer.'

Logan leaned back against the iron railings, checking his phone as an elderly lady laid a small wreath of paper flowers outside Balmain House Hotel.

TARA:
> Rearranged the P/T meeting for tomorrow night so you're not getting away with it THAT easy.

Well, she was still speaking to him, so that was good. He thumbed out a reply:

> I'm still at the crime scene. One of them anyway.

> Am I too late for chips?

SEND.

PC Kent emerged from the MCU, wafting her face with a leaflet on 'How To Spot A Terrorist'. 'PNC checks out. Darryl Merickson, 423 Headland Court, no priors, lives with his grandmother.' She jerked her head in the vague direction of town. 'Had a sneaky look at his dad. Talk about "a man of strong opinions" – currently doing four years for assault. Didn't like the way an Asian gentleman "barged in" at karaoke to sing "Livin' On A Prayer". Cos apparently that's his song.' Her expression soured. 'Oh, aye: Dad's got "strong opinions" all right.'

Logan frowned at the van. 'What do we think about Darryl's story?'

She looked both ways, then leaned in, voice all whispery, as if she was about to share a massive secret. 'Just between me and you, Guv, I *think* we might be witnessing a racist tosser coming to terms with the fact that brown people don't deserve to be firebombed.' Then back to normal again, in the shadow of a burnt-out hotel. 'Just a shame it took ten litres of unleaded, one dead, and eight injured to get there.'

'Urgh… Why does tragedy bring out all the *damaged* people? If it's not kids with abusive dads, it's racists and wanknuggets. Sometimes all three.'

'That's moths for you.' She did a bit more wafting. 'You want me to let him go?'

Logan's phone *ding-buzz*ed in his hand.

Tara:

>We've had our tea.
>
>Half an hour and the Lizz-Ness Monster is going to bed.
>
>FINGER OUT if you want to read her a story!

'Sod.'

'Guv?' PC Kent was staring at him. 'What do you want me to do about Darryl Merickson?'

'Hmm...? Oh, right. Well, it's not like we're *holding* him, or anything. Free to go any time he likes.'

A nod. 'Guv.'

She disappeared into the MCU again, and Logan had a bash at composing a reply to Tara's text.

> Don't think I'm going to make it home for storytime. Tell Elizabeth I'm sorry.
>
> Honestly, this case is

His thumbs stopped as little hairs pricked across the back of his neck.

Someone was watching.

Logan raised his eyes from the screen.

There – on the other side of the road – another young man, but unlike Mr Hairy, AKA: Darryl Merickson, this one wasn't armed with a bouquet of cheap flowers and a mylar party balloon. Instead he had a carrier bag from the same off-licence as those pirates, earlier. And muscles. Lots of them. Showing them off in a tight wife-beater vest with 'HARRY'S PROTEIN SUPPLEMENTS' on it. Arms like tattooed anacondas. And one of those halfwit haircuts, where it's shaved at the sides and shaped like a bunnet on top. Plus moustache.

Strangely, even with the all the muscles, tattoos, and facial hair, he somehow managed to look like a primary schoolboy. Assuming the school had a very lax policy about steroids.

But he wasn't *actually* looking at Logan – he was staring up at what was left of the hotel.

Fair enough.

The Mobile Command Unit's side door popped open and

out lumbered Darryl, with his balloon and half-bald flowers, followed by PC Kent.

It must've been the sound of the door clunking shut again, but Mr Muscles glanced towards the MCU, caught Logan's eyes, and gave a wee start.

And now he *was* staring at Logan.

The Number 2 bus grumbled down Broomhill Road, heading for 'AUCHINYELL & RGU', partially blocking Logan's view as Mr Muscles flickered between the passengers, through the windows.

Still staring. Eyes are getting wider.

Darryl Merickson frowned. Looking out into the street, as if he was missing something important here. 'What?'

But when the Number 2 had passed, Mr Muscles wasn't there any more. Vanished. Gone. Flushed away.

Logan stepped out into the road ... and there he was, running after the bus. Waving. Trying to attract the driver's attention.

Nothing suspicious about it all.

And while that haircut should've been illegal, it probably wasn't an arrestable offence. More a cry for help.

Anyway...

Logan returned to the pavement. 'Right, thank you for your time, Mr Merickson.'

Darryl went up on his tiptoes, peering after the Number 2 as it shrank into the distance. 'What?'

'Nothing to worry about. You take care, OK?'

He stayed where he was, looking from Logan to the road and back again. Shrugged. Then squatted in front of the hotel railings and added his drooping flowers to the growing mass of tributes, tying his balloon next to that strangled teddy bear.

Then stepped back to take it all in. Closed his eyes and shook his head. 'Kids...'

Maybe this was one of those 'teachable moments'? But given that Darryl clearly wasn't the sharpest spoon in the cutlery drawer, it was probably best to lay it on a bit thick.

Logan made a big show of looking up at the hotel's blackened remains. 'This is what happens when someone thinks it's OK to hate people based on the colour of their skin. Or their religion. Or their sexuality, gender, nationality, football team: whatever it is they don't like.' Pointing at the ruins. 'Convince yourself that they're *lesser* than you and you can commit atrocities.' Dramatic pause... 'Even kill kids.'

Darryl's face hardened, then a nod. A grunt. And off he stomped.

Hopefully to be a bit less of a prick.

PC Kent scrunched up one side of her face. 'Not exactly *subtle*, Guv.'

'Some people don't work well with nuance.'

'Suppose.' She had a good peer down the road, where the Number 2 was little more than a little red lump. 'So, what *was* that all about?'

'Just some guy missed his bus.' So there'd been no need to go charging out into the road, like an idiot.

But it'd been a *long* day.

Know what? Steevie was right: a twelve-hour shift *was* enough for any man, and Logan had been at this for *fourteen*, so it was time to sod-this-for-a-game-of-soldiers, sign out, and be home in time to read Elizabeth that gory story about the little skeleton boy she liked so much.

Because kids were weird.

But yeah: enough was—

Logan's phone *ding-buzz*ed. Probably Tara.

He pulled it out and sagged. Not Tara.

DCI Rutherford:

Can you check on the search teams?

DCI Hardie's come down with the plague so now I'm stuck in his stupid protest march oversight meeting.

Wonderful.
So much for getting home anytime soon.

A fat yellow sun skimmed the horizon, casting long blue shadows and a warm golden light that sparkled across the swollen river. Making the fog-banks of midges *glow*.

DS Doreen Taylor had thrown caution to the wind and stripped her SOC suit to the waist, showing off a damp 'Kermit For President' T-shirt that clung to her rounded tummy and industrial bra. Wilting perm held back in a sweat-stringed ponytail. Perspiration *actually dripping* off her as she chugged a bottle of water. Standing hip-deep in a forest of nettles at the side of the River Don.

The rest of her four-person team waded their way along the riverbank behind her, wearing thick red rubber gauntlets as they poked and shoved at the stinging undergrowth.

Out in the middle of the river, DS Marshall's team picked their way through an archipelago of reeds. Bracing themselves against the current with big search poles.

Someone had clearly taken a Health-and-Safety course, because all four of them were roped together and wearing bright-orange life jackets. Because it was better to look like a right numpty than get washed out to sea.

Doreen drained the last dregs from her bottle and surfaced with a gasp. 'Jings...' Wiping a damp hand across her shiny face. Then wafting the hem of her soggy T-shirt. 'Like a *sauna* in here.'

Hard not to smile at that. 'Did you actually say "Jings"?'

'And the *midges*! Don't believe them when they say these bloody suits are bug-proof. Little sods are eating me alive!' Scratching, scratching, scratching.

'I'm guessing you haven't found anything?'

'If we had, we wouldn't keep it to ourselves, trust me! Sooner I'm out of this one-woman, bug-infested sweat-lodge the better.' She kicked at the nettles with a black welly boot. 'This is a *massive* jamboree of jobbies. A carnival of crap. A...' She frowned, then sagged. 'Nope: that's all I've got the energy for.'

'Parade of poop?'

Doreen grimaced out at the shining clouds of vampiric bugs. 'By my reckoning we've got ... maybe forty minutes? before it's black as a politician's heart out here. Don't fancy searching this stuff by torchlight. Not with the river at full whoosh.'

'Just do what you can, OK?' Hand up. 'I know, I know: it's horrible, but if some dog-walker finds Charles MacGarioch's mouldering corpse tomorrow morning, washed up on the riverbank, we'll never hear the end of it.'

'Not going to happen: your boy's long gone. Body wouldn't even have made it past the weir.' Doreen tossed the empty bottle to Logan. 'He's made us look like a right ... tombola of turds.' Then she wrestled her wet arms back into her squelchy sleeves, pulled her zip up, did the same with her hood, and waded out into the ocean of nettles again. Leaving Logan alone on the bank.

She was right – there was no point risking officers' lives searching the river in the dark. But the media were still going to crucify them for it.

He turned around, elbows and hands raised to shoulder height as he shuffled his way back to the path, doing his best to avoid brushing any of the vicious plants. Because an SOC suit

107

might be nettle-resistant, but his fighting one most certainly wasn't.

Soon as he was back on sting-free tarmac, Logan pulled out his phone and called Rutherford.

It rang and rang and rang and rang as he marched back towards the car, but *finally* the DCI's voice slumped out of the speaker. Sounding about as full of life as a baked jobbie. *'Logan?'*

'Still no sign of MacGarioch?'

A cough. *'He's not washed up, yet?'*

'Going to be dark soon. And the river's swollen. And I'd rather not fill in six tonnes of paperwork because we got one of the search team drowned.'

Rutherford gave a little snort. *'You want paperwork? This protest march I've inherited from Hardie is an utter buggerfest. Bad enough when it was just hand-knitted lefties campaigning against climate change, but now I've got a bunch of far-right prickwanks holding an anti-migrant rally too. And both lots of bastards want to do it right down the middle of Union Street!'* A fit of coughing rattled down the phone. Followed by some heavy breathing. Then: *'You got any idea how much paperwork that generates?'*

'Not a competition, Guv.'

There was a groan, then more coughing. *'Sorry. Been one of those days.'* Poor sod sounded as if he was about ready for a post mortem. *'Speaking of which: how long you been on for?'*

Logan checked his watch. 'Since half six.'

'Look, we don't need you for Morning Prayers tomorrow. Have a long lie; just make sure you're in for nine, all right?' The call went silent for a moment, then an almighty barrage of coughs blasted in Logan's ear, going on and on and on – the salvo finishing with a wheezing whimper.

'You OK?'

Nothing from the other end.

Logan kept walking, following the river upstream towards the car park. 'Guv?'

Nope.

He turned around, peering back towards the search team – just visible in the distance, their outlines growing indistinct in the dying light.

'Guv, are you OK?'

'Have to be, don't I.' A pained sigh. *'Consider yourself off duty, Inspector. Nine sharp tomorrow morning! We're going to noise-up everyone MacGarioch's ever met.'*

Thank God for that: time to go home.

Logan let himself in through the front door, closed and locked it behind him. Sagged there for a moment, until the siren scent of his fresh fish supper dragged him upright again. Crisply rustling in its cardboard box, with 'WEE JIMMY SWANKY'S ~ CHIPPER TO THE STARS' printed on the top and 'SCOTLAND'S REAL NATIONAL DISH!' on every side.

Dark in here.

He clicked on the lights.

Sighed.

Picked the little pair of red Paddington wellies off the floor and put them in the rack with all the other shoes, boots, and trainers. Slipped out of his fighting-suit jacket and hung it up with everyone's coats.

Because to hell with laying it by upstairs. Not when there were hot chips needing eaten.

'Hello?'

No reply.

But familiar music thrummed out through the living-room door. Sinister and … scuttley. Which could only mean one thing.

He grimaced. Braced himself. And crept inside.

They'd closed all the curtains, shutting out the twilight, so they could bathe in the well-worn creepy glow of *Witchfire* on DVD. Even though, strictly speaking, the film was in *no way* age-appropriate for a six-year-old. Especially the 'spiders' scene – currently scurrying its way across the TV – which always gave Logan the willies.

Apart from that, it was a nice room: painted a cheerful yellow, with three well-stuffed bookcases, a coffee table littered with toys and magazines, and a couple of red velvety couches. One of which was occupied by The Stinkers.

Tara had taken the centre spot, sagging back with her head on a couch pillow, eyes closed, glasses squint, gob open. Looking unnaturally pale in the flickering spidery light – freckles standing out against her heart-shaped face. Strong jaw. Long, wavy, dark-red hair.

She had a book open in her lap, and a small child snuggled into her side – also asleep with the gob hanging open. It wasn't the only thing she'd inherited from her mother. She had the same red hair and freckles, but those were definitely her daddy's ears.

Poor wee sod.

That soppy warm fuzziness ballooned in his chest, making his wizened old heart tingle as if Tara and Elizabeth had just poured space dust all over it. And all they were doing was sitting there, snoozing it up as the film got to the *really* horrible bit.

Gah...

Logan grabbed the remote and killed the TV.

Of course, what he really *should* do is wake them up. Send them both off to do their teeth and go to bed. But they looked so peaceful.

Plus, if they were awake, they'd lay siege to his chips.

And as the great Greek philosopher Aristotle said in his fourth-century-BC treatise, *Nicomachean Ethics*: sod that.

Because blood might be thicker than water, but chips were thicker than both.

Twelve

Bastard.

Andrew dumped another chunk of bush into the incinerator – leaves crackling and hissing as the flames took hold. It was just one of those cheapies Asda sold from time to time: a galvanised bin with wee feet on it and holes drilled along the sides. But it did the job.

And the garden looked a lot better than it had when he'd woken up this morning. Seething.

Fucking DS *Fucking* Davis.

Who the hell did he think he was, making Andrew wet himself? Like he was a wee boy, back in primary six, and the bullies pinned him to the playground wall…

Bastard was lucky Andrew didn't Release The Beast and pound the living crap out of him, right there in the kid's bedroom. Cop or not.

Yeah…

He could've totally taken Davis.

Wouldn't even have been close.

Another branch met the fire.

It was only a wee garden, round the back of their wee house, in a wee forgotten corner of Dyce, but it'd turned into a jungle these last couple of years. Well overdue a good clear-out.

At least now you could see the view – what there was of it, at this time of night – a smear of grey field with the lights

112

of Bucksburn twinkling in the middle distance, through the trees. And up above, a sea of deep, deep indigo blue, speckled with cold indifferent stars.

The moon glared out, from just above the horizon. Septic and angry. Swollen and mocking. Because DS Davis made him piss himself.

Andrew snarled another chunk of garden into the incinerator, jamming it down, making angry orange sparks swarm into the air. Spiralling off into the night.

One caught the back of his hand, landing on the raw patch where he'd skinned his knuckles hacking branches off that stupid hedge. Stinging like a burning wasp.

'Fucking … *fuck!*' Sticking the knuckle in his mouth and sucking on the broken skin. Tasting hot iron and bitter smoke.

Should call the cops on the bastard, *that's* what. Dial one of those anonymous tip-off lines and tell them all about what DS Davis did to that *poor* woman.

Yeah, but Davis *was* the cops, remember?

Who were they going to believe – their detective-sergeant buddy, or Andrew: a normal, decent, hardworking bloke?

Course they wouldn't believe him.

They'd fit him up, just like every other poor—

'Andy?'

He forced his face into a smile, and turned. 'Hey, Mum.'

She shuffled out of the kitchen door, carrying a steaming mug of something. Wearing baggy jeans and a cheery-pink sweatshirt with 'ARBROATH THIRTEEN TWENTY' embroidered across it. Her thinning hair kept in an unflattering bob, even though he'd *begged* her to let him cut it properly. Because it *wasn't* too much trouble. And he really *did* know what he was doing.

Wouldn't let him sneak a few vials of Botox from the salon

for her either. But why should a woman her age look thirty years older than she really was?

Mum handed him the mug, then beamed out at the garden. 'Ooh, it's *lovely*, Andy.'

'It's a start, anyway.'

'Don't be much longer, though. Can't have you catching your death out here.'

On a night as hot and clammy as a tramp's armpit?

'It's OK. Got the fire to keep me toasty, the smoke to keep the midges away, and you to keep me topped up with tea.' He took a sip. 'Mmmm, delicious. Lovely, thanks.'

'Oh, really...' Mum frowned at him, brushing a couple of leaves off his Mr McPork T-shirt. 'What are you wearing that scruffy old thing for?'

He looked down at the pig mascot, with its butcher's cleaver and 'I'VE GOT SOME MEAT FOR YOU, BABY' – the print all cracked and faded. 'I'm only gardening.'

'It's full of holes.' She gazed up into his eyes, like he was the most precious thing in the whole stinking world. 'Maybe I should get you a sweater?'

Christ no.

'Won't be long, Mum. Promise. Just want to get this all tidied away, and maybe we can have breakfast on the patio tomorrow? I can make pancakes, if you like. Pretend we're on holiday?'

She stood on her tippytoes and kissed him on the cheek. 'You're a good boy, looking after your old mum.'

Yeah, he was.

And that's when the KL919 decided to spoil the mood – lighting up the sky as it came in to land at Aberdeen Airport. Its flight path didn't take it right over the house, but the big Embraer ERJ-190 twin-jet roared over the field on the other side of the garden wall. Getting lower and lower, wheels down, ready to land. A huge blue-and-white carrion crow.

Mum's face darkened, shooting her fist into the air with the first two fingers extended. Bellowing it out against the engines' whine: 'FUCK OFF BACK TO AMSTERDAM, YOU HERRING-MUNCHING DUTCH *BASTARDS*!'

But the pilot didn't – they never did – he just carried on with his final descent, over the airport fence, and onto the runway.

As soon as the plane was gone, the thunder faded from Mum's eyes. She reached up and patted Andrew's cheek. 'Don't be too late.' Then off she shuffled. A fifty-year-old woman in an eighty-year-old's body.

How was that fair?

He waited till she was safely inside, with the door shut, before grabbing the old metal pole and ramming it into the fire. Yanking it round and round, stirring the burning sticks, sending a swarm of sparks leaping into the tacky air. Going round and round. Whipping it up. Heat building and building. Till the whole world blazed around him...

Then he fetched the bin-bag from under the patio table.

Opened it and pulled out a copy of that morning's *Press and Journal*, *Aberdeen Examiner*, and the latest *Evening Express* as well. All three papers rumpled and creased where he'd been through them twice – reading and rereading every article, just to be sure.

Not one of them even *mentioned* Natasha Agapova.

Andrew tossed them into the incinerator, feeding the flames.

Then dipped back into the bin-bag for the two pairs of fancy panties and the lacy bra. They went into the fire, then the dirty stocking.

Quick look left and right to make sure no one was watching,

and the pants from Natasha's washing basket got one last sniff for luck before the blaze took them.

What a waste.

Next to burn was every single thing he'd been wearing last night – from the black cargo pants and hoodie, right down to his socks and pants. Fizzling and smoking, then *whoomp*, they finally caught – polyester turning the smoke oily black.

Then the wee rucksack.

Only two more things in the bag.

The Knife wouldn't burn, but a thorough spraying with bleach and it would get chucked in the river tomorrow.

Which left the most damning bit of evidence.

Andrew pulled his night-vision goggles from the bag.

Only they were, like, nearly *three hundred quid*.

Maybe a good going over with antibacterial wipes would do it? But there was one thing he absolutely could *not* keep.

He popped open the small rectangular cover on the goggles' housing, and ejected the micro SD card hidden inside.

Because even thick bastards like DS Davis's mates might find a recording of Andrew breaking into the victim's home a *little* suspicious.

He clutched the fingernail-sized card in his fist.

What if dumping it in the incinerator wasn't enough? Police IT guys could recover all sorts of things these days. You saw them do it on the telly all the time.

Have to record over everything a few times, first... Or download one of those file shredders off the internet.

Yeah, but the card had some of his favourite creeps on it.

That didn't sodding matter.

The choice was 'getting away with this' or 'ending up in prison for the rest of his life'.

Besides, it wasn't like this was the end of Andrew's creeping career, was it? Could make a new video *tomorrow*, if he wanted…

Yeah, but maybe one last look for old-times' sake? Before he destroyed everything.

Andrew's bedroom was at the back of the house, meaning he had a perfect view of the garden incinerator, smouldering away, giving off an evil orange glow.

Sitting at his childhood desk, he reached out and lowered the blinds, shutting the outside world away. Because even though it was highly sodding unlikely someone would march across the field, climb the garden wall, and scramble through the hacked-back bushes, to peer in through his bedroom window and watch him sitting here in the nip, having a wank – better safe than sorry.

It wasn't a big bedroom, but then it wasn't a big house.

Which is why, even though he had black satin sheets, his bed was a single. Posters for the films he'd loved growing up, lined the walls: *Nanny McPhee* and *Kung Fu Panda* rubbing shoulders with *The Dark Knight* and *Reservoir Dogs*.

To start with, he'd put Post-its over their eyes, so they couldn't see him sitting there, all naked, bashing away, but they were used to it now.

Quick check to make sure the bedroom door was locked, and Andrew fired up the laptop he'd nicked from that woman in Danestone – the one who'd stayed out all night, instead of coming home while he hid in her wardrobe.

One of his non-good-night creeps.

But then he'd needed a new computer anyway, and you'd have to be an idiot to steal something like that from a woman you'd just given a 'treat'.

Too much risk of being tied back to the event.

So: the blinds were down, the door locked, his clothes

neatly folded and put away. He had his hand lotion and his box of tissues ready. Headphones on.

But before he gave *himself* a 'treat' – probably best to check the footage from last night. Yes, it would ruin the mood, but better to get it out of the way now, rather than leaving it hanging over him.

Deep breath.

Then Andrew clicked play.

A fancy-looking garden filled the laptop's screen. Much bigger than the one here. Better-kept as well, because rich wankers like this always had little men to do the gardening for them, didn't they. The scene was from above, looking down at trees and bushes and the back of the house, all rendered in a sickly shade of night-vision green.

Then Andrew jumped from the fence, into a manicured border. Freezing as the security light clacked on.

Count to ten...

And the lights clacked off again.

Soon as they did, he was on the move – hoofing-it across the lawn to the back door without setting the motion sensors off again. Because people never set this stuff up properly.

There, he dropped to one knee and a gloved hand appeared on screen, holding an Electric Pick Gun. Then an angry buzzing noise as it vibrated in the lock, and the back door swung open.

You know, probably didn't need to see the whole thing in real time.

He clicked fast-forward and the video whizzed through the utility room to the kitchen, then into the hall – focussing for a moment on the security system. A fancy bit of kit, and expensive with it. But no sodding use if you didn't *arm* the thing.

The camera whooshed around the ground floor, then swept

upstairs. Mirror. Empty bedroom. Box room. Then the kid's room. Then Natasha Agapova's *boudoir*.

Andrew slowed the video for the exciting underwear rummage, then sat back, chewing on his thumb as Natasha and DS Davis arrived.

'*Excuse me? Excuse me, Miss Agapova?* Natasha *Agapova?*'

'*Go away, I'm not in the mood.*'

'*No. Sorry. Yes. But I'm with the police, see? Detective Sergeant Davis. Can I come in? I'm afraid I have some bad news.*'

Did he sodding ever.

Just hearing the man's voice was enough to make Andrew's balls clench again. He hit mute, and watched in silence as the camera scurried down the corridor to hide in the child's bedroom, behind the door.

Holding his breath as the footage replayed the horrible scene where DS Davis almost caught him. Not daring to exhale until the vicious bastard headed back downstairs again.

Andrew sagged in his seat, willy drooping like a little wrinkly chipolata.

Maybe it'd be better to shred *everything* right now? Get rid of it all. Leaving nothing behind to connect him to the house, or Natasha, or the terrifying monster with the warrant card.

Onscreen, the night-vision goggles rushed to the window, peering out between the curtains. Zooming in on DS Davis as he dragged his unconscious victim to the boot of his car.

Wait a minute...

Andrew thumped the spacebar, pausing the video.

DS Davis's Vauxhall Astra filled the laptop's screen, and right at the bottom of the image, clearly visible and sharp as The Knife, was the car's number plate.

Will you look at that.

A wee smile tugged at the corner of Andrew's face.

Maybe he didn't have to delete the footage after all?

Maybe this video was his own personal Cashline machine, and DS Davis was the banker.

And *maybe* the vicious, violent bastard wasn't so scary after all.

Because how difficult could it be to track someone down from their number plate? Pretty sure there were AI tools on the dodgier bits of the internet that would do it in seconds.

Piece of cake.

Andrew cracked his knuckles and got to work...

The moon had barely risen, just skimmed its way along the horizon. It was still swollen and baleful, but now it was beautiful too. Because the night had *gold* in its mouth.

Andrew sidled over to the garden incinerator and peeked inside. Nothing left but ash and some blackened rubble – all of which was getting bagged up and ditched in a roadside bin somewhere, tomorrow, while he was out getting some stuff to celebrate his newfound wealth.

Maybe pick up some prawns and steak and champagne. Hell, why not a lobster too? Live a little.

Mum would like that.

But first:

Andrew settled his bum against the patio table, grinning as he tapped away at his phone – slipping into DS Davis's DMs on a secure messaging app, because he wasn't an idiot.

YOU DON'T KNOW WHO I AM BUT I KNOW WHAT YOU DID

SEND.

Perfect.

Andrew took a sip of Red Bull – as if he wasn't fizzing enough already – and settled back to wait.

Not for long though, because the reply came dinging right back.

UNKNOWN:
You've got the wrong number.

Oh really?

His thumbs flew across the screen.

NATASHA AGAPOVA SAYS DIFFERENT

I'VE GOT YOU ON VIDEO!!!

WANT PROOF???

Didn't take more than a couple of seconds to bring up a still of DS Davis dragging Natasha out to the kerb, with a lovely view of the bastard's face.

SEND.

And off it went, scurrying through the aether, like a bubonic rat. Bringing the plague to DS Davis's life.

This time the reply took a *lot* longer.

Andrew saved the contact into his phone, giving it an inconspicuous name to avoid suspicion.

Ding.

MURDERING BASTARD:
What do you want?

There we go.

THOUSAND QUID TO START WITH

IN CASH!!!

THEN WE'LL SEE

SEND.
Ding.

MURDERING BASTARD:
When. Where.

Maybe best not to give the bastard time to plot and plan.

> DUTHIE PARK
>
> 20 MINUTES
>
> INSTRUCTIONS TO FOLLOW

SEND.

Well, they'd follow soon as Andrew had figured out what they were. But arranging an anonymous ransom drop had to be fairly straightforward – happened all the time in films.

Bound to be websites telling you how to do it, if you knew where to look.

Because Andrew wasn't an idiot – after what DS Davis did to Natasha Agapova? He was taking *zero* risks.

Ding.

MURDERING BASTARD:
> How am I supposed to get my hands on £1,000, in cash, in twenty minutes?

Sorry, mate.

> YOUR PROBLEM NOT MINE
>
> DUTHIE PARK
>
> 20 MINUTES

SEND.

Out in the field, a dark, pointy shape turned into a fox, bounding through the hip-high barley, on its way towards the airport.

It paused, nose up, as if catching a whiff of just how all-conquering and impressive Andrew was.

He toasted the fox with the can of Red Bull, one predator to another.

Still nothing back from Davis.

Off in the distance, a door opened, letting a bass-pounding thump of music out, then clunked shut, leaving nothing but silence behind.

Andrew checked his phone.

Five minutes and counting.

Maybe he'd over-egged it, and twenty minutes *wasn't* enough time to get that kind of cash together? Not like the banks were open, was it? And you could only take out a few hundred at a cash machine.

Yeah, this might've been a mistake.

Should send Davis another DM, telling him tomorrow would be—

Ding.

MURDERING BASTARD:
OK.

Oh yeah.

Andrew threw his head back and howled at the moon.

Out in the field, the fox hunkered down, disappearing into the barley, then sprinted away, leaving the stalks shivering in its wake.

DS Davis was now *officially* screwed, and soon as Andrew had finished bleeding him dry, he'd turn the bastard in – cos the cops couldn't cover for him with the whole thing on video.

Or even better: bleed Davis dry, then sell the film to the papers. Get one last payday. And then the cops wouldn't have a choice. No way they could cover this up with Davis's face splashed all over the *Daily Mail*, or *The Sun*.

Ha!

Turned out Andrew's visit to Natasha's house hadn't been such a disaster after all...

— do not feed the seagulls —

13

Something went *'Gnnnnnnnnnnnnn!'* … *'Gnnnnnnnnnnnnn!'* in the darkness. Then David Bowie barged into Logan's bedroom and tried to radio an astronaut.

Urgh…

Logan cracked open one eye and squinted up at the ceiling. Blinked a few times. Smacked his lips, because apparently the Jobbie Fairy had paid his mouth a visit sometime during the night. Shame it hadn't tidied up before leaving, because the room was a bit of a mess: hardback books piled up by the chest of drawers, clothes piled up on the wicker chair in the corner, shoeboxes and assorted gubbins piled up on top of the freestanding wardrobes, and seventy-five percent of the duvet piled up on top of Tara. Because she was a thieving sod.

Leaving all of Logan's naked bits on show.

The curtains were drawn, but bright light spilled in around the edges, making the walls glow a cheery yellow.

And still 'Space Oddity' wibbled on.

God's sake.

Logan's hand quested across his bedside cabinet, past the lamp and the alarm-clock radio, to grab the mobile phone making all the racket. Stabbing the button with his thumb. *'What?'*

Silence.

Then a wee whispery voice: *'Sarge? It's Tufty. Erm... Where are you?'*

'About to jam a cactus up your Large Hadron Collider!' Glowering at the clock. 'It's five past seven!'

'Yeah. And Morning Prayers start at seven, and you're—'

'Having a long lie!'

At which point, Tara rolled over, peering out from Fort Duvet, nose all wrinkled, mouth pinched tight, hair frizzing every-which-way like a ruptured gonk. 'Don't make me *kill* someone!'

'It's bloody Tufty.' Back to the phone. 'What – do – you – *want?*'

'Only DCI Rutherford's a no-show and we're all kinda twiddling our thumbs, wondering what we're meant to do today. You know: Operation Iowa?'

Wonderful.

No prizes for guessing why Rutherford hadn't turned up this morning. After all that coughing yesterday? The bugger was off sick.

'I thought maybe The Princess Of Darkness would take charge, but she does has a feet up on the table and reading the paper. Oh and a scratching under the bra.'

Logan scrunched his eyes shut again. 'Who else is there?'

'We've got Harmsworth, and Lund, and Barrett, and—'

'*Senior officers*, you corrugated Fraggle. Anyone over the rank of sergeant?'

A wee fuzzy monster hopped up onto the end of the bed, big floofy tail pluming in the air as she padded along the sliver of duvet Tara hadn't annexed yet. Cthulhu clambered onto Logan's scar-scrambled stomach. Pausing to blink at him with lovely amber eyes. Before tiptoeing across his chest and head-butting his chin. Purring all the way.

'Oh, I see… No. It's like a haunted pirate ship here this morning. Arrrrrrr… Avast, me absent hearties!'

Cthulhu rubbed her cheek against Logan's phone, claiming it as her own, then gnawed at his wrist to make him put down her property. And those cat teeth were sharp.

'Ow! You little horror…'

Tufty's voice drooped. 'Sorry, Sarge.'

'No, not…' Logan swapped his phone to the other hand – out of biting range – and ruffled the fluff between Cthulhu's ears.

More purring.

Suppose there was no point pretending this would all go away: someone had to take charge.

He let a big sigh rattle free. 'Better put her on: The Evil Empress Of Poopland.'

'Thanks, Sarge.' There was a scrunching noise, and Tufty went all muffled. 'Sarge? It's the sarge, for you.'

Steel groaned in the background. 'Oh aye? What's that lazy buntfumper want now?'

'He's in bed.'

'Give.' More scrunching, then Steel came through loud and sleazy. 'You having a breakfast knee-trembler, and need some advice how to satisfy Ginger McHotpants, there?'

'Where's DCI McCulloch?'

'I generally find nibbling the inside of a thigh to be a good starting point, especially if—'

'McCulloch: where is he?'

'What am I, his mum?' Something on her end went hisssssss, then whooomph. Which probably meant she was puffing away on that stupid vape again. 'Got to say, it's pretty unprofessional: skiving off Morning Prayers for whatever squelchy deviance you heterosexuals get up to of a morning. Some of us have been here for hours.'

Cthulhu jumped down from his chest and did a bit of cat yoga – showing everyone her bumhole in Downward Dog.

Logan swung his legs out of bed, then sat there, yawning. Ratcheting the heel of his free hand into one eye socket. 'Get someone round Rutherford's house and make sure he's OK. Then I want everyone doing something *useful*: search teams back out there; door-to-doors in Bridge of Don, Tillydrone and Hillhead; and someone needs to canvass every A-and-E and minor-injuries unit in the northeast. See if Charles MacGarioch's turned up looking for treatment.' He blinked at the bedside clock – 07:08 – then yawned again. 'I'll be there in fifteen.'

'Yes, your Majesty, three bags full.' Hissssss … whooomph. 'Anything else? Want me to polish your bumhole while I'm at it?'

'And no vaping in the office!'

He hung up and sagged for a moment.

Before hauling his naked, unpolished, arse out of bed.

Nearly half an hour later, Logan marched into the office, with a takeaway coffee in one hand and a rowie in the other.

Tufty had been right – it *was* like a ghost ship in here, only with fewer parrots and no rum. And more in the way of desks and cubicles and whiteboards and filing cabinets and office chairs. So maybe not *quite* so piratey after all.

A small knot of support staff crewed the phones and HOLMES suite, but one of them sounded as if she was trying to expel a lung. But that was it as far as the dayshift was concerned. Everyone else was out.

Logan picked his way between the desks to the corner where DCI Rutherford and his team usually sat – the snotty heart of Operation Iowa.

No one there, of course.

He took a bite of rowie, chewing on salty-fatty-stodgy

goodness as he picked through Rutherford's in-box. Which seemed to be the usual depressing mix of memos and circulars and reports and—

'*DI McRae.*' A hard voice, right behind him. Pronouncing his name like some form of venereal disease.

Logan turned, nice and slow, not making any sudden movements, and there was Chief Superintendent Pine with her arms folded, and jaw set. Eyes pinched.

Oh joy.

He swallowed. 'Boss.'

She made a big thing of checking the office clock. 'Morning Prayers?'

'DCI Rutherford told me to skip them and come in at nine. It'd been a long day.'

'I see.' Pine unfolded her arms as a bit of the chill seeped away. But only a bit. 'We need a result on this one by *close of play*, Logan.'

You never knew your luck.

'Do our best, ma-am.'

'Especially after yesterday's fiasco.' She jerked her head towards Rutherford's desk. 'I take it you've seen the papers?'

A copy of the *Aberdeen Examiner* sat in front of the monitor, unfolded so the front page was on full view: 'SUNDAE DRIVER IN CITY CENTRE CAR CHASE CARNAGE' with a big photo of Mr FreezyWhip being hauled out of the river by that crane. Then two small pics from someone's mobile phone showing the chase, and a map illustrating the route.

Logan puffed out his cheeks. 'Well ... I'd hardly call Tillydrone the "city centre", but—'

'You'll be pleased to hear that I've arranged for another eight officers to join us from P and Q Divisions – for the protest this weekend.' Parking her bum against the desk and smiling at him as if they were the best of chums.

131

Which was suspicious.

'Will I?' He pulled his chin in. 'In a *general* sense or...?'

'With Rutherford off on the sick, I'll need someone to take the reins.'

Aristotle strikes again.

'Yeah... With respect, Boss, that kind of public-order operation is *way* above my pay grade, so—'

'You'll be equally pleased to hear that you're now officially acting up: Detective *Chief* Inspector McRae.'

Oh God, it got worse.

He forced a smile. 'I see.'

'Given the rate of attrition round here, you'd better select a couple of acting DIs as well. Delegation is the key to a healthy work–life balance, after all.'

And worse.

He tried not to wince, he really did. 'Ma-am.'

Her voice softened. 'I know. But what choice do we have? I'm trying to find us more officers, but everyone's got the same problem. And while I'd love to issue a statement asking members of the public to stop breaking the law till we're all feeling better, I worry the criminal element *might* take that as an invitation to go on a spree.' Pine gave his fighting suit the once-over with a critical eye. 'Which reminds me – I want everyone in uniform till the staffing crisis is over. Let's at least pretend we've got more officers out there than we do.' Pointing. 'That includes you and your team.'

And even worse again.

'Ma-am.'

'Excellent.' She hopped down from the desk. 'Now, I'm away to bully Dumfries-and-Galloway into giving us a few bodies. Till then, try to find Charles Sodding MacGarioch.' And away she marched. 'And for *Christ's* sake, don't let anyone else get sick!'

He waited till she was gone, before folding over, covering his face with his hands, and boinking his head off the desk.

Should've stayed in bloody bed...

Abandoning DCI Rutherford's plague pit of bad news and extra responsibility, Logan sat at his *own* desk, with his own cartoons and holiday-planner pinned to his cubicle walls, and a photo of Tara and Elizabeth in a wee Lego frame, and mountains and mountains of paperwork – liberated from Rutherford's so-called filing system.

Only instead of working his way diligently through it, like a *responsible* acting detective chief inspector, Logan was frowning away at that copy of the *Aberdeen Examiner* Pine had been nodding at.

Which wasn't exactly making his morning any happier.

A familiar voice gravelled its way over the cubicle wall. *'Oh aye? This what they call working now, is it?'* Steel.

Logan didn't bother looking up, just turned the page. 'It is when they're writing about *my* case, yes.'

In addition to that horrible front page, the *Examiner* had devoted an entire centre-page spread to 'ARE OUR COPS OUT OF CONTROL?' with a photo of the police van being towed away from yesterday's crash site, and a blurred snap of Mr FreezyWhip swerving to avoid the kids on bikes.

Another section screamed 'POLICE PURSUIT "COULD HAVE KILLED US" SAY PANICKED PENSIONERS' above a group-shot of the oldies in their tinfoil blankets.

While a third went with, '"INNOCENT BOY" HUNTED BY "CRUEL COPS" CLAIMS GRANDMOTHER' featuring a picture of Charles MacGarioch, standing outside the flat on Gort Lane, with his arm around his much smaller nan.

Which was *such* a load of bollocks.

Steel peered at the article, lip curled like she'd accidentally eaten something nasty. 'Surprised they ID'd the racist wee shite.'

'Hard not to – every bugger for three miles saw us chasing him.'

Logan turned the page.

And there, nestled between articles on a council scandal and a local 'business tycoon' being done for historical sex offences, was 'POLICE APPEAL FOR HELP FINDING MISSING TEENAGER'. And there was Charles MacGarioch again, this time looking angelic in his school uniform.

The text that went with it didn't help.

Logan gave the paper a wee shake, then read out loud: '"The popular teenager from Tillydrone, who regularly volunteers at his local foodbank," of course he sodding does, "took a job at Gillmore's Fish and Chips, on Tillydrone Avenue, to support his disabled grandmother after her benefits were *cruelly* cut during the first round of austerity..."' A snort. 'He sets fire to a hotel *with people in it*, and they're trying to make out he's some sort of Mother Teresa! They're going to look bloody silly when we charge the bastard.'

Steel snatched the paper from Logan's hands, elbows propped on the cubicle wall as she skimmed it. 'So, tell them. Put out a statement – "Dear Journalist Morons: Charles MacGarioch is a rancid, bigoted, arsonist pish-wank, who tried to murder a bunch of asylum seekers. Stop chrome-plating his bumhole and tell the sodding truth for a change, you pricks."'

He tried to grab the paper back. 'Have you not got work to do?'

But she danced backwards clear of his hands. 'Blah, blah, blah.' Still reading. 'I hear Chief Soupy Perky-Pine wants a couple of acting DIs.' Steel gazed nobly at the ceiling. 'Just saying: while I do not *seek* office, if my country *needs* me, I *am* prepared to put my *personal wishes* aside and accept this *great responsibility.*'

Bet she was. It…

Hang on.

'How did *you* know? Only told me five minutes ago.'

'I have my sources.' Smiling like a Cheshire cat full of cream. And sparrows.

'Good for you.' Logan gathered up a bunch of Rutherford's Operation Iowa files and plonked them on the paper in Steel's hands. 'Meanwhile: you can go through the HOLMES actions and get some of your lazy buggers to start ticking them off.' Then made himself scarce, before she could say anything…

14

The path scrunched beneath Logan's shoes, and he descended through the woods towards the riverbank. Air gritty with the scent of wild garlic that had gone past its best. That slightly sour taste lingering with every breath.

Surprised the students hadn't smoked it all, to be honest.

Kids these days, with their clean living and learning things…

The River Don had calmed down a bit since yesterday and entered its meandering phase, coiling like a glistening intestine around the Hillhead halls of residence. Couldn't see the accommodation blocks from down here, but someone was blasting rap music through an open window, somewhere above. Which was a bit of a shock, seeing as it was only five past eight on a Wednesday morning. Surely most of the buggers would be fast asleep till noon?

And yes, that was a terrible stereotype, but sod them. If Logan had to be up at sparrow's-fart o'clock, why should anyone else get a long lie?

Up ahead, four SOC-suited figures picked their way along the water's edge, poking away with their poking sticks. Surrounded by clouds of glowing midges as sunlight poured like chip fat through gaps in the tree canopy. Making everything sizzle and wilt.

The river was only a stone's throw across at this point, and

DS Marshall's team searched the opposite bank. Their SOC suits shining uncomfortably bright.

Blinking after the relative shade of the woods, Logan stepped into the deep-fried light, off the path and down onto a teeny-tiny beach – just about big enough for a single person to lie on. As long as they didn't mind their towel getting wet.

Both teams searched on, completely ignoring him.

'Hello?'

Everyone looked up, but only one of them waded out of the shallows, and onto the tiny beach.

Doreen peeled back her hood and unhooked one side of her mask, letting it dangle free from her other ear. Face all red and drippy. '*Please* tell me you found the scumbag, and we can stop looking.' She lowered the suit's zip, exposing pasty-white sweaty skin and a cast-iron sports bra. 'Only been at it half an hour, and my Smurf suit's like a fish tank.' Flapping the open side of it to cool down. 'And where's this flipping drone from Tayside we were promised?'

Good question.

Logan scanned the riverbank. 'MacGarioch must've clambered out *somewhere.*'

'Gah...' More flapping. 'I'm seriously considering "accidentally" falling in, for a cool down.'

'You hear about Rutherford?'

'Off on the sick? Lucky sod.'

'Which means I'm now, officially, acting up.'

She gave him a sympathetic grimace.

Time to spread the love. 'So, by the powers vested in me, I hereby anoint you: Acting Detective Inspector Taylor.' Logan made the sign of the cross. 'God bless you and all who sail in you.' Then hooked a thumb across the river. 'Biohazard too.'

But instead of groaning and complaining, Doreen *actually*

smiled. Stood up a little taller. 'Does that mean I can ditch the search?'

'Nope.' Pointing at her team. 'You're down one body already. Can't afford to lose anyone else.'

And the smile turned into a grimace again. 'How am I supposed to Detective Inspector things if I'm stuck in a sweat-soggy Tyvek onesie with squelchy wellies? This is—'

'HOY! OVER HERE!'

They both turned, and there was DS Marshall's team, jumping up and down on the other side of the river, waving their arms about like idiots.

'WHAT?'

Doreen's Airwave gave three bleeps. She dug the sweaty handset from her SOC suit and pressed the button. 'Safe to talk.'

DS Marshall's voice crackled out of the speaker. *'Think you owe me a pint; we've got something.'*

Hallelujah.

She flashed a grin at Logan, then lowered the handset for a bit of old-school shouting across the water instead. 'BIOHAZARD: I COULD KISS YOU!' Going much quieter for, 'If you weren't so ugly. And farty. And Bob-like.'

Logan waded his way through the waist-deep undergrowth on the other side of the river, doing his chicken-wings impersonation again to keep his hands away from anything stingy, scratchy, or covered in yuck.

The bank was a *lot* steeper over here too, meaning every step carried the risk of a humiliating and painful plummet into the river below.

He navigated his way downhill, step by careful step, towards the clump of excited SOC suits.

Doreen's team stood about on the opposite bank, watching and waiting. And, more importantly, not *doing* anything.

Logan shoved his way through a clump of particularly amorous brambles and staggered to a halt, two inches away from pitching head-first into the river.

Detective Sergeant Robert Marshall, AKA: Biohazard Bob, was waiting for him. A thick-set bloke with big, sticky-out, taxi-door ears; a massive bald patch; and a furrowed mono-brow; all perched on an unsolved-Rubik's-Cube head.

Like Doreen, he'd unzipped his SOC suit to the waist, only instead of a sports bra he'd opted for a T-shirt. 'TIMMY & THE TIMEONAUTS ~ DUCKING ABOUT IN SPACE AND TIME' with his nips clearly visible through the soggy white material. A sniff. 'Took your time.'

'Bloody right I did: got *no* intention of going for a sploosh for your entertainment.' Logan scanned the slippery river-bank. 'What you got?'

'Over here.' He led the way to a cluster of rocks and dead branches that reached about seven feet out into the water.

It looked a bit like a half-arsed beavers' dam, made of crud washed downstream on the swollen river. A flash of bright-red-and-white leather glimmered at the far end, caught on a branch. There was more of it submerged below – but the silt-stirred water blurred the outline, making anything more than six inches beneath the surface fade from view.

One of Biohazard's team stood on the bank, clickity-clacking away with a large digital camera. Recording the scene.

Logan frowned out at the dam. 'Body?'

''Bout to find out.' He jerked his thumb towards the patch of mystery leather. 'You want to?'

Maybe yes, maybe no.

'Should really get Scenes down here first: tape off the area, common approach path, organise a diving team, health-and-safety audit, hazard report, risk-analysis briefing...'

'By which time it'll be half-past next Friday.'

139

And it might not even *be* anything.

Given how short they were on people and resources, doubt the Chief Super would be pleased if he wasted hundreds of man-hours on a red-and-white-leather herring.

Logan nodded. 'Give us your wellies.'

He wobbled his way along the accidental beavers' dam, arms out for balance, shirtsleeves rolled up, borrowed wellies on his feet, nitrile gloves on his hands, and that huge digital camera slung around his neck. Gritting his teeth, because the chunks of branch and bits of stick were not exactly stable.

Both teams watched him from their own side of the river, no doubt praying for Logan to fall in. Because people were bastards.

Halfway along, and they were going to get their wish, because the branch beneath his boot gave a rice-crispy bout of snap-crackle-and-pop, bits crumbling off it as it rolled out from under him, leaving Logan stumbling forward, arms cart-wheeling, camera dragging him down. Then crash and splash as the branch hit and floated off downstream.

One of Biohazard's team waved at him. 'Watch the camera! Watch the camera!'

Sod the bloody camera.

Logan stumbled headlong, grabbing at random sticks and lumps of wood and ... thump. His knee hit a rock, stinging like an absolute *wanker*. But it was enough to stop him following the branch into the Don.

He stayed where he was, eyes closed, breath hissing between clenched teeth. 'Stupid, bloody, idiotic...' Ow. He gave it a count of five.

Doreen's voice wafted across the river. 'You OK?'

'Of course I'm not O-sodding-K!' He struggled into a bent-back crouch, glowering at that stupid chunk of traitorous leather. Muttering away to himself as he inched along the rickety dam. 'Bet it's not even him. Bet it's just a ... seat cushion or some shite...' Going much slower now, testing every foothold before trusting his weight on it.

All the way to the far end.

OK.

Wedging his wellies in place, Logan switched on the camera and clacked-off half a dozen shots. Zooming in on the red-and-white patch, visible through the silty water.

This time it was Biohazard's turn, using his hands as loud-hailers: 'SEE ANYTHING?'

'Give us a bloody chance!'

If they thought this was so sodding easy, they should come out here and try it themselves.

Logan squatted down as far as possible, one welly jammed against a weed-slimy rock, just beneath the surface, the other into the gap between two branches. And reached...

And reached...

And stretched...

And was going for a swim in the river, wasn't he. Ruining a perfectly good fighting suit and digital camera along the way...

And finally, his fingertips latch onto the leather whatever-it-was.

Thank Christ for that.

He pulled, but nothing happened.

Oh, come on.

He tightened his grip, hauling and heaving, then tugging and jerking, then straining and swearing, bracing himself as best he could against the wobbly branches and slimy rock, and *really* yanking the bloody thing towards him. Until the whole thing wrenched free in a gunfire crackle of snapping twigs and splintering wood and Logan nearly went in the river again.

There was a whoosh of water, spattering out of the red-and-white leather as it burst into the air. The thing had sleeves, so definitely not a seat cushion – a jacket, identical to the one Charles MacGarioch was wearing when he jumped out his bedroom window.

Biohazard tutted. 'Is that *it?*'

A chorus of moans and whinges rose from the search teams on both sides of the river.

Not sure if they were disappointed because there wasn't a body attached, or because Logan wasn't currently floating downstream towards the North Sea.

Logan leaned forward again, still holding the jacket in one hand as he stared into the underwater hole it had occupied.

No body lurking there, either.

Sod.

Logan shuffled around in his hunched-over crouch, and picked his way back along the dam to the shore, where he tossed the jacket to Biohazard.

'Gah...!' He caught it, but the thing was still piddling water, so Biohazard had to dance backwards, scooting uphill and holding the thing out at arm's length to keep his socks dry. Because that's what happens when you've lent your wellington boots to someone. 'Did you *have* to?'

'Yup.' While it was hanging there, Logan searched the jacket's pockets: one waterlogged mobile phone; one pack-of-three, fruit-flavoured, ribbed-for-her-pleasure, go-longer-numbing-gel condoms; one ruined 20-pack of cigarettes; and one set of car keys, with a plastic 99-cone key ring that looked an awful lot like the one on top of Mr FreezyWhip.

He held up the keys, jiggling them so they sparkled. 'And you definitely didn't find any sign of him getting out further upstream?'

'Naw. You'd leave signs, wouldn't you?' Biohazard glanced up the bank. 'Footprints in the mud, crushed vegetation, wading through the long grass... Stuff like that.'

'Then MacGarioch's still alive.'

Biohazard turned and waved at one of his team – anonymous in their SOC suit and mask. 'Bernie: chuck us a big evidence bag. Waterproof.' Then back to Logan. 'And how do you deduce *that*, Oh Great One?'

Logan jiggled the keys again. 'He took these out of the van's ignition and stuck them in his pocket on the way downstream. You don't do that if you're drowning.' Watching as the jacket was bagged-up. 'He planked his leathers here, because a bright-red-and-white jacket's going to stick out like an infected toe. And Charles MacGarioch wants to stay as invisible as possible.'

Logan held out the keys and Bernie bagged those too. 'Keep looking. He clambered ashore somewhere between here and the sea – and if we're lucky, *someone* saw him.'

Biohazard seemed to think about that for a minute, then rolled his eyes. 'Fine. But I want my wellies back!'

XV

Didn't matter how much sunshine there was, an industrial estate was an industrial estate was an industrial estate. Or, in layman's terms: the view was shite.

Colin Miller (56) shoved his way out of the newsroom and strutted down the corridor, rocking a dark-blue linen suit today. Grey shirt. Orange tie. Because real men weren't afraid of a little colour. No portfolio of stories clutched under his arm this time – nah, Mr Ring Binder had stayed home, on the desk – instead he was armed with a notepad and a mug of Colombia's finest clutched in his stiff-fingered black-leather hands.

Aye, that's *coffee*, no' cocaine.

He turned the corner and blinked at the silly bastard sat on his arse outside the editor's office. Again.

Louis from the Art Department (26), wearing the same stripy jumper, sneakers, and Poundland jeans as yesterday. Complete with his collection of mountboards.

Still, at least he hadn't pished himself.

Colin made for the door marked 'LEGAL', cos the buggers got all gastrointestinal when he published anything that might get the paper sued. 'Hoy, Louis: you better no' still be here from last night.'

The beardy wee shite jerked upright in his seat, swivelling around. 'Erm... No?'

144

Aye…

Colin abandoned Legal for a minute, and marched up to the editor's door instead. Gave it a wee knock. Wiggled the handle – locked. Then a proper thump with the side of his fist, putting a bit of welly into it. 'WAKEY-WAKEY!' Really pounding on it now. 'POOR LOUIS NEEDS A SLASH!'

Poor Louis jumped to his feet. 'Don't tell her that!'

Daft bastard.

'IS IT OK IF HE DOES IT OUT HERE, OR WOULD YOU RATHER HE PISSES THROUGH YOUR KEY-HOLE?'

'God's sake, Colin!'

A grin. Abandoning the performance to lean back against her door instead. 'Relax: she's no' in, yet.' Nodding at the car park. 'Her Majesty's Porsche *still* hasnae arrived.'

'Oh…' Louis sank into his seat again.

'See that's the problem with editors today: nae work ethic. Aye, they're stuffed up the bahookie with management-speak and buzzword-salad, but see doing some *actual* work? There's no' a single *one* of the buggers knows a "mutton" from a "nut" or an "orphan" from a "running turn".'

Cluelessness radiated off the useless fud. 'Sorry?'

'Have youse even *tried* calling her at home? Maybe asking nicely if she's planning on gracing us with her presence any time before the next ice age?'

'Oh…'

Course he hadn't.

No wonder the whole Newspaper Industry was going down the crapper – naebody had a sodding clue.

'Away with you!' Colin pointed off down the corridor. 'The great Natasha Agapova *isnae in*; go design us something better than a right-wing shite-rag knock-off, ya stripy wee fanny.'

Pink riding high in his cheeks, Louis got to his sneakered

feet and shuffled off, with many a backward look. Cos the boy was about as cool as a bucket of burning jobbies.

Colin gave him a wee wave, then, soon as Louis was gone, rolled his eyes and knocked on Legal's door.

Kids today...

16

'...*to tell us all about her new book,* PC Munro and the Beekeeper's Crypt, *which is a great read if you're the kind of person who likes books...*'

'Grandholm Drive' always sounded so much grander than it really was. Probably because it had the word 'grand', right there in the title. But it didn't have fancy houses, or imposing buildings, or buildings of *any* kind – just trees and scrub and weeds, either side of the patched tarmac.

Which was just as well, because *technically* Logan was committing an offence under Section 3 of the Road Traffic Act 1988, by holding a printout against the steering wheel while driving. Making for the bridge back into Tillydrone. Eyes flicking down to check the list of Charles MacGarioch's known associates, complete with contact details and any recorded offences.

The question was: which one to interview first?

Visit the nearest address, then spiral outwards, or work through them alphabetically, one by one?

'...*coming up in the last twenty minutes of the show! So stick around for that.*'

Off to the left, the high-rise blocks of Tillydrone poked into the air, like the pins on an upturned plug, sunlight sparkling off their windows. But according to Logan's list, none of MacGarioch's mates lived there.

Which was odd. You'd think he'd have made at least *one* local friend growing up.

'Now, here's a blast from the past for all you old rockers out there. It's Twenty-Five Cartridges and their 1973 number one chart-smasher: "Lovehammer"!'

The Gordon Brae bridge appeared between the trees, its modern slab of concrete hovering above a hot-pink sea of rosebay willowherb. Some of which was still half-drowned after last week's rains.

Power-chords whanged out of the car's speakers, joined by a thumping drumbeat and a whirling synthesiser. Building until the singer barged in over the top, aggressive and adenoidal:

> *'Baby! Baby I got love for you!*
> *So much love, give you all of my love!*
> *Gotta lay down, Baby, and feel my—'*

Logan's phone triggered the car's Bluetooth hands-free thing, cutting the song off mid-unsubtle-sexual-reference. He poked the green button. 'Hello?'

'Sarge? It is I: Tufty!'

Idiot.

'Told you to stop doing that.'

A sort of pre-bridge faded into view, like a damp under-pass, choked with drooping weeds. Docken and ragwort ran rampant, up and down the embankment, in swathes of sickly green and fire-bomb yellow.

'Sorry, Sarge.' Not sounding it in the least. *'The Empress of Pokey Filth said you wanted someone to do the hospital rounds? I does has an results for you.'*

Logan pulled up at the junction, waiting for a line of traffic to pass. 'If you're expecting a drum roll, you've called the wrong person.'

'Oh, right.' Some rustling noises crinkled out of the car's

speakers. *'Well, first I thought about getting in touch with all the GP practices too – because they sometimes treat people, don't they – but then I remembered that most don't open till nine, so MacGarioch couldn't—'*

'While we're still young, Tufty.'

OK: gap in the traffic, time to pull...

It was that bloody clown car again, heading north towards Danestone, but this time the driver had another clown in the passenger seat. All done up in the full regalia, complete with bright-red honkable nose. And an expression you could sour milk with from three hundred paces.

Going by the grim-faced glares, maybe they were on their way to murder someone?

Mind you, not sure you could take hitmen seriously if they dressed like that. Suppose, with all the make-up, it'd be harder to identify who was underneath though, so it made sense from an anonymity / getting-away-with-it point of view.

But then clowns *registered* their 'look', didn't they – there was a BBC Two documentary about it – painting their face on an egg, so no one copied it. There was even a central registry in Wookey Hole and a place in London...

The clown car 'backfired', letting free a wee cloud of baby-blue smoke as it puttered away up the road.

Wonder if *assassin* clowns would do the same? Made sense, didn't it? Couldn't have someone else claiming credit for your kills. Wouldn't be sporting.

'...asked everyone to keep their eyes to the ground and their ears peeled.'

What?

No idea what the wee loon had been wanging on about.

Logan gave himself a shake and turned left, across the pre-bridge, making for Tillydrone. 'Sorry – lost you there. Went through a tunnel.'

'I said, "Charles MacGarioch did not has a going to hospital." Or, if he did, he didn't match the description or photo I emailed out. But I asked them—'

'To keep an eye out. I know. I heard.'

And finally it was time for the main-course bridge, spanning the swollen River Don. Silty grey water flashing like a welder's arc in the morning glare – sharp and stinging. Logan narrowed his eyes and flipped down the sun visor.

'Saa-aarge?'

'Acting Detective Chief Inspector McRae, to you.'

'That's what I wanted to ask, Sarge. See, I know you've had this big promotion and you does therefore has need of: An Sidekick!'

Now that he was closer, those tower blocks looked more like stacked electronic components than an upturned plug. Part of some vast crackling impersonal machine.

Up ahead, the bridge ended at the junction where Charles MacGarioch almost smashed through those gormless boys on their bikes. The road now bore two sets of tyre marks, tattooed in black across the greying tarmac, where Mr FreezyWhip and the police van screeched around the corner and up the hill.

'Sarge? You still there?'

'Thought you were DS Steel's sidekick.'

'Please, Sarge. You know what she's like. And I'd make a perfect Dr Watson! I could drive the car and get you coffee and be all impressed by your detective-ing.' He swapped the wheedling whine for on an old-man doctor voice: '"Good grief, Chief Inspector," I ejaculated, "how the devil did you deduce that?"'

'Abso-sodding-lutely not.'

'But you does has to has a sidekick: it's the law! And—'

'Go do something useful. Like chase up Sweeny in the Media Office – we need a press-release drafted on the search for MacGarioch before the buggers start screaming for one.'

What else? 'And then go poke Forensic IT: I want Charles MacGarioch's digital world gone through with a rotary culti-vator. Oh, and while you're at it: call Tayside. What's happened to the drone operator they promised us?' That should keep Tufty busy for a while. 'Well? Off you trot.'

Then Logan hung up on him, before he could complain or whinge some more.

Bluetooth-connection-thingy over, the radio faded up again, on a whanging-guitar chorus:

'*...with my Lovehammer. Lovehammer!*
Gonna fill you up with my love!
My Lovehammer! Lovehammer!
Baby gonna give you my Lovehammer!'

The entrance to Gort Lane was just up ahead, and Logan nipped through a gap in the traffic onto the road where Charles MacGarioch grew up – apparently friendless. Somehow, without all the rushing about and police dogs and sirens, it looked a bit ... smaller than yesterday.

'*Baby, Baby, you know that it's true,*
My Love-love-love-lovehammer,
Hammers ... only for you!'

Which was the drummer's cue to launch into a bang-and-crash-wallop solo. Which was a bit of a relief after all the screechy nasal roaring, to be honest.

Logan headed up the road, to Block Four, where the 'RESIDENTS PARKING ONLY' still lay bent flat against the sun-bleached grass, as Captain Adenoidal started up again:

'*Baby! Baby, can you handle my love?*
All this love, it's all of my love!
Wanna show you my love, gonna give you my—'

'Nope.' Logan killed the engine and blessed silence returned.

He climbed out into the dusty heat, clunked the car door shut, plipped the locks, and headed into the relative cool of the stairwell.

The rear door was propped open, letting a tiny hint of a breeze waft in, bringing with it the shriek-and-giggle of happy wee kids, and the '*thud-adudadududa...*' of that life-saving trampoline.

He was halfway up the first flight of stairs when his phone *ding-buzz*ed with an incoming text.

COLIN MILLER:

> Wee birdy tells me you fished something from the river this morning.

How the hell did he find out so quickly? Like a sodding psychic.

Logan's thumbs rattled a reply:

> You've got a sodding cheek after that hitjob in the paper this morning.

> 'CARNAGE'?!?!?!

SEND.

He'd barely made it to the first floor when the reply came *ding-buzz*ing back.

COLIN MILLER:

> You chased an ice-cream truck halfway across Aberdeen – course we're going to write about it.

> >%)

> Come on: what did you find?

No chance.

Logan stuck his phone back in his pocket and kept on climbing.

Hard to believe that a police search team had ransacked the place yesterday – normally they left places looking like a tipped-out wheelie bin, but clearly Mrs Victoria MacGarioch was the houseproud type, so every doily, antimacassar, and creepy little cat ornament was back in its place. No sign of fingerprint powder or size-eleven bootprints.

The lady of the house was ensconced in her armchair, in front of the telly, wearing the same grey-tracksuit-and-brown-cardigan as yesterday. Squinting through milk-bottle-bottom glasses at some antiques / attic / reality / competition programme – puffing away on a cigarette as Logan bumped through the door.

Doing his best not to spill anything.

Been a while since he'd last made tea in a pot. Let alone one with Princess Diana's face plastered all over the outside.

Mrs MacGarioch pointed her walking stick at the sideboard, and Logan eased the tray into a wee gap between the feline figurines. Most of which were *remarkably* ugly.

'Here we go.' He poured tea into a delicate china cup that featured King Charles's regal mug. Nodding at the collection of maudlin moggies. 'See you're a cat person? All the best people are.'

She sniffed, eyes fixed on the TV screen. 'Can't stand animals. They're parasites, eating your food and piddling everywhere.'

OK...

He added milk from the jug: Queen Elizabeth, and sugar from the bowl: Prince Philip. 'It can't have been easy, raising Charles all on your own.'

'*And* they shed hair all over the place.' Accepting the proffered cup without so much as a thank you. 'His dad was no use. Feckless. Lazy. Took off, first sign our Diana was pregnant.' Mrs MacGarioch gazed up at a framed photo of all the Windsors on a balcony at Buckingham Palace, doing a bit of ceremonial waving. 'No sense of *family*. No sense of *duty*.'

Logan helped himself to a cup: Princess Margaret, with a splash of the Queen and no Royal Consort.

'Not that Diana was much better.' Mrs MacGarioch glowered into her tea. 'Dropped Charles off here for what she *swore* was just a long weekend, so she could go on holiday with her friends to Ibiza.' Back to the TV. 'That was sixteen years ago.'

Ooh – potential line of inquiry alert.

Logan kept his voice casual. 'Does she keep in touch? With Charles.'

'Not unless he's got a Ouija board under the bed.' Taking a big sook on her cigarette. 'Got herself killed in a car crash on Corfu. That's one of the Greek islands.' A proud, smoky sniff. '*Prince Philip* was born there.'

As if that somehow made her daughter's death worthwhile…

'Any other family?'

The wrinkles around Mrs MacGarioch's mouth deepened. 'I told that … fat, *ugly* policeman all this. The sweaty one.'

That would be Harmsworth. 'Yes, but you know what fat ugly people are like. Can't trust them.'

She pursed her lips for a moment, rearranging the creases. Then nodded. 'I had a brother once, but he got cancer in his … downstairs.'

'What about Charles's dad? Or maybe his dad's side of the family?'

'They moved to Australia. "*Moved.*"' A snort. 'Ran away, more like. Don't know which bit, don't care. Nineteen years and he's never sent my Charles so much as a birthday card!'

'How about—'

'What kind of father does that? Just abandons his kid? Dumps him, like yesterday's rubbish and sods off to start a new family somewhere else?'

Good question. And a bit of a sore point. But Logan just took another sip of tea and moved on. 'Girlfriend? Boyfriend?'

Mrs MacGarioch sat up straight, wattles wobbling. 'Not under *this* roof! And my Charles isn't some sort of nancy gayboy, thank you very much!'

'That's—'

'The very *idea*. With all those pictures of half-naked women on his walls? And he *had* a girlfriend, for your information.' The proud sniff was back. 'But I put a stop to that. You can tell when someone's no good. Like that horrible Markle woman.'

'You didn't approve?'

'Coming between a son and his father; poisoning Harry with all this woke, American, "mental health" nonsense. We never had "mental health" in my day, we kept calm and carried on!'

As if she'd ever been in the war. She was, what … seventy? Seventy-five, tops.

'"*Mental health.*"' Mrs MacGarioch ground her cigarette out on the bones of its fallen comrades. 'They should bring back National Service!'

Logan produced his notebook. 'I'm going to need her details.'

'I don't know, do I. "Keira" something. And don't ask me what she looks like, because they all look alike.'

Right…

He closed the notebook again, because there was no way he'd be writing *that* down. 'I'll just take a look in Charles's room, then. Leave you to …' pointing at the TV, 'whatever that is.'

Then got the hell out of there.

17

It looked as if Mrs MacGarioch had worked her magic in Charles's room as well, clearing up after the search team's 'enthusiastic rummaging'. She'd changed the bed, picked everything up off the floor, and tidied the desk – though there were obvious holes where the computer, games console, and every single game had been confiscated.

With any luck they'd be getting analysed right now, rather than played with.

Just in case the search team had missed something, Logan snapped on a pair of blue nitrile gloves and had a wee peek under the mattress.

Nothing there.

There was nothing interesting in the rolling-drawer things under the bed, either. Unless you were fascinated by neatly folded T-shirts, ironed pants, and paired socks.

So Logan tried the bedside cabinet – checking behind and beneath it. Then did the same with every drawer.

Nope.

The wardrobe was full of shirts, trousers, and jackets; a scuffed mountain of trainers; and an open six-pack of Lynx Africa. Three were missing, so Charles had already squirted his way through half the packet. Probably all in one day, going by how much it honked in here when they broke the door down yesterday.

One last place to try: Logan squatted down in each of the room's four corners and tugged at the carpet, but it was all securely nailed down. No access to loose floorboards and secret hidey-holes.

Pfff...

He opened the window, leaned on the sill, and peered out.

There was the trampoline, two storeys below, with a half a dozen little kids boinging up and down on it.

God knew how Charles MacGarioch managed to make it all the way from here. And, OK, the 'second floor' didn't *sound* very high, but the ground was a long, long, *long* way down.

Splat.

Logan plonked himself on the edge of Charles's bed, looking around at the posters and children's books. No adult books. Not meaning '*dirty*' books – doubt his granny would approve of anything racier than a Catherine Cookson – but books for grown-ups. These were all for kids, and teenagers.

Mind you, MacGarioch was only nineteen.

Hell of an age to kill someone.

Maybe—

A *ding-buzz* sounded from Logan's pocket, and when he pulled his phone out, 'IT'S TUFTALICIOUS!' glowed in the middle of the screen. The little sod had done something to his phone again.

Checked With Forensic IT · STOP

Not Gained Access To Computer Yet · STOP

Have Asked Them Nicely To Be Less Pants · STOP

Great. So much for a 'pineapple suppository'.

Ding-buzz.

Tᴜꜰᴛʏ-ᴅᴏᴏᴅʟᴇ-ᴅᴏᴏᴏᴏᴏ!:
  Press Release On Search Underway · STOP

  Sweeny May Be Having Nervous Breakdown · STOP

  Tayside Say Drone Operator Ill With Diseases · STOP

Oh, for goodness' sake...

Logan flopped back on Charles's bed, with his feet still on the floor.

What were they supposed to do now?

No drone, no forensic IT, and no idea where Charles MacGarioch had disappeared to.

  ...

It was odd, seeing the room from this angle. The video game posters were OK, but there was something *slightly* obscene about the female popstars – looming over him in their bikinis and/or underwear.

One, near the head of the bed, was particularly pneumatic: in her early twenties; blonde hair; and a bikini that was more straps than fabric, festooned with sequins. She was kneeling on a beach, while a lake of fire burned behind her. Oiled-up and pouting. Coming off as 'creepy and predatory' when she'd probably been aiming for 'sultry and alluring'.

Maybe Charles MacGarioch *liked* that kind of thing, though?

She'd been Sellotaped to the wallpaper – like all the other posters in here – but Miss Bikini-Pop-Star must've been there a while, because the tape on the corner nearest the pillows had curled away from the wall a bit.

Lying there, half on the bed, Logan reached up and smoothed it back into place.

Hmm...

Parallel lines marred the surface of the poster, just above the tape, where the ink had flaked away. Hard to see, because of the flame-lit beach, but definitely there.

Wasn't easy, what with the blue nitrile gloves and everything, but after a bit of fiddling, he peeled the Sellotape away from the wallpaper again, slipped a finger under the poster's edge, and eased the other side off too.

Most of Miss Bikini-Pop-Star's right leg curved out from the wall, revealing a photo hidden underneath. Six by four – the kind you could get printed out on a self-service machine at most supermarkets.

It was Charles MacGarioch and a young woman, the pair of them posing for a selfie on the dodgems at some travelling funfair. Can't have been the permanent one, down the beach, because there were trees off to one side and what looked like a big out-of-focus stripy Union Jack thing in the background.

Charles was grinning away as she planted a duck's-arse-pout kiss on his cheek. They were much the same age, both with a smattering of plukes about the forehead, only while he was pale as cheap vanilla ice cream, she was a rich salted caramel, with long wavy black hair, a button nose, and disco eye make-up.

The photo was held in place with Blu Tack, rather than tape, and when Logan popped it free an acne rash of little greasy spots marked the wallpaper underneath. As if it'd been taken down many times, then hidden away again.

Logan smoothed Miss Bikini-Pop-Star's poster back into place, then turned the photo over.

'CHARLIE & KEIRA 4 EVA!' and a love heart with an arrow through it.

He frowned at the photo again.

So, this was the mysterious Keira.

Seemed like an odd romantic partner for someone who'd just carried out a horrific, racially motivated attack.

Oh for God's sake. So that's what his granny meant – 'they all look alike' – she was being a rancid racist shiteflap.

Might be a motive? Charles falls in love; his racist nan throws a bucket of cold water over it; he breaks up with Keira; they fight, things are said; Charles lashes out and gets a sort of twisted revenge-by-proxy at the Balmain House Hotel...?

Made sense, in a teenaged-boys-are-sodding-insane kind of way. Worth having a word with her, anyway.

But as Keira wasn't on the list of known associates, they'd have to find out who she was first.

Logan pulled out his phone and took a snap of the photograph, then slipped the original into a small evidence bag.

Right, time to get out of here.

He stepped back through into the living room, where the property-attic-auction bollocks had been replaced by a house-makeover reality thing, featuring a glamorous American couple with hard hats and sledgehammers, whacking the crap out of a partition wall.

A voiceover accompanied the footage – woman's voice, spiced with the crayfish vowels of the deep south. '...*and if there's one thing we've learned from doing* gazillions *of these projects, it's: don't count your* cockroaches *till they've hatched...*'

Logan thumped the bedroom door shut, a little louder than was strictly necessary. 'Mrs MacGarioch, this girl you didn't approve of, the one who was leading Charles astray. I need her surname.'

Because it was worth another try, while he was here.

Onscreen, the woman's sledgehammer battered through a rusty old pipe, and a deluge of bugs cascaded into the room – screams ringing out as both presenters danced away from the skittering waterfall in a barrage of swear-concealing bleeps.

Victoria MacGarioch smiled at the telly, clearly enjoying the cockroach rodeo. 'What?'

'Charles's girlfriend: Keira, what was her last name?'

'Told you: don't know, do I.' She shifted in her armchair, as if those bugs were crawling up her spine. 'Something ethnic.' Then grabbed the remote and cranked up the volume, not looking at him even once.

A man's voice, dripping with Mom's apple pie and non-existent gun control boomed out of the TV, loud enough to be physically painful: '*I mean, we seen roaches before, but nothing like* this. *It's like a gosh-darn creepy-crawly* sea *of the things!*'

'"Ethnic" in what way?'

No reply.

'Mrs MacGarioch?'

The couple on the telly scrambled from the room, then out of the house. Bursting through the front door to jiggle about in the front yard, brushing real and imagined bugs from their clothes. High-stepping over a 'TRUMP PENCE 2020 ~ KEEP AMERICA GREAT!' lawn sign, while a grubby Stars-and-Stripes flew overhead.

'Mrs MacGarioch?'

She lit a fresh cigarette and hissed a cloud of smoke at the screen. As if he wasn't even there.

Looked as if the audience was over.

'OK... Thanks for your time.'

He let himself out.

The council had given the flat a temporary-replacement front door, that was barely a step up from boarding the place up, but Logan made sure it was closed and secure, before heading downstairs.

He'd almost made it to the ground floor, when his phone launched into 'Ode To Joy' which wasn't really appropriate today.

'Hello?'

'*Where are you?*'

He checked the caller ID – 'CHIEF SUPT. PINE'. Oh joy.

'Just paid Charles MacGarioch's granny a visit, Boss. Might have a lead that's worth chasing if—'

'No: why aren't you here? The meeting started five minutes ago.'

He stepped out into the lobby and stopped. 'Meeting?'

'MAPPA meeting about the protest this weekend. You're supposed to be chairing it.'

'What? No one told me about any—'

'Honestly, Logan, I expect you to be across your responsibilities, now you're an acting chief inspector.'

He pinched the bridge of his nose. 'With all due respect, Boss, I'm not psychic! I can't just magically know what—'

'We're in Conference Room One. I'm prepared to hold the fort till you get here, but put a rocket under it. I've got better things to do than cover for you.'

'But...'

She'd hung up.

Wonderful.

Logan sagged like a discarded sock, staring up at the underside of the stairs above.

Because who *didn't* want to spend hours and hours and hours wasting their life away in a Multi-Agency Public Protection Arrangements meeting?

Being an acting chief inspector sucked arse.

Episode 18 | Penny's Riverside Adventure! | (NSFW)

[Be sure to like, comment, and subscribe!]

Up above, the sky was *completely* blue and shiny, and the river sparkled in the baking sunshine. More like Benidorm or Ibiza than a little pebble beach on the side of the River Dee, a stiletto's throw from Duthie Park, in the shadow of the railway bridge.

Shame about the bloody seagulls, though. A pair of the useless fat bastards wheeled overhead, *scrawwwwwwwk*ing away, which was going to make the sound *so* much more difficult to fix in the edit.

Carol checked her reflection in a pocket mirror.

Looking great, babe: gorgeous fake eyelashes; contoured blusher; anything blotchy well hidden beneath a good layer of pancake foundation; perfect blonde hair with just a hint of dark roots on show, cos that was dead trendy right now; and bright-fuchsia lipstick. And OK, the six-inch heels made walking on all these pebbles kinda risky, but they made her legs and bum look *spectacular*.

Carol practised her 'Hello Boys' pout, then popped the mirror back in the pocket of her ankle-length trench coat. Nearly went on her arse, as her heels slipped on the stupid rocks. 'Could we no've gone down the beach? Break my sodding ankle on this shite...'

Kyle grinned back at her. 'Nah, come on, Caz; be brilliant, this.' She should dump him really. I mean, a twenty-two-year-old should be a *man*, not a glekit wee nyaff. She deserved to be with ... a muscle-bound high-flying hunk, not some scarecrow-in-a-tracksuit who looked as if his lightbulb wasn't entirely screwed in.

But she needed a cameraman, and he had his own laptop to do the editing, so there you go.

Kyle fiddled with the handheld gimbal mount, fixing his iPhone into place. Poking away at the screen, then holding the thing up, ready to go. 'You wanna rehearse or something?'

Cheeky sod.

'You saying I don't know my business? I know my business. Cos I'm a *professional*.' Treating him to a contemptuous hair flick. 'Let's do this.'

She unbuttoned her trench coat, revealing a lime-green bikini skimpy enough to give the *Pope* palpitations, slipped out of the coat, and laid it carefully out of shot, on the bank, amongst the weeds. 'Make sure you get me and the river and the bridge.' Pointing across the river. 'No one wants to see that bloody sports club, *or* football pitch, *or* care home.'

'Gotcha.' Kyle shifted about, framing the scene.

Carol wobbled along the pebbles a bit, arms out for balance, because she was definitely going to break an ankle in these bloody heels.

Catwalk turn.

Hands on hips.

Sassy pose.

Pouty lips.

Girly voice – because God forbid men should have to deal with an actual grown-up confident woman: 'Hey, *lovely* subscribers, it's your favourite Only Fans sensation, *Penny Thistle*, with...'

Oh, for Christ's sake.

Kyle was waving at her.

She dropped the sugar-and-spice shit. *'What?'*

'Wasn't recording. Gotta wait till I say "action", yeah?'

'Gahhh! I was *perfect*!' But she gave herself a little shake, resumed opening positions – back to the camera, arms by her sides – because she was a professional. 'Well? Go on then!'

'Aaaaaaaaaaand ... action!'

Turn, pose, pout – girly voice: 'Hey, *lovely* subscribers, it's your favourite *Only Fans sensation*, Penny Thistle, with another video just...'

Cheesy organ music blared out from the road above, as some inconsiderate bastard drove past.

She glared up the riverbank, past the rippling pink sea of rosebay willowherb, to where a multicoloured car was puttering past, going *'bang'* and letting out puffs of pink and blue smoke.

Then a loudhailer added to the din: *'Roll up! Roll up! The greatest show on Earth: for two more nights only, in Westburn Park!'*

Carol stomped a high-heeled foot. 'OH FOR *FUCK'S* SAKE!'

Kyle lowered the camera. 'Cut.'

She clenched her entire body and howled it at whatever clowns were ruining her scene: 'WE'RE TRYING TO SHOOT A VIDEO HERE, YA BUNCH OF PRICKWANKS!'

'Come see the Rumplington Brothers' Circus of Delights! All the fun of the fair!'

Carol jammed both middle fingers up towards the disappearing car, teeth bared, everything trembling as the last puffs of baby blue and pale pink faded away.

Then a snarl.

And a grunt.

Shake it off.

'I'm a professional. I'm a professional.' Deep breath. She turned her back on the camera again. Act one beginners: positions, please. 'OK.'

Kyle gave her a moment, then: *'Aaaaaand … action!'*

Sodding turn, frigging pose, shitting pout, and girly *bastarding* voice: 'Hey, lovely subscribers, it's your *favourite* Only Fans sensation, *Penny Thistle*! With another video *just* for you.' Carol bit her lip and squeezed out a giggle, setting everything jiggling. 'Hope you *like* it.'

She turned and wobbled out into the water – which wasn't easy because A: heels, and B: even on a hot summer's day, the river was still barely above freezing.

Carol did a playful sweep around, grin fixed on her face like the bloody thing was welded there, splashing water at the camera, then scooping up a handful and pouring it across her chest.

GOD SAKE THAT WAS COLD!

Smile, Carol: give the punters what they want.

At least now her nipples jutted out like fruit pastels. The dirty bastards would love that.

Another giggle.

Then a saucy look left and right, to make sure 'no one's watching'. Even though that was the whole point of filming it. Hamming it up like something off one of them old-fashioned silent movies:

Oh, am I all on my *own*?

But it's so *hot* in the sunshine.

Too hot for little old *me*.

Carol unhooked the catch at the front of her bikini top and slowwwwwwwwwwwly peeled it open. Teasing as she eye-fucked the camera.

Three, two, one:

She pulled both sides wide open, exposing her pierced assets.

Kyle gawped. 'Bloody hell...'

'Oh for Christ's ... *frigging* ... CUT!' Carol stomped a foot at the stupid bastard with his stupid haircut and his stupid bloody tracksuit. 'You're not supposed to talk! It spoils it for the subscribers if they're mid-*wank* and your stupid man-voice blares in their ear!'

He lowered the camera and stared. 'It's ... but...' Pointing, eyes wide. 'Ohhh...'

'They're just *breasts*, Kyle. You've seen them before!' She pulled them in and up, sunlight glinting off the twin piercings. 'I mean, obviously I'm *flattered*, but—'

'No! Look.' Still with his finger trained on her chest.

Only it wasn't really, was it. He wasn't looking *at* them, he was looking *through* her.

Bloody rude.

She turned, and there was the Edinburgh train, rumbling onto the bridge, making for Aberdeen station. A whole host of people peered out the windows, ogling as she basically flashed the whole train.

Carol flinched and slapped her hands over her naked breasts, because...

Actually, why bother?

All publicity was good publicity, right?

So let the people see a bit of *flesh*. House prices were through the sodding roof, and every new subscriber put her one step closer to escaping Mum and Dad's place.

Made sound financial sense, when you thought about it.

She let go of her boobs and gave the train a wave, throwing in a jiggle for good measure. 'FIRST TASTE'S FREE!' Smile, pout, pose. Lowering her voice, even though there's no way anyone would've heard over the huge diesel engines. 'The rest you have to *pay* for.'

Kyle made a revolting *hl-urk*ing noise. 'Think I'm gonna hurl...'

'It's called *advertising*, Kyle. Jesus you're such a...'

Wait a minute – what he'd been pointing at: it was a man.

Carol covered her breasts again, sharpish. Taking a slippery step backwards, her heel catching between two stones and sending her crashing down on her backside in the river. Sending up an explosion of spray that glittered and sparkled in the sun.

Sitting there, holding her boobs, staring at the man.

But he wasn't staring back, because he was facedown in the water. His legs were stranded on the bank, but his top half floated – left arm stretched out towards the sea, right folded under his face. Dressed all in black, like a ninja or something.

The back of his head was one big *raw* wound, hair sticky with dark-crimson blood around the edges of a great big dip. About the size of a soup bowl. With flashes of pink and grey poking through the soggy mess.

Probably startled by the splash, one of the seagulls got its courage back, swooping down to land on the body's back, right between the shoulder blades. Cocking its head as it eyed up the chunks of gore.

Then that big yellow beak stabbed forward and helped itself to a tasty, glistening treat.

At which point Kyle was loudly and prodigiously sick.

'Oh, well that's just *great*.' Carol glowered at the seagull as it went in for another beakful. 'Knew we should've gone down the bloody beach.'

19

In Dante's *Divine Comedy*, there are nine circles of Hell.

The first is Limbo: home to people who aren't Christians, so they can't get into Heaven, but weren't dicks when they were alive so can't be punished in Hell. Level Two is for the lustful. Three is stuffed full of gluttons. Four is where the avaricious are held to account. Five is all the angry sods. Six: heretics. Seven seethes with violent bastards – though Dante is a bit of a wanker when it comes to defining what 'violence' actually means. Eight is slick with fraudsters. And the ninth circle is a frozen lake, where traitors spend eternity with only their heads poking out of the ice...

But what Dante *didn't* know was that if you took a dirty big drill, and bored your way through the ice, down, down, down a thousand feet or more, you would eventually come to a small stuffy cavern, where lies the tenth and *final* circle of Hell. Also known as the MAPPA meeting on this Saturday's upcoming protest march.

Oh, it might've looked a lot like the room where Logan and Pine and Rutherford and Sweeny had grimaced their way through a post-press-conference debrief, but it was full of demons, all hell-bent on making Logan's afterlife a sodding misery.

One of them was on his feet now – a baldy prick in black-rimmed glasses, with 'KEITH LONGFELLOW ~ ABERDEEN

City Council Liaison Management Services' on his name badge – wanging on about key performance indicators and stakeholder engagement.

Every seat in the place was packed with some other poor sod, in their shirtsleeves and lanyards, listening to Keith drone on.

Like Jessica, from the Road Department – frizzy-haired with a splodge of ketchup on her top – who kept trying to say something, but Keith was in full monologue-mode with no intention of ceding the floor to anyone.

So they all sat there, wilting in the stale meeting-room air, with their mugs of nasty coffee and plates of disappointing biscuits.

To start with, Logan had taken down everyone's names and which department they represented: Fire, Ambulance, Public Transport, Traffic Wardens, Licensed Premises, Waste & Recycling, the business community, etc. etc. etc... Full of good intentions – planning to make detailed notes on their various flipchart and PowerPoint presentations.

But it'd been nearly an hour and a half now and he'd already started doodling skulls and kittens on his conference notepad, as Keith tried to break the World Record for Most Boring Arsehole In The World.

There weren't even any biscuits left.

No decent ones, anyway.

Chocolate bourbons.

Which looked more like dog biscuits than people ones. Ironic, given that chocolate was poisonous to dogs and—

Logan's phone *ding-buzz*ed, skittering slightly on the tabletop as the caller ID flashed up: 'It's Tufty Time!'

It wasn't enough to distract Keith, though. '...and we have to *maintain* that draw factor long after all these protestors have gone away. We should be embracing this as an *opportunity* to showcase Aberdeen as a destination not just for protest, but for *fine dining*, and *culture*, and *recreational activities...*'

Ding-buzz.

This time, 'Mmmm... Tuftalicious!' glowed away in the middle of the screen.

How?

How did the little sod manage to make *Logan's* phone change caller ID every time? All the texts came from the same bloody number.

'...tangible benefits to *key stakeholders* that will remain long after the placards have been put away...'

Oliver, from Waste and Recycling, helped himself to the second-last bourbon. He was one of those young go-getter types, with a slick short-back-and-sides, ratty little nose, and a mole on his cheek big as a badger. 'This is all well and good, Frank, but have you any idea how much crap's going to be left behind after the march? How am I supposed to clean that up without extra funds?'

Jessica banged the table. 'That's what *I've* been trying to say!'

Keith smiled at them both, as if they were boisterous but well-meaning children. 'You have to see the *bigger picture*, people. With all eyes on Aberdeen this is our chance to show-case the city in a *positive* and *cooperative* light. I propose setting up an engagement committee to explore—'

'What if we just cancel it?'

Everyone turned to stare at Logan, as if he'd grown antlers.

'Think about it:' counting the points off on his fingers, 'it's going to cost a fortune, it's going to disrupt the city for hours, it's going to leave a massive mess, it's going to be a nightmare to police, and it's got several potential flashpoints for violence, public disorder, and property damage.'

Silence.

Mouths *actually* fell open.

'Look, it's—'

Which is when his phone decided to launch into Bowie's 'Space Oddity' as 'BEHOLD THE MAGNIFICENT TUFTY!' filled the screen. And the wee shite *knew* he was in a meeting.

Logan stabbed 'DECLINE'.

Keith clutched his lanyard, like a string of pearls. 'This isn't a *police state*, Chief Inspector! We don't *ban* peaceful protest in this country, though God knows the previous government tried their best. It's simply—'

'Here we go,' Oliver from Waste and Recycling threw his hands in the air, '*typical* nationalist bias. I think you'll find it's the SNP who've been in power for—'

'—suggestion. How can we call ourselves a democratic nation if we curtail the public's right to—'

'Don't be a prick, Oliver.' Jessica from the Roads Department was on her feet, fists clenched. 'You know as well as I do that the Scottish Government's powers are restricted by Westminster's *repressive* grip on—'

'—matter of *civic pride*, Chief Inspector. And I *insist* that no move be taken to curtail those inalienable rights!'

Logan held his hands up. 'I just asked the question, OK? It's not as if I'm—'

Then the door clattered open and an out-of-breath Tufty stumbled into the room, bringing himself up short before he crashed into Jessica's back. 'Eek...'

Keith stuck his nose in the air. '*Excuse me*, but I think you'll find we've got this meeting room booked till *twelve*, so—'

'Sarge!' Tufty pulled a face at Logan. 'Sarge, we've got a hot one. On the riverbank.' Raising his eyebrows for an ominous pause. '*Something*'s washed up...'

Something...?

That could only mean one thing: Charles MacGarioch's body.

And an excuse to escape The Tenth Circle of Hades.

Logan grabbed his notes, and phone, and pen, and the last forlorn bourbon biscuit, definitely *not* grinning as he hurried for the door. 'Sorry everyone: duty calls.'

'But, Chief Inspector, what about our—'

He clunked the door shut behind him, and got the hell out of there...

The pool car skirled along Market Street, siren wailing, blue lights flashing, as Detective Sergeant Simon Rennie drove like a coked-up squirrel.

His peroxide-hedgehog hair stood to attention at the front, but was deserting its post at the back. He'd put on a bit of weight since the third kid, but had tried to compensate for the extra chin with a little bleached Vandyke beard. Which was a bit ... mid-life-crisis-ish. As if Spike from *Buffy the Vampire Slayer* had awoken one morning to discover he'd somehow turned into Guy Fieri.

Tufty sat in the back, munching away on the rescued bourbon biscuit as a reward for rescuing Logan from the MAPPA Meeting Of Doom.

Which left Logan in the passenger seat, one hand wrapped around his Airwave handset, the other around the grab handle above the door as Rennie threw them around the four-way junction at the end of the road – narrowly missing a massive articulated lorry hauling offshore containers away from the harbour – and roared off down North Esplanade West.

'Will you slow down! Already got one corpse on the go today, don't need another three.' Logan pressed the Airwave's button again, voice raised above the siren. 'I don't care if they found the body or not, they don't get to film the bloody thing: keep them back. We need that scene secured!'

Offices and industrial units flashed by on the right, a line of trees and the shining ribbon of the River Dee on the left – with the granite-grey mass of Torry lurking behind it.

Steel's voice grated through the Airwave. *'Oh, aye, thanks for pointing that out. Here was me selling tickets and letting everyone take selfies with the remains. What a silly-billy I am!'*

'We got an ETA on the Procurator Fiscal, or the Pathologist yet?'

'How the buggerlumping hell would I know?'

Tufty sooked air through his biscuity teeth. 'That's a quid in the jar.'

The pool car flashed through the lights outside the big Jewsons in a blare of angry horns.

A bunch of fish workers were out lounging on the riverbank, still dressed in their overalls, blood-and-guts aprons, hairnets, and wellies. Enjoying a tea break in the sunshine. They sat up to watch the car go by.

Tufty gave them a cheery wave.

'No' my job to do the managerial stuff, remember? I'm just a lowly Sergeant.'

'Can you grow up and do your job?'

The car wheeched on, past a bunch of glass-and-concrete office blocks with their glittering modern facades, trying to kid on there weren't fish-processing units hidden in the little side streets behind them. With big plastic bins full of fish guts, heads, and bones for the seagulls to feast upon.

Mind you, suppose they were a dying breed, these days. Back when Logan was a humble probationer, patrolling the streets with Big Annie Dunbar to stop him doing anything stupid.

Wonder what happened to her...

The traffic thickened up ahead – anticipating the approaching roundabout – cars and trucks and lorries creeping down the left lane, while the right was clogged by some tit in a black

BMW. The driver more interested in dawdling along, contemplating his bumhole, than getting the hell out of the way of a patrol car with its lights and siren blaring.

And still nothing back from Steel.

Logan pressed the button again. 'Hello?'

'You made Doreen and bloody Biohazard acting DIs, and not me!'

'It was their turn.'

Rennie leaned on the horn. 'COME ON: MOVE IT!'

'I'm the only bastard here with the experience! I've been a Detective Chief Inspector, *for pricking cock's sake! And—'*

'And look what happened last time!'

Either the BMW driver had finally woken up, or realised he wasn't the centre of the sodding universe, but his indicators flashed left, then right, then left again. No one was letting him in, though, so in the end – still indicating the wrong way – he bumped up onto the central reservation.

Rennie accelerated into the gap.

The pool car roared past warehouses and the BP garage, then out onto the roundabout, cutting across the nose of a skip lorry, and onto Riverside Drive.

Then the road dipped beneath the old Wellington Bridge, following the river inland...

And still not a peep from Steel.

Logan sighed. 'OK. Sorry. That was... But it's your own fault for being a pain in my hoop.'

No reply: just the car's roaring engine and wailing siren.

A series of pseudo-art-deco office blocks whisked by on the right. On the other side of the river, up a steep forty/fifty-foot embankment, sat a neat row of granite tenements, then a bunch of flats where Craiginches Prison used to be. Because nothing in this sodding city could ever stay the same.

'You there?'

The pseudo-art-deco offices gave way to an eight-storey block of pseudo-art-deco flats, then a pseudo-art-deco warehouse. Because Riverside Drive liked to pick a theme and stick with it.

They whooshed beneath the railway bridge, and the east-most edge of Duthie Park appeared – a playground area with shrieking kids, bored mums, and an over-excited spaniel.

Still no response from Steel.

Tufty leaned through from the back of the car. 'She doesn't like people talking about "The Great Fall From Grace", Sarge. Gets her all … dark and bitey.' He patted Rennie's shoulder, and pointed. 'That's us over there.'

Rennie's eyes narrowed. 'Yes, thank you, *Constable*, I did manage to work it out for myself.'

Would be hard not to: a pair of patrol cars blocked off the lay-by and two uniformed officers were busy erecting a line of blue-and-white 'POLICE' tape. Cordoning off access to the crime scene.

They weren't the only cars parked there, though – a ratty Honda Civic festered between them, its rear driver's-side wing held on by what looked like cable-ties.

Rennie double parked, blocking it in, and killed the engine. Radiating smugness. 'In *record* time.'

Idiot.

Logan climbed out into the hammering sun, one hand making a visor above his eyes to cut the glare down a bit.

Green exploded everywhere. Trees in full leaf, bushes in full … bush. Weeds running rampant all the way down the bank to the water's edge. The south entrance to Duthie Park sat on the other side of the road, with its fancy granite chess-piece gateposts, and lacy wrought-iron railings. Which was probably going to cause problems later. But for now, Logan tipped a nod at the PCs erecting the outer cordon and marched across the lay-by, past a vandalised phone box, and over to the much plainer railings – there to keep stupid people from tumbling downhill into the river.

From up here, there was an almost uninterrupted view of the water below. Bramble, nettles, and rosebay willowherb choked the steep bank, partially hiding a narrow pebble beach below. But the main action was thirty-odd feet off to the left, downriver, where another pair of uniforms did battle with a roll of black-and-yellow tape: 'CRIME SCENE – DO NOT ENTER'. Trying to erect an inner cordon. With nothing convenient to tie it to, they'd stuck a pair of orange traffic cones on the bank and fixed one side to them. God knows why, but instead of leaving it there, they'd decided to enclose the crime scene by wading out into the water with great-big sticks they could jam into the riverbed.

Because when you were thick as mince, health-and-safety didn't count.

What they were *trying* to enclose floated facedown in the water – legs up on the bank. Dressed all in black and definitely dead. A huge feathery seagull swooped down onto the body, but one of the PCs yelled and waved their arms at the thing till it flapped into the air again. Screaming avian obscenities as it climbed. Circling overhead. No doubt waiting for another chance and plotting revenge.

Upriver, a familiar rumpled figure was talking to a bare-footed woman in a trench coat and an emaciated baboon in a tracksuit. That would be WhatsHerFace and Thingumy – the couple who discovered the body.

Steel might've been sulking, but at least she was *doing* something.

Logan snapped on a pair of gloves and leaned out over the railings, scanning the undergrowth.

'Guv?' Rennie sidled up, keeping his voice low. Presumably so Tufty wouldn't hear. 'What we looking for?'

'Unless he jumped off a train, someone must've chucked the body in from somewhere.'

'Eh?' Chin in, making that ridiculous bleached Vandyke bristle. 'But he was... Nah: Charles MacGarioch went in the water, remember? When the ice-cream van crashed?'

Just when you thought Rennie couldn't get any thicker...

'That was the River *Don*, you vulcanised Flump! *This*,' putting on a singsong lilt, to really sell the sarcasm, 'is the River *Dee*. Dee – Don. Don – Dee.' Logan treated him to a withering scowl. 'What: you think he got swept out to sea, then back again, all the way through the harbour, and a mile-and-a-half upriver? Like he's been on a wee cruise trip for corpses?' Waving a hand at the half-floating body. 'Oh, and did he stop off somewhere along the way to change into *completely different clothes*? Or did the little fishies help him with that?'

At least Rennie had the decency to blush as he peered at the remains. 'Ah...'

'Exactly.' Logan turned to Tufty. 'Where's the common approach path?'

'Erm...' The wee loon bounced on his tiptoes, scanning the riverbank, then pointed. 'That way, Sarge.'

One last wither for the Idiot Rennie. '"Charles MacGarioch"...' Then Logan followed Tufty's finger, to where twin lines of yellow-and-black tape bordered a trampled path through the weeds, all the way down to the pebbled beach. Climbing over the railing, he took his time, moving sideways like a worried goat, or a cautious haggis, because it was nearly vertical here – arms out to keep his balance on the descent, because there was nothing the lower ranks loved more than a stuck-up DCI tobogganing through nettles on his arse.

20

Logan stepped out onto the click-clatter of little round stones, blinking at the bitter-sharp parmesan stink of fresh vomit.

He skirted the half-chewed spatter, and across the slithery beach, to the traffic cones. Staying behind the glaring-yellow strip of tape as the two uniforms wanked about with the other ends.

PC Ferguson was a nondescript bloke with an underwhelming moustache and all the grace of a tumble-dryer. PC Greig: a good six inches shorter, with a pageboy haircut, sharp little nose, and blinky eyes – making her look as if one of The Beatles had sex with a sparrow.

Ferguson and Greig were both knee-deep in the river, wobbling about, trying to get their Gandalf's staffs to stay upright in the fast-flowing water. And failing.

'Hoy!' Logan waved at the pair of them. 'What on earth are you doing?'

PC Greig shoogled her stick. 'Inner cordon, Guv.'

'Who are you protecting the body from, *mermaids*? Get out of the bloody water, before you fall in and drown.'

While they splish-splashed back to shore, Logan had a good frown at the body. Back of the guy's head looked like half a pound of raw stewing steak, mixed with strawberry Angel Delight.

So that's what the seagull had been after.

Which probably explained the vomit.

Ferguson waded ashore, 'Hi, Guv. It's—' and promptly fell over on the beach. Sending pebbles rattling. 'Buggering...'

'You're bloody hopeless.' Greig rolled her eyes and hauled him to his feet. Then nodded at Logan. 'What's the plan?'

'Better get the road closed – you can see all this from the lay-by. No entry to Riverside Drive from the Duthie Park Roundabout and ... other side of the railway bridge. And get on to the park – I want those gates shut and padlocked.' He looked up at the bright blue sky and its hungry, circling seagulls. 'We need a crime-scene tent down here ASAP too, before the TV people turn up with their sodding drones.'

'Guv.' And away she wobbled, keeping a firm grip on Ferguson, in case he went Alpha Oscar Tango again.

Soon as they were gone, Rennie slithered over, with Tufty in tow. The peroxide idiot pouted at the body. 'So if it isn't MacGarioch, who is it?'

As if Logan was supposed to know.

Time for another withering Paddington scowl.

Tufty held a hand up. 'I has chased-up Scenes, Sarge. They *is* on their way, but did give an ETA of twenty minutes, on account of Ernie has-ing the squits.'

'Make sure he's got bicycle clips on his SOC suit then.' Logan looked out at the shining river. They weren't that far from the harbour, here. Less than a mile, for sure. Which meant something else to deal with: 'Is the tide coming in or going out?'

'On it.' Tufty whipped out his phone and wandered off, poking away with his tongue sticking out.

Rennie made a show of getting *his* mobile out too. 'And *I'll* get cracking on the misper list: see if anyone's lost a ...' squinting at the body, 'six-foot, IC-one, male, dark hair, undercut, last seen wearing black cargo pants, black boots, and a black sweatshirt.'

'Hmm...' Logan stepped right up to the cordon. All in black: the guy was even wearing black nitrile gloves – like the ones tattoo artists used. So not wanting to be seen, or leave any fingerprints. Dressed for cat-burglaring. 'While you're at it, see if there's been a string of thefts-by-housebreaking anywhere around here. Could be our victim picked on the wrong property? Householder fights back, things get out of hand, "oh no", panics, dumps the body.' Turning to look uphill, at the trees towering above. 'Which *probably* means within three or four streets of the park. You don't take the guy you just accidentally killed on a magical mystery tour.'

'Unless you're in some sort of fugue state, cos of the shock?'

That was true.

Logan patted him on the shoulder. 'Better make it *all* of Aberdeen, then.'

Which was when Rennie realised that he'd just vastly increased his workload. A groan, a sag, and off he sodded.

Over in the middle distance, Tufty waved. 'SARGE!' Jumping up and down to attract attention. 'TIDE'S COMING IN!'

Of course it sodding was.

Scenes better get here quick then, or he'd have to compromise the crime scene to secure the body. And the Procurator Fiscal would *love* that. Not to mention their horror-show Pathologist. But they'd love it even less if he let the remains float away.

Maybe—

'*Hoy.*' A gravelly voice, right behind him.

'Jesus!' Logan skittered sideways. Turned. 'Don't *do* that! Sneaking up on people...'

'I called in Scenes, by the way.' Steel glowered up at him. 'And the PF, *and* Dr Death, even though it's no' my spudging job.'

'How can you creep about on this stuff?' Just moving his feet set pebbles rattling. 'Like a horrible terrier-haired ninja.'

The scowl deepened.

Not far up the pebble beach, Tufty was turning slowly in place, with his phone out. Probably taking panoramic crime-scene photos that had better not end up on Twitter. Then the phone rang in his hands, making him jump and drop it with a high-pitched 'Eeep!' Scrambling to catch the thing before it shattered on the stones. He stuck a finger in his ear, and answered it, waving at WhatsHerFace and Thingumy as he passed.

The seagulls circled high above, like albino vultures.

The river flowed.

The sun shone.

And Steel just stood there, regarding Logan with a look cold enough to reverse global warming in a single glance.

Sigh. 'If this is about Doreen and Biohazard being acting DIs, don't.'

She stuck her nose in the air. 'Oh aye: like *I* care.'

One of the gulls broke away from its mate, swooping down at the remains, hoping for another tasty gobbet.

Steel snatched a golf-ball-sized lump of rock from the beach and hurled it – the stone wheeching off on a perfect intercept course.

Almost got it too, but the feathery velociraptor jinked clear a heartbeat before the pebble hit. Flapping away from the gory buffet in an explosion of *scrawk*ing and *kee-ow~kee-ow~kee-ow...*

'Nah.' Steel brushed grit off her hands. 'All the extra responsibility and work for none of the extra pay?' Turning and slouching away. 'Kiss my sharny arse.'

Because no one sulked like Detective Sergeant Roberta Steel.

As if they didn't have more than enough to worry about.

Like the unidentified body with its head bashed in. And if *that* was an accidental death, Logan's bum was made of cheese.

This was murder.

He dug out his Airwave handset and pressed the button. 'DCI McRae to Control: better tell the Chief Super we've got another problem...'

A lot had changed in the last two-and-a-bit hours. The patrol cars had been joined by Scenes' grubby Transit van, a mud-spattered black Range Rover, and two unmarked Vauxhalls that looked as if a strong sneeze would make bits fall off.

With the road closed from the roundabout to the railway bridge, they weren't restricted to the lay-by, so they'd spread out along the front of Duthie Park. Where the gates were locked and secured with a line of blue-and-white 'POLICE' tape.

And because the road was shut, the usual collection of Outside Broadcast Units were nowhere to be seen. So were all the press vehicles. Which made a nice change.

It also meant that the media scrum was trapped behind the park's fancy iron railings. Penned in like nosy zoo animals, poking their cameras over the bars.

A small crowd of lookie-loos had joined in – after all, it was a lovely day, so why go picnic in the park with your loved ones, when you could gawp at a bit of human tragedy?

Logan shifted his phone from one side to the other, ducking behind Scenes' Transit, out of the cameras' glare. 'Biohazard? You still there?'

There was a wee pause, then: *'Are you serious?'*

'Yup.'

He leaned on the railing.

The river was higher now, raised by the incoming tide, but Scenes had still managed to get a blue-plastic marquee erected over the riverbank, extending out into the water. A couple of SOC-suited figures headed inside, carrying a body bag. Good luck to them, with the sun beating down it had to be like a kiln in there.

'*And you're* definitely *not shitting with me?*'

'Doreen's now officially in sole charge of the search. Get your farty arse back to the ranch and commandeer an incident room. I want a Murder Board, HOLMES instance, and some bodies ready to go by the time I get there.'

Suspicion scuttled down the phone. '*But* I'm *running the team, right?*'

'Reporting to me, but yeah: you're running the team.'

A drone whined past overhead, its dead gimbal eye taking in the scene, 'SKY NEWS' emblazoned down the side.

Tempting to flip it the Vs, but that *probably* wouldn't go down well back at headquarters.

Biohazard barked out a wee laugh. '*Only been acting DI a couple of hours and I'm already leading a murder case!*'

'The Chief Super still has to OK it.'

'*Doreen's gonna poop breeze blocks when she finds out!*' You could almost hear him rubbing his hands. '*There's me swanking about the air-conditioned office, while she's stuck here sweating her boobs off in a Tyvek romper suit.*'

'Don't wind her up, it's not nice. You're—'

'*Hold on, I can see her on the other side of the river...*' There was a scrunching sound, and everything got a bit muffled. '*HOY! DOREEN! GUESS WHO'S OUTTA HERE? ME!*' Followed by a jagged burst of maniacal laughter. '*I GOT A MURDER TO RUN! ... THAT'S RIGHT! THE SEARCH IS ALLLL YOURS, BABY!*' Then Biohazard was back on the phone again. '*Ooh, she does not look happy.*' Giggling away to himself. Then: *'How big a team do I get to lord it over, Guv? A dozen? Two dozen?'*

'You'll be sodding lucky. Do the best you can, OK?'

Going by today's staffing crisis, that would probably be three officers, a stapler, and a bottle of Tipp-Ex.

Tufty appeared from somewhere behind Scenes' Transit, bearing two large wax-paper cups. Somehow, he'd managed to swap his fighting suit for the full Police-Scotland-uniform black, complete with peaked cap, stabproof vest, high-vis waistcoat, and overstuffed utility belt.

'Got to go. Official duties call.' Logan hung up, then frowned at Tufty. 'How did you...?'

The wee spud did a wiggly turn, showing off his new outfit. 'The Monstrous Mildewed Maiden made me fetch a bunch of stuff from the station, and I always keep a spare T-shirt and trousers in my locker. That and clean socks. And pants.' A sage nod. 'In this job, you *never* know when clean pants might come in handy.' A pause. A blink. 'Oh, and:' he held out one of the cups, 'ta-daaaa!'

Logan raised an eyebrow. 'If this is meant to be a bribe, you can stop right there. *Rennie*'s my sidekick.'

That made him deflate a bit. 'Oh...'

'Mind you,' Logan accepted the cup, 'shame to waste it.' Taking a sip of iced coffee far nicer than anything they served in the tenth circle of Hell.

Then the pair of them stood there, drinking their drinks, while not very much happened on the riverbank down below.

The Sky News drone whined past again, doing a slow pan this time.

Tufty produced his phone. 'DS Rennie did get me to dig out details on everyone reported missing since last Sunday.'

Course he did.

'Lazy sod.'

A pout. 'But I did work hard!' Holding out the phone. 'Look I did make maps and graphs and everything!'

'Not you: *Rennie.*'

The pout turned into a smile. 'Oh. That's OK then.' Tufty poked at the screen. 'I did also research every burglary in the Greater Aberdeen Area for the last six months. In case our victim is of the cat-stealing variety. Then I did a geographical analysis, cos you can totes profile someone based on where they dump a body. Did you know most people won't cross running water to do it? Like they is *witches* or something.'

'Are you getting to the point, or do I have to beat you to death with your own truncheon?'

'Right: results.' He scrolled and scrolled and scrolled some more. 'Here we go. Missing persons is a dead end: we've got a schoolteacher – female; a bus driver – in his sixties; a fifteen-year-old girl; a violinist – five foot four; and a mother of two. None of them matches our victim.'

'Anyone work in a tattoo parlour?'

'No. Should they?'

So much for the gloves being a clue. 'Apparently not.'

'Oh, OK. Which leads us onto *burglaries.*' Poke, scroll, fiddle. 'There's heaps and heaps of shopliftings, but we can discount all of those, cos people don't usually do it in the middle of the night. And the only places still open are twenty-four-hour supermarkets, casinos, clubs, and all-night petrol stations. And they *ain't* gonna kill someone for robbing them.'

Oh, to be a naive wee PC again.

'Yeah...' Logan took a scoof of chilled coffee. 'Remind me to introduce you to the guys who own Secret Service, on Windmill Brae. Steal from *their* club and we're fishing you out of Rubislaw Quarry. In bits.'

'And then I did a pattern analysis to see when and where the break-ins happened, cos I was told to look for our victim going on a spree. And that does give us these.' He held his phone out again, showing a map of Aberdeen with clusters of red dots superimposed over it. 'Biggest splodges are multiple hits on the same night.'

Not a *massive* amount of help.

'Suppose it's a start.'

'And then I did put my *Thinking* Head on.'

A pair of figures emerged from the marquee, not wearing the standard white SOC Tyvek suits, but pale blue ones. Or 'going the full Smurf' as it was known.

'And my Thinking Head did ask: "Who else does wear all black, Lovely Tufty, but does not burglarise cats?"'

The lead Smurf stopped, just inside the cordon, and threw back her hood. Took off her safety goggles and mask, then shook her hair free. Which didn't help much, because it was stringy with sweat. Isobel needed her roots done, too – the greys were beginning to show. But the crows' feet and laughter lines didn't change the fact that she was still a very attractive woman. Until you got to know her.

'And *I* said, "I does has no idea, Mr Thinking Head. Who?" And my Thinking Head did go: "Muggers!"'

Smurf Number Two performed the same unhooding procedure, only with far less catwalk-model poise. But then Sheila Dalrymple was one of those tall, thin, *angular* people, who seemed to be constructed entirely out of coat-hangers; with trendy glasses and a wide flat face. Carrying their mobile pathology kit in a blue plastic evidence crate.

'And I did said, "That's a very clever point, Mr Thinking Head." Because Mr Thinking Head is very clever indeed.'

Isobel said something to one of the Scenes team, pointing back towards town.

They nodded, then scuttled off to make a phone call.

Tufty held out his phone again, where a couple of small

dots were superimposed on a map of Duthie Park. 'So I did a search on muggings in the vicinity, because if you mug someone you mug them when they're on foot, right? Cos it's hard to mug someone who's in a car. They can just drive away.'

Instructions issued, Isobel scrunched her way across the pebbles to the common approach path.

'Only there wasn't a lot of them, when I checked. I think muggers want somewhere with more foot traffic after dark, and the park isn't really a shortcut *to* or *from* anywhere.' A wee shrug. 'Sorry.'

Isobel clambered up the steep bank to the lay-by, with Sheila struggling along behind her – having a lot more difficulty, carrying that crate.

Logan lowered his voice to a whisper and sidled closer to Tufty. 'Try to not say anything stupid, OK?'

Isobel pulled herself over the railing, snapped off her purple nitrile gloves, and nodded at the pair of them. 'Acting Detective Chief Inspector, Constable.'

A wave from Tufty. 'Hi, Doc.'

She gave him a scowl in return. 'That's *Professor* McAllister.' Then started towards her filthy Range Rover, but Logan held up a hand, blocking her way. Politely.

'Anything you can tell us?'

'Of course.' She regarded his hand with disdain. 'I can tell you that we do post-mortem examinations in this city, rather than indulge in random guesswork.'

Helpful.

'Isobel, you must've noticed *something*. Come on, we won't hold you to it. Just … any idea on time of death?'

There was a long, imperious pause.

'You *do* know how we estimate time of death, don't you?

188

With a rectal thermometer and some complicated mathematics. Which we do back at the mortuary, *not* knee-deep in a river.'

Logan pinched his eyebrows in and up, in a sort of spanked-puppy-dog look.

Her mouth pinched. Then a breath hissed out. 'But I *suppose* I can *speculate* that the remains have been in the water for a number of hours – probably overnight, going by the lividity and level of predation by marine fauna. Cause of death is yet to be determined, but if he was alive when the trauma to the back of the head occurred, he wouldn't be for long.'

Sheila Dalrymple struggled over the railings and staggered to a halt, joining the congregation. 'Verily, 'twas a mighty blow he suffered. Near rent his skull in twain, it did.'

Everyone stared at her.

'Don't do that.' Logan turned back to Isobel. 'What about ID? When you went through the guy's pockets: driver's licence, credit card, library membership...?' He got nothing back but a flat, dead stare. 'Fine: how quickly can you get fingerprints and DNA?'

Her eyes narrowed, in a way that suggested she was about to tell them to fornicate somewhere far from here. Then: 'DNA will depend on the lab. But don't expect miracles – everyone's got the flu, so they're woefully understaffed. As for fingerprints? Wait until the body's dried out, then we'll see.'

'Don't suppose you've got a photo of his face? Pocket contents?'

A tut from Sheila. 'I' faith, some villain had plundered our fallen friend's possessions long afore we lay our hands upon his damp apparel.'

'What?'

Isobel sighed. 'The victim's pockets were all inside out. Are we to assume you weren't responsible? It's not uncommon for police officers to conveniently "forget" the importance of crime-scene management.'

'We didn't touch him!'

'Then 'twas truly a villain that performed the vile search –' Sheila leaned in for a conspiratorial wink, '*perhaps* even the miscreant you and your stout fellows seek!'

Isobel massaged her temples. 'Sheila, I need you to chase up the duty undertakers. Make sure they're on their way to collect the remains, OK? Please.'

A nod. 'Be of good cheer, my lady, for I shall stir their *sluggardly* pot!' And off she stalked, taking her crate with her.

Soon as she was gone, Isobel let loose a long-suffering breath. 'Someone gave her a box-set of romantasy novels. That Diana Gabaldon has a *lot* to answer for.' She undid her SOC-suit zip, revealing a sweaty grey shirt and purple tie. 'We took some reference shots before putting the remains in a body bag. Sheila will email them to you. But I doubt they'll help with identification – going by the extensive edemata and ecchymosis, he was severely beaten for an extended period.'

Tufty binged upright. 'Rapist!'

Eh?

Isobel peered at him. 'Your constable appears to have Tourette's.'

'No, no, no, no.' The wee loon shook his head. 'We were playing "Who Dresses All In Black In The Dead Of Night?"'

'I don't think that's a very funny game, *Constable*.'

Logan stepped in, before she eviscerated the daft sod. 'It isn't meant to be. And Constable Quirrel's got a point; see if you can light a bonfire under the lab – I need to know if our victim's DNA matches any rape kits.'

She stood there, frowning for a moment. Then pulled her shoulders back. 'I require a favour.'

'Do you now?'

'I understand you're having a gathering on Sunday. A barbecue. I want you to invite Colin.'

'Ah...' Logan grimaced. 'I'm not sure that's entirely appropriate, with—'

'For goodness' sake, it's been twenty years! If Colin can get over the fact you and I used to be sexually intimate, surely you can too.'

Wow.

OK.

He tried again. 'It *might* not be appropriate, because half the guests are *police officers* and your Colin spends most of his time writing articles about how useless we are!'

'Oh. I see.' Isobel didn't even blush. 'Well, I want you to invite him anyway. All his work friends have been made redundant, and he needs some sort of outside interest.' She rustled off, without so much as a 'thank you'.

'*Fine.* But I want those DNA results ASAP!'

If she heard that, it didn't show. Instead she climbed into the Range Rover, started the engine, and growled away into the scorching afternoon.

'Sa-arge,' Tufty fluttered his eyelashes, 'about that barbecue...?'

'No. Now go find me some rapists.'

21

'...denies all involvement and says he looks forward to clearing his name when the case comes to court in September.'

The pool car puttered up Holburn Street, stuck behind an extremely large man on a bicycle, doing five miles per hour in a drench of sweat and soggy Lycra cycling shorts.

Silly sod.

Had to be thirty degrees out there. And everyone knew Scottish people started melting if it got above eighteen.

Rennie's hand kept twitching towards the horn, as if that would make their rolling roadblock go any faster. But then he'd been in a grump since they'd left the lay-by. What with doing all the driving while Tufty lounged in the back. Making him little more than a bleached-blond chauffeur.

'...revelations that NHS trusts across Scotland are declaring a state of emergency, as admissions hit an all-time high for the year...'

Logan went back to gazing out the window.

This bit of Holburn Street was a bit on the shabby side, to be honest. But it could've been worse. At least it wasn't all charity shops, vape shops, phone shops, bookies, and boarded-up units, like Union Street.

Tufty leaned through from the back. 'Do you know what *I* think?'

'Hmmph.' Rennie glowered across the car at Logan. 'Did you *have* to bring him?'

'Couldn't exactly leave the wee loon behind. Imagine the trouble he'd get into.'

'...*struggling to keep up with the number of patients. Joanna Parkinson, leader of the Scottish Conservatives, has blamed "decades of SNP underinvestment" for the situation...*'

'Yeah, but he should be *Biohazard's* problem, now. Not ours.'

'No, but listen,' Tufty tapped both headrests, '*I* think we should go back to the station, because it'll be *way* easier to cross-reference sexual assaults and offender profiles within geographically specific parameters.' He bit his bottom lip and grinned at the same time, making him look like a demented hamster. 'And I does has leftover Chicken Jalfrezi and naan bread in the CID fridge for lunch. We did get a celebratory curry last night, because Kate said ... *yes!*' Bouncing up and down in his seat. 'I does has a bidie-in! How cool is that?' Serious face. 'But mostly the sexual assaults thing.'

'...*Fordyce, MSP for Aberdeen South and North Kincardine invited her to "awa and bile her heid".*'

Logan smiled. 'Congratulations.'

Rennie just humphed again.

The lights were with them, for a change, and they crawled across the three-way junction where Holburn Street crashed into the tail end of Alford Place and the start of Union Street.

Back in the day, Aberdeen's main thoroughfare was vibrant and alive, now it was all grey and moribund. Seemed as if every day there was something else closing down, or 'To Let, May Sell'.

'...*following a riot at her concert in Glasgow. The American pop star, and vocal Trump critic, has received numerous death threats...*'

Still stuck behind their one-man Tour de France, Rennie's thumb stroked back and forth across the car's horn. As if he was trying to arouse it. 'We're *not* going back to the station.

Call the support team: get one of them to do it. We've got bigger haddock to batter.'

Which was true.

After all, Charles MacGarioch's friends weren't going to interview themselves. And every single one of them would need talking to.

Tufty's bottom lip poked out, no doubt mourning that leftover curry, then he whumped back in his seat, and pulled out his phone. Noodling away at the screen. Probably playing some daft game. Because no one could just sit *quietly* any more, could they. They always had to be *entertained*.

Rennie glared in the rear-view mirror. 'Constable! I said call the—'

'Has-ing a bash at it online, Sarge.' Poking and scrolling. 'Searchity search, search, search…'

'*…and three people were stabbed. The First Minister has called for calm, calling the outbreak of violence this week "a cowardly and racist attack"…*'

Logan unfolded the list of Charles MacGarioch's known associates and scanned down it for the closest address. Then pointed at the traffic lights. 'Left here.'

Rennie switched lanes, accelerating past Mr Soggy Spandex, then wheeching around the corner onto Rose Street with its collection of takeaways and sitty-ins. Each one a siren's call to Logan's empty stomach.

Well, it was a long time since breakfast, and a couple of mouldy meeting-room custard creams did *not* count as tenses.

'*…claim the arson attack on the refugee support centre, in Edinburgh's Cowgate last night, was inspired by the burning of a hotel housing migrants in Aberdeen.*'

There was a sports shop on the junction with Thistle Street, where two women in overalls were removing a big sheet of plywood from a shattered window. Presumably to replace it with one of the units strapped on the back of their tartan van – the one with 'Auchterturra Glazing Company Ltd' down the side.

'Though most politicians have condemned the events, Ian Wilson-Vale, of Vision for Britain, said:'

A full-on twat bloviated out of the car's speakers. Like a fart made flesh. *'People are angry that our proud country doesn't feel like it's theirs any more. These are* legitimate *concerns, and the government isn't helping by pretending everyone who feels that way is somehow "racist" or part of the "far right".'*

Sitting in the back, Tufty noodled on. 'Doodley, dooodley, searchity poo…'

'Following his comments, Marion Lewis – minister for Culture, Media and Sport – is facing calls to resign after she was picked up on a live microphone after her interview with BBC Breakfast News *this morning:'*

A tired female voice grumbled out of the radio, the audio muffled and crackling: *'Christ, that man's a bigoted moron. The real question is: why would anyone elect a racist [BLEEP]-wit [BLEEP]-[BLEEP]ing [BLEEP] like Ian [BLEEP]-For-Brains Witless-Vile?'*

'The minister wasn't available for comment. But her department did issue the following statement:'

'Searchity, bingity, bongity, boo, spidgity, spodgity, spudge…'

Rennie rolled his eyes. 'The idiot's right about one thing: we should drop him off at the station.' Nodding in agreement with himself. 'Biohazard's going to need all the help he can get. I mean, how are we supposed to set up *yet another* murder inquiry with no flipping officers to staff it?'

With difficulty.

Logan pointed. 'Straight through at Skene Street.'

'"…for calm, rather than seeking to divide our country by stoking the flames of isolationism, xenophobia, and hatred."'

They crossed just as the lights changed, onto Esslemont Avenue, with the austere granite lump of Aberdeen Grammar School on one side and a long run of grim-grey tenement flats on the other.

Rennie slowed to avoid mowing down a middle-aged man with a shark's fin haircut. 'Suppose we could get officers to double up, but you know what the press are gonna say if they find out we're half-arsing it. Unless it turns out our victim *was* a rapey pervert. Then they'll probably give the killer a medal.'

'What a time to be alive.'

'*...sex scandal engulfing American politics as a third Republican senator is questioned by the FBI...*'

Tufty looked up from his phone. 'Do you want the depressing news, or the depressinger news? One hundred and sixty-three unsolved rapes still on the books.'

'Christ...'

Rennie boinked a fist off the steering wheel. 'You know what we should do? Mandatory DNA database for every male in the country. And anyone *entering* the country too. Soon as you set foot on Scottish soil: DNA swab, thank you very much; into the database you go.' Sniff. 'Fingerprints too. That'd help the clear-up rate.'

'Oooh...' Tufty scooted forwards again. 'Maybe you could fit everyone with ankle monitors as well? Or tracker chips? Make sure you know where they are at all of the times.'

'Good idea!'

Logan thumped Rennie on the arm. 'He's being *sarcastic*, you coagulated Moomin.'

A scowl. 'Doesn't stop it being a good idea.'

Soon as they passed the Grammar School, Esslemont Avenue narrowed to a grey trench – four-storey tenements on both sides, facing off across the road. The ones on the right were armed with satellite dishes, all pointing their antenna spears back towards the town centre, but the left was completely unarmed.

Now there was a metaphor...

Logan folded the list and stuck it back in his pocket. 'Anywhere you can find a space.'

Rennie squeezed the pool car in behind a pair of huge communal black bins, tightly sealed against the brain-eating seagull menace.

'Right.' Logan scrunched around in his seat. 'You find any rapes in Duthie Park?'

'Doing my best, Sarge.' Poking and frowning away at the phone's screen. 'Location fields aren't searchable by geographic proximity ... you can only list addresses alphabetically. Who *coded* this? The API's rubbish!' Poke, poke, poke. 'See, *this* is why I wanted to go back to DHQ... That and the curry.'

Rennie climbed out of the car, then poked his head back in, smiling like a hungry wolf. 'Then you'd better sit here and go through them, one by one, hadn't you, *Constable*.' He held up a paw. 'Don't worry, I'll crack a window for you. Wouldn't want someone calling the RSPCA on me.' Then thunked his door shut, leaving Logan and Tufty alone in the car.

'Sa-arge?' The wee loon curled his top lip. 'Is he *always* this much of a snudge?'

'No barking at passers-by. And try not to chew the upholstery.' Logan slipped out onto the pavement, wagging a finger through the open door. '*Stay...*'

Clunk.

Bloody hell...

The riverbank had been hot, but it was nothing compared to this. All that granite must've spent the last few days soaking up the heat, and now the tenements were like massive radiators, pounding out even more warmth as the sun baked down.

Other than the satellite dishes, and occasional downpipe, the flats were devoid of fancy ornamentation. Here and there, windows lay wide open, trying to coax in the non-existent breeze, letting music and TV shows ooze out into the sticky air.

Rennie turned around a couple of times, a Labrador in an ill-fitting suit, looking up at the buildings. 'Where we going, Guv?'

'Go easy on the wee loon.' Heading across the road. 'Not his fault you're jealous.'

'*Not* jealous.' Rennie scurried after him. 'If anyone's jealous, it's *him*. Because I'm so great.'

Yeah, you keep telling yourself that.

'And the RSPCA don't operate in Scotland – it's the *SSPCA* up here. If you're going to make fun of people, at least get your references right.' Logan stopped outside number sixty-five. Checked the paperwork again. 'Jericho McQueen: one of Charles MacGarioch's little friends. We start here then we work our way through the list. Someone's got to know where the racist wee shite's hiding. We're…'

The main door to number sixty-five swung open and an auld mannie in baggy jeans and a polo shirt scuffed out, bald as a boiled egg, hauling a tartan shopping trolley behind him.

'Here.' Logan stepped forward, catching the door before it bit into the trolley's flanks. 'Let me get that for you.'

Mr Bald-And-Baggy wrestled his trolley free, then gave the pair of them a good squint. 'You Jehovah's Witnesses or cops?' Waving that away before they could answer. 'Don't care, long as you give that idiot in Two B a hard time. He's an ASBO waiting to happen. And a wanker. That's a sin, right: wanking?' He waved that away too. 'Course it is. *Everything*'s a sin with you miserable bastards.'

With those kind parting words, he shambled off, hiding that shiny head beneath a green woolly bunnet.

'That was lucky.' Logan stepped into the building's lobby,

which was nice enough if you liked brown. Brown woodwork, brown tiles on the floor, chocolate-mousse-coloured paint on the walls. A framed picture of a teeny kitten in a teacup hung at the foot of the stairs – a nugget of sweetcorn in a four-storey jobbie.

He popped his head outside again. 'You just going to stand there gawping, or can we get on with this?'

Rennie stared after the old man. 'Rude auld bugger. I mean, do I *look* like a Jehovah's Witness?'

Not unless they'd really let themselves go.

'Anyway,' Rennie joined Logan in the lobby, 'before we start: who's playing "good cop"; and who's the *crazy, nothing-to-lose, loose-cannon* that doesn't take any shit and won't stop till he gets a result?'

'How about we play "professional cop", "other professional cop"? You know, for a change.' Heading upstairs.

Rennie trotted along behind him. 'You've no respect for tradition, that's your problem.'

'No, *my* problem is that I'm surrounded by idiots.'

'And halfwits?'

'Halfwits?' Logan snorted. 'I dream of being lucky enough to work with *halfwits*.'

The first-floor landing was another study in turd-brown, this time featuring a picture of a baby rabbit, sitting in the middle of a salad bowl, eating the lettuce.

And on they climbed.

'I'd need three of you mooshed together to count as a halfwit.'

Rennie grinned. 'I miss our little talks, Guv. We should work together more often.'

The second floor had a duckling peeking out of a shoe, and yet more brown. And the armpit-sweaty fug of cannabis hanging in the air.

Not Logan's problem.

One floor to go.

'Guv?' Rennie dawdled a bit at the back. 'We still on for Sunday? Unless the city's like something off *Mad Max* after the protest, of course. *Welcome to the Teuchterdome!*'

'Emma bringing her tattie salad?'

'Coleslaw. And I've got two of those big things of beer from Costco. Like a mini keg?'

The top landing boasted a puppy wearing a bowtie and a soppy expression to enliven the poop-inspired decor.

Logan stopped outside Jericho McQueen's flat, and pointed at the door.

Rennie gave it a knock. 'Anything I should know before we go in?'

'I like her tattie salad better. Oh, and Steel's bringing, and I quote, "homemade lesbian sausages".'

'Urgh...'

The door opened an inch and a wrinkled face peered out – narrowing her eyes as she clocked their fighting suits. 'If yer here tae ask aboot my eternal soul: I gied it tae a wee mannie wie a forky tail and horns twa wicks ago.'

'Is Jericho in?' Logan held up his hands. 'He's not in any trouble, we just need to have a word about one of his friends.'

Suspicion seeped onto the landing, thicker than the smell of weed downstairs. 'Oh, aye?'

Silence.

Then a sigh.

And the door swung open all the way.

The wrinkled face belonged to a woman in her mid-eighties, with a tan corduroy skirt, Sex-Pistols T-shirt, thick-rimmed glasses, and a red cardigan. 'Suppose ye'd better come in. But wipe yer mochit feet!'

It was always nice to feel wanted...

22

The living room struggled under the weight of a dark wooden table, bookcase, and mantelpiece stuffed full of ugly ceramic angels. Which made a change from ugly china cats. But unlike Victoria MacGarioch's flat, there wasn't a single photo of the royal family on display. Or anyone else, come to that. Instead, a brass urn had pride of place on the mahogany sideboard, in a wreath of white plastic roses.

A ridiculously large TV took up one whole corner, the screen filled with some sort of be-jumpered Scandi crime drama – paused mid-gruesome discovery.

Logan shifted on the saggy, striped couch, not drinking the tea they hadn't been offered.

Why did no one on the telly have the faintest clue about crime-scene management? Never mind an SOC suit, *Politisjefinspector* Melancholy Ugly-Sweatersdóttir wasn't even wearing *gloves*.

Rennie stood in front of the window, looking out and down at the street below. Presumably lording it over Tufty.

Which left Mrs McQueen: sitting in pinched stillness on the room's only armchair as the clock ticked.

Yup: great to feel wanted.

Finally, the living-room door opened and in slouched a young man whose DIY beard kit fluffed out from a puppy-fat face. It went with little pink eyes and a nose that looked as if it'd been broken more than once. He hadn't bothered to dress for company, scuffing his way to the couch in a Lego *Ninjago* T-shirt, Spider-Man boxer shorts, and nothing else. Collapsing into the seat beside Logan, with a yawn and a scratch, hair sticking out in all directions.

And even though his skin was pale and lumpy as a tub of cottage cheese, his accent sounded like a wobbly Detroit-gang-banger-from-the-projects knock-off: 'Go see's a Coke, Gran.'

'Get it yersel, ya lazy wee gype. Staggerin' in at aw hours.'

'Gra-aaaa-annnn…' Whining and whinging.

'Oh, in the name o' the hairy Christ…' She levered herself out of her armchair and lumbered from the room.

Rennie got his notebook out – pen at the ready.

'Jericho.' Logan put on his best non-threatening-we're-all-friends-here voice. 'You're one of Charles MacGarioch's mates, right?'

'Might be. Don't mean I've done nothing. Even if *he* has. Which he hasn't.'

'Any idea where he might've got to?'

A lopsided shrug. 'Dunno: at his nan's or his bitch's, innit? I ain't his keeper, bro.'

Logan kept his face perfectly still, because giving the wee shite a bollocking for referring to women as 'bitches' wouldn't help catch Charles MacGarioch. And Soban Yūsuf deserved better than that. 'Sure you didn't see him yesterday? Or maybe he popped past early this morning, when everyone else was asleep?'

'Nah: whatever you's trying to pin on Charlie is *sod all* to do with me. Jericho was *working* all night.' He mimed playing twin turntables, while holding imaginary headphones to his ear. As if talking about himself in the third person, in a borrowed accent, didn't make him enough of a tosser. 'Got me, like, a hunnerd-an-fifty witnesses, innit?'

'That's cool.' Logan leaned in, as if he was about to share a secret: 'Where's he hiding?'

'Don't know. Wouldn't tell you if I did. Cos Jericho don't *clype* on his homies.'

Time to try concerned-parent mode. 'It's only going to get worse for him, Jericho. The longer Charlie's in the wind, the harder they're going to crack down when they find him. Help *us* to help *him*.'

Jericho stiffened. 'You deaf, bro? Jericho – don't – clype.'

'I can respect that.' OK, so concerned-parent didn't work, how about gossipy-mate? 'How long have you two known each other?'

'Since. You know?' He looked across the room, at the urn sitting on the sideboard. 'We was in that support thing, for kids that didn't have no mums and dads. Growed up with our nans or grandads ... aunties, that kinda shit.'

'Must've been tough.'

'Nah.' Jericho looked over his shoulder at the door, a wee smile on his face. 'She's a daft old bitch, and her taste in music is *well* crap, but I love her, you know? She bin good to me all these years. Jericho would fuckin' *die* for that woman.'

Fair enough.

Logan produced his phone and called up the photo he'd found in MacGarioch's bedroom. 'Charlie found himself someone to love too.' Holding the screen out.

'Yeah, he's a lucky guy.' Jericho did that stupid finger-clack thing rappers used to do about a decade ago. 'She is *unjustifiably* hot. *Spicy* trembles, you know what I'm saying?'

Not even vaguely.

Turning the phone back the right way, Logan frowned at

the screen. Ooh, look at me: being all confused. 'Keira still lives at home, doesn't she?'

'Nah, man. She's got her own place in Powis, innit. Sharing with them vegans and shit.'

A nod. 'Sweet.' Now all they needed was a last name and an address.

'*Totally.*' His grin pulled that horrible ratty pseudo-beard even further out of shape. 'Likes to mess with them, cos she brings home, you know leftover *steak* from the restaurant and leaves it in the fridge for them to freak out about.' Jericho waved his hands about and put on a hippy voice. '"It's a *dead animal*, man! I'm like *totally shocked* and *offended*!" Ha!'

'Yeah. Of course. She works at the…' Logan scrunched his face up, throwing in a little shake of the head. 'I always forget the name of the place.'

'"The Star-Sprinkled Heavens". Which is well wanky, but you gotta make wedge, right?'

Rennie did a little squint-shouldered pose. 'You got *that* right, bruv.' Making devil's horns with both hands and half-folding his arms so they pointed at forty-five degrees, as he launched into a rap:

> '*She's called Keira, like Knightley,*
> *Cos she's hot and she's spicy,*
> *But you treat her politely,*
> *Ask nicely, go lightly,*
> *And her surname is…?*'

Oh, for God's sake.

Jericho *stared* at him, as if the daft bastard had just grown an erect penis in the middle of his forehead. Which might have been less embarrassing.

'Ah, nah.' Jericho shook his head. 'Nah, nah, nah.' Jumping

to his feet and jabbing a finger at Rennie's stupid face. 'You bastards is *playing* me! Like I is some sort of fuckin' *idiot*!'

Logan poured on the oil. 'Forget about him, *he's* the idiot. It's OK: you and me were just chatting and—'

'Jericho ain't no clype!' The pointing finger swung around to the living-room door. 'Get yo *lying* police asses out my nan's crib!'

At which point that very door swung open and in scuffed Mrs McQueen, carrying an ice-filled glass in one hand and a can of off-brand Coke in the other.

She took one look at her grandson, then Rennie, then Logan. 'What?'

'It's nothing.' Logan stood, making soothing gestures. 'We're cool. Everyone just needs to calm down and we can—'

'Gran, these police wankers is trying to get us to clype on Charlie! I want them *gone*, like.'

Her mouth pinched – tight as a tourniquet. 'You heard the boy: out.'

'Well … how was I supposed to know?' Rennie stumbled out onto the pavement, courtesy of a not-too-subtle shove.

Logan followed him into the sun-baked street. The glare almost blinding after the brown gloom of the stairwell. 'A *rap*? Are you insane?'

'It's not... He's...' Sulky pout. 'Wasn't going to cooperate anyway.'

'He *was* cooperating! Till you did your Slim Shifty impersonation.' Logan stomped off towards the pool car.

'At least we found out where MacGarioch's girlfriend works, right? They'll give us her last name, and Bob's your wingwang.'

Idiot.

'Jericho McQueen's probably up there, right now, on the phone, *warning* Keira that we're looking for her boyfriend!'

Rennie loped around to the driver's side, casting a pitying look across the roof as if Logan was the one who's daft. 'It's *literally* in all the papers. Charles MacGarioch's face was on the morning TV news bulletins. Trust me: she knows.'

'You're still an idiot.' Logan hauled open the passenger door and thumped into a four-wheeled air-fryer. Peeling off his jacket before he reached medium-rare. 'Now *she* knows *we* know about her and Charles.'

Tufty was still in the back seat, still poking away at his phone, and still wearing the full Police-Scotland-black outfit with stabproof and high-vis. Little sod must've been sweltering, but there wasn't even a drop of sweat on his pointy face.

He'd nicked the map from the pool car's glove box and spread it across his knees – Aberdeen, laid out in all its sprawling glory – only now the city was peppered with teeny tags made of torn-up Post-it notes. Two colours: yellow, and pink.

Rennie whumped in behind the wheel. 'Yeah, but does that really matter?' Digging out his own phone and fiddling with it. 'They're not an item any more – you said the racist old-bag grandma broke them up.' He held the phone to his ear. 'Might make this "Keira" a bit bitter and ready to dob her ex in. I mean, what kind of tit doesn't stand up for his woman, when some rancid—' He sat forward, putting on a polite, slightly plummy voice. 'Hello, yes, is that the Star-Sprinkled Heavens? … Good. … Yes. … Lovely, thank you. … Can I ask, I know it's a bit cheeky, but is Keira working this lunchtime? She's my wife's favourite. … Now, that *is* a shame. … Oh, she *will*?' Flashing a thumbs-up at Logan. 'Smashing. … Tell you what, let me check with my wife and I'll phone you back about booking that table. … OK, thanks. … Thanks. … Bye.' He hung up. 'The mysterious Keira won't be in till this evening.'

'Subtle.'

'Oh yeah.' Rennie gave his head a wee shoogle. 'This isn't my *first* dance recital.' Then he stuck a hand into the back of the car, snapping his fingers like a prick. 'You finished yet?'

Tufty applied another nib of torn yellow Post-it. 'Almost.' Then sat back and peered at the map.

A sniff. 'Told you he was useless.'

The wee loon pulled a face. 'See, I'm thinking there's maybe a case for *not* reporting it.' Running a finger around the map. 'If you've just accidentally-on-purpose killed the guy who broke into your house to rape you – or your wife, girlfriend, mother, child – do you ditch the body in the river *then* call the police to say "Help! We've been attacked!"?'

True. 'Not if you wanted to get away with it.'

Another yellow nib. 'So maybe you don't report it at all? Or maybe you report it as something else, cos you need a crime number for the insurance? Which is why I did go back to the housebreakings again.'

Logan sat up. 'Anything for last night?'

'Near Duthie Park?'

'Preferably.'

'No.' Tufty tore a teeny square of yellow from a Post-it and stuck it down near the airport. 'Last night we've got three in Rubislaw, one in Northfield, one in Stoneywood, and two in Danestone.' Tapping each location in turn. 'Busy night for thieves of a cat-like nature.'

'Then we start in Rosemount and work our way out.' Logan thumped Rennie. 'Drive.'

A groan. 'Should we not be leaving this to Biohazard?'

'Where's your team spirit? Besides, like you say: Keira won't be at work till this evening. Maybe we can get this thing solved before then?'

After all, you never knew your luck…

23

Logan stepped out of the front door of number eighty-six, into a fancy portico with granite pillars, because the houses in this bit of Rubislaw weren't exactly modest. Big flash homes with big flash gardens and big flash cars parked outside.

Mr Copeland followed him out into the sunshine – wringing his hands. Mid-seventies, in a 'LochSkian Hotel' polo shirt, shorts, baldy head, and hairy knees. 'It's all *quite* distressing, really.'

Logan tucked his notebook away. 'It might be an idea to get a decent padlock on your shed. You never know when thieves will strike.'

'Oh yes, definitely. Definitely.' Nodding so hard his wattles wobbled. '*Thank you*, Officer.'

Greasy, lying, hairy-kneed fraud that he was.

A quick nod, and Logan wandered off, down the driveway and around the corner, onto Forest Road.

How thick did he think Logan was? Someone broke into his shed and made off with a ride-on lawn mower worth *three-thousand-pounds*, a chainsaw, a petrol strimmer, pole saw, and over two grand's worth of power tools?

Aye, right.

The front lawn was nowhere near big enough for a ride-on mower – most of it was lock-block parking for the two Jags and a Lexus – and the back garden had been covered in paving slabs. OK: it was a very *nice* patio, but doubt it needed a lot of mowing.

Should put a flag on the crime number, in case the insurance company got in touch.

Why was it, the richer some people got, the fewer morals they had?

Of course, maybe that's how they got to *be* rich in the first place...

Forest Road was even swankier, with huge granite mansions, baronial palaces, Edwardian halls, and the odd Schloss thrown in for good luck. And it was lined with trees, so there was a nice bit of shade from the punishing sun.

Good for strolling along with your hands in your pockets.

Logan's phone *ding-buzz*ed as he took a left onto Rubislaw Den North. Which was posher still. You'd need a serious lottery win to afford anything in this part of Aberdeen. Or old family money.

Ah, a boy could dream...

He checked his phone, pulling up the new message as he wandered through the leopard-spot shade. Not a text this time, but an email.

Sᴇᴇɪʟᴀ Dᴀʟʀʏᴍᴘʟᴇ:

> Well met, good fellow; I trust the day finds ye hale and hearty.
>
> Attached, please find, these photographic representations of our sorry victim's physiognomy as recorded by mine device of miraculous wire-free communication this very morning. {official pics to follow}

My mistress hath scheduled a post-mortem ere the cock crows ten tomorrow's morn. And greatly pleased we would be to have thy presence for this grand affair!

Your obedient servant,

Miss Sheila J. Dalrymple

Swear to God, she was drinking on the job.

Logan clicked on the attachment, starting the download.

Over on the other side of the street, a woman jogged by in her Gucci tracksuit and Chanel sweatband, with a ridiculous-looking cockapoo trotting along beside her on an extending leash. No doubt impressed by Logan's fighting suit, she gave him a cheery smile on the way past.

Little did she know that his entire outfit came from the big Asda in Garthdee.

But he returned her greeting anyway, the smile vanishing from his face as Sheila Dalrymple's attachment finally appeared.

Bloody hell...

Logan leaned against the cool trunk of the nearest tree. Frowning at the screen.

It was a portrait shot: the body lay on its back on the pebbled beach. Even with the flash on, the camera hadn't been able to adjust for the watery blue light that seeped in through the SOC-marquee walls, draining colour from the remains.

Which was probably a blessing.

The features were lopsided – barely recognisable through all the swelling. One cheek looked broken, and the eye socket above it was virtually gone too. The mouth nothing but a mess of tattered flesh. The nose almost non-existent.

It wasn't just a beating: whoever this poor sod was, they'd been subjected to a *horrific* level of violence. Didn't matter what they'd done: no one deserved that.

Because the body had been lying facedown in the river, all the blood had pooled in the lowermost tissues. Turning the skin there beetroot-purple, while everything above it was the colour of frozen butter.

Logan huffed out a long breath and scrolled through the other photos.

Number Two was a close-up of the eyes, ballooned up to scarlet slits. Number Three showed the left ear, almost completely ripped from the victim's head. And last, Number Four. The poor sod's right hand – with every single finger on it broken and dislocated.

Even with the sun softening the tarmac, the day had turned a lot colder.

Logan took a breath, hit 'FORWARD', and thumbed out an email to Biohazard.

> This is your victim. PM's at 10:00 tomorrow (don't be late, or Prof. McAllister will dissect you!).
>
> Looks like either blind rage, or a punishment beating. Maybe torture?
>
> Get onto the labs and chase the crap out of them for that DNA!

Soon as the email registered as 'SENT' Logan pocketed his phone and marched up the road – it wasn't a strolling kind of day any more.

He'd made it about halfway, when the pool car appeared, something thin and poppy piffling out of the open driver's window.

'Doodle-dee-doo, doodle-dee-doo,
Cos I love you, doodle-dee-doo,
My heart is on fire, hot like vindaloo!
Doodle-dee, doodle-dee, doodle-dee-doo...'

Rennie took one look at Logan's face and killed the radio. 'What's wrong?'

Could just show him the photos, but there was a risk – after the whole DNA-Test-Every-Man-In-Scotland rant – he'd want to celebrate, and that would *not* go well.

Logan forced a smile instead. 'Someone "broke into" an old man's Shed of Lies.'

'Ah, OK.' He hooked a thumb over his shoulder. 'Mine was a crotchety pair of auld farts whose home-help *allegedly* made off with a set of silver cutlery and two crystal decanters. Silly sods didn't get their key back before stiffing her a month's wages for breaking a casserole dish.' Grin. 'Why are rich people such *twats*?'

A question for the ages.

Logan climbed into the passenger seat. 'So, if *my* OAP was working an insurance fiddle, and *yours* were—'

'The technical term is "twats".'

'That just leaves the wee loon.'

Rennie put the car in gear, and off they went.

Bayview Road wasn't as swanky as Rubislaw Den North, but then not much in Aberdeen was. It was still pretty grand, though. Even if whoever named the street was a lying sod. That or they had a massive ladder, because the only thing visible from here were the large granite houses. And even they were partially hidden behind hedges and trees.

Rennie peered through the windscreen. 'Where is the little spud?'

'Play nice. Or I'll promote *him* to Head Sidekick and you can go help Doreen search the riverbank.'

'God... *Total* shudderfest.'

Two doors down, a gate opened in a seven-foot-high hedge and out lolloped the little spud in question.

THIS HOUSE OF BURNING BONES

He paused on the pavement, turned, and waved back towards the house. Then closed the gate and stood there, face upturned, beaming back at the sun.

Rennie ponked the horn.

Tufty gave *them* a wave as well, then scurried up the road and clambered into the back. 'Afternoon, Sarges.' Rubbing his tummy with happy hands. 'Mr and Mrs Knowles did has the loveliest of finger sandwiches and teeny quiches and strawberry tarts and meringues with rhubarb cream!' Sigh. 'Couldn't eat another thing.'

There was a scowl from the driver's seat, but Rennie kept his gob shut. His stomach rumbled a complaint, though.

It wasn't wrong.

Logan gave the mirror a stare. 'What about the break-in?'

'Some poophead jimmied the patio door in the dead of night, and tried to make off with their DVD player.'

Interesting. '*Tried* to?'

'They does also has a *very big dog*. And Captain Woofalot doesn't like burglars.'

Rennie raised an eyebrow. 'Bingo.'

'No: no "bingo". Mr Knowles is in a wheelchair, Mrs Knowles is in a leg brace, and they're *both* in their eighties.' Pausing for a chin stroke. 'Unless she beat him to death with her walking stick, I don't think they're our killers. Plus, it's difficult to dump a body when you drive a mobility scooter...'

Rennie's face tightened, but the threat of being demoted to squelchy-riverbank-searching kept him silent.

Tufty consulted the Post-it-note map. 'Northfield?'

'Northfield.' And now it was Logan's stomach's turn to howl. 'But we're stopping somewhere for lunch, first.'

Rennie took a scoof of Irn-Bru. '...but the thing that worries me is: what happens if it all kicks off like last time? Cos that's what these bastards want, isn't it – anti-migrant riots on the streets, smashing in corner-shop windows, burning people out their homes. And all the time they're raking in the cash!'

This bit of Northfield was a lot less swanky than Rubislaw Den. Instead of granite mansions, the pool car sat between twin terraces of beige-and-brown harling. Two-storey, flat-faced, with the occasional tiny awning bolted above the front door. No mature trees, or towering green hedges here. Instead, most of the gardens had been lock-blocked, or tarmacked-over for off-street parking. Hatchbacks and vans, instead of Range Rovers and BMWs.

'And you know what?' Rennie took a bite of pie, chewing through the words. 'Bet half of it comes from Russia too. Destabilising the West, one knuckle-dragging racist arsehole at a time.'

To be fair, they were very nice pies.

And it was easier to let him rant on by himself – just throwing in the occasional, 'Uh-huh,' every now and then to show willing – than actually pay attention to whatever it was he was *wanging* on about this time.

Logan shifted his pie around a little, using the paper bag as a container to keep the grease off his fingers. Steak mince. The king of pies. Hot, gristle-free, savoury, dark, and delicious, from the bakery on Byron Square.

Munch, munch, munch.

It was just the two of them in the car, the back seat lying vacant while Tufty was out doing a bit of work for a change.

That would teach the little sod to stuff himself full of fancy finger sandwiches and tasty pastries.

'Tell you,' Rennie swigged more Irn-Bru, 'we should make it illegal to own a newspaper, or radio station, or any of that shite, if you don't live *and* pay tax in the UK.'

Logan's phone *ding-buzz*ed on the dashboard. He checked it, one-handed, leaving the other free to provide another tasty munch of crisp pastry and beefy gravy.

'And they're forever bleating on about being "patriotic", and "having pride in our country"! How are we supposed to be proud of it, when it's full of *wankers* like Charles MacGarioch and those hostel-burning pricks in Edinburgh? What, we're supposed to just turn a blind eye and salute the sodding King?'

TARA:

> Don't forget: P/T conference is TONIGHT!
>
> New time = 1930
>
> Will you be home first?

Good question.

'And don't get me started on the politicians!' Rennie tore at his pie, getting flakes of pastry all down his clip-on tie. 'Pretending they're "men of the people" – half these tossers went to private school!'

Logan pecked out a reply with one thumb:

> Do my best.
>
> If I'm not home by 7 – go without me and I'll meet you there.
>
> ...
>
> Promise.

SEND.

'Working class? Never done a hard day's work in their bloody lives!'

Ding-buzz.

Tara:
Logan!

Yeah… Had a feeling that wouldn't go down well.

'You know *why* they want to drag us all back to the seventies? It's cos *that's* when they were *kids* – no responsibilities, no worries, no mortgages, or any of that shite. Mummy looked after their every need, and you could call people "nig-nog" and get away with it.' A grunt. Some angry chewing. 'Bunch of fucks.'

Logan's thumb ticked across the teeny keyboard:

> Picked up another murder this afternoon. A really nasty one.

> But I WILL be there, I swear on Cthulhu's fuzzy whiskers.

And you couldn't get a more solemn oath than that.
Send.

The rear door creaked open and in thumped Tufty – all black and fluorescent yellow, like a radioactive liquorice allsort. 'Mr Bhattacharjee thinks it was one of the kids from a couple of streets over. They wriggled in through the bathroom window, ransacked his mum's bedroom – she wasn't there, on account of being in hospital with the lurgie – and made off with her life's savings. About two and a half grand, stashed under the mattress.'

Logan popped his phone back on the dashboard. 'Think he might be our killer?'

'Doesn't drive. And it's going to look weird if you call an Uber and ask if it's OK to pop a body in the boot.'

True.

Logan polished off the last morsel of pie. 'Starting to think this housebreaking idea of yours is a washout.'

'Was only a hypothesis, Sarge.'

Rennie crammed in the final toenail-curl of pastry, chewing as he scrunched up the paper bag and lobbed it over his shoulder. Where it *just* missed Tufty's head. 'Stoneywood, ho!'

And off they went again.

24

Logan clunked the pool car's door shut, shielding his eyes from the sun's glare as a white plane with a red-tartan tail scrambled into the sky, propellers going like the clappers.

The tiny bungalow they'd parked outside sat in the middle of a row of dilapidated wooden sheds. Isolated from the rest of the street. As if the other houses were scared of catching something.

It didn't even have a strip of pavement outside.

This was 'SAOR ALBA', according to the nameplate screwed to the wall by the gate. Grey harled walls, lichen-greened slate roof, the woodwork peeling and in need of a paint. The front garden was a bit of a mess too. But the building backed onto a field of barley – rapidly losing its green tinge as it slowly baked – so at least the view was nice. If you didn't mind being on the Aberdeen Airport flight path…

Rennie climbed out and pulled on a pair of shades. 'Lonnnng way from Duthie Park.'

With insights like that, it was *amazing* he hadn't made Inspector yet.

Logan opened the garden gate, setting it groaning and squealing like a haunted pig, then marched over to the front door. Rapping on the wood with his knuckles.

'This is all a waste of time, isn't it.' Rennie scuffed down the short path, following him. 'Stupid idea.' Casting a scowl back towards Tufty – currently gazing out across the field, like a badly dressed garden gnome.

A muffled, '*Hold on...*' came through the door, then it swung open and a small woman appeared. Sixty-something? With grey hair, jeans, clogs, and a lime-green sweatshirt that had 'END OF EMPIRE' embroidered across the chest, along with some twee thistles. Looking rumpled and a bit confused as she blinked out at Logan and Rennie ... then sagged in disappointment.

Again: always nice to feel wanted.

Logan pulled on a professional smile. 'Mrs Shaw? We're here about your break-in.'

'Oh?' Peering around them at the street beyond, clearly looking for something. Or someone. It can't have been Tufty, though, because seeing him just caused her to sag even more. 'I thought you lot didn't bother your backsides for anything less than a full-on murder these days.'

Logan spread his arms wide. 'And yet: here we are.'

She let out a tut, then a long-suffering sigh. 'You'd better come in then.'

Wow.

The tiny room looked as if someone had been through it with a petrol strimmer. Film posters hung in tatters from the walls, the bed lay on its side, the mattress slashed. Every drawer hung wide open, their contents flung about; wardrobe too.

A small desk – the kind kids were given to do their homework at was missing a leg, leaving it tipped back at a drunken angle. All *its* drawers were open too, but there was no sign of the contents. Nothing computery on the floor or wedged on top of other broken things.

Mrs Shaw turned in place, flapping her arms like a lime-green penguin. 'I mean *look* at it! What sort of animal does this to a wee boy's bedroom?' Pointing at the piles of clothes. 'All his *things.*'

Logan stepped back out into the hall.

It was tiny too. But then this was a tiny house.

Paintings of Scottish pastoral scenes dotted the walls, between five doors leading off. Two hung open, revealing a tidy little lounge and a tidy little kitchen.

He tried the other three: tidy little bathroom, tidy little linen closet, and a tidy little bedroom.

Hmmm...

Logan stepped back into the maelstrom, where Mrs Shaw was picking up a pair of black boxer shorts – folding them, then turning around again, trying to find somewhere tidy to put the things.

'And they didn't touch *anything* else? Just your son's room?'

She put the boxer shorts on the wonky desk and plucked another pair of pants from the floor. 'I don't know what Andrew will say when he gets home. They took his new laptop!'

'But you didn't hear anything?'

'Well, I was fast asleep, wasn't I. Soon as I've taken my pills, I'm out like a badger.' Her shoulders dipped. 'Came through to see if Andrew wanted a boiled egg for his breakfast and found ... this.'

Not the best start to the day.

Logan snapped on a pair of gloves. 'And where was your son when all this happened?'

'Oh, he was out. Probably at a girl's house.' A smile. 'Thinks I don't know, but he's just like his father: proper ladies' man. Well, he is *very* handsome.'

She rescued a photo from the messy floor and held it out: a professional headshot, eight-by-ten, of a young man with a strangely ... *plastic* face. Tidy little beard to go with the tidy little house, black hair swept back from a perfectly smooth forehead, plucked eyebrows, teeth so white they probably glowed in the dark. Sort of handsome, in a Made-By-Mattel way.

A curly signature was superimposed over the bottom of the image, with the words 'ANDREW WALLACE SHAW ~ AVAILABLE FOR MODELLING AND ACTING WORK' and a mobile number.

So much for 'wee boy'.

Mrs Shaw let out a wistful breath. 'Not that his dad hung around for very long. Wandering eye to go with the wandering hands.'

Logan turned – surveying the wreckage again. 'Jealous or jilted boyfriend, maybe? Or a girl he's dumped?'

That got him a scowl. 'My Andrew's not some sort of ... homewrecker! He's been raised *right*. A *good* boy. I made *certain* of that!'

'I'm sure he is, but we have to ask this stuff.' Logan had a poke around in the debris. Clothes mostly, with the occasional airport paperback thrown in. 'How did they get in? Your burglar.'

'Don't know. I was asleep, remember? But when I woke up the back door was lying wide open. And you can tell the insurance people I *always* lock it!' She folded another pair of scattered undies. 'All they ever do is work out ways not to pay what they owe. What's the point of insurance if they never honour their end of it?'

'Uh-huh.'

Something went *crunch* under his foot.

Logan lifted a V-neck T-shirt out of the way and frowned at what he'd stepped on. An oval tube, wide as a hardback book, but plastic, camouflage-coloured, with some sort of elasticated strapping attached to one end.

He was bending down to pick it up when his phone burst into song, blaring out 'Ecce Homo, Qui Est Faba'. Which could only mean one thing: Biohazard.

'Sorry: I'd better take this.' Poking the green icon. 'DI Marshall, what can I do for you?'

'If you're not safe to talk, find somewhere you are.'

Yeah… That didn't sound good.

Logan put his hand over the microphone. 'Wonder if I could bother you for a cup of tea, Mrs Shaw. If it's not too much bother, of course?'

She rolled her eyes. 'And I thought it was just lazy writing on all those TV shows.' But she shuffled off anyway.

He closed the door behind her. 'OK. Safe to talk.'

'Got a rush job back from the labs: DNA on our victim. No ID as yet, but we've got a hit on five *unsolved rapes.'*

'Shite…' Checking the door was *definitely* shut. 'Sounds as if Tufty was right.'

'He's a creeper – gets into people's houses in the wee small hours. Targets single mothers.' A grunt. *'We're going to need more bodies – preferably female officers – to visit the victims and check for alibis. Don't want to add to the trauma.'*

That wasn't going to be an easy conversation.

'I'll see what I can do.' Logan picked up whatever it was he'd stood on, turning it over in his hand.

Looked like a pair of binoculars, only much higher-tech. The lenses were all cracked, and so was the camouflage-green casing as if someone had stamped and stamped and stamped on it. Leaving wires poking out and bits of circuit board on show.

'Not sure if it'll come as a relief or not – knowing someone's battered the bastard to death and chucked him in the river.'

'Better not mention that bit. At least, not till we get an OK from the PF…' Logan weighed the fancy binoculars in his hand. Looked around at the wreckage. 'Biohazard: this creeper of yours – do the victims remember anything *specific* about him?'

'*Hold on...*' There were some rustling noises. '*Dead of night... Here we go: dressed all in black, wearing a ski-mask with big sharp teeth printed on it. Like a monster's grin. Threatens them with a dirty big knife – "Make a sound and I'll slit your throat, then rape your kids..."*' A breath. '*Jesus.*'

'Yeah.'

'*Whoever did for this fucker: we should throw them a parade.*'

'The victims say anything else?'

'*Only that it was dark the whole time – he never put the lights on.*'

Yeah, but how did he navigate a strange house in the dark...?

Wires and circuit boards.

Maybe they *weren't* binoculars? Maybe they were night-vision goggles.

And maybe Mrs Shaw's 'wee boy' wasn't such an angel after all...

Logan leaned back against the pool car, phone to his ear. 'No comment.'

A wave of noise washed across the street as an orange-and-white jet swooped down towards the airport – roaring in over the field, then disappearing behind a block of flats at the end of the road.

Sadly, the din faded away, and Colin Miller became audible again: '*Seems like it's your day for finding treats from the deep, but. First it's Charles MacGarioch's jacket, now his body.*'

'And again: no comment.'

'*C'mon Laz, don't be an arse. Haven't had my meeting with the new owner, yet – assuming she ever deigns to turn up. Be nice if I had a wee scooparoonie to show off my skills, but.*'

There was still no sign of Tufty or Rennie. Hopefully the pair of them were doing a decent job of pretending to be an SOC team. Only without the scrunchy white suits and grubby Transit van.

'You should get your ears checked, Colin. Man your age – hearing's the first thing to go. That and the willy.'

'*OK, how about this: any comment on the old dears you traumatised yesterday, chasing that ice-cream truck into the river?*'

Logan scowled out at the barley. 'No one was *traumatised*! No matter what crap you printed this morning.'

A rumbling howl grew louder, and an aeroplane appeared from behind the flats, outbound this time – white-and-green, with a shamrock on the tail – clawing its way into the clear blue sky. Wings shining in the blazing sun.

'*They could'a died, man. If Charles MacGarioch hadn't swerved intae the Don, they'd be geriatric mince by now. People are saying he's a hero, like.* Sacrificing *himself, instead of ploughing through them OAPs.*'

A *hero*?

'Ha! That's me laughing at you. Did you hear it? Ha!'

'*Then there's those wee boys on the bikes. Could'a driven straight through them an' all. Didn't, though, did he.*'

'Charles MacGarioch is *not* a hero. He's a...' Logan clamped his gob shut, before something classified fell out.

'*Oh aye?*' Colin adopted a sly, sleekit tone. '*You know: it might help yer cause if you was to tell me why youse were after him in the first place. Put his "heroism" in a wee bitty context? Especially now he's dead – drowned as a result of your police chase.*'

Logan gazed out across the barley.

The Aer Lingus flight had shrunk to little more than a shining dot in the distance.

A tortoiseshell cat bustled across the hot tarmac, tail swaying, disappearing into one of the tatty wooden sheds.

And Colin didn't say a word. Letting him stew.

OK. Who knew – maybe it *would* help.

'Strictly off the record? And I mean one hundred percent in *no way* for publication?'

There was a wee pause, then: '*Agreed.*'

'The body we fished out of the Dee wasn't Charles MacGarioch. So, if you publish that, A: you're going to traumatise his grandmother for nothing, and B: you'll look like an idiot when the details come out.'

No response.

Logan turned his back on the sun. 'Isobel tells me you're a sad lonely git with no friends.'

'*Are you* positive *it's no' him?*'

'She wants me to invite you to the barbecue at my place, Sunday.'

'*Cos if you're screwing with me...?*'

Oh, for Christ's sake: you try to do someone a favour.

'Of course it's not sodding him. I'm a police officer; unlike you shifty journalist bastards, we actually tell the truth.'

Most of the time, anyway.

'*Aye, fair enough.*' A grunt. '*And I'm no' "sad and lonely", I'm just a bit... Our new owner's doing that fire-and-rehire crap, and half the guys I work with are out.* Apparently, *proper, trained, experienced journalists are "too expensive". Why pay* them, *when you can "hire" a bunch of spotty unpaid interns to churn out click-bait instead?*'

'Yeah, well, it's Sunday from one. Feel free to bring a bottle of something swanky.'

The bungalow's front door swung open, and out lumbered Tufty, listing to one side under the weight of the pool car's SOC kit – like an oversized make-up case in dented stainless steel, with a handle that was almost solid duct-tape.

Rennie was right behind him, carrying a slithery armful of evidence bags.

'Got to go.' Logan hung up, not waiting for a goodbye.

Mrs Shaw shuffled into the doorway, peering about again. Probably expecting her wee boy to turn up at any moment.

Seemed a bit cruel not to tell her, but until they knew for sure? No point breaking her heart for nothing.

Logan gave her a little wave instead.

She nodded back, then disappeared inside – into the gloom.

Tufty popped the boot and heaved the SOC kit inside, with Rennie tumbling his collection of evidence bags in after it.

'Find anything?'

'Plenty fingerprints.' Tufty wrinkled his nose. 'Don't know about DNA, though – been a while since I did the course.'

'Not you, you desiccated Clanger. Simon?'

Rennie shuffled his haul. 'Got those night-vision goggles; box of black nitrile gloves, still in the Amazon packaging; squirty thing of bleach...' He pulled one of the bags out and held it aloft. 'While *here*, we have an electric bump gun.' Then gave Tufty a patronising smile. 'It's a device used for quickly picking locks.' Back to Logan: 'There's also a collection of women's lacy underwear. And one ski-mask, complete with printed-on pointy shark teeth.' He held that one up too – a disembodied mouth grinned out at them.

So they'd have to break Mrs Shaw's heart after all.

Logan at the bungalow, with its overgrown garden and tiny little rooms. 'Call Scenes – I want them out here right now.'

'Guv.' Rennie marched away, phone out, already dialling.

'You OK, Sarge?' Tufty closed the boot. 'Only you look all *squinky*. Thought you'd be happy.'

'This whole thing just got a shed-heap more complicated.' He drooped back against the car. 'Whoever killed Andrew Shaw, they're probably someone he tried to rape. Or someone he *did* rape. Or a victim's spouse, maybe relative.' Gesturing at the field and the street and the manky sheds. 'But why come all the way out here to trash Shaw's bedroom? Hardly counts as revenge if you've already beaten the bastard to death – you do it because you're *looking* for something.'

'Ah, I seeeeeee.' Tufty poked the boot. 'When I dusted the night-vision goggles for prints, I finded an empty SD card slot on the side. Maybe Shaw recorded his outings so he could "enjoy" them later?' A grimace. 'You know, on his own. Playing "Shuffle Mr Wibbly".'

Probably.

Which means this wasn't a crime of passion.

If Andrew Shaw had broken into their house and they killed him in the heat of the moment, he would've have had the goggles on him – there'd be no need to search his room.

No: whoever did it, they found out who he was, hunted him down, tortured and killed him. Then broke into his mum's house and got rid of any evidence he'd brutalised *their* family in the first place. Which explained why the laptop and all the computer equipment were missing too.

And that pointed the finger in a very horrible direction.

Logan took a deep breath. 'Tufty: do me a favour and go through the five rape victims' statements. See if any of them are police officers, OK? Or related to one?'

'Police?' Both of Tufty's eyebrows clambered up his pointy wee face. 'Sarge.' And off he trotted.

Logan let his head fall back, to stare up at the shiny blue sky.

Maybe they'd get lucky, and he'd be completely wrong about this?

Yeah…

The whirling *clatter*-and-*thrummmmm* of rotors rushed closer, then a bright red-white-and-blue Super Puma helicopter snarled overhead, whisking oil workers away to some far-distant oil field, in the middle of the North Sea.

'Jammy sods.'

227

25

SOC-suited figures rustled from their manky Transit van to Andrew Shaw's house – carting empty evidence crates one way, and full ones the other.

They weren't the only newcomers. A patrol car had joined the party and brought a couple of rusty Vauxhalls with it. Now their occupants were going door-to-door and searching the field behind the house.

Giving them a bit of space, Logan retreated to the car park, outside the block of flats, in the scattered shade of a drooping tree.

'A cop...' Biohazard had clearly got the Chief Super's memo, because he'd changed into regulation black, only without the stabproof vest and utility belt, because he was a fancy-pants DI now. His bare arms already going red as he paced the pavement – one hand massaging his forehead. 'Oh, for Christ's ... buggering...' He stopped and stared at Logan. 'A *cop?*'

'Maybe. Maybe not. Who else could track down a rapist like that? Private investigator? Journalist?'

'But a *cop?*'

'Might be worth checking the Police National Computer – see if "Andrew Wallace Shaw" has turned up in any search results lately.'

'Nooooooo...' Biohazard crumpled forwards, like a rumpled

question mark. 'Guv, maybe Doreen *would* be better as SIO on this one? I don't mind searching the riverbank, honest I don't. It's quite calming really...'

Fat chance.

'You should get someone to contact Shaw's dentist. Whoever killed him did a number on his teeth, but you might ID the body if there's any work intact. A fiver says he had veneers fitted. And talk to his GP surgery: we're looking for any old broken bones or scars.' What else? 'See if you can find his car too: must've left it somewhere.'

Biohazard groaned. 'This whole thing's a proper sodding poisoned chalice full of ... jobbies.' He straightened up and pointed at the bungalow. 'I catch the killer and he's a cop: everyone hates me, horrible press, career suicide. I *don't* catch the killer: everyone hates me, horrible press, career suicide.'

Logan patted him on the back. 'That's the spirit.'

'But, *Guv*...' Like a puppy, destined for a hessian sack and the nearest river.

But before Acting DI Marshall could start whimpering, Tufty scampered over from the pool car, holding out his Airwave handset. 'Sarge? Got a call for you; someone called PC Kent?'

No idea why they didn't just dial his direct number. Or even who PC Kent was. But it was that kind of day.

He took the handset and poked the button. 'Safe to talk.'

A Peterhead accent jerked out of the speaker: '*Sir? I mean, Boss. No: Guv. Yes. Hello? It's Hilary. PC Kent? Watching Balmain House Hotel? Where the fire was?*'

Ah, *that* PC Kent.

'What can I do for you, Hilary?'

'*Yeah, Guv? I've got the hotel owner here, and he's ... "feelin' nae pain", if you get my drift. Maybe, you could ... you know? Cos he's demanding access and I'm telling him no, and he's not taking*

229

that for an answer; and he wants to speak to whoever's in charge; and there's only me here; and when I asked the station for backup, they just said to call my SIO; only I don't really have one, cos I'm on loan from Peterhead, like I said; and the owner's becoming "agitated"; and I get the feeling everyone's going to disapprove if I twat *him one. So...?'*

'No twatting members of the public!'

Suppose it wouldn't *hurt* to lend a hand.

After all, everything was under control here, Scenes would be at it for ages, yet. And Biohazard was a big boy now, and ugly enough to cope on his own.

'We'll be there soon as we can.'

'Unless you secretly want *me to twat him one, Guv? I can, you know. Be delighted to, actually. We Blue Tooners do "reasonable force" really* well.'

'Definitely not! Sit tight till we get there, and don't let him into that building.' Because today was bad enough, without some drunken sod crashing through the burnt-out hotel's floor and killing himself.

'Thanks, Guv.'

Logan handed the Airwave back to Tufty. Huffed out a breath. Then gave Biohazard a 'buck-up' thump on the arm. 'You'll be fine. Just make sure no one cocks anything up. We want a clean result on this one, OK?'

A grimace. 'Oh, thanks a sodding heap.'

They left him to it – marching across the sticky tarmac to the pool car.

Rennie had all the doors wide open, but the thing was still hot as a crematorium as Logan thumped into the passenger seat.

The peroxide twit looked up from his phone. 'Emma says *she'll* do tattie salad if Tara makes whatever-it-is: with the little bits of pasta that look like maggots?'

And didn't *that* sound delicious…

Logan clunked his door shut. 'Buckle up: we've got a sozzled hotel owner to rescue from a Peterheadcase!'

Trees lined North Anderson Drive, their leaves: muted green, beneath a layer of summer dust. Set too far back from the dual carriageway to cast any shade.

The pool car cruised up the hill, past the fire station and some sort of council art installation featuring an endless line of orange traffic cones. Probably making a statement about the futility of human existence.

A parpy-trumpet indie-rock number tootled out of the radio, upbeat and jolly. Tufty nodding along in the back with a vacant smile on his face. Rennie tapping his fingers on the steering wheel. Logan's shoe marking time in the footwell.

Then three-beeps blared across the beat – announcing an incoming call on Logan's Airwave as they slowed for the semi-organised chaos that was the King's Cross Roundabout. He clicked off the radio, prompting disappointed noises from the idiots. 'Grow up.' And answered the call. 'Safe to talk.'

'Guv? It's Doreen.'

He checked the handset's screen: it was indeed.

'If you're calling to complain about the search: tough. There's no point—'

'We've found something.'

And with that, everyone sat up straighter.

'Brig of Balgownie. Charles MacGarioch was last seen wearing a black T-shirt, right?'

'Four Mechanical Mice.'

'That's what I thought.' There were some rustling noises, then: *'Found it caught in a shopping trolley, wedged against the bank. Ripped down the back, so looks like it was torn off.'*

That didn't sound good.

Rennie eased them closer to the roundabout, hunched over the wheel, rocking back and forward, looking for a gap in the traffic.

'Sure he didn't just *take* it off?'

'Not unless he's Edward Scissorhands. I've called Scenes – see if we can get DNA or something – but the only working van's sodding about somewhere in Stoneywood. Any chance you can light an acting-chief-inspector-sized fire under their arses?'

'Not really. They've got a serial rapist's house to process.'

Over on the pavement, a leathery couple were out walking a sausage dog – her in a bikini, him in budgie-smugglers, both in sun hats and flip-flops. Grey haired and saggy. So it wasn't just their feet going flip and flop.

What the hell was *wrong* with people?

No one wanted to see—

'Guv?'

Logan snapped back. 'Erm... Who's doing door-to-doors in Hillhead?'

'Spudgun's team.'

Rennie flickered the car's police lights, whooping the siren a couple of times to cheat his way into the swirl of vehicles and straight across the roundabout. Bit naughty, but at least Logan didn't have to look at Mr and Mrs Baggy-Wrinkles any more.

'OK. Tell Spudgun to shift focus to Bridge of Don and Seaton. Chances are, if MacGarioch's made it ashore, naked from the waist up, he's going to be pretty distinctive.'

'On one of the hottest days of the year? It's "taps-aff" weather, Guv. Half the buggers in Aberdeen will be wandering around like pre-boiled lobsters.'

As the Bikini/Budgie-Smugglers proved.

'My money's on him washing straight out to sea. Maybe he's hit his head on a rock or a log or something, and it's away to the briny deep he goes.'

Logan grimaced. 'Yeah, thanks for that.' But she wasn't wrong. 'OK: keep searching. Got to hope MacGarioch's made it out alive. Or if he *is* hurt, he's somewhere we can get to him.'

A whine slithered into Doreen's voice. *'Come on, Guv, I've gone boil-in-the-bag in this sodding SOC suit. Everything squelches!'*

'You want me to make Spudgun acting DI instead?'

She let loose a wee theatrical sob, then a massive sigh. *'Yes, Guv. Searching it is, Guv. Thank you, Guv.'*

Should think so too.

Outside the Balmain House Hotel, that mass of tribute teddy bears and grief bouquets had spread along the railings like a gaily coloured cancer.

Rennie parked behind the Mobile Command Unit, which didn't look so mobile any more, because someone had slashed the tyres.

Weren't people *lovely*?

A couple of young men finished off cable-tying a replica Aberdeen FC shirt to the railings, with the front facing the scorched remains, so the world could see that they'd had 'Yōsuf' printed across the back.

They posed for a couple of selfies – bent-knees-and-victory-Vs – in front of the maudlin display. Grinning away like the morons they were.

Photos taken, they sloped off, leaving the crime scene dead and deserted. No sign of a drunken hotel owner *or* PC Kent.

Not sure if that was a good thing or not...

Logan climbed out into the furnace afternoon.

Soon as his foot hit the pavement, Kent emerged from the MCU – her brown-blonde hair looking a lot more dishevelled than yesterday. 'Guv.' She nodded at Tufty and Rennie as they shuffled up. 'Other people.'

The knuckles on her right hand were scuffed, and a little swollen patch reddened across her chin.

'Hilary, when you said, "reasonable force" how reasonable was it?'

A happy sigh. '*Very* reasonable.' Kent hooked a thumb at the No-Longer-Mobile Command Unit. 'He's inside, having a wee rest, if you want?'

'Might as well. As we've come all this way…'

Logan followed her into a stuffy funk of stale booze, unwashed clothes, and warm dust. Which probably had something to do with the man slumped across the table. Eyes closed and gob wide open, snorking away as a puddle of drool spread. A half-drunk mug of something brown sitting beside his head.

Kent plucked the mug from the tabletop, then banged her hand down hard. 'WAKEY, WAKEY, MR MURRAY!'

'Gnnnnggffff…?' He jerked upright, then collapsed back into his seat. Blinking. A string of dribble still connecting his mouth to the tabletop like a fleshy balloon. Mid-fifties, maybe? With double bags under his eyes and a proper soup-strainer moustache. Scrapes on his left cheek and forehead. His polo shirt was all rumpled too, collar half-up, half-down; stains on his chinos – hole in one knee.

He wobbled a bit, as if the MCU was driving down a rutted track. One eye screwed shut as he peered around at the four of them. Or possibly eight, depending on how drunk he was.

Rennie and Tufty stationed themselves by the kettle, looking hopeful, as PC Kent loomed over their guest.

Meanwhile, Logan clunked the door shut and locked the thing, *before* leaning back against it – because you only made *that* mistake once – and folded his arms.

Kent wobbled the mug. 'Thought I'd sober him up a bit, before deciding whether to charge him or not. Isn't that right, Mr Murray?'

He answered with a rattling belch, filling the van with a rancid miasma of garlic and old whisky.

Logan coughed, one hand windscreen-wipering in an attempt to waft it away. 'Didn't drive here, did he?'

'Only lives across the road. Lucky he didn't get squashed by a builder's lorry on the way, though.' She clicked her fingers under the man's nose a few times. 'Mr Murray? Mr Murray: you wanted to talk to someone in charge – this is Detective Chief Inspector McRae.'

A baleful one-eyed glare turned in Logan's direction. 'Wanna make... Wanna make a complaint. ... Police ... *brutality.*'

Logan tutted. 'Is this *true*, Officer Kent?'

'Mr Murray became a little "boisterous" when I wouldn't let him into the crime scene.' She produced her notebook, flicking through to the relevant page. 'He felt the exclusion order shouldn't apply to him, on account of it being his "bloody buggering hotel in the first bloody place" and that we're "a bunch of buggering wanks" if we think we can keep him "bloody out" of his own "bloody buggering hotel". Guv.' She tapped the plastic rectangle fixed to her stabproof vest. 'I got the whole thing on camera, if it helps?' Because sometimes Body-Worn Video was your friend. 'Oh, and he got the scratches-and-scrapes tripping over the kerb, before I even spoke to him. That's on film too.'

A sigh. 'Oh dear, Mr Murray: that doesn't sound very good, does it? In fact, it *kind of* sounds as if Officer Kent here should charge you with a number of offences.'

Mr Murray waved a trembling hand in the vague direction of the ruins. 'Do you ... unnerstand ... unnerstand someone ... *died*? ... In my hotel! ... Someone died...' His pink eyes shimmered. 'I only tried... It's not ... not fair.' And tears rolled down his injured cheek.

Poor sod.

Logan swapped the stern-police-officer act for a much kinder tone. 'But I think, if you apologised, she might be persuaded not to arrest you. Isn't that right, Officer Kent?'

'Hmmm... Don't know, Guv. He was *very* boisterous.'

Mr Murray covered his face with his hands, shoulders jerking with every sob that wracked free. 'I'm sorry! Please, I'm so sorry...'

Because Charles MacGarioch ruined every life he touched.

'Hey, it's OK. Shhh...' Logan patted Mr Murray on the back. 'Officer Quirrel will see you home.'

Tufty cast a longing look at the unboiled kettle, then pulled on a brave smile. 'Come on, let's get you safely to your beddybyes.'

It took a bit of hauling and levering, but eventually he got Mr Murray to his feet, where he wobbled and swayed, as if ready to timber down at any moment ... before staggering out into the sunshine – with most of his weight supported by the wee loon.

Soon as they'd gone, Rennie popped the lid off the kettle, peered inside, then dug a two-litre bottle of water from one of the cupboards and filled it up.

Logan waited till he'd plugged it in. 'Milk, no sugar.' Then followed Tufty and his drunken friend out into the sunshine. Watching from the pavement as they steered a meandering course across the road, like a tiny tug towing a drunken cruise ship.

PC Kent stepped down from the MCU. 'Sure we shouldn't do him anyway, Guv?'

'Nah. What's that going to achieve? Poor sod's already lost his hotel.'

The flotilla arrived at the far shore, where Mr Murray performed an ungainly pirouette and thunked sideways into a Subaru estate. Before being hauled upright again and steered towards the bland granite building opposite, with is drooping 'FOR SALE' sign.

Kent tucked her hands into her stabproof's armpits. Looking off into the distance and acting all casual. 'Don't suppose I can stop doing this anytime soon, can I, Guv? Got to be more interesting-slash-important things to do than guarding a burnt-out craphole.'

Given how short staffed they were?

'Yeah, probably.' Logan turned back towards the MCU. 'It's...'

Wait a minute.

He swivelled around again. 'Other side of the road: this guy look familiar to you?'

It was Mr Muscles, from yesterday. With the daft haircut and porn moustache. The one who'd missed his bus. Staring up at the blackened corpse of Balmain House Hotel. Clutching another carrier bag from the off-licence.

Today's wife-beater vest had 'COLONEL MICHIGAN'S GYM' and the silhouette of a boxer on it.

He must've realised they were watching him, because his gaze drifted down from the scorched granite remains to Logan and PC Kent.

Then a look of horror crawled across his face.

The bag fell from his hand, bursting against the kerb – and a spray of lager frothed out into the warm afternoon.

Then Mr Muscles was off: sprinting away down Broomhill Road. Like the four horsemen were after him.

Shite...

Because that wasn't suspicious *at all*.

26

'STOP, POLICE!' Logan ducked out between two parked cars, heading for the other side of the road, legging it after Mr Muscles.

AAAAAAAAAAAAAAAAArgh!

The Seat Ibiza barrelling up Broomhill Road slammed on its brakes, nose dipping as it left skidmarks on the tarmac, and the driver probably did the same in his pants. Eyes wide, mouth hanging open as Logan stared back at him.

OK.

That was close.

Logan forced a smile, then ran for the other pavement, heading after Mr Muscles, breath-and-blood whooming in his ears, feet slapping against the concrete slabs.

A weird echo grew and grew, and there was PC Kent, raggity bun bobbing along behind. It might've taken her a while to build momentum – what with all full kit on – but she was motoring now. Doing that high-step knees-and-elbows thing sprinters did on the telly. 'Who ... who are ... who are we ... chasing?'

You'd think it would be sodding obvious. But Logan pointed anyway. 'Arnold Bloody Schwarzenegger!' Then pulled out his Airwave handset. 'DS McRae ... to Control.'

Mr Muscles went left at the junction, by the newsagent's, abandoning Broomhill Road for the more genteel Balmoral Place. And they were gaining on him.

Logan and Kent motorbiked around the corner, momentum taking them out into the middle of the quiet street. Doing their best to break the twenty-mile-an-hour speed limit.

A voice burst out of the Airwave: *'Safe to talk?'*

Mr Muscles jinked out into the middle of the road too – avoiding a pair of old ladies, blocking the pavement so they could shout at each other. Glancing over his shoulder as he drifted across the dotted line.

'In pursuit ... of I-C-One male ... five nine ... heavily muscled ... tattooed arms...'

Mr Muscles hammered on, playing chicken with a black Porsche coming the other way.

Brakes screeched, the horn blaring as the car slithered to a halt – pretty much blocking the road – about three feet short of flattening him.

He didn't even slow down.

Instead, Mr Muscles took a running leap, left foot landing square in the middle of the bonnet; the right whacking into the rubber seal at the top of the windscreen, sending cracks flashing across the glass; his left foot left a dirty big dent in the roof; and he was down the other side.

Still running.

The driver scrambled out from behind the wheel, shaking her fist and stamping her heels. 'LOOK WHAT YOU DID TO MY CAR! YOU BLOODY IDIOT! COME BACK HERE!'

Mr Muscles ... did not.

He kept going.

But Logan and PC Kent had to detour around, up onto the pavement, then back down again after they'd passed the dented Porsche.

There must've been an alley off to the side, because a pair of little girls shot out of it on their bicycles – one bike wrapped in rainbow-coloured tape, the other all pale-pink and sparkly, like a *Twilight* vampire. Both with tasselled handlebars and a plastic unicorn's horn cable-tied to the front.

Mr Muscles clattered straight into the pair of them, in a flailing mess of arms and legs and chains and wheels and swearing. Tumbling across the tarmac.

Hallelujah.

Logan closed the gap. 'I need ... need backup to ... Holburn Street and ... Balmoral Place!'

Oh yeah: Mr Muscles was screwed now.

His lead had completely vanished and in thirty seconds, Logan and PC Kent would be all over him like sleaze on a politician.

He fought clear of the wreckage. Looked left, then right. Probably weighing up the odds. Then grabbed the nearest girl's bike – pink-and-sparkly – and jumped on. Standing in the seat as he pedalled away with all his might.

So much for sleaze.

Logan hurdled the other bike and one of the girls. 'Suspect is now on ... a stolen ... girl's bicycle.' Ragged breath. 'STOP, POLICE!'

The over-pumped lump looked back over his shoulder at that, which was probably a mistake, because one of the road's many potholes grabbed the front tyre, and sent him straight over the betasselled handlebars.

He hit the tarmac with a crunching *thwack*.

Got you.

Logan and Kent were almost there when he struggled to his feet, bringing the bike with him – front wheel all twisted and bent.

Scarlet gushed out of his flattened nose and shattered mouth, a scattering of bloodied teeth still embedded in the road at his feet.

But Mr Muscles wasn't done yet.

He roared out a froth of bright red, swinging the bike like a sparkly sledgehammer.

'Shite!' Logan hit the deck, but it slammed right into PC Kent's stabproof vest, hurling her sideways into an ugly VW people carrier.

She bounced off the bodywork. The bike kept on going: straight through the rear driver's-side window with a firework *tshhhhhh...* Cubes of glass sparkling in the sunlight as the car alarm yowled, hazards flashing.

Not waiting around, Mr Muscles staggered into a run, one tattooed arm held against his chest.

Logan shoved himself upright. 'STOP! ... POLICE!'

As if anyone ever did.

Instead, Mr Muscles barrelled straight through the 'STOP' sign at the end of the road.

A tartan-liveried glazier's van screeched to a standstill, inches away from bursting him like a gore-filled water balloon.

He thumped his good hand against the bonnet, spinning around to glance at Logan again, keeping the momentum going as he ran across—

BANG.

The Toyota Hilux smashed right into him, sending his body whirling into the air like an Action Man hurled by an angry child. He cartwheeled over the truck's cab and its load bay – full of broken bricks, and jagged spears of rusty rebar – then hit the road with a sickening *crunch.*

Far too late, the Hilux jammed on its brakes, jerking sideways into the glazier's van with an almighty crash of broken double-glazing units.

Little cubes of safety glass pattered down across the tarmac.

Horns blared.

Someone screamed.

Behind the Hilux, a minibus pulled up about two feet short

of the battered body. Driver gripping the wheel, face trans-
formed into a gargoyle grimace, staring at what was left of Mr
Muscles. Then all the schoolkids in the back piled forwards for
a good gawp – phones out, filming away like the horrible little
ghouls they were.

Logan hurpled into the middle of the road, arms out like a
crossing guard. Holding the traffic back as he hurried over to
the broken-limbed, twisted mess of fractured bones and torn
flesh, in a spreading pool of dark, dark blood.

Because things weren't bad enough already…

— bluebottles, asbestos, and blood —

Chapter Twenty-Seven

*in which Tufty does a Good Deed and has
a poke about in a Very Messy Place*

Tufty propped Mr Murray against the wall. Holding him there
with one hand while the other went a-rummaging for house
keys.

And yes, it would've been a lot easier if Sergeant Rennie,
or the Sarge, or Officer Kent had offered to help – because
assisting Mr Murray across the road from his burnt-out hotel
was a bit like wrestling drunken jelly – but Tufty did has *an
initiative*. So he could totally do this.

Aha! Keys.

The name on the fob was the same as the faded sign above
the door: 'DUNRENOVATIN', so this had to be the place.

He unlocked the door and shoved it open, then turned to
give the Sarge a wave, but he was busy talking to PC Kent.

Droop.

Ah well.

'Come on, let's get you inside.'

Tufty took a firm hold of Mr Murray's arm and hauled him
upright – wibble-wobble – then steered him over the threshold
and into a dark and dusty hallway.

Oooh, *atmospheric.*

Envelopes and flyers spilled out from the edges of a sisal mat, like they'd been kicked onto the black-and-white tiles. Or at least the tiles *looked* black-and-white, it was hard to tell under all that dirt. A fancy staircase swooped upwards, discarded books and empty bottles lining the steps. Spooky high ceilings.

Cobwebs colonised every corner, blurring the edges as they sagged under ancient layers of dust.

This must've been a big fancy house at one time, abandoned long ago to the mice, spiders, and ghosts...

Ah well.

Tufty folded his new friend over the newel post at the foot of the stairs, then scurried back to close the front door with a *clunk.*

Doo, doo doo-doo. *Click, click.*

Keeping an eye out for disembodied hands or Cousin Itts, Tufty tiptoed to the bottom step. 'Hello? Anyone home?'

The house swallowed his words before they could echo.

'HELLO-OH?'

No reply.

'Mr Murray, is there someone here who can look after you?'

Being draped over like that, made his words all muffled and breathy: ''Lone... Aaaaaaaall 'lone.'

In which case Tufty would just have to save the day.

He pulled Mr Murray upright again. 'Right: bed.'

'No. No, no, no, no, no...' Mr Murray waved his hands like a fly was trying to scoot up his nose. '*Whisky.*' And off he lurched, stiff-legged as a wind-up penguin, to a door at the back of the hall.

'Mr Murray?' Tufty followed him into a kitchen that was even dustier. No fancy gadgets, no R2-D2 cookie jars or Dalek tea cosies, not even a cooker – just a hole where it used to be. Going by the fust-and-dust outline on the wall, a big American-style fridge freezer once lived here – now replaced by a battered under-the-counter job that buzzed like it was full of wasps. But what the kitchen *did* have were a cheap kettle, a cheap toaster, and a cheap microwave, perched on the grubby worktops; a crispy layer of dead flies on the windowsill, and a bunch of chubby bluebottles banging their heads against the grubby glass.

Oh, and bottles. Lots and lots and lots of bottles. An army of them, all empty and lined up on parade. Most of Mr Murray's squaddies looked like the kind of wine supermarkets flogged for under a fiver, with the odd bottle of Old Sporran McRotgut acting as captains and generals.

Clearly, in the battle against sobriety, Mr Murray believed quantity triumphed over quality.

He grabbed a bottle from the ranks, staggering slightly as he held it up to the thin grey light. Empty. So was the next one. And the one after that.

Tufty put on his best helpful voice: 'I really think you'd be better off having a nice lie down, Mr Murray.'

'Got to ... got to have *something* ... somewhere...' He inspected the troops again.

A mound of letters was heaped up by the toaster. And though it was a *little* nosey to look, they all seemed to be stamped 'FINAL DEMAND!'

Tufty peered out through a slightly less dirty bit of the window at a back garden smothered in weeds and bushes and things.

Three doors led off the kitchen – one back into the hall, one out into the jungle, while the third lay slightly ajar.

And as the Horror-Haired Queen of Grumbling Doom was always telling them: '*It's no'* snooping *if you're a police officer, it's* investigating.'

So he left Mr Murray clinking his way through the soldiers, and slipped through the beckoning doorway. Having an investigate.

It might've been a drawing room back in the Long-ago, but now it was a storage place for spiderhouses and mouse droppings, slowly suffocating under a blanket of fuzzy grey. Shadows on the wall remembered paintings and maybe a large flatscreen TV? Bet there'd been heaps of fancy furniture in here: bookcases and writing desks and chesterfield couches. Now though, there was just a saggy brown corduroy couch and a coffee table made from old milk crates, with a teeny portable CRT telly on top. Indoor aerial. Not even a DVD player.

A bouquet of *long*-dead flowers wilted in a vase on the mantelpiece, all papery grey-and-brown, next to a photo frame – lying facedown in the dust.

In this haunted house, even the ghosts were sad...

Tufty stepped back into the kitchen, where Mr Murray was still hunting for a non-empty warrior to ride into battle with him.

'Hey, come on. Why don't we get you upstairs, OK?' Tufty plucked a hollow general from Mr Murray's hand, took his arm, and steered him towards the door. 'There we go. You'll feel much better after a snooze.'

Or hungover as a Klingon's bumhole.

But it was the thought that counted.

The main bedroom was every bit as miserable-and-fusty as the rest of the house: shadowed walls; discarded clothes in the corner; and a bed cobbled together from pallets and old panel doors, with a droopy mattress on top.

Breathing hard, after half-carrying him all the way up the stairs, Tufty flopped Mr Murray onto the bed. Setting the pallets creaking.

Lying there, flat on his back, he stared up at the ceiling. Which had to be rotating *pretty* fast, given how blootered he was.

Then Mr Murray popped out a wet burp, that sounded like it contained lumps. He smacked his lips and grimaced.

Hmmm...

Maybe not the best of ideas?

Luckily though, the room had an en suite, and when Tufty pushed the door open it was totes fancy and stuff, with a claw-foot bath, and a swanky shower cabinet, and a bidet for washing your bum. Ooh-la-la! Très swish.

Shame it was all so grubby.

But it would do.

He hauled Mr Murray up again and waddle-walked him into the echoing room.

Another lumpy burp. 'Sleeeeeeeeep.'

'Why don't we put *you* in the recovery position in here instead? That'll be fun, won't it?' Helping him down onto the cool tiles. 'This way, if you vom, it'll be easier for you to clean up in the morning. And you probably won't choke on any chunks.'

Probably.

It took a bit of pulling and shoving to get all of Mr Murray's limbs and body in the right place so his airways would be clear – cos people-origami was tougher than it looked – but finally Tufty wrangled him into place, then stood back to admire the results.

Now *that* was some fine recovery-positioning.

By the time he'd fetched the duvet from the bedroom, Mr Murray was already snoozing it up, snorks and grunts echoing off the uncleaned tiles.

Like a sleepy warthog.

Tufty draped the duvet over him, then tiptoed away.

Maybe it wouldn't hurt to do a *little* more investigating, you know, while he was here?

There was another bedroom on the first floor, but it was even more empty than Mr Murray's – no bed or mattress, just dust and arachnids.

Then a single bedroom – but the only way to tell was a tatty Kylie Minogue poster curling away from the ancient zoo-animal wallpaper; not a single bit of furniture.

Then a sewing room – going by the bobbins and grey-furred reels scattered about the untreated floorboards, because even the carpet was missing.

Then a big family bathroom – just as swanky as Mr Murray's en suite, but it clearly hadn't been used or cleaned in years. A thick drift of flies littered the grimy windowsill, and a weird, meaty-sewagey stink slithered out of the drains and toilet pan.

Moving on...

Tufty climbed up to the top floor, with its sloped ceilings and dormer windows.

First up: a box room. You could tell, because that's what it was full of. Cardboard ones of all shapes and sizes, looking tired and brittle. Like Mr Murray.

Then the home gym. Or, at least, it had a rusty exercise bike sitting in the middle of the empty space. Being slowly consumed by cobwebs and teeny-weeny flakes of neglect.

Tufty opened the last door.

Blinked at the contents.

Then closed it again.

Nah.

OK: one more go.

It was a child's bedroom, and unlike every other room in the house, it was still fully furnished. A bed, a wardrobe, a toy box, a Mr Men duvet, an orange teddy bear, a rocking horse, a desk and chair, a bookcase full of well-thumbed paperbacks. *Winnie-the-Pooh* and Narnia, *Alice in Wonderland* and *The Wizard of Oz*... All the classics.

But Mr Murray complained about being '*Aaaaaaaall 'lone.*'

And there was *no way* Social Services would let a kid live here. Mr Murray was probably a lovely bloke, but he could barely look after himself, never mind a wee boy or girl.

Tufty ran a finger along the windowsill.

Clean.

Not so much as a spiff of dirt.

Now that *was* weird. And sort of creepy. But mostly sad.

From up here, you could see right into the burnt-out skeleton of Balmain House Hotel. Hard not to imagine flames screaming up into the sky as the poor sods staying there coughed and spluttered for the exits...

Back downstairs, Tufty wandered into the drawing room again, making for the mantelpiece with its dead flowers and facedown frame.

He turned the picture over.

A much younger Mr Murray grinned up at him, hugging a cheery, slightly chubby blonde woman. She had a fair-haired toddler on her hip, an orange teddy clutched in his wee sausage fingers.

Tufty frowned at the photo for a bit. Then up at the ceiling.

Then put the frame back on the mantelpiece, upright, so the happy family smiled out into the graveyard room.

Poor Mr Murray.

Tufty scuffed out into the hall, stopping at the end of the stairs. 'OK, MR MURRAY: YOU TAKE CARE OF YOURSELF. TRY NOT TO DROWN IN YOUR OWN SICK!'

He stood there for a minute, one foot on the bottom step.

A rasping snore *rattled* through the building – amplified by the en suite's tiled walls. Then another. And another. Getting louder and louder as Mr Murray really let rip.

Tufty shrugged and let himself out.

Standing on the sun-drenched doorstep, he locked the door again, then posted the keys through the letterbox.

There we go.

At least that was *one* good deed done today...

XXVIII

'FUCK!'

Natasha jerked awake.

This was not right.

This was not good.

This was … oh Jesus.

Where the *fuck* were her clothes? Grit and stones dug into the skin on her back and thighs, scraped against her elbows and heels as she thrashed in place, making something metal clink and rattle.

The bastard – the one who came to her house with a message about that dickhead Adrian – what the hell had he done?

She was blind. And deaf?

And suffocating.

Get to your bloody feet!

But her arms weren't working properly. Every time she tried to move them it dragged her neck about. As if her wrists were … tied to her throat or something. Like some twisted version of Edvard Munch's *The Scream*.

'HELP ME!' Bellowing into the darkness.

But the sound came out all muffled and distorted.

He'd put something over her head. A bag, maybe? Something sticky and salty.

Wait, wait, wait.

Breathe.

Just lie the fuck *still* for a moment and breathe.

You're not an idiot. Or a *victim*, OK?

Whatever this shit is, you can beat it.

Every breath hissed in and whoomphed out. Caught inside the bag.

Breathe…

She clenched her fists, then released them again, fingertips pressing against whatever it was that covered her head.

Leather. Felt like leather. Something thick, held together with stitches. Not a bag: a *mask*.

Still couldn't move her wrists.

Didn't matter – one thing at a time.

Yeah, but it was quite a big bloody thing.

She jerked her hands to one side, then the other, then in opposite directions, and every time something dug into her neck. Like it was surrounded by a band of steel.

Sticking her right elbow in the air meant her fingertips could feel their way along the collar: metal, a good two-inches thick, with rings set into it, and a sort of handcuff thing around her left wrist to hold that in place. It was the same on the right.

Shackled.

Sweat trickled down her cheek.

Christ it was like a bloody oven in here.

Elbows down again, she traced the outline of her mouth, only it wasn't her mouth it was a zip. With some sort of *thing* attached to the pull tab, stopping it from moving. Something metal. Heart-shaped.

Like this was a fucking *joke*.

OK, further up … another pair of zips, one over each eye. Only these ones weren't fixed shut. She pulled the right one open and light flooded the world.

Then the other.

Fuck.

Not sure if that made things better or worse.

Natasha blinked away the sticky gunk and squinted up at the wooden beams and grey corrugated roof above her head.

Bluebottles droned through the hot dead air.

It was some sort of tumbledown outbuilding, maybe a dozen foot square, built from chunks of stone, held together with crumbling mortar and smaller rocks. It had one of those heavy sliding doors, rust-streaked and hanging from a buckled metal rail. But it wasn't much of a barrier, given the great-big hole in the wall next to it – some sort of partially collapsed window – that let the sun stream in.

Her eyes drifted down, across the scabs and scrapes and bruises that rampaged over her naked stomach and thighs.

The bastard had taken her dress, but at least he'd left the underwear. That was something, right?

Maybe.

All she had to do now was climb out through the hole, get the hell out of here, find help, get Detective Sergeant Dickhead Davis arrested, then arrange for someone to rape the bastard to death in the prison showers.

See how he fucking liked it.

Come on, Natasha: up.

She rolled over onto her side, shoving at the dirt floor with her elbows, getting both legs under her. Heaving herself upright. Which wasn't bloody easy, with both arms out of action.

She only managed two steps towards the window before something grabbed her throat and jerked her to a stop.

That rattling, clanking noise rang out again.

Natasha turned.

A six-foot length of thick chain stretched from her collar to a galvanised bin full of concrete.

Bracing her bare feet against the floor, she pulled. Strained.

The bloody thing didn't move.

She glared at it.

Stepped closer and shoved it with her knee.

Solid.

Her anchor probably weighed twice what she did.

One of those big fat bluebottles settled on her shoulder, where the skin was scraped and weeping. Having itself a nice little feed.

'FUCK OFF YOU BASTARD!'

All that came out were some mumbled vowels, but it was still enough to make the fly abandon its meal and growl into the air. Circling. Waiting for its turn to land and feast again.

Don't cry.

Don't blub like some little baby.

You can *do* this.

Just need some time to think, is all.

The caved-in window overlooked a weed-choked court-yard, with a slightly less crappy outbuilding on the right. A bunch of rotting pallets were stacked outside it, beside a hulk of farm machinery that probably hadn't moved in decades. Then there was a small gap, with a view out across a scrubby field – neglected and overgrown, tall purple spears of fireweed burning against the blue sky.

A big agricultural shed sat opposite Natasha's prison, its concrete panels half-skinned in wasp-peeled wooden slats, beneath a roof of corrugated asbestos sheeting.

Finally, off to the left, a beige-and-brown static caravan formed the final side of the square. Its windows opaque with dirt and dust. Lichen reached out from the corners and joints, spreading across the walls like mould on a corpse.

You didn't need to be bloody psychic to know something very, *very* bad had happened here.

And that there'd be worse to come…

29

Logan held up a hand as the recovery van reversed perfectly into place, and its brake lights flared. Then the driver hopped out and connected his winch to the glazier's van.

Normally, just after half five on a Wednesday afternoon, Holburn Street would be a constant stream of traffic. Instead, it was all 'ROAD CLOSED ~ ACCESS ONLY', and 'DIVERSION →' from Bloomfield Road to Abergeldie Terrace. They'd shut off chunks of Balmoral Place and Balmoral Road too, making an inverted crucifix with Mr Muscles playing the part of Christ.

Or at least he had been until the ambulance whisked him away, lights flickering and siren wailing.

Now, the only vehicles left within the cordon were the Toyota Hilux, the glazier's van, and 'CAPTAIN TOWAWAY ~ "IF YOU'VE HAD A CRASH, WE'LL COME IN A FLASH!"'

Two patrol cars sat just outside – blocking Holburn Street at either end. One officer from each car kept the vulgar public away, while the other two swept up all the broken glass. Carefully avoiding the glistening red puddle slowly baking into the tarmac where Mr Muscles came to an almost-dead halt.

Two Outside Broadcast Units had parked on the City Centre side of the barricade – ITV and Channel 4 – and a few hacks milled about outside the cordon on the Garthdee side, but the only thing that seemed to be actively recording was a BBC drone.

Suppose, once the body was removed, all the exciting news had already happened.

The recovery winch whined and *poing*ed as it hauled the Auchterturra Glazing Company's van up onto the load bay. Struggling a bit, because the Toyota Hilux had crushed the rear wheel arch and twisted the tyre round nearly ninety degrees.

The Hilux, on the other hand, only had a wee dent in the radiator to show for both impacts. So maybe...

Sod.

A familiar black Mercedes purred up to the barrier on Balmoral Road.

Sergeant Brookminster climbed out, scanning the street as if he was on the President's Secret Service detail, before catching Logan's eye, nodding, then opened the rear passenger door.

Here we go.

Chief Superintendent Pine stepped into the sun. Hung up on whoever it was she'd been talking to, and marched towards the crash scene, leaving Brookminster to mind the car.

Logan muffled a sigh, then stood a little straighter.

Pine stalked across the road, keeping her voice down. 'I hope you've got a *really* good explanation for this *massive* cock-up.'

'Boss. How nice of you to come out and show your support.'

Her eyes bugged.

Then she grabbed him by the arm and hustled him away, into the mouth of Balmoral Place. Presumably because the head-height walls on both sides of the little road offered a bit of shelter from the press.

She let go and poked him in the chest. 'Your sarcasm is *not* appreciated. I've got one of the city's major arteries closed off, a massive incident underway, and an unidentified man who might not live to see the evening news, never mind tomorrow!' She jabbed her poking finger at the bloodsplatch. 'Now what the *hell* were you thinking?'

Logan bit the inside of his cheek, before anything unwise escaped. Took a deep breath. Then: 'Our RTC victim was hanging about Balmain House Hotel yesterday. He was back again today, and when he clocked me and PC Kent, he ran. Bang: drops his shopping and sprints off down the road.'

'You didn't have to *give chase!*'

'Oh, and you'd just let him go, would you? Nothing suspicious to see here?'

Pine glowered back. 'That's not the point.'

'People only run because they don't want to be caught.' Actually, you know what? Screw diplomacy. This *wasn't* his fault. 'And it's not like we chucked the guy in front of that truck! *We* were shouting at him to stop.'

She marched off five or six paces, then back again. 'What did he do? Other than run.'

Good question.

'Don't know yet. Don't even have a name – no wallet, no ID on him. Only a couple of fivers, a snotty hanky, and a small bunch of keys.'

'Urgh...' Pine covered her face. 'He's going to be an *aid worker,* isn't he. Or a volunteer with handicapped kids...' She dropped her hands, eyes narrowed. 'Thought I told you "everyone in uniform"?'

'I'd have nipped home to change, but I've been kinda busy.'

'Oh, haven't you *just.*' She did another half-lap. 'We can't paint this guy as a suspect in Operation Iowa. Not till we've got some proof he was involved in burning the hotel.' A frown. 'He *was* involved, wasn't he?'

Logan gave her a shrug.

'Wonderful.' Pine stared up into the pale blue sky. 'Was

our caseload not bad enough without you complicating everything? One dead body a day not sufficiently *challenging* without ...' waving her arms about, '*this*?'

'Sorry, Boss.'

She drooped. 'I know, I know.' Sigh. 'Where's PC Kent?'

'Sent her back to the station; doing a formal statement and incident report. If it helps, she's got the whole chase on her BWV.'

'Suppose that's something.' Pine went back to pacing, one finger tapping away at her forehead. 'You'd better head off and do the same. I'll hold down the fort here, till we get the road opened again.'

Good grief: a senior officer who was *actually* prepared to help. 'Thanks, Boss.' He flashed her a pained smile and got out of there before she changed her mind.

He'd barely gone a couple of paces up Balmoral Place before her voice rang out behind him:

'*And no more complications!*'

Well, you never knew your luck, did you...?

Logan slumped along Balmoral Place, sticking to the pavement this time. The dented Porsche was gone, along with its angry driver, and so had the quarrelling OAPs. Leaving behind the chirp of birdsong and the sound of violins and a choir, coming from one of the houses – mournful, *dark* music that clashed with the vibrant gardens and flowering shrubs.

And fitted today perfectly.

A voice from across the road: '*Aye, aye.*'

Great.

Colin Miller lurked against a tree, suit jacket hooked on a finger, over his shoulder, as if out for a stroll on the piazza in Venice. He gave Logan a wee salute with his free hand. 'Miss me?'

Nope.

Logan kept going. 'Can we not, today? Haven't got the energy for sparring.'

'Busy day for you, the day.' Colin fell in beside him. 'It's no' bad going, though: murder-victim-discovered-in-the-river mid-morning, ID'd by teatime.'

'We haven't ID'd anyone.'

Wink. '*Course* you haven't.'

'Thought you were meeting your new owner.'

'Aye, right. The great Ms Agapova *still* hasnae shown. Probably off swanking it up with her posh-and-or-rich chums.' A sniff. 'She's just doing it to torture me.' Then Colin put on an Australian accent so bad it would strip the hair off a koala at thirty paces: '"Nah-but-yeah, keep the poor bugger hangin', he'll be fair-dinkum sweating through his Grundies, waitin' for the chop. *Rippa!*"'

Logan frowned. 'Didn't know she was Welsh.'

They wandered past the metal signs – one blocking the road, the other directing traffic to go down Braemar Place instead – and the funereal melody faded away, replaced by the squeals and shrieks of little children playing instead.

'And how come you can still churn out your squalid little rag without an editor?'

'Editors are like colonoscopies. Aye, sometimes they might be necessary, but most of the time they're just a pain in the arse.' Colin gave Logan the side-eye. 'This barbecue invite: better no' be some sort of half-arsed bribe, so I'll go easy on youse in the paper.'

'Told you – it was Isobel's idea.' Shrug. 'But it wouldn't hurt you to be less of a dick about everything.'

'It's my *job* to be a dick about everything. See: it's *your* job to catch bad guys and impose the will of the state. I'm there to hold you to account. Otherwise, who's gonnae keep you buggers honest?' The screeching got louder, followed by a flotilla of shimmering bubbles, wafting out from behind a high wall. 'So your deid man in the river's Andrew Shaw.'

Logan stopped and stared at him.

Grin. 'People phone and email the paper all the time. They see all youse daft buggers in your SOC suits, tramping in and out of their neighbour's house? They *tend* to notice something's up.'

'We search lots of houses, all the time. Doesn't mean it's—'

'Andrew Wallace Shaw: thirty-two. Gigolo-Joe-looking motherfucker – all Botox and Brylcreem. Works at Brenda's Hair and Beauty Palace on Chapel Street, doing perms and colouring. Very good at it, so I'm told.' Frown. 'No' any more, like. On account of him being deid.'

Logan headed off again. 'You're fishing, Colin.'

'Nah, I'm no'.' Radiating smugness.

'One of your little birdies?'

'Gotta protect my sources, but. Only thing I *can* tell you is: it's no' Isobel. She wouldnae tell me shite, even if my job was on the line. Which it probably is, byraway.'

Logan turned right at the crossroads, heading up Broomhill Road, back towards the Mobile Command Unit. On the other side of the road, a wee man was out changing the display on the newsagent's sandwich board to 'CITY CAR CHASE ENDS IN CARNAGE!'

Colin scowled. 'I mind the day when being a journalist *meant* something. Now we're all bloody "Content Creators" and "Engagement Engineers". I shite you not – "Engagement Engineers"!' A snort. 'Used to be about digging out the facts, no fear or favour; speaking truth to power, sticking up for the little guy... Now it's all "How many tweets did you put out the day?", "How many likes and retweets did you get?", "How many bloody comments?"'

'You saying that headline wasn't you?'

'Course it sodding wasn't. Think I don't know the difference between an ice-cream van and a car? Can't have a car chase with a pair of sodding *vans*. And you never *ever* put a dog's cock on a headline!'

OK...

No idea what *that* meant, and no desire to find out.

The wee man unfurled a new poster for the sandwich board's back face, too: 'UK BRACED FOR MORE RACE RIOTS'.

Colin snarled, shoulders up. 'And don't get me started on *that* bollocks. Whipping up fear while simultaneously promoting the bloody thing you've just told everyone to be afraid of! Tell youse, it's—'

'*Hello?*' A voice honked out, right behind them. One of those teenage-boy noises that wobbled about from bass to treble mid-word. '*Out of the way! Excuse me. Thanks.*'

Logan stepped aside and a young man trundled past, wheeling a pushchair and talking on a mobile phone at the same time. His AFC tracksuit was two sizes too big, flapping about in his wake as he clomped away at speed, on massive trainers, heading up Broomhill Road. Taking his World War One haircut, yodelly voice, and schoolboy zits with him. 'No! ... Because it's *your* turn to change the nappies! I *always* change the nappies. ... Yeah, well I want to go on the school trip to Belgium too – how about we prioritise *my* needs for a change, Sharlene?'

Kids today...

Colin dug his free hand deep in his pocket. 'And when did it become OK to dumb *down* everything? Who decided we're all thick as breeze blocks?'

'Did you just come here to whinge?'

'Hmmm? Oh.' A frown. Then Colin jerked his head back,

over his shoulder. 'Yeah: yer man, back there, Mr Tarmac Tartare. This mean youse've finally got a suspect for the hotel fire?'

'Off the record?'

A nod.

'Can't say. And I don't mean that in a police "we can't talk about ongoing investigations" way: we don't know. He was standing right there,' Logan pointed at the pavement, opposite the burnt-out hotel, 'watching the place, and when he saw us, he legged it. Don't even know who he is.'

'What is it with you bastards and chasing folk till something shitey happens?'

They crossed the end of Balmoral Terrace, slowing up as the crime scene loomed. The pool car was still tucked in behind the MCU, so at least Rennie and Tufty hadn't sodded off with it when he'd sent them back to the station.

Small mercies.

Colin pulled his lips in, as if tasting a fine wine. Then spat out, 'I was thinking … *steak*. How many people you got coming to this thing, Sunday?'

'About twenty, twenty-five?'

'Aye, maybe burgers, then. And some beer. No point wasting quality wine on you bunch of philistines.'

'Speaking of whipping up fear – you heard any rumours about this protest march? Rumblings? Plots?'

'What: racist arse-nuggets versus anti-fascists; climate change deniers versus eco nutters; pro-war – anti-war; far-right wankers – woke socialist tossers; sharks and the jets…?' He bared his teeth. 'Hope you've got the Fire Brigade standing by. Isobel and me are barricading the doors and sheltering-in-place till it's all over.'

Logan headed across the road. 'Thanks for that. Very helpful.'

'I'm no' an informer, Laz. Got to keep my shiny shield of impartiality polished to an impeccable sheen.' A quick shifty glance, left and right. 'But wouldn't hurt to have a *wee* lookie at Graeme Anderson. You know, on the off chance...?'

The name was familiar, but not sure why.

Find out soon enough, though.

'OK. Thanks, Colin.'

'Aye, well – one: you didn't hear it from me, and two: you *owe* me. Again. And don't you forget it!'

30

The pale granite lumps of the Central Library and Saint Mark's gave way to the pale granite lump of His Majesty's Theatre – whose name was finally topical again after seventy years. About a dozen little kids skipped along the pavement towards it, all wearing knitted pink onesies with oversized ears – being shepherded by a trio of adults dressed as the Grim Reaper. Scythes glinting in the baking light as a heat haze shimmered above the tarmac on Rosemount Viaduct.

Bet sweat was *cascading* down their bumcracks.

Going by the posters outside the theatre, they were off to see 'SKELETON BOB & THE UNFEASIBLY LARGE SHEEP!'

Jammy bastards.

Because Logan was heading back to the office, windows rolled down, radio chattering away to itself.

'*...but here's a wee traffic update before the six o'clock bulletin: Holburn Street has just reopened! So that's the good news. The bad news is you've got another hour of me to endure, before Stevie B's* Preload Playlist.' Honks and twiddles and whooshing noises blared out of the speakers in a 'comedic' fashion. '*Tell you what, let's squeeze in a quick tune, shall we? Here's the Brigadoon Tourist Board with their new single: "The Whale That Ate The World". Aaaaaaaaaall aboard!*'

Cue indie guitars and someone wanging the hell out of a drumkit.

Wonder if there was a special school DJs went to, where they learned how to be massive arseholes? *Honk-honk, ding, wibble!* And now here's another heeeeeeeeeeelarious wind-up call!

Tossers.

Well, maybe not *all* of them, but still...

A singer joined the music:

> *'Still afloat, in my old boat, and I can't stop,*
> *Antidote, for every note, over-the-top,*
> *Scapegoat, it's so cutthroat,*
> *and I-I-I-I-I ride these waves!'*

Logan's Airwave joined in with a trio of bleeps. He pulled the thing out. Fumbling with the buttons one-handed and switching the radio off at the same time.

When he looked up again, the bus shelter was stampeding straight towards the pool car's bonnet.

Logan stamped on the brakes – the nearside front wheel skiffing off the kerb as he wrenched the steering wheel right. Getting out of the bus lane and back where he was meant to be.

No one saw that, right?

Hopefully...

He pressed the Airwave button and told a teeny white lie: 'Safe to talk.'

Rennie's voice joined him in the car. *'Got some updates for you, Guv.'*

Logan checked the dashboard clock: nearly six o'clock. 'Thought you'd have gone home by now.'

'Urgh... Sore point. Half of us are on compulsory green shifts. And that's not the worst of it: we're all back in frigging uniform! Itchy trousers and nylon T-shirts, because "we need a visible police presence to reassure the public"...' A wet raspberry noise rattled free. *'Sod the public. What did the public ever do for me?'*

'What is it with people whinging at me today?' Straight through at the roundabout onto Schoolhill, past the Cowdray Hall with its columned war memorial and carved lion statue – currently wearing a traffic cone on its head, because why should Glasgow's Duke of Wellington get all the fun? 'I'm *not* your agony aunt. If you need therapy I can easily swap you out for Tufty. The wee loon did good today, with the sex-offender-break-ins thing.'

'*No! It's fine. Team player all the way, Guv.*' Some rustling of paperwork. '*Got a positive match on the victim's remains. DNA matches samples from the bedroom – hairbrush, manscaping razor, that kinda stuff. The body in the river is* definitely *Andrew Shaw.*'

Really?

'Pathology said "definitely"?'

'*Course they didn't. They couched it in "high probability that"s and "on the balance of probability it's likely"s, but unless our victim broke into Shaw's bedroom to shave their balls, it's definitely him.*'

Now there was an image.

Looked as if Mrs Shaw's heart was getting broken after all.

'Someone needs to deliver the death message to his mother.'

'*Biohazard's on his way now.*' Rennie puffed out a heavy breath. '*Don't envy him that one: "Sorry, Missus, your wee boy's dead – someone bashed his brains in and dumped him in the river. Oh, and by the way, turns out you raised a rapey wee shite."*'

Yeah…

Logan checked the clock again. 'Get your bum out front – I'll pick you up on Broad Street.'

'*Cool.*' He lowered his voice. '*And don't worry: I won't tell You-Know-Who. We can have some decent grown-up conversation without Constable Sodding Quirrel wanging on about particle physics and who'd win in a fight: Stephen Hawking or Davros. I mean, everyone knows Davros's chair is equipped with Dalek—*'

Logan ended the call.

He dawdled past the old Robert Gordon's building – now turned into some sort of 'tech hub' – and the 'UNIQUE DEVELOPMENT OPPORTUNITY' that used to be the old student union, and the old … whatever it was the Academy shopping centre used to be before it became a shopping centre. Probably an academy, going by the name. Then past the hairdressers that used to be a museum and art gallery.

Giving Rennie time to escape from the office and meet him out front.

And yes, *technically* Logan was meant to go back to the station and give a formal statement about what happened on Holburn Street, but there were things to be getting on with.

A *ding-buzz* sounded deep in his pocket, but he wasn't daft enough to read text messages while driving.

Not after nearly totalling a bus stop…

Schoolhill turned into a pedestrian-and-cycle zone at the crossroads with Back Wynd and Harriet Street, but Logan flickered the pool car's blue lights and drove down it anyway.

Rebel that he was.

St Nicholas Kirk appeared between the graveyard trees, then he was at the bottom of the hill, waiting for the lights to change as sweaty people with carrier bags streamed from one bit of the Bon Accord Centre across the road to the other bit.

A rookery of nuns in black habits were busking outside the Bank of Scotland, playing a weird mash-up of punk, folk, and techno, singing away as they rocked out on guitars, decks, tambourine, double bass, and a cajon. They seemed to be having a great time, even if no one was paying any attention to them.

On the opposite side of the street, a miserable clown handed out flyers. Clearly regretting his career choice and wishing he'd become a nun instead.

The lights changed and Schoolhill turned into Upperkirkgate.

Logan did some more dawdling.

Sure there used to be a Blackwell's bookshop here. God knew what it was now – maybe the games shop? And what happened to the Tasty Tattie?

That was the trouble with getting older: everything changed...

Well, except for The Kirkgate bar.

At the top of the street, Logan turned right, and Marischal College reared into view, a jagged granite confection of narrow windows, mini-spires, and assorted pointy bits, all sparkling in the early evening sunshine. Facing off against the miserable row of ugly grey Rubik's cubes that went up to replace the old council buildings.

Like a jobbie, plonked down beside a wedding cake.

And speaking of jobbies – there was Rennie, leaning back against the plinth that Robert the Bruce's horse stood on. Brucie himself, sat in the saddle, cast in bronze, holding aloft the 1319 Stocket Charter ... but to be honest, it looked as if the statue was trying to send a message to someone in the horrible office building opposite.

Like the final scene of a very strange romcom.

Rennie probably thought he looked dead cool, standing there, with one foot up on the granite behind him, in the full Police Scotland uniform, wearing a pair of oversized sunglasses that gave him the air of a seventies lothario.

Logan pulled up and Rennie peered out over the top of his shades, before swaggering over and popping the passenger door.

What a knob.

'Guv.' He was in the middle of fastening his seatbelt, when a smaller, *pointier* figure scurried across the pedestrian area, waving at them.

Tufty.

He piled in the back. 'That was close! Thought I was going to miss you, there.'

Rennie's mouth pinched, back stiffening.

Logan turned in his seat. 'I think DS Rennie was hoping for some quality time.'

Big grin from Tufty. 'Don't mind me.'

Rennie took off his sunglasses and glared. 'Oh, but we *do*.'

'No fighting, children.' Putting the car in gear and heading for Union Street.

'Don't you have anything *better* to do, Constable?'

'Depends on your definition of "better", Sarge.' Tufty leaned forwards, so his head poked through the gap between the seats. 'The Ominous Harbinger Of Ultimate Doom is on a bit of a rampage at the moment, on account of having to be back in uniform, so it's best to stay out of the way.' He gave Rennie a wee pat on the shoulder. '"The Ominous Harbinger Of Ultimate Doom": that's Detective Sergeant Steel. It's one of the nicknames me and Sarge have for her.'

'I *know* who she is! I've worked with her longer than—'

'Apparently all her uniform trousers have "shrunk in the wash" again, so she's got IBS. Incredibly Belligerent Sergeant syndrome.'

'And for your information: *I* was calling her "Wrinkles McBumFace" when you were still in short trousers!'

Logan stopped at the lights, watching the buses rumble across the box junction and the flattened corpse of a big fat seagull. Too slow or too old to get out of the way of whatever turned it into a feathery pedestal mat. 'Can the pair of you just, for one *teeny tiny* minute, focus on the case?'

Rennie snorted. 'Which one?' Holding up both hands to count them off: 'We've got Andrew Shaw's murder, Charles MacGarioch on the run, drugs in Lithuanian teddy bears, the break-ins at all those sports shops, car thefts, burglaries—'

'All right, all right. We get it.' He scowled up at the lights, drumming his fingers against the steering wheel.

OK.

'I need a PNC check on one Graeme Anderson.'

Tufty whipped his phone out. 'Sarge.'

Logan looked across the car. 'This restaurant Charles MacGarioch's girlfriend works at – think it'll be open by now?'

Rennie popped his oversized shades back on. 'I could eat.'

A long, flat-fronted, granite terrace curved along one side of Bon-Accord Crescent. Two storeys up and one storey down – where each basement level was set back behind its own little lightwell, with steps leading down below road level. Mullioned windows and grand double doors; olde-worlde lamp-posts and iron railings. Looking out over a verdant triangle of parkland. Even if most of it was hidden behind a swathe of trees.

The restaurant menu was mounted to the railings, beside an open gate and stairs down to a welcoming mini-courtyard with sculptural pot plants and a wee seating area.

Rennie leaned in for a good squint at the glazed frame as Logan locked the car and joined Tufty on the pavement.

The wee loon held up his phone. 'Graeme Anderson: forty-three, Libra, history of DV and possession-with-intent. Got four years for putting a junior doctor in a wheelchair.'

'Doesn't he sound nice.'

'I had a sneaky wee look at his socials, Sarge. He does not has a very nice *at all*.'

Rennie whistled. 'Sodding hell... "Tempura haddock, with triple-cooked chips, crushed petit pois, and sauce gribiche" – guess how much.'

'Here.' Logan tossed him the car keys.

'Oh no. I'm not keeping a dog *and* barking.' He lobbed them at Tufty instead. '*You* can play chauffeur.'

'Eeek...' There was a bit of juggling as Tufty fumbled the catch. Then a clatter as they hit the deck. Then some scrambling to pick them up again. 'Bad keys: naughty!' He pocketed the things. 'Anyway, so Anderson's always liking horrible posts from Vision for Britain and the Anglo Saxon Defence Group and the People's Sovereign Army. He's what nice polite people call a *complete* arseholish turd-wit.'

'Seriously,' Rennie pointed at the menu, '*thirty-six quid*. For a fish supper!'

Logan descended the steps into the little suntrap, where heat radiated from its granite walls, making his forehead prickle with sweat. 'THE STAR-SPRINKLED HEAVENS' gleamed in gold letters above the restaurant door.

Tufty bimbled down after him. 'Think Anderson might even be treasurer of the local ASDG chapter...' A pause. 'Ooh, ooh! Can we go arrest him for something?'

'Don't know yet.'

He opened the door and stepped into air-conditioned opulence.

It was all low lighting, polished wood, decorative glass, and dark-blue walls in here. Something soothing and classical wafted out from hidden speakers, while a constellation of LEDs glittered in the midnight ceiling.

The maître d' stood up behind her desk, smiling as Logan entered. White-haired and maternal, arms open wide. '*Welcome* to the Star-Sprinkled Heavens. Can I take your coats and ask what name your table is reserved under?'

Logan presented his warrant card. 'I understand Keira's working tonight?'

'Oh dear...'

'It's OK, she's not in any trouble. We just think she might've seen something that can help with a case we're working on.'

A prim little nod. 'I'll just be a minute.' Off she bustled, through a door behind the reception desk, leaving Logan and Tufty alone.

Until Rennie squeezed in. 'And you won't *believe* what they want for a steak. Eighty-seven quid for a ribeye! And you don't even get tatties – you have to buy all your vegetables and sauces on top of that.' Curling his lip as he looked around. 'Me and Emma found a place in Union Square last week and it was sixteen ninety-nine a head. *All-you-can-eat.*'

Somehow doubt it would be quite the same dining experience as this place…

Tufty noodled on his phone.

Logan counted the LED stars.

No one paid any attention to Rennie.

So he had to spoil the silence: 'And another thing—'

Thankfully, that was as far as he got, because the door through to the dining room opened, releasing the murmur of conversation and clitter-scraik of cutlery on plates as the early-dinner crowd got stuck-in to their overpriced meals.

A young woman slipped into reception, wearing a smart white shirt, tweed waistcoat, black trousers, and the half-apron of a French waiter. Keira looked a lot younger and shorter in real life, especially without the heavy make-up. Her long black hair was pulled back in a neat French pleat, and she shuffled her sensible brogues on the carpet. Not meeting anyone's eyes.

Logan tried a non-threatening smile. 'Keira?'

'Hello?' Sounding even younger still, a wee nervous tremor in her voice as she snuck a look at Tweedle-Spud and Tweedle-Twit in their police uniforms.

'It's OK: we just need to ask you a few questions, then you can get back to work.'

She bit her bottom lip at the maître d'. 'Is it OK?'

A matronly nod. 'Of course it is. Why don't you take them out the back? Give yourself a bit of privacy.'

Which no doubt had the added benefit of getting the police out of reception before any guests saw them and started suspecting something was very wrong in Restaurantland.

Keira gave her a little curtsey, then swept a hand towards a small, unassuming door, as if leading them to their table. 'Please, follow me, gentlemen.'

'The back' turned out to be a narrow gully between the kitchen's extractor ports, the outer wall of the toilets, and the bins. Marinating in the smell of mouldering food waste. Beyond that, the neighbouring properties' eight-foot-high walls enclosed a small 'STAFF ONLY' car park jammed with rusty old hatchbacks – festering in the blistering sunshine.

A stringy wee bloke squatted atop a couple of old veg boxes, knees level with his shoulders, sooking on an old-fashioned cigarette and fiddling with his phone. Getting ash all down his long black waterproof apron. Fingers chapped red and raw, like uncooked beef sausages.

He looked up and scowled as Keira stepped out through the emergency exit, then went back to his mobile. 'Tell Benny to sod off: I'm on my *statutory* break.'

She held the door open for Logan and his halfwits. 'Bruno, can you give me a minute, please? I ... I need to speak to someone.'

'Then you can sod off too. I'm – on – my – break!'

A cruel smile twisted Keira's face, and just like that, the trembling, shy little girl vanished, replaced by a much harder version. 'Either you *do* one, or I tell the nice policemen here all about what you've got hidden in the bottom of your locker.'

Bruno's head snapped up at that. Eyes widening as he saw Rennie and Tufty, standing there in the full Police Scotland getup. He scrambled to his feet. 'All right, all right! Jesus. You're such a beeeee-atch!'

She clicked her fingers at him. 'Give us a fag, too. Don't be a stingy prick.'

He slumped and flumped, then tapped a cigarette from his pack and handed it over. Glowering as he lit the thing. 'Can I *go* now?' Bruno stuck out his weedy little chest, nose in the air as he squeezed past Logan. 'I ain't got nothing in no locker. She's just being a biatch.' Then off he scurried, no doubt keen to get rid of whatever it was he definitely *didn't* have planked in his locker.

'*He's* the bitch.' Keira took a long slow draw on the cigarette she'd bullied out of the kitchen's pot washer. She whoomphed a lungful of smoke in Logan's direction. And her transformation from a polite little girl into an arrogant wee shite was complete.

Her chin came up. 'What? You never see a Nubian goddess before?'

OK...

31

Logan wrinkled his nose against the triple stinks of cigarette smoke, festering bins, and old chip fat. 'Have you got a last name, Keira? Or are you more like Adele and Madonna?'

She blinked back at him, head tilted, cool as a bitter sorbet. Then shrugged. 'Longmore. Fourteen F, Allenvale Court, Gairn Terrace, Aberdeen, AB Ten, Six EW.'

Logan checked to see if anyone was writing that down – Rennie and Tufty both had their notebooks ready, biros already scribbling.

Keira stuck her chin out. 'I look after my grandad.'

Not according to Jericho McQueen.

'Thought you shared a flat with a bunch of vegans?'

'Nah. That's what I tell the *Thirsty* Boys: Jericho, Spencer, Wallace, and the rest. Think they can get it on with *this* fine ass?' Patting herself on the bottom. 'No way I'm telling them where I live!'

Fair enough.

'What about Charles MacGarioch.'

There was a tiny pause, then: 'Never heard of him.'

'Really?' Logan called up the photo from MacGarioch's bedroom. 'Because I heard you two were an item.'

Her mouth pinched as she considered the picture. 'Maybe. Why? What you think he's done?' Keira flicked a cylinder of ash onto Bruno's vacated perch. 'Not that it's anything to do with *me*. Whatever it is.'

'Where is he?'

'How would I know?' Throwing it back, hard and fast.

'Because you're his girlfriend.'

'You're the ones chased him into the river.' She leaned back against the wall, wearing that cruel smile again. 'What, you cops think we can't read the papers? I hear he's a proper hero for saving those kids and those oldies.' Another long inhale. 'Anyway: haven't seen him in ages. His bitch grandma's *scared* of people like me. Says I'm a black whore, trying to corrupt her poor little darling.' A snarl. 'Racist cow.'

Logan nodded. 'Yeah... That was *kind of* the impression I got too.' Maybe try appealing to old affections? 'We need to talk to Charles, Keira. And it's in *his* best interests to talk to *us*. You want to help him, don't you?'

She sent another cloud of smoke Logan's way. 'How'd you find me?'

'Keira, it's important, OK? After the crash yesterday: he could be hurt. What if he's got ... internal bleeding, or a concussion?'

'And whose fault would *that* be?'

One more go: 'He could be *dying, right now*, and not even know it. You want that to happen?'

She smoked and smoked and smoked, burning through her extorted cigarette, making it *hisssss*. Looking off into the middle distance, towards the centre of town. Forehead creased between the concealer-plastered zits. 'Charlie always said he wanted to go to Ireland. The south bit, where all the Guinness and leprechauns is.' A smile broke free – a genuine one this time, nothing malicious about it. 'Had this great-big dream of getting his own B-and-B. I'd do the meals and he'd look after the rooms. We'd both get fat and pop-out a whole heap of kids...' She dropped the spent butt, grinding it out against the concrete. 'Course, we'd need to wait for his granny to snuff it – Charlie won't abandon the old cow, and no way she's moving to Ireland. Surrounded by all them foreigners? Living in the EU? She'd rather claw her cobwebbed fanny out with a carving fork.'

'When did you last see him?'

'*Months* ago.' Keira pulled one shoulder up to her ear. 'His nan's debts were getting him down; old bag never was any good with money. Tried picking up extra shifts at the chippy, but it's not exactly *wedge*, is it? Minimum wage and all the second-hand grease you can scrape off your hair?' She dug into her apron and pulled out a tube of extra-strong mints. Popped one, frowned at the packet, then extended the open end to Logan.

'Thanks.' He offered a business card in exchange. 'If you hear from Charlie, or anything, can you let me know? We're *genuinely* worried about him.'

She eyed the thing, as if it might bite. 'You never said why you're after him.'

'Someone tipped us off he'd been involved in something a bit shady. We went round to get his side of the story.' OK, so strictly speaking that wasn't *exactly* true, but it wasn't exactly a lie, either.

Keira plucked the card from Logan's fingers, turning it over to read the mobile number printed on the back in biro. Then filed it away with her mints. '*If* he calls.'

'Thanks.' Nodding at the restaurant. 'We'll leave you to it.'

Logan shooed Rennie and Tufty through the emergency exit, into a short corridor with scuffed white walls and doors marked 'MANAGER' and 'STORES' on one side, 'STAFF/ CHANGING' and 'KITCHEN' on the other. And dead ahead: 'FRONT OF HOUSE ~ REMEMBER: YOUR SMILE MAKES ALL THE DIFFERENCE!'

Because it wasn't just Police Scotland who were addicted to 'motivational' wank.

Soon as they were all inside, Rennie flattened himself against the wall, snuck back to the emergency exit and cracked it open a sliver. Ear pressed against the gap.

Oh for God's sake.

Logan dropped his voice to a whisper. 'What are you doing, you idiot?'

The idiot stuck a finger to his lips, so quiet he was barely audible: 'Seeing if she calls MacGarioch to tell him we were here...'

Tufty hooked his thumbs into his utility belt, rocking on his heels like an old-timey prospector. 'I got a job in a chip shop after school. Worked my way up from peeling tatties to doing the pizzas. Very responsible job, doing the pizzas.' Nodding at the wisdom of that. 'It's not all deep-fried Mars Bars, you know.'

Rennie scowled. 'Will you shut up? Trying to listen, here.'

'We used to do deep-fried Crunchies too. Mmmm...' Then a grimace. 'Cadbury's Creme Eggs were a step too far, though. Like a weenie hand grenade full of napalm, they were.'

Halfwits. Logan was surrounded by halfwits.

He ignored the reminder to smile and pushed his way into reception, anyway.

The maître d', on the other hand, flashed her dentures as he emerged from the door, pointing at the phone currently pressed to her ear, as if he couldn't see it. But he gave her a thank-you wave anyway.

Tufty tottered after him. 'They'd burn straight through the roof of your mouth. Remember the fizzy acid blood in *Aliens*? That. Only all chocolate and fondanty.'

Bet Inspector Morse never had to put up with this nonsense.

•

Sunlight streamed through the canopy of leaves at the side of the road, stirred by a faint breeze, making the dalmatian spots ripple across the pool car and tarmac.

Tufty lounged against the driver's door, hands in his pockets, eyes closed, face up, a wee smile on his daft pointy face.

Across the road, a well-heeled couple headed downstairs to The Star-Sprinkled Heavens for ferociously expensive fish-and-chips.

And there was *still* no sign of bloody Rennie. Two more minutes, and that was it – they were leaving. With or without him.

Logan cupped a hand over his phone, cutting a bit of the glare, and squinted at Tara's latest message:

P/T meeting = 1930 remember?

Don't be late or there WILL be spanking!

And NOT the fun kind!!!!!

He poked out a reply.

That's the plan.

I'll have to go back to work afterwards, though.

Sorry.

SEND.

And that was it: time up.

He knocked on the car roof. 'Let's go: some of us have things to do.'

Tufty jumbled in behind the wheel, grinning and pointing at himself with both thumbs. 'Oh yeah: promoted to sidekick.' Starting the car as Logan settled into the passenger seat. 'Where to, Holmes? Is the game afoot?'

Logan checked the list of Charles MacGarioch's associates.

'Kincorth. Then I need to be in Countesswells for half seven. Sharp.'

'Huzzah!' Wriggling his bum, like a happy terrier. 'Sa-arge, now that I is your *official* sidekick, and I did has the genius idea about rapists and burglaries … can I come to the barbecue on Sunday?'

'No.'

He drooped. 'But *why*?'

Logan gave him a Paddington Stare. 'You *know* why.'

And with that, the happy terrier realised it was on the way to the vet to get snipped. 'Oh.' A sniff. Then a shrug. 'Still promoted to sidekick, though.' He put the car in gear and pulled away from the kerb.

Which is when Rennie decided to finally put in an appearance, wandering up the steps from The Star-Sprinkled Heavens' subterranean lair. Eyes popping as he watched the car leaving without him.

He sprinted for the back door, yanking it open and diving inside. 'What the hell?' Thumping Tufty on the arm. 'Constable!'

'Ow!'

'Don't blame *him*.' Logan pointed. 'It's your own fault for wanking about.'

'That was really *sore*.' Still rubbing his arm, Tufty headed off down Bon-Accord Crescent, following the road around to the left as it turned into a narrow lane.

Rennie struggled with the seatbelt. 'And for your *information*, I wasn't "wanking about", I was conducting an impromptu covert surveillance operation. Or an ICSO, as it's known in Secret Service circles.' *Click.* 'Because, of course, Keira was lying. I can tell when a girl's telling porkies a mile off – their lips move.'

Tufty took a right, heading downhill on Bon-Accord Street,

making for the lights with a frown on his face. 'Bit misogynistic, Sarge.'

'I've got three daughters and a wife with a shoe addiction, Constable: I *know* when women are lying.' He sat forward. 'So it was logical to assume that Keira Longmore would get in touch with Charles MacGarioch, soon as we'd gone.'

Might as well indulge the lad: 'And *did* she?'

'Called her grandad to check he was OK after the men from the Council had been to fix the living-room window.'

'Oh, the *horror*.'

'Hmm...' Rennie squinted off into the middle distance, as if that made him look any less daft. 'Course, *maybe* she wasn't talking to her grandad at all? Maybe it was *MacGarioch*. And maybe "the men from the Council" is code for us – the police – and "fixing the living-room window" means ... we've been round asking questions?'

'Bit of a stretch.'

Rennie dug out his Airwave. 'Going to run a PNC check – see what she's been done for...'

Tufty clicked on the radio. 'Meantime, let's have us some tunes!'

XXXII

Come on you *fucker*...

Natasha shoved her heels into the dirt floor and pushed. Straining away from the bloody anchor, the chain grasped in an awkward fist-over-fist grip because her wrists were still shackled to that bastard collar.

Heaving and hauling.

Toes digging into the baked earth.

Putting all her weight into it.

Legs trembling with the effort.

Sweat trickling down her face, inside the mask.

More on her grubby arms and legs.

...

The anchor ground its way towards her – less than an inch, but that was something, right?

Christ knew how long she'd been at it, in the baking heat of this stone oven, but her throat was like a tube of burning sandpaper, her tongue twice the size it should've been. Breath howling in the confines of the soggy leather.

And what she wouldn't do for a drink. For a nice tall tumbler of water, ice cubes clinking, condensation sparkling on the chilled glass...

Hell, she'd even take the arch arsehole Adrian back. Two-faced, thieving, cheating bastard that he was.

As she stood there, hunched over and wheezing, bluebottles settled onto her bare skin. Feeding on the salt and scabs.

A glass of water and a shower and a soft, soft bed...

Come on: couldn't build a media empire by lying down and dying. You got there by *fighting*.

And DS Davis would be back soon enough, with the next instalment of whatever horror he had planned. Fucking police *wanker*.

Did his cop mates know what he got up to? Did they know he was a dirty, criminal, violent bastard? Or would they all pretend it came as a massive shock when the story broke. One more rotten apple in a barrel full of shits.

She bent her knees and tightened her grip on the chain, *growling* with the effort, then *yelling*, *snarling*, and *howling* inside the suffocating mask.

The anchor rasped forward another fraction of an inch.

One more go...

But the bloody thing wouldn't move. A chunk of stone poked out of the hard dirt floor – not far, barely the height of a cigarette pack – but it was two or three feet wide, and the galvanised bucket full of concrete was wedged right up against it.

She tugged and yanked and pulled and swore and screamed and wrenched on the bloody chain, but the bastard wouldn't go any further.

She let go, staggered a couple of paces closer to her anchor, raising her foot to kick the bastard...

But what would that achieve? Oh yeah, it'd be *great* to shatter the bones in her foot, cos that would make life *so* much easier, wouldn't it? Being unable to walk on top of everything else...

So she whumped down onto the ground instead. Sitting there with her chest against her knees. Breath jagged and catching.

Do *not* cry.

Do *not* give the bastard the satisfaction.

But the tears came anyway, because this was gonna be a *shitty* way to die.

33

Logan stepped out of the front door, shutting it behind him.

It was a little terrace of six houses, next to another identical one, and a third that looked a bit like a schoolhouse.

This bit of Kincorth was all uphill, the front gardens bordered by a steep slope down to the road below. Then a nice little strip of parkland, then another road, then more houses, descending all the way to the River Dee. Though the water itself was hidden behind a ripple of bright-green trees.

Still a nice view, though.

About a dozen teenagers had set up a picnic site on the yellowing grass, complete with camp chairs, tartan rugs, barbecues, cool boxes, and a Swingball set.

Smaller kids scampered around the trees and bushes, giggling and screeching as they hunted each other with Super Soakers and bubble guns.

Everyone was in shorts and T-shirts, enjoying the sun, while the enticing scents of charcoal and sizzling chicken wafted through the warm air, and a handful of Bluetooth speakers pumped out cheery tunes.

Had to admit, it was kinda idyllic.

Shame to spoil things by asking about a racist, arsonist, wee shite like Charles MacGarioch.

Logan headed down the steps, and across the road, rolling

up his shirtsleeves, because it was far too Mediterranean out here to wear a suit jacket.

'Sarge.' Tufty joined him at the edge of the small park, doing a hoppity-skip to get his feet left-righting at the same time as Logan's. Because clearly it would kill him to act like a normal, *sensible* human being for ten minutes.

'Twit.' Logan strolled onto the grass, one hand shading his eyes, voice raised above the music: 'Randolph Hay?'

Over by the barbecue, a young man in a camping chair raised his tin of Stella in reply. Long red hair, tucked back behind his ears; squint front tooth; the kind of nose you'd normally find on busts of Roman emperors; and a 'F&#K CAPITALISM!' T-shirt. A brightly coloured tattoo rampaged all down one arm: Norman Picklestripes 'being intimate' with Betsy. Randolph took a scoof of lager. 'I go by Ralph, though. You guys want a cold one?' Pointing at the little kids. 'We got non-alcoholic for the weenies?'

'Can we talk?'

Ralph stood. 'Course. Course.' Grabbing a weenie as they hurled past, he wheeched them up into the air, upside down. Giving them a wee shoogle till they shrieked with delight. 'Watch my chair, OK? Don't let the Bumbersnatch steal it!'

The weenie giggled and wriggled as Ralph lowered them into his vacated seat.

Then Mr F&#k Capitalism led Logan and Tufty away, across a road, to the next small chunk of park. He leaned against a tree trunk; took a swig from his can. Keeping an eye on the weenies. 'So, you want to talk about Charlie.' Grinning as Logan raised an eyebrow. 'The Orphan Grapevine's been ringing.'

Quick check to make sure Tufty was writing this down.

'You're one of the support group.'

'Family holiday, staying with friends in Cornwall. Mum and

Dad had a run-in with a London estate agent going way too fast on a twisty country road after a liquid lunch.' He toasted them with his Stella. 'I was five. And in the back seat.'

'I'm sorry.'

'Meh...' Shrug. 'There are worse origin stories, believe me.' Another swig. 'Haven't seen Charlie for about ... week and a half? Talking about a trip to the circus in Westburn Park. Get the whole gang together and hit the final night.'

Logan tucked his hands into his pockets, keeping it casual. As if there weren't a shortarse police constable, in the full uniform kit, taking notes. 'He say anything about money worries?'

'We used to hang out all the time – the whole lot of us. Broken little people, looking for our tribe. But it's hard to do that when people start disappearing off to university.' Ralph made a spreading-out gesture with one hand. 'So yeah...' Drifting away for a moment, creases deepening between his eyebrows. Then back again. 'Charlie's a good guy. I mean you'll *never* find anyone more loyal: literally give you the shirt off his back – seen him do it. But he's not winning *Celebrity Mastermind* anytime soon, if you get my meaning. Always coming up with get-rich-quick schemes; always having to bum a couple of quid for the bus fare home.'

Logan looked out across the park, to where there was nothing more pressing or important in the whole world than getting your little sister or brother soaking wet, or pretending to be a dinosaur. 'What do you think he'd have made of the protest this weekend? Environmentalism, capitalism, immigration...? Would he be pro or anti?'

'Charlie?' A laugh. 'Wants to be the next Steve Jobs; doesn't really understand how the market economy works. Recycles, but dreams of jetting-off to exotic, far-away lands on a private jet. And as for migrants: you've met Keira, right? Her dad's from Ghana; mum's from Inverurie, via Algeria. Charlie's nan might be a weapons-grade right-wing "friend of Nigel", but Charlie's cool.'

OK, time to ask the *big* question. 'Any idea where he might be hiding? We're worried he hurt himself when he drove that ice-cream van into the river. Could be serious.'

'Ah.' Ralph frowned at the treetops, one finger tapping against his tin of Stella as the silence stretched. Then he scrunched up his face, and drained the can. Decision made. 'After Charlie's mum died, he used to run away a lot. Not far – you know the Wallace Tower, in Seaton Park? There was a loose bit of plywood boarding-up the windows, so he'd squeeze through the gap and spend the night. Don't know if you can still do that. Maybe?'

'Thanks. You've been a huge help.' Logan offered a business card. 'If he does get in touch?'

'Understand – I'm not *clyping* on Charlie, I'm only trying to help him.' Ralph took the card. 'The daft sod's his own worst enemy...'

Tufty climbed back in behind the wheel, looking across the pool car and out through Logan's window, towards the park – where Ralph was chasing a couple of weenies around the makeshift picnic area, arms in the air, making monster noises and pretending he was going to eat them, while they laughed and screeched.

'Do you think a Bumbersnatch is related to the fuminous *Bandersnatch*? Perhaps the slithy toves did gyre and gimble in Kincorth?' Sniff. 'Or is it just a coincidence?'

Silence.

Logan didn't even move.

In the back, Rennie was graveyard still.

Both doing their best *not* to encourage him.

Finally, Tufty shrugged, started the car, and launched into a lumpy three-point turn.

With the moment broken, Rennie pointed. 'Right: Seaton ho!'

Logan pressed buttons on his Airwave, and waited for the bleeps. 'Sergeant Moore, safe to talk?'

'Fit like, Boss Mannie?'

'Spudgun: need you to grab a couple of bodies and stakeout the Wallace Tower in Seaton Park. Low key. No lights or sirens.'

Three-point completed, Tufty headed back towards the Bridge of Dee.

'Oh aye? We looking for anything in particular?'

'Charles MacGarioch used to hide out there as a kid. Might be nothing, but worth a punt.'

'Could go in mob-handed if you like?'

'Not unless you know he's *definitely* there. Don't want to spook him, otherwise.'

'See what I can do.'

'Thanks, Spudgun.' Logan ended the call. 'Fingers crossed.'

A snort from Rennie. 'Yeah, because when have we ever been *that* lucky?'

Good point.

The peroxide idiot sat forward, poking his head between the seats. 'If we're gonna do a stakeout, we should order pizza!' Rubbing his hands. 'And none of that meat-free bollocks: eighteen-inch American hot, with extra spicy sausage and jalapenos.'

'Nope.'

Rennie pouted. 'Oh come on, Guv – don't even get proper *cheese* at home any more. Emma's gone all vegan-bolshy.'

'I mean "nope" as in "we're not going on a stakeout."

Spudgun's a big boy now: doesn't need us to hold his hand.' Logan pointed through the windscreen. '*Countesswells* ho.'

'Eh? But what's more important than catching Charles MacGarioch?'

Tufty took a left, pootling down Abbotswell Drive towards the bridge. 'We does has a prior appointment.'

'But...?'

Logan shook his head. 'Don't make me "nope" you again. It's...' His phone *ding-buzz*ed an incoming text. 'Hold on.'

SGT. BROOKMINSTER:

> URGENT MEMO – ALL SENIOR OFFICERS!!!
>
> Uniforms MUST B worn @ all times till staffing issues resolved!
>
> The Chief Super thanks U 4 Ur cooperation!

Bet she did.

Urgh...

Suppose there was only one thing for it, then.

'But we've got a quick stop to make first.'

The pool car scrunched to a halt on the driveway and Logan scrambled out, running for the front door. Unlocking it and letting himself into the house. Peeling off his suit jacket as he charged upstairs.

Dumping it on the bed, unclipping his tie, then stripping down to his socks and pants, before hauling on his itchy uniform trousers. While Cthulhu watched from atop the laundry basket, head on one side, tail twitching, as if he was insane.

Clingy, black, police-issue T-shirt on, Logan straightened his epaulettes and rushed downstairs again. Sitting on the bottom step to lace up his black boots.

Into the kitchen.

He tore open a sachet of chicken and extruded the gelatinous slab into Cthulhu's bowl – giving her a wee stroke and a kiss on her fuzzy little head as she tucked in.

Then into the hallway again, grabbing his lanyard and peaked cap before wheeching out the front door, slamming it behind him.

Locking it.

Then leaping back into the passenger seat.

Logan banged a hand on the dashboard. 'Drive. Drive!'

And Tufty did.

Kirkenwell Academy was a concrete monstrosity that looked about as welcoming as a prison block.

Actually, strike that – HMP Grampian was *much* nicer than this miserable series of grey boxes masquerading as a school. A pair of three-storey blocks were bolted together at right angles, with a bunch of other, smaller wings sticking out in random directions. All flat roofs and dirt-streaked walls. Over a dozen ancient Portakabins clustered about the edges – no doubt a temporary measure when they were erected, twenty or thirty years ago.

Rusty chain-link fencing was a bit of a theme: eight-feet tall; dividing the secondary school from the primary; wrapping around the rhomboid of tarmac that passed for a playground; and enclosing a tatty patch of grass that was just big enough for a couple of five-a-side football pitches and a weedy running track.

The pool car pitched and lurched between potholes.

A miserable OAP, dressed in brown overalls, was scraping great sticky globs of chewing gum off the school sign: 'KIRKENWELL ACADEMY ~ WHERE DREAMS GROW AND FLOURISH'.

Tufty gave him a wave on the way past and got nothing but a stony look in return. 'Yeah...' He scooted down in his seat. 'Is it just me, or can anyone else hear banjo music? Backa-dow-dow-dow dow dow-dow-dow...' Following the pitted road to the back of the school, where a leprous patchwork of tarmac pretended to be a car park. Crowded with rundown estate cars, sagging hatchbacks, and the occasional flatbed truck. Surrounded by yet more chain link.

A *deeply* unattractive, bread-van-style Citroën Berlingo was parked by the gated entrance to the school grounds – a sticker in the rear window boasting 'MY OTHER CAR IS A POLICE VAN'.

Suppose it would've been too much to hope that Tara was the one running late for a change.

Logan undid his seatbelt, setting the dinger off. 'Close to the gate as you can.'

Tufty drove right up to it – slamming on his brakes at the last moment – and Logan jumped out into the oppressive evening air. Tasting toasted dust at the back of his throat as he battered through the gate into a fenced-off compound. Pulling on his peaked cap as his phone *ding-buzz*ed another incoming text message.

Probably Tara, wanting to know where the hell he was, but there was no time to check it.

The compound's barricade of chain link was topped with barbed wire, protecting a squat building about the size of a garage forecourt. It'd been painted white once, long, long ago, but now grass grew in the flat roof's gutters.

Weirdly, all the windows were coated in that stuff boy racers used to hide the interior of their wankmobiles – the sort of pinky-orange film that was only see-through if you were looking out.

The door was marked: 'STRICTLY STAFF ONLY!'

but some helpful soul had taped a pair of laminated signs to the wall: '← PARENT TEACHER MEETINGS: SECONDARY' and 'PARENT TEACHER MEETINGS: PRIMARY →'

Logan went right – jogging around the side of the teachers' bunker to what looked like the entrance to a prison exercise yard. But it was a bare-and-basic playground instead, with some hopscotchy things painted on the potholed tarmac, and a couple of wonky climbing frames. Though those were cordoned off with yellow-and-black-striped tape and signs screaming: 'WARNING – UNSAFE!'

He shoved through the squealing gate, and loped across the playground to Kirkenwell Academy's primary school, also known as a sprawl of interconnected Portakabins, squatting in what used to be a five-a-side football pitch – going by the goalposts that still stood at either end – though the grass had been smothered with landscape fabric and bark chips.

At some point, they'd had a bash at cheering things up, by painting each 'temporary' building a different colour, like the houses in Balamory, but they'd long since faded and weathered to a grubby palette of off-greys.

One of the cabins, at the front of the depressing pack, was covered in posters that the kids had clearly drawn themselves – because they were rubbish – and above the door a sign declared: 'ALL VISITORS MUST REPORT TO RECEPTION!'

Logan stopped just outside. Took a deep breath. And stepped into the mildew-sock-and-armpit funk of a cobbled-together primary school.

Rows and rows of empty coat hooks lined the walls, with hard wooden-slat benches below. Five doors off, each painted a different colour: 'RED ZONE', 'BLUE ZONE', 'GREEN ZONE', 'YELLOW ZONE', and 'TOILETS'. A handful of desks made a pushed-together island in the middle of the room, where a beanbag-faced woman in a pink cardigan and perm sat facing the door, knitting. Looking as if she'd be happier at the foot of a guillotine, watching a bunch of French aristocrats get twelve inches shorter.

Instead, she had to make do with supervising a cardboard box full of name badges – each of which had a blob of blue, yellow, red, or green on it. Which presumably corresponded to each of the 'zones'.

Logan risked a smile. 'Hi.'

She didn't look up, needles *click*er-*clack*ing away. 'Name badge.'

OK...

He had a rummage through the box, but the closest he could find was one with 'LOGAN MACRAY' and a big green blotch on it. With a heavy sigh, he pinned the thing to his lanyard and marched through the door to the Green Zone.

Which turned out to be yet another Portakabin – shock horror – with scruffy green carpet tiles and some fairly awful kids' paintings on the walls. About three dozen little desks were lined up in neat rows, each with its own small plastic chair. A door at the back of the class promised access to a 'COOLDOWN AREA'.

Could do with one of those back at Divisional Headquarters. And a naughty step wouldn't go amiss...

To add a touch of sophistication and luxury, they'd laid out two bowls of crisps, a stack of plastic cups, and a beaker of diluting orange. All three of which looked cheap and nasty.

A handful of teachers milled around – easy to spot by their lanyards, general air of depression, and predilection for corduroy. Except for one: a young woman with huge bouffant black hair and denim dungarees, who seemed to be mainlining Energizer batteries.

The parents, on the other hand, looked bored and uncomfortable, each with a fidgety little child in tow.

A baldy bloke in shorts and a golfing jumper grinned. 'Aye, aye. A'bidy behave, it's the polis.'

And with that, everyone stopped talking to stare at Logan. Thanks, mate.

Logan tucked his hat under his arm, gave them all a friendly nod, then wandered over to where Tara and the LizMonster were examining a wall of what might've been Pokemon. Or self-portraits. Difficult to tell.

Elizabeth was in her school uniform – grey trousers, white polo shirt, stripy tie – but Tara had gone casual in jeans, boots, and an old Atomic Killer Cockroach T-shirt. And she was still the most stylish thing in the room.

Logan gave the pair of them a wee salute. 'Acting Detective Chief Inspector McRae, reporting for duty – bang on time, as usual.'

Tara checked the wall clock. 'Skin of the teeth, more like.' But she gave Logan a kiss anyway. No tongues, because it was schooltime.

'Hey, monster.' He ruffled WhizzyLizzy's hair.

'Da-aaa-aaad!' Scooting out of reach and fiddling her locks back into place.

He held up his new badge. 'Well, I say "McRae", apparently I've changed my name.'

Tara pursed her lips, one eyebrow raised. '*Full* uniform? Really?'

'The Chief Super insisted. Says there's so many of us off on the sick right now, the public need reassurance.' He posed. 'Are you reassured?'

'Just don't go arresting anyone, OK?'

Elizabeth grabbed his hand, pulling him towards the front of the room. Still a bit lispy, on account of not having all her front teeth back yet. 'Come on, Dad, we're going to be late for our first appointment!'

Urgh…

Tara poked him. 'You're the one who wanted to have a kid.'

And so it began…

34

Mr Blackwell's 'office' for this evening was a desk by the whiteboard. He fidgeted with a pen – spinning it round and around in his long thin fingers, like a middle-aged majorette. The rest of him was long and thin too. In fact he was tall enough to have outgrown most of his hair, leaving a pair of hefty eyebrows and a droopy moustache behind.

The biro/baton went for another spin. '…but perhaps Elizabeth needs to pay a *little* more attention to her fractions and long division.'

Logan's phone *ding-buzz*ed in his pocket, but teachers tended to get huffy if they thought people weren't hanging on their every word, so he left it where it was.

'Now,' Mr Blackwell swapped the spinning pen from one hand to the other, 'I know that's considered *advanced* for six-year-olds, but Elizabeth's a bright girl and there's no reason she can't *excel* with a little motivation.' Big smile. 'You like music, don't you? Of course you do, everyone likes music.'

Tara nodded, and after a wee pause, Logan did too. Humouring him.

'Well, there you are! *Mathematics* is the music of the cosmos. Its rhythms are the rhythms of quantum physics and black holes, biology and ecology.' Spreading his arms wide, the pen never missing a beat. 'Everything around us *sings* to mathematics' tune! And I want every child who comes through that door to sing along.'

Mr Blackwell stood there, as if he was expecting a round of applause.

He didn't get one.

'I see.' A frown. 'Perhaps that's the wrong analogy for you? Ermmm...' He snapped his fingers. 'Aha! Do you like *sport*?'

Oh God...

Mrs Greenwald looked like a part-time rugby player, with bear-like hands, broad shoulders, and a slight stoop that took her down to a mere six foot. Index and middle finger yellowed with cigarette tar. A wee paunch that implied she spent more time in the pub than the classroom. Face like a wet weekend in Huntly, voice like a bucket full of gravel, as she moaned on and on and on. '...and we were meant to have a school trip to the Science Museum, in London. *Then* it was downgraded to Dynamic Earth in Edinburgh. *Now* I don't even have the budget for an afternoon at Satrosphere, and it's only down the road!' She glowered out through the window. 'We've got a proper science lab, you know. With benches, and Bunsen burners, and ... flipping oscilloscopes. Only the roof's made of reinforced autoclaved aerated concrete, so I'm stuck in here making volcanoes out of papier-mâché and bicarbonate of soda. *How is that science?*'

Maybe, if Logan pulled the fire alarm, they could all go home?

The Energizer Bunny with frizzy hair and dungarees turned out to be Mrs McIntosh, a snub-nosed dynamo of a woman whose can-do attitude and beaming smile hinted at either lots of prescription drugs or an impending psychosis. Possibly both.

She eyed Logan's uniform, then gave him a massive wink. 'Not going to arrest me, are you? For being too much fun!' Then nudged Elizabeth. 'Right, Lizzy?'

He kept his voice flat as a mortuary table. 'I think you're safe, there.'

'You see, I think English *should* be fun! Shakespeare doesn't have to be stuffy – *Hamlet* was the *EastEnders* of its day!' Popping on an atrocious Mockney accent as she squatted down in front of Elizabeth: 'To be, or not to be, and all that, innit?' Then mangled out an even more Dick Van Dykeian 'Leave it aaart, you muppet!'

Mrs McIntosh bounded upright again. 'Now, have you thought about our special summer theatre camp?'

Christ, no.

Elizabeth dragged Logan out through the back door, and onto the woodchip. 'Hurry! Hurry!'

They'd plonked a toilet block behind the primary-school warren: a small Portakabin divided in two – one half marked 'BOYS' the other 'GIRLS'. Neither of which looked particularly sanitary. The harsh-plastic scent of pine disinfectant and floral air freshener struggled to conceal the fact that little children weren't always the best at 'getting their presents in the porcelain Santa'.

An older man lurked outside the loos, puffing away on a roll-up – holding it in his cupped hand like a true secret smoker. His ragged shirt cuffs were stained with smears of green, yellow, and pink. Blue-and-red dirt under his fingernails. Late fifties, with a sensible grey haircut, John Lennon glasses, and white stubble on his chin. Wearing a blazer-and-tie as if he'd lost a bet and this was the forfeit.

Logan let the little monster hustle him over to the toilets. 'Well, it's your own fault for drinking all that orange juice.'

'Not helping!'

The man looked up, mid-puff, and wheeched the cigarette around behind his back. Hiding it. Forcing a smile as he wafted away the smoke. 'Fallen foul of the rozzers, eh, Elizabeth?'

'Can't stop: back teeth are floating!'

Logan let go of her hand and she sprinted for the door to the girls'.

Soon as she'd gone, the man's cigarette reappeared for one final draw. Then he ground the tiny butt out against the sole of his shoe.

Another *ding-buzz* came from Logan's pocket, but he sagged against the wall instead.

Mr DirtyCuffs jerked a thumb at the toilets. 'A police escort? She not a bit young for Public Enemy Number One?'

'My daughter. Who spends *way* too much time with her Aunty Roberta.'

'Ah.' A nod. 'Enjoy it while you can. In six years' time the hormones kick in and "Daddy's Little Girl" turns into "Satan's Gangly Monster."' He dug out a small tobacco tin and dropped the mangled butt inside, where it joined a row of roll-ups, awaiting their turn.

Logan pointed at the piddle-palace Portakabin. 'Are you…?'

Because if not, hanging around outside a kids' toilet might be considered *slightly* suspicious.

'Humphrey Fordyce-Adams, to give the full Sunday School moniker. Art and Design. Oh.' He offered the tin. 'You smoke?'

'Gave it up.'

'Very wise.' Sparking up a fresh one. 'For a minute there, thought you might be here about Ruby.'

Logan whipped out his notebook. 'Is one of the kids in trouble?'

'*Music teacher*: Ruby Burrows, didn't turn up for work last Monday. Thought maybe something bad had happened – you know what they say, "stress, booze, and razorblades make uncomfortable bedfellows". Shame, I liked her.' He gave Logan the side-eye. 'Not like *that*.' Then raised his eyebrows. 'Well, maybe once. After the End-Of-Term-Piss-Up party.' Grin. 'But that's teachers for you.'

'Yeah.' Logan looked back towards the classrooms. 'I've certainly met some … interesting characters this evening.'

'You mean Nichole?'

No idea.

Humphrey Fordyce-Adams – which was a ridiculous name for a man not currently wearing red trousers and a shooting waistcoat – tried again. 'Mrs McIntosh: English?' Miming a big frizzy helmet. 'Hair. Dungers? Nah, she's OK.' He took a very non-blue-blooded draw on his fag. 'Believe it or not, we're all very nice here. Well, *"Doctor"* Buchan's a bit of a prick, but there's always one, isn't there?'

'Usually lucky if it's only one.'

'Yeah, well, he's only subbing till Ruby gets back. Then he can sod off home to whatever rock he slithered out from under.' Humphrey examined Logan through the smoke. 'Don't remember you from last year.'

'Elizabeth's a Cults Primary kid – temporarily assigned to—'

'*This* hellhole.' A bitter laugh. 'Oh, yeah: they'll close and refurbish every school in the city before they finally get round to us.' Flicking ash towards the main building. 'Assuming they don't just bulldoze the place, salt the earth, and erase all mention of Kirkenwell Academy for Weird Little—'

The toilet door thumped open and Elizabeth scuffed out, looking a lot happier than when she scurried in.

Humphrey hid his cigarette again. 'Teeth back where they should be?'

'Phew. That was close!' She gave him a wave. 'Sorry for not

saying hello, Mr Fordyce-Adams: but I had to see a man about a racehorse.'

Far too much time with her Aunty Roberta.

Logan peered. 'Have you washed your hands, you filthy little horror?'

She held them out for inspection: front side, then back, before grabbing his in her *slightly* clammy fingers.

Urgh...

He nodded at Humphrey. 'Suppose we'll see you inside.'

'Mr Fordyce-Adams is *famous*, Dad. He's got a painting in the Royal Academy!'

A gracious, pantomime bow. 'My Warhol-allotted fifteen minutes of fame.' Followed by a grimace. 'Turns out not everyone enjoys it.'

Very true.

There wasn't really anything to say to that, so Logan escorted Elizabeth back to the miserable lump of manky Portakabins for another round of pointless meetings.

As if he didn't get enough of that at work...

Dr Buchan – the aforementioned 'prick' – had a whole room all to himself. The walls were painted a scuffed yellow, the carpet tiles blotched with stains and worn down to the adhesive in places. A trio of shelving racks played host to the cheaper kinds of musical instrument: recorders, little metal chime blocks, a couple of tambourines, and a whole bunch of triangles. There was even a battered old upright piano, the floor sagging beneath it. But to be fair, the ceiling sagged in the opposite corner, so it all sort of evened out.

Humphrey was right – this whole place needed redecorating with a bulldozer.

'Hold on a minute.' Dr Buchan perched on the piano's deflated stool, wearing a semiquaver pin in his tartan tie.

A towering skeleton of a man, with surgeon's fingers and a bandage on his right wrist. Thin glasses, high forehead. And a nose designed for looking down. 'Do you *seriously* mean to tell me that you *don't have a piano* in the house? I thought you were one of our more ... affluent parents.'

Tara frowned. 'Well, we've never really—'

'Because it doesn't have to be a *Steinway*, even a decent Blüthner upright would do.' He rubbed at his bandage. 'You can't expect Elizabeth to master an instrument if she can't practise at home.' Dr Buchan's face soured even further. 'God knows I'm wasting my time with most of the children here, but it would be nice if parents would *occasionally* meet me halfway.' That nose cranked upwards a couple more inches. 'Music isn't "nothing" – a mere *bagatelle* to fritter away your time on – it's *life* itself! It's—'

Logan's phone burst into 'Space Oddity'.

Oh, thank God for that. Tufty might've been a daft little spud, but he knew how to pick his moments.

Dr Buchan sharpened the edge on his withering teacher's voice: 'We do encourage visitors to *switch off* their mobile devices *before* entering school premises, Mr McRae.'

'Police business.' He pulled out his phone, and marched from the room, back into the reception area, as David Bowie warbled on.

The Guillotine Knitting Club had disappeared, taking her crummy box of crappy badges with her. But even that hadn't made the place any less miserable.

Logan poked the green button. 'What?'

'*Is everything OK, Sarge? Only we've been sitting out here for ages and Sergeant Rennie's getting all fidgety. He's pacing up and down the car park as we speak.*' Tufty's voice went all whispery. '*I think he does need to has a wee.*'

Logan wandered over to the nearest window, looking out

at the dismal playground. 'Could be worse: you could be sat in here, listening to some wank-faced prick lecture you about how you're crap parents because you don't have a grand piano in every room.'

'I've been going over DCI Rutherford's files, and—'

'How did you get those?'

'You had them all piled up on your desk, Sarge. I had a good snoot through, back at the ranch. Before you picked me and Sergeant Rennie up?' Nosey wee sod. *'Anyway, being a most excellent side-kick, I has worked up an online calendar for all his meetings and reviews and assessments and court appearances and stuff. Only I suppose you can't really do his court appearances, as they'll probably want to ask questions about the cases and you weren't involved in those, so we should probably request a continuation on anything where we don't want the accused going free.'*

Fair point.

'Thank you.'

'So, just to let you know: you've got another MAPPA meeting tomorrow morning about the protest, a case review for the people-smuggling thing, another one for Operation Hedgehog, then the car-thefts thing, the break-ins-at-all-those-sports-shops thing, the drugs-coming-in-in-Lithuanian-teddy-bears thing, and Professional Standards want a word about The Dastardly Queen Of Ultimate Sticky.'

Of course they did.

Logan closed his eyes and massaged his forehead. 'What's Steel done now?'

'Inappropriate language of a sexual nature to female co-workers and canteen staff.'

To be honest: knowing her, it could be worse.

'OK: tell Rennie to tie a knot in it, and I'll be with you soon as I can.' He checked his watch. 'Call it fifteen minutes.'

He hung up. And, as he already had his phone out, it would be daft not to at least *check* his messages.

SPUDGUN:

> In place at Wallace Tower.
>
> Got Sporky and Guthrie hiding in bushes with binoculars and popcorn.
>
> Bored already.
>
> Will keep you updated.
>
> Urgh...!

DOREEN:

> I had to send Baker and Ducat home – sick.
>
> Need more bodies!!!
>
> Need to call off search.
>
> Need HOLIDAY!

Yeah, she was probably right. If Charles MacGarioch's body had washed up on the riverbank *surely* they'd have found it by now.

The final message on the list was from an unknown number:

> Hi. I was thinking ~> you only have those old pics of Charlie right? In the paper they're all ancient.
>
> Got a couple from drinks last week. Attch:

Which means the unknown number was probably Randolph 'I go by Ralph' Hay.

He'd attached a couple of jpegs, but the internet was running like a three-legged sloth, so they'd be a while downloading.

They were still chugging away when the door to the Yellow Zone opened, and Tara and Elizabeth escaped from Dr Buchan's pus-coloured lair.

Tara closed the door behind her, slumped against it, then narrowed her eyes at Logan. 'You *rotten* sod.'

'Duty called.' He held up his phone. 'Literally.'

'We're going to have to get a piano, aren't we.'

Elizabeth skipped on the spot. 'Dr Buchan's what Aunty Roberta would call "a—"'

'Oh no you don't, young lady.' Logan shook a warning 'dad' finger at her. 'We're not having that kind of language in an educational setting.'

Those pictures were *still* downloading.

He glanced at the coloured doors. 'How many of these spudging things have we still got to go?'

'Millions…'

'*No*, Mum,' Elizabeth frowned up at her, 'only Drama, Art, History, and Computer Science.'

'Is it too late to put you up for adoption?'

A shrug. 'Probably.'

Logan's phone bleeped, announcing that the attachments were finally ready to view. 'OK, but I can only stay fifteen minutes: got Rennie and Tufty waiting outside.'

Tara gave him *her* version of the Paddington Stare, which had far more of the homicidal Father Jack about it.

He raised a hand. 'Unless you *want* murderers running about the city, murdering people in a murdery way?'

She rolled her eyes instead. '*Fine*.'

'Thought so.' Logan shot Elizabeth with a finger gun. 'OK, Fizzy Lizzy Bing-Bong: who're we meeting next?' Sneaking a quick glance at his phone as she checked the photocopied schedule.

Attachment Number One was a photo of half a dozen

THIS HOUSE OF BURNING BONES

young people, in a pub – no idea which one – all gathered around a table grinning at the camera with their glasses raised. Pints, mostly.

There were more revellers off to both sides, but in the middle sat: Ralph, Jericho, Charles, and…

Oh sodding hell.

35

Logan jammed his phone back in his pocket. 'I have to go. Sorry.'

'But Da-ad!'

He hunkered down, so they were eye to eye. 'Who does Daddy love most in the whole wide world?'

Elizabeth didn't even have to think about it: 'Cthulhu.'

'True.' He gave her tummy a prod. 'But who does Daddy love *almost* as much as Cthulhu?'

'Mummy.'

'Nah, she's a poo-head.'

Tara walloped him one. 'Hey!'

A big grin from the Lizzasaurus Rex. 'Is it Elizabeth Tobermory Strachan-McRae?'

So he gave her a wee kiss on the head. 'Darn tootin'.' Then stood and shot Tara a grimace.

'Go.'

Logan marched for the door, already dialling.

'But remember what I said about spanking!'

He thumped out into the playground, where the air was hot and claggy and smelled of *freedom*. Phone to his ear, waiting for the halfwit Tufty to—

Logan stumbled to a halt, inches away from falling over a little girl. Well, not *little*, little. Maybe twelve years old? Dressed in black jeans, black biker boots, black leather wrist things, and a black T-shirt with Marceline from *Adventure Time* on it. She'd even dyed her hair jet-black, like Undertaker Barbie.

She glowered up at him, from a ghost-white face with coal-coloured lipstick. 'Hey, watch where you're...' Then her eyes widened in their smoked shadows. 'Ooh, it's *you*! It really *is* you. They said it was, but then you didn't show yesterday, so I thought maybe they were lying, but it's *you*, and...' Then she must've remembered that babbling Goths weren't cool, so bobbed one shoulder and sniffed instead. 'Yeah. I mean, ... 'sup?'

'Sorry.' He pointed at the gate through to the teachers' bunker. 'I've got to—'

'You don't *remember* me?' Bottom lip trembling.

Not even vaguely.

'Erm... Yes?'

The Ghost Goth Girl looked away, chin jutting out like a chalk cliff. Shoulders back. 'We rescued those kids from the Livestock Mart. You know, from those tits in masks?'

What?

Logan stared at her.

Nah.

Couldn't be.

'*Rebecca?* But you were, like,' he held a hand out, as if patting a weenie kid on the head, 'and didn't you have big red hair?'

A gigantic smile crashed through her teenage cool. 'You *do* remember!' And Rebecca launched herself at Logan, wrapping him up in a hug, even though she only came about halfway up his chest.

OK.

Weird.

...

Actually, given what they'd been through together, pretty sodding understandable.

Logan hugged her back.

In the happy silence, a tiny tinny voice squawked out of his phone: *'Sarge? Hello?'*

He looked down at those dyed black roots, and the Darth Vader outfit. 'Are you OK?'

She let go and stepped back, wiping her nose on the back of one hand. 'So, it's true – your daughter goes here, right?' Rebecca's pale chin came up again. 'Want you to know: anyone messes with her, they mess with me. And I will *fuck* their shit up.'

'That's ... very kind of you.'

'Hello, Sarge? Can you hear me?'

God's sake.

Logan groaned. 'I'm *really* sorry – I've got to run.'

Rebecca nodded. 'You got tits to arrest.'

'But it's been great seeing you again!' He pointed at her, smiling as he backed towards the gate. 'Don't do drugs; stay in school; and so on and so forth.'

'Sarge? Knock once for yes, twice for no...'

She waved at him.

He waved back.

Then turned and hoofed it, phone pressed against his ear. 'Start the car – we need to move. *Now.*'

'The game's afoot!'

But not in a good way.

Logan hung up and shoved through the gate, jogged his way around the teachers' Portakabin of Mystery, and out into the crappy car park. Pausing for a moment to check the photo Ralph sent, one last time, just to make sure.

The fourth person sitting at the table – turned in his seat to speak to someone just out of the picture: sharing a joke, going by the rosy cheeks and shining eyes – was wearing a backwards baseball cap and a wife-beater vest with 'COLONEL

Michigan's Gym' printed across the chest above a little silhouette of a boxer.

Mr Muscles.

The poor bastard who'd got himself smeared halfway across Holburn Street only three-and-a-bit hours ago.

Sodding hell indeed...

XXXVI

The world was full of flies. Fat and greasy, glittering blue-and-green. Circling in the air above her. Landing to feed on the darkening bruises and scraped flesh.

The sun still burned, high in the sky, but it was hidden behind the grey corrugated roof now – baking down, making every breath thick and stifling through the leather mask. Blood *whump-whump-whump*ing in her ears.

And Natasha lay on her back, chained to her bloody anchor, blinking up at the flies and the cobwebs.

Nothing to eat. Nothing to drink.

How long could a human being live without water? Prisoners on hunger strike could last for weeks and weeks, but *water* was different.

Some special-forces bloke on the idiot box claimed it takes about three days to die from dehydration. Especially if it's hot. First your kidneys shut down, then your liver, then your brain shrivels, and finally your heart can't cope any more.

Bang: that's you.

Now every breath grated its way down her outback throat, stirring the dust.

At least the smell had faded. Or she'd got used to it.

Taking a crap on the floor wasn't exactly dignified...

Especially with both wrists manacled to the metal collar around her throat. Limping around to the opposite side of her anchor – moving as far away as the chain would allow. Scrabbling about on the hard-packed dirt to get her pants down round her ankles, so she wouldn't get them covered in it, then another complicated humiliating fight to get the things back up again.

Then retreating from the stench, to the end of her tether. Lying on the floor trying not to cry as what she left back there ... baked in the never-ending heat.

Attracting even more flies.

A juddering squeal made the bastards leap into the air, to buzz and drone with their shitty mates.

The rust-streaked wooden door rattled back on its metal runner, letting a harsh slab of sunlight crash into Natasha's prison. Scalding her legs.

Could barely move them out the way.

So she just lay there and groaned instead.

Detective Sergeant Davis took one step inside and recoiled back again, one hand wafting the foetid air from his face. 'Fuck's sake...'

And he was gone again, leaving the door wide open.

As if that did her any good.

He was back – maybe five minutes later? – with a bucket of water, soap suds spilling out over the side. Heaving it over her like he was rinsing a car. Startling the flies.

It was so dry in here that the liquid didn't soak straight into the parched earth, it sat on top of the dusty surface in spark-ling droplets.

She tried to scoop some up, even if it was full of soap, but it just turned to gritty mud in her fingers.

DS Davis's lip curled. 'God, you're disgusting.'

'Water...' The word barely more than a croak. 'Please... *Please...*'

He stared at her. Then squatted down. 'You want *mercy*? After what *you've* done?'

'Please...'

'Did those migrants get any mercy? The ones you burned?' He snorted. 'Oh, maybe you didn't strike the match yourself, but you fanned the flames. Threw petrol on it. All that *hate* and *bile*. You spoon-fed it to whatever slack-jawed Neanderthal did the actual dirty work.'

Natasha reached her muddy fingers towards him. 'Water...'

'Publishing story after story, whipping up the racist wankers till they went out and torched a hotel.' Davis stood. 'THEY BURNED CHILDREN!'

Children? How on earth was that her—

'BITCH!' He lurched forwards – a booted foot slammed into her ribs hard enough to flip her onto her side. A jagged *pop* inside her chest, stabbing carpet tacks into the flesh with every Sahara breath.

She curled up on the gritty floor and the boot hammered into her back. Then again. And again. Sharp explosions slicing through her lungs, crackling out like bloody fireworks as a dry scream howled free.

Then nothing.

No more kicks.

Nothing but the ache and tear of her tortured back.

Davis spat a glob of white onto the earth by her head, breathing hard. 'You've been getting away with it for far too long. Maybe it's *your* turn to burn?'

There was a metallic clang-and-clatter as he picked up the bucket again, then the scuff of boots on the parched floor.

The door squealed and rattled shut.

The flies began to settle again.

And only *then* did Natasha allow herself to cry.

37

The pool car whipped up Anderson Drive, lights flickering. Tufty poked the horn, making the siren *whonk* and *whyeeeeeoooow*, parting the traffic in front of them like a short-arsed Moses.

He was hunched over the wheel, as if that would make the car go faster.

Logan shifted in his seat, one finger in his ear to block out the excess noise, because it was almost impossible to hear Ralph Hay's voice over the phone. 'That's great, thanks.'

'*No problems. Hope it helps.*'

Logan hung up.

Soon as he did, Tufty flipped the switch, setting the siren wailing full time as they shot through the King's Gate Roundabout.

Right.

Logan waved a hand at the backseat. 'Rennie: I need a PNC check on one Spencer Findlater.'

'On it.'

Tufty accelerated up the hill, overtaking a minibus and a Mackie's lorry, eyes firmly fixed on the road. 'Sa-arge, not that I'm not enjoying the wheech, but *why* are we wheeching? I mean, this Spencer bloke hasn't woken up or anything, so it's not like we can question him.'

'Because you heard Randolph Hay – Charles MacGarioch

is hyper-loyal to his friends.' Pointing towards Aberdeen Royal Infirmary. 'Well, his friend's just been in a horrible accident; of course he's going to visit Spencer in hospital.'

'Yeah,' Tufty killed the siren, 'but nobody knows he's *in* hospital except *us*, Sarge. And we only found out thirty seconds ago.'

Logan opened his mouth, then shut it again.

The wee loon had a point.

'Sod.'

'OK, got him.' Rennie poked his head through from the back, reading off his phone. 'Spencer Findlater, nineteen: handful of warnings for getting into fights; almost ended up in a Young Offenders Institution for torching wheelie bins when he was a kid; bunch of shoplifting; all about the same time.' A grunt. 'Guess he didn't handle losing his parents very well.'

'You got an address?'

'Not a million miles away: Four Arnage Court.'

'OK.' Logan gave Tufty a poke. 'You heard the man.'

Arnage Court wrapped around three sides of a nice big rectangle of grass, dotted with trees and some saggy rhododendrons. Someone had been at the road sign, adding a 'C' to the start of the first word.

Three-storey blocks lined the court – each one made up of four or five units, with six flats apiece and a central stairwell. If you were lucky enough to live on the upper floors, you got a balcony of your very own, but the ground floor had access straight out onto a shared garden area. Where all the recycling bins lived.

There were even more bins lined up along the overgrown hedge outside the first block. About twenty feet of them. All black and wheelie and waiting for collection.

Rennie whistled as they drove slowly by. 'That's a *lot* of bins to burn...'

Tufty parked behind a fusty Transit with 'SANDY THE HOOSE BUILDER' on the side and a peeling graphic of a cartoon joiner. 'Think the arson connection's relevant? You know, with the hotel?'

They climbed out into the stifling heat, and Rennie popped on his stupid sunglasses again. 'Maybe, maybe not. Everyone goes through a "burning things" phase. Right?'

Logan stared at him.

Tufty raised both eyebrows.

Rennie pulled his chin in. 'What?' Following Logan through the knee-high gate and up to the front door. 'Oh, come on! It's not just me. *Everybody* does it.'

'Enough.' Logan rang the bell for Flat Four. 'We're about to tell some poor sod their grandchild's been mangled in an accident. Either you're on your best behaviour, or you're waiting in the car. But you're *not* going up there to act the prick, do I make myself clear?'

Maybe a bit close to the bone, but he deserved it.

Pink scoured its way up Rennie's neck. 'Sorry, Guv.'

Should think so too.

A black cat sauntered past, tail in the air, pausing only to mark its territory against a brown garden-waste bin.

A woman tottered along the pavement, coughing and hacking away.

Somewhere in the distance, children were chanting a skipping song:

'*Your dad is a big fat tosser,*
He did a wank upon a saucer,
Your mum cooked it for your tea,
With bogies and a big jobbie!

How many jobbies did you eat?
One, two, three, four...'

Logan was reaching for the bell again when a man's voice growled out of the intercom, old and mushy and distorted by the cheap speaker:

'Yeah, what? ... Erm... What you ... want?'

'Mr Findlater?'

No reply.

Tufty raised his hand. 'You've got to press the button, Sarge.'

'Hmmph.' Logan pressed the button. 'Mr Findlater, can we come in, please? We need to talk...'

'Oh for ... erm ... fuck's sake.'

But he *buzzzzz*ed them in anyway.

Mr Findlater must've been a bear of a man when he was younger, but now he was bent like a paperclip as he shuffled back to his baggy armchair. Most of his hair had gone, leaving a straggly collar-length droop behind, but his face was a thing to scare children – lumpen craggy features and a nose that had been broken so many times it barely counted as a nose any more. His burgundy cardigan had faded to the colour of old blood, and even though it had to be in the mid-thirties outside, he was bundled up in a shirt and jumper too. His brown cords were worn through at the knees, much like the carpet.

There was a second armchair – clearly part of the same set, but a lot less scuffed, dusty, and sagging – and a wooden dining chair, all three facing a small TV. Though it wasn't on.

A bookcase lurked in the corner, stuffed full of record-your-own video tapes. Each one carefully labelled in faded ink along the spine.

Having completed his wobbly journey, the old man collapsed into his seat.

Logan sat on the edge of the wooden chair. 'Mr Findlater, I'm—'

'Frank.' Now that it wasn't filtered through the intercom's wiring, his voice was a low, dark rumble. 'S' Frank.'

'Frank. I'm afraid there's been an accident.'

Blank look.

'Your grandson, Spencer? He was hit by a car this afternoon and he's in hospital.'

'Hospital? ... Man...' He shook his head, blinking, as if trying to get spots out of his vision. 'I've been ... having ... erm ... tests.'

Rennie wandered over to the other armchair, lowering himself into—

'NO!' Mr Findlater was on his feet, no longer folded over and trembling, but huge and broad and powerful. 'DON'T YOU *FUCKIN'* DARE!'

Rennie scrambled out of the seat, before his bum could even touch down. 'OK, it's OK.'

'YOU STAY OUT OF HER CHAIR!'

'OK, I'm sorry!' Hands up in surrender. 'Won't go near it. See? Promise.' He backed away from the seat.

'*Nobody* sits there.' Glowering at the empty space.

As the anger faded, so did Mr Findlater – the towering monster shrinking until only the trembling old man remained.

He juddered his way back into his own chair.

Well, that was... Yeah.

Logan cleared his throat. 'Mr ... Frank, is there anyone we can call? A carer, or somebody?'

'Spencer takes ... Spencer's my grandson. ... He takes care of me.'

'But Spencer's in *hospital*, Frank.'

A frown crumpled that monolith brow. 'I … erm … I been in hospital. … They ran … tests.'

'Tell you what, Frank, why don't I make you a nice cup of tea?' Logan stood. 'Would you like a tea?'

But Mr Findlater seemed to have drifted away, squinting at the blank TV instead, as if something was already playing there.

'Right.' Heading for the living-room door.

Tufty scurried over. 'I'll get the teas in, if you like?' Playing the good sidekick.

'You stay here and keep an eye on Sergeant Rennie. Just in case.' Then Logan slipped out into the hall.

It was an awkward, fat 'L' shape, with a mess of eight doors leading off.

The first one opened on a cupboard full of dusty bed linen.

The second revealed a kitchen that was more like a corridor, lined with grunky, old-fashioned cupboards and cabinets.

Logan closed the door and tried again: another cupboard, full of boxed crap this time.

Number four led out onto the balcony, where a knackered bicycle slowly decomposed, along with a couple of clothes horses and some tins of paint. But then they'd squeezed past those when they'd come through the door at the far end, from the stairwell. So that was no use.

Fifth: a bathroom, with an ancient, stained, salmon-pink suite and peeling lino floor.

Which left two to try.

Eenie, meenie…

Logan tried the one furthest away: an old-fashioned bedroom with floral pillows-and-bedspread that looked as if they hadn't been washed in a while, and a view out over the rear green.

Which left door number eight.

Logan stepped into a small bedroom, that clearly belonged to a *much* younger person.

Like Charles MacGarioch and Andrew Shaw, Spencer Findlater had papered his walls with posters, but instead of films, soft-porn popstars, and computer games, he'd gone with oiled-up bodybuilders – men flexing away in their swimming trunks, showing off their veiny muscles and leathery tans.

A collection of free weights were neatly stacked beneath the window. The single bed wore an old *Transformers* duvet cover.

But what was *most* striking about the place were the heaps and heaps and heaps of dirty-big tubs of whey protein. Each one large enough to hold a child's severed head.

There had to be at least two hundred of them in here. Lots of different brands, most still in their shrink-wrapped pack-of-six cases – complete with delivery notes.

Logan snapped on a pair of gloves, hefted a multi-pack off the nearest stack, and turned it over to read the delivery address.

It was the sports shop on Thistle Street – the one getting its windows replaced this afternoon.

Hmmm...

Bet every delivery note in here would turn out to be from a sports shop that'd been broken into.

Which at least solved that one...

Logan opened the built-in wardrobe and searched through the clothes. Other than yet more tubs of whey protein, stashed under piles of athletic leisure wear – most of which still had the security tags attached – there was nothing exciting.

So he tried the mattress instead.

Levering it up from the bed frame exposed a bunch of magazines with titles like *Muscle Mag* and *Flex* and *UK Beef*. Which *sounded* like gay porn, but a quick rifle through proved

323

that although they *were* full of oiled-up men in their pants, it was all about bodybuilding.

And yeah, teenaged boys were known to have a one-track mind, but this was ridiculous.

Just to be safe, Logan knelt on Optimus Prime's face and peeled back the posters above the bed. But there were no hidden photos, or anything else. Just a couple of startled spiders.

He checked under the bed instead.

Ooh, a holdall.

That looked a bit more promising.

Logan pulled the thing out and unzipped it.

A black tracksuit sat on the top. And when Logan lifted it out, there was a hammer, a pair of black trainers with little sparkling cubes of broken glass embedded in their treads, and a pair of black leather gloves. All carrying a faint … unleaded smell.

Sod.

OK.

He put everything back where he'd found it, zipped the holdall up again, and slid it under the bed.

Stood.

Snapped off his gloves and pocketed them. Before retreating from Spencer Findlater's bedroom and closing the door behind him.

Logan eased back into the living room, carrying a mug of tea and a digestive biscuit on a wee plate.

Someone had turned the TV on, and now Tufty, Rennie, and Mr Findlater sat there, watching some old boxing match. Well, Mr Findlater and Tufty were sitting – the old man in his sagging armchair, the wee loon on the dining-room chair – while

Rennie stood off to one side. Clearly not wanting to risk another shouting-at.

The picture was a bit grainy, and there was a stripe down one side, but that didn't seem to bother them as two huge men battered the living crap out of each other in the ring.

Mr Findlater's shoulders twitched in time with every punch thrown by the guy in the red shorts.

Rennie looked up from the screen. Reaching for the mug in Logan's hand. 'Cheers, Guv.'

'Not *for* you.'

'Oh…' The idiot drooped for a second, then perked right up again. 'Anyway, you'll never guess: but we're in the company of *genuine* sporting greatness. This,' Rennie put on an OTT announcer's voice and shoogled both hands towards their host, 'is the *one*, the *only*: Francis "Big Frank" *Findlaterrrrrrrrrrr*!'

Never heard of him.

Logan handed 'Big Frank' the mug and the old man took it without moving his eyes from the screen.

'Thought I recognised the name when we came in, but then I saw all the videos.' Rennie hooked a thumb at the bookcase. 'Big Frank had golden gloves, man. He could put a guy *twice* his size on his arse in three rounds. Biff, bang, crash, wallop!'

Logan hunkered down beside Mr Findlater's armchair. 'Frank, do you know where Spencer was on Sunday night, Monday morning? Can you remember for me?'

Nothing. Not even a frown.

'Course it all went south after the Roxborough fight. Roxborough was aye a cheating bastard, though. Got a six-month ban for what he did, but poor Frank never fought again.'

'Frank? Where was Spencer on Sunday night? Was he out?'

Something flickered inside Mr Findlater and he resurfaced from the boxing ring. 'Spencer's in hospital. … He's… Police came round … erm … came round and told me … Spencer's in hospital.' His forehead furrowed. 'They do all these … tests…'

Logan patted his arm. 'I know, Frank. I'm sorry.'

And then he was gone again.

38

'...yeah, no: anonymous tip-off.' Logan paced the grass square, outside Big Frank's building – from a wilting tree to a drooping rhododendron and back again. Lying to his superior officer. 'Someone thinks they saw Spencer Findlater coming out of Capercaillie Sports on George Street after the break-in.'

Which *might*'ve been true.

Who could tell?

Nearly nine o'clock, and the sun was sinking towards the horizon, painting everything with a warm golden-syrup glow. Making the air a bit … sticky.

Rennie and Tufty loitered by the pool car, forbidden to come any closer so they had plausible deniability if it ever came out that Logan had fiddled the facts slightly.

Finally, Chief Superintendent Pine came to a decision: *'All right, I'll get you a search warrant for Findlater's flat.'*

'Thanks, Boss. And he's one of Charles MacGarioch's mates, so it might be an idea to test anything they find for accelerants too.' Keeping it nice and casual, as if he'd just thought of it. 'Belt and braces.'

A sigh rattled down the phone. *'Anything else while I've got my chequebook out?'*

'Now you mention it...' He stopped pacing and looked up at Flat Four. 'With Spencer in hospital, there's no one to look after his grandad, and he won't last the week if we leave him on his own. He'll either starve to death or burn the house down.'

'You want me to sort out a care package at five to nine, on a Wednesday night? Yes, thanks for that.' There was an ominous pause. *'Speaking of Charles MacGarioch...?'*

'Still working on it, Boss.' Back to pacing again.

'And while I've got you, would you care to explain why I've got three officers sitting on their thumbs in Seaton Park, playing I Spy?'

'Ah...' The truth *probably* wasn't the best option in this case either. Not unless he wanted Pine to pull the op, because 'they're probably bored' didn't exactly make his team sound very professional. 'Well, of course, as you know... Erm...' Why on earth did Spudgun let them play games on a stakeout? Worse: why did he let senior bloody management catch them doing it?

Surely there had to be a...

Aha!

'As you *know*, Boss: I Spy is a recommended attention-centric activity for ICSOs like this. Boredom leads to a lack of focus – people start missing things – but playing *I Spy* requires constant observation and evaluation of your surroundings, which is what they're actually there to do in the first place. Ma-am.'

That sounded believable, didn't it?

'ICSO?'

'Impromptu Covert Surveillance Operation.'

'I see...' Her voice took on a vindictive little smile. *'Very convincing. I look forward to you giving a presentation on that at our next Divisional Training Management Meeting.'*

Sod...

Logan buried a groan. 'Yes, Boss.'

'What happens if Charles MacGarioch doesn't show up at your ICSO? I haven't got enough officers as it is, without wasting resources on a red herring.' She huffed out a breath. *'I'm*

pretty sure half the buggers off on the sick are swinging the lead – pretending they've got the plague, so they don't have to do any sodding work. Well, maybe not half, but a good twenty percent, anyway. The point is: I can't afford to have three of the officers I do have tied up all night on a no-show.'

'Like you say: "What choice do we have?" If he turns up and we're not there to catch him, we're screwed.'

Logan wandered back towards the car while she considered that.

He'd made it as far as the road, before Pine rejoined the conversation:

'Sergeant Moore and his team have all been on since zero-seven-hundred. Your op can run till ten, then you need to swap them out for other officers. Everyone's running on fumes as it is.'

Well, that went better than expected.

'I think I can—'

'But you're only getting two nightshift bodies. And I want everyone in for Morning Prayers! That includes you.'

Suppose it was better than nothing.

'Yes, Boss.'

'Which means you clock off at ten as well. No one's handing out Hero Points for running yourself into the ground.'

He checked his watch. Just over an hour to go, before home-time. 'Thanks, Boss.'

'Now, if you'll excuse me, I've got a care package to organise...'

She hung up, and Logan sagged for a moment.

Could've been worse.

Right: he straightened up and marched across the road.

Tufty jingled the car keys. 'Where to, Sarge?'

Logan opened the passenger door. 'ARI – let's go pay Big Frank's grandson a visit.'

'Seriously?' Rennie pulled a face. 'But he's *unconscious*, Guv, it's—'

'Then you can stay here, or walk back to the station if you like?'

The idiot scrambled into the back.

'Thought so.'

The Critical Care Unit smelled of disinfectant, drain cleaner, and despair. Having all the blinds drawn didn't help – shutting out the sinking sun, and replacing every bit of natural light with dimmed LED bulbs.

The muffled sound of trainers on the terrazzo floor squeaked out under the part-glazed door to Ward 201, bringing with them the *whirr* and *bleep* and *hissss* of machinery designed to keep the hospital's most vulnerable patients alive.

Rennie drooped against the corridor wall, fiddling on his phone, while Logan waited by the locked door for the doctor to slouch over here and let them in.

Inside, a small cluster of beds sat in the middle of the room, fanning out in a circle. Each one had about three times the amount of space you'd get anywhere else in the hospital – presumably to make it easier for a crash team to surround the patient – with banks of equipment and high-tech screens and computers on arms and all that whizzy life-saving stuff. A handful of private booths ran around the outside, not quite as Robocop, but still advanced compared to the normal wards.

There were a lot more nurses in attendance too, bustling about between the beds, while their charges lay flat on their backs, zonked on sedatives, and wired up to all that whirring, bleeping, hissing kit.

The doctor paused to check some poor sod's notes, then dragged her pink Crocs over to the door. With the facemask and surgical cap on, there wasn't much of her on show, just a pair of eyes with dark bags underneath, and a few wisps of brown curly hair that had escaped from its prison. Blue scrubs and rumpled PPE.

Logan waved through the glazed partition, but she just glowered back, pointed at her own mask, then jabbed a finger towards the door.

Following the pointing digit led to a wall-mounted dispenser full of individually wrapped N95 masks.

He plucked two from the stack and handed one to Rennie.

The doctor waited till they were both masked-up before opening the door and slipping out into the corridor. Her voice sounded as if it had just run a marathon, with a fridge-freezer strapped to its back. 'This better be important.'

'Dr Emslie?' Logan flashed his warrant card. 'Detective Chief Inspector McRae: we're here about Spencer Findlater.'

She glanced back at the ward. 'He's only just out of surgery, and to be honest, it's eighty-twenty he doesn't make it.'

Rennie snorted. 'You're kidding.'

Dr Emslie squared her shoulders. 'You want a list of what's *broken*, Sergeant? Cos we'll be here for a while. Then there's the list of what's ruptured, torn, detached, perforated, and *leaking*.' Giving him a scowl. 'You smash two tons of metal into someone, hurl them through the air like a rag doll, and whack them against tarmac *at speed*, and see how optimistic you feel.'

Pink flushed across Rennie's ears, making them glow. 'Was only thirty miles an hour.'

'Want to try it? We can go out to the car park, right now, and flag down the nearest flatbed truck!'

Logan raised his hands. 'OK, OK, let's just turn the heat down a bit.' Poking Rennie. 'You: go wait outside.'

A wee grumbling mumble sounded behind Rennie's mask, then off he flounced. With all the grace of a sulky teenager.

Dr Emslie glared at his departing back.

'Sorry about that.' Logan forced a smile. 'Been a long week.'

'Oh, please: *do* tell me about it.' She gave herself a wee shake. 'Spencer Findlater's been placed in a medically induced coma. So if you're planning on interviewing, or arresting him anytime soon – you're shit out of luck.'

Bit harsh.

'Can I see him?'

'No you *can't* bloody see him! What do you think this is: a petting zoo? They're not exhibits, they're human beings.'

'But—'

'He's – just – out – of – *surgery*!' The glare returned. 'And how do I know you're not asymptomatic? How do I know you're not going to spread Covid all over my ward, wiping out half the unfortunate bastards in there?'

'But—'

'Cos that's what it is, OK? It isn't "the flu", or "the sniffles", or "the Lurgie", or "Captain Trips", it's Covid! *That's* why half the bloody city's off sick.' Getting louder. 'Just because every wanker, newspaper, and politician wants to pretend it's magically gone away, that doesn't make it happen!'

'OK...' Logan backed off a couple of paces. 'Look: Spencer might get a visitor. If he does, I need you to call us *immediately*.' Digging out his phone and bringing up the photo of Charles MacGarioch and his fellow orphans in the pub. Zooming in on Charles's face till it filled the screen.

'He dangerous?'

'Hard to say.'

Dr Emslie rolled her eyes. 'Well, that *is* helpful. Thank you *so* much.' She produced her own phone with a long-suffering sigh. 'Send me a copy and I'll get Marilyn to print out some posters.'

It took a couple of goes, but eventually they got the image transferred.

Logan put his mobile away. 'Officers on-site will keep an eye out too, but with all these entrances...?'

'Because my job isn't difficult enough?' She threw a sharp, stabbing gesture at the ward door. 'I've got a skeleton staff, full beds, and a bunch of people already calling in sick for tomorrow. Aberdeen's like a *bloody plague pit*...' On either side of the mask, her jaw muscles clenched. A deep breath and Dr Emslie shook her head, then looked away. 'Fine: we'll shout if we see him.' Her arm came up, pointing away down the corridor. 'Now, if you wouldn't mind sodding off – I've got a bunch of dying people to save.'

She turned to go.

Then stopped.

'And don't you *dare* come back here without a mask on!'

And with that jolly farewell, Dr Emslie slapped her pass against the security reader and shoved back into the ward. Pulling the door shut behind her, in case Logan, or his germs, tried to follow.

He lowered his voice to a whisper. 'And a merry Christmas to you too.'

Then marched off towards the exit, taking his cooties with him.

39

In an ideal world, the biggest hospital in the northeast of Scotland would've had a fancy front entrance. Something that spoke of Aberdeen's position as the energy capital of Europe. Something that reflected all the oil money that had flowed through the city since the seventies. Something that gave a little nod to the billions of pounds of tax revenue generated for the UK Treasury.

But it was, to be honest, a bit of a shithole – more like the pedestrian entrance to an underground car park, with a pair of sliding doors surrounded by an array of half-arsed signs.

Auld mannies and wifies were lined up in the fading light, still wearing their baffies and dressing gowns, grimly puffing on cigarette after cigarette, in bloody-minded defiance of all the posters telling them not to.

Back in the day, there'd been a nice big overhang to shelter beneath and enjoy your fag out of the wind and snow and rain. But the Health Trust had filled it all in, leaving the patients with nowhere to stand and indulge their vices but outside in the open air. And it *still* wasn't enough to deter these Wrinkled Priests and Craggy Priestesses of Sainted Lady Nicotine.

Logan stepped out into the sunlight, phone to his ear, waiting for Doreen to pick up.

Her voice groaned out of the speaker. *'If you're calling to make my life even more depressing: don't, OK? The only thing keeping me upright is visions of a phenomenally large G-and-T when I get home. With lots and lots and* lots *of ice.'*

He headed for the multistorey opposite – a weird, elongated-OXO-cube of a thing, wrapped in sheets of holey metal. 'No sign of Charles MacGarioch?'

'Guv, I swear to God, if we do find his body, I'm going to kick the crap out of it before we call anyone.'

Bit unprofessional. But understandable.

'How far you got to go?'

'Dunno – maybe a quarter mile? We're well past the bridge anyway.' A knackered sigh. *'Sun's going down: it's all long blue shadows and a zillion midges out here. Going to be dangerous if we keep going much longer. And I know it's going to be twilight till eleven, but that's sod-all use for searching.'* Doreen gave a little sob. *'Just want to pour the sweat out of my wellies, lie down, and cry…'*

'OK – Give it another twenty minutes, then head back to the station. We're calling it quits at ten, today.'

'I'm too tired and squelchy to celebrate.'

Logan hurried across the road. 'Just do me a favour and get someone to have a quick march along the last bit of riverbank, OK? In case his body's just lying about.'

'He's not here, Guv. You've got dog walkers crawling over every bit of this … what is it, an estuary? Where the beach-and-all-that-bollocks starts? If he was here, they'd have found him by now.'

Yeah, she was probably right.

Biohazard sounded as if he was about to pop an aneurism. *'And then there's that* stupid *woman in the bikini, wanging on about finding the body like it's a sodding marketing opportunity! You name a broadcaster: she's had a bash at selling them her story.'*

The lift dinged, and Logan stepped out onto the rooftop level of the hospital car park. Which wasn't *quite* as tall as the big number thirteen painted on the wall made it sound, given each 'floor' was only half the OXO cube's width, and a half-step above the one before. But it was still high enough to have a great view out across the city and off to the sea, where a row of bright-orange supply ships glowed against the greying water. A flash of pale pink marked distant wind turbines, hanging motionless on the horizon, caught by the sinking sun. Though you did have to peer through the holes in the tinfoil wrapper to see them.

'*Christ's sake: she makes her money doing soft porn videos for sadwanks! And now we're supposed to pretend she's some sort of hard-hitting journalist? Kate Adie in a frigging thong?*'

Nearly half nine, and this bit of the car park was deserted, except for the pool car. Which Tufty had parked in the furthest corner from the lifts, for some stupid reason.

Rennie paced up and down in the distance, on the phone to someone. Rubbing his forehead and making soothing noises, so probably getting a telling-off.

The wee loon, on the other hand, had his arms out like a tightrope walker, wobbling his way along the edge of the inner parking spaces. Keeping himself 'busy'.

'*They interviewed her on the BBC, Guv!*'

'Have you tried asking her nicely to stop?'

'*Oh,* apparently *her fans have a right to know all about it. She even took video. Of the remains!*'

'So confiscate her phone. It's evidence in an ongoing murder investigation.'

'*I did. She and her halfwit boyfriend already uploaded a "report" to YouTube before they even called us. In her bikini!*' Biohazard made a noise like a ruptured coffee machine. '*We're trying to get it taken down, but you know what that's like.*'

'Just … do what you can, OK?'

Logan hung up and strolled across the rooftop level. The

sun might've been skimming the horizon, but the black surface of the parking bays radiated heat up his trouser legs.

Tufty nodded as he approached. 'Sarge.'

'This what passes for "being productive" these days?'

The daft wee sod tapped his own forehead, still wobbling along the white line. Indulging in a faux-French accent that probably counted as a hate crime: 'Zee leetle grey cells, they are a-working 'ard, monsieur Lestrade.'

'Lestrade was *Sherlock Holmes*, not Poirot, you reticulated Clanger.' Logan cupped his hands into a makeshift loud-hailer and bellowed a 'HOY!' across the car park. 'WE'RE LEAVING!'

Over by the ramp down to the next level, Rennie waved. Ending his call before hurrying back to the car.

Tufty climbed in behind the wheel and started her up. 'Where to avec les automobile, monsieur?'

Good question.

Logan puffed out his cheeks, and sank into the passenger seat. 'Back to the ranch. We've got half an hour till home time, and I still need to file a report on Spencer Findlater's accident.'

Rennie bundled himself into the back. 'Did you say "home time"? Are we getting home? Cos Emma would very much like that.' Checking his watch. 'Better yet, Donna, Lola, and Charlize will be in bed: we can veg in front of the telly for a change.' Rennie closed his eyes, an expression of bliss on his silly face. 'Eating ice cream in our pants...'

Now, there was an image to put you off your Cornetto.

By the time the pool car emerged from the multistorey car park, the road was shrouded in gloom. Sunlight might still be skimming the top layers, but it had abandoned the ground to evening's muggy grasp.

They wended their way around the half-empty staff car park, past various ugly grey lumps of Aberdeen Royal Infirmary outbuildings, and off the hospital estate. Heading back towards the centre of town.

Not exactly the prettiest bit of the city, but it could be worse. Especially if you liked grey.

Things got a bit greener, as they approached the junction with Argyle Place and Argyle Crescent. Then the pool car popped across the lights, and they were surrounded by it: Victoria Park on the right, Westburn Park on the left. Trees overhanging the road on both sides, shadows lengthening beneath them.

Something was going on in Westburn Park – lights flickering and strobing in the growing gloom.

Logan rolled down his window and the sound of Wurlitzer music whumped through the sticky evening air, accompanied by the clatter-whoosh of funfair rides and the happy screams and cries of the people playing on them.

A mini-rollercoaster was visible through the trees, along with waltzers, spinny-swingy things, dodgems, coconut shies and other entertainments of dubious honesty.

And, rising above it all, the red-white-and-blue stripes of a big top, lit up from the inside like an alien spaceship.

Happy families wandered about, eating candyfloss and chips. Completely unfazed by all the death and destruction in the world. Not worrying about asylum seekers trapped in a burning building, or young men with their heads caved in, or rape and trauma and abuse and war and famine and dying alone with dementia…

'…Sarge?'

Logan blinked.

OK.

Tufty had obviously just asked him a question, but no idea what it was.

The wee loon frowned across the car at him. 'You OK?'

'Sorry. Miles away.'

'I did has an scheduling query: that MAPPA meeting isn't till nine thirty, so do you want to visit the last of Charles MacGarioch's friends first thing tomorrow, before it kicks off?'

'Might as well. Unless you've got a cunning plan to get me out of the thing?' Hopefully... But going by the expression on Tufty's face, probably not. 'Never mind.'

The glowing big top faded in Logan's wing mirror, swallowed by trees. He huffed out a long breath. 'Being a police officer is a little bit like joining the circus. When you're a probationer, you're on the dodgems – yeah, you take a bashing, but it's *exciting*. Thrilling, even. Then you're a PC and riding the rollercoaster: you've got no control over speed or direction, it's all ups and downs, but it still feels as if you're going somewhere. And maybe you start to think: one day I'm going to ride the Ferris wheel and I'll finally see the big picture. Or maybe I'll even get to be Ringmaster, controlling the whole show...'

Westburn Road turned into Hutcheon Street, with its terraced flats on one side and the decaying carcasses of derelict factories on the other.

'But what *actually* happens when you get promoted, is they lock you in the coconut shy and hurl meetings at you till you fall off your perch.' Logan sniffed. 'The only constant is: you're always surrounded by bloody clowns.'

XL

Colin Miller (56) had a wee sip of coffee – his own blend of Guatemalan, Kenyan, and Mexican beans, cos it didn't hurt to be a bit classy now and then – wandered across the patio, and frowned out at the garden.

A cluster of scarlet roses glowed against the dark-green foliage, like blood spatter...

Patches puffled along the edge of a border, snuffling away, stubby tail wagging as she explored the same old familiar world with the kind of excitement only a springer spaniel could muster.

The sky still glowed a ghostly blue, but Mr Sun had sodded off for the day, leaving only the solar-powered lights to illuminate their massive garden.

Quite proud of that, actually. Took a lot of work to get the place looking this good. And it wasn't easy having green fingers when you were missing great chunks off four of the buggers.

Colin tightened his grip on the mug, black leather gloves squeaking on the pale china.

They didn't really go with the old Pink Floyd T-shirt and chinos, but you sort of got used to them. In the end.

There was a *clunk*, and Professor Isobel McAllister (53) emerged through the French doors from the kitchen. Glass of Merlot in one hand, casual but stylish in a burgundy short-sleeve

340

V-neck dress. Hair tucked behind her ears. Wearing the little square glasses she only used at home. Flip-flops were a bit of a sartorial low point, but Isobel was still the most beautiful woman in the whole frigging world, so you could excuse the occasional faux pas.

A few more creases bloomed between her eyebrows. 'You're not out here smoking those stinky cigars again, are you?'

He went back to frowning at the roses. 'Ever wonder why you bother?'

'Because they're bad for you. Always trust a pathologist when they say you should stop doing something – we've seen enough people's innards to know what we're talking about.' She took a sip of wine, then transferred the glass to her other hand and slipped her naked fingers between his gloved ones.

'No' quite what I meant.' Sigh. 'Kinda get the feeling our new owner's screwing with me. Dangling the job over my head, you know? "Here's a meeting to see if you still get to work here, or if you're out on your arse like all your mates. Only I'm no' gonnae turn up for it, *or* reschedule. Instead you can bloody sweat."' The coffee turned bitter in his mouth. 'Natash Aga-frigging-pova. The *Scottish Daily Post* used to be a decent paper, till she got her hands on it – now it's nothing but a right-wing tabloid shite-rag, obsessed with fuckin' celebrities and fearmongering and "the world's full of paedos and foreigners and everything you don't like is *woke*..."' He dumped his mug on the patio table. 'Now she's gonna do the same with the *Examiner*. I seen the mock-ups. And I'm expected to *beg* for my job?'

Isobel pouted for a moment. 'Do you want me to be honest, or supportive?'

He smiled. 'Supportive?'

'I'm sure this is just a misunderstanding, and they'll sort it out tomorrow.'

Aye, maybe...

'And honest?'

'I don't normally approve of rough language, but: screw them.' Another sip of wine. 'You used to love working there and now you hate it. So quit. Tell them to fashion their job into a cylinder and insert it rectally – with force. And no lubrication.'

He winked. 'I love it when you talk dirty.'

'You could write that book you've been droning on about for years.'

'I don't *drone*. I ponder and muse, cogitate and deliberate, contemplate and—'

'Well, why not? *Are* you happy?'

Working with children pretending to be journalists, churning out tweets and blogposts and *'you won't believe what these film-stars look like now!'*, chasing deadlines, never writing about the things that really matter...

Was he happy?

'No.'

Isobel nodded. 'There you go, then.' And as if that settled everything, she spun around – making her skirt flare, showing off a bit of leg – and headed inside again, leaving him out here in the gloom, alone.

'Aye.' He picked up his half-empty mug. 'There I go.'

End of an era.

No more newspapers for Ace Reporter Colin Miller...

Or maybe the mug was half full?

Colin nodded, then took Schrödinger's mug back into the kitchen.

No Isobel – moved on to another part of the house, leaving her empty wine glass behind.

Downlighters sparkled off their swanky high-end gadgets, and the kind of coffee machine you normally only saw in posh restaurants. Lots of warm wood and terracotta walls, a marble worktop imported all the way from Tuscany. Photos of the family holidays, Rosie (12) getting her brown belt in karate, Alfie (10)'s first violin recital, and dropping Sean (19) off at university.

See, that was your metaphor, right there: one day your wee boy's taking his first steps, the next he's away studying medicine in Edinburgh. Things change.

Maybe it was time *he* changed too.

Colin rinsed his mug and Isobel's glass, stuck them in the dishwasher, then grabbed his car keys from the drawer.

Aye: he *could* just hand in his notice tomorrow, but where was the fun in that? Going by Agapova's record, she'd probably be 'working from home' again, anyway. And if you're gonnae tell someone to roll their job sideways and stick it up their arse, you want to do it to their face.

Colin stuck his head out into the hall. 'I'm just heading out for a bit. Go stick a bottle of fizz on ice – when I get back, we're celebrating!'

Colin turned his BMW M2 Coupé – red as the roses, with active M differential, rear-wheel drive, and TwinPower turbo inline six-cylinder engine – onto the driveway outside Natasha Agapova's house.

A true-crime podcast rumbled out of the car's Harman Kardon fourteen-speaker sound system, keeping him company on the journey out here.

'*...and when we opened the second trench, there were the missing village children: twenty-two dead little bodies, all lined up in a row, with their heads pointing towards the chancel, their feet bound in silver chains, and iron stakes driven straight through their sternums.*'

'*Wow. Not their hearts? Cos you'd think it would be their hearts.*'

'*Well, you see that's the* fascinating *thing about the Church of Our Lady and Saint Peter—*'

He switched it off.

Had to admit, Agapova's house was bigger than theirs. But where Colin and Isobel had a stylish Georgian sandstone mansion, *this* was a modern kit-build with all the class of a drunken jakey. Couldn't be more than a couple years old, set in a big garden that sloped down to some woods.

Aye, it might've been big, but the garden was pish. No thought put into the planting at all.

It was one of a small cluster of equally fancy-but-styleless properties a few miles out past Peterculter. An enclave for captains of industry, movers and shakers, and the nouveau riche glitterati.

AKA: pricks.

He followed the snaking driveway up to the house, with its two-storey floor-to-ceiling glazed entrance hall, and parked right outside.

No sign of any other cars, but there was a double garage bolted onto the side, so the Rolls and Ferrari were probably safely locked away in case the squirrels got at them.

Kinda looked like every light in the house was on, blazing out into the dark, but the only figure visible belonged to a *massive* teddy bear, dressed like an offshore worker in boots, gloves, T-shirt, and hard hat.

Cos editors were weird.

Colin climbed out, thunked the car door shut, and went to shoot his cuffs... Only he didn't have any, cos he was wearing a T-shirt.

Buggering hell.

Should've changed into a suit and tie – pulled on the full armour. Given Natasha Bloody Agapova a glimpse of what she'd thrown away with her stupid power games.

Ah well: too late for that, now.

He swaggered over to her front door and thumbed the bell.

The overture to Mozart's *Le Nozze Di Figaro* blared out, somewhere inside the house.

Talk about *pretentious*. *'Ooh, look at me, a* bing-bong *isn't classy enough!'*

The thirty-second clip played itself out, and silence returned.

Off in the woods, a deer barked – like a cross between a grunt and a belch.

And there was *still* no sign of Agapova, tripping downstairs to answer the sodding door.

Well, he hadn't come all the way out here to just go home again without telling her where to shove her crappy job.

He gave the bell another go, and Mozart started up again.

Still no answer.

Right: time to go old-school.

He raised a hand to knock. But perhaps a bit of *drama* wouldn't go amiss? So hammered on the thing with his fist instead...

It swung open on the first thump. Never mind locked, it wasn't even *latched*.

'Hello?' He shoved the door all the way. 'HOY! AGAPOVA!'

Nothing.

That great-big teddy bear stared at him with its dead button eyes.

Colin stepped across the threshold into the double-height hallway. The cold-blue glow of twilight wasn't bright enough to compete with the LED spotlights in here, turning the front wall of glass into a mirror.

'HELLO?'

Still nothing.

He pulled off his left glove, revealing a hand truncated by two joints on his pinkie, and one on his ring finger. Leaving shiny stubs behind, lightly puckered where the skin was stitched back together.

Colin stuck the tip of his thumb and index finger in his gob and let loose a shrill, deafening whistle.

Then stood there as the house swallowed it.

Aye, something wasn't right here.

The hall sideboard played host to a couple of oversized fancy vases – maybe African, going by the patterns worked into the glaze? – but another two lay broken on the floor, pieces scattered out across the pale carpet.

And in between the shattered curls of pottery, lurked dark-red smears and droplets, staining the deep pile. A smudged handprint on the sideboard. Another on the wall.

Shite.

The blood was already mahogany coloured, each individual drip: dry and shiny as a little beetle, so probably not fresh. But Colin gave them a wide berth as he tiptoed further into the room.

'MRS AGAPOVA? ARE YOU ALL RIGHT? HELLO?'

A pair of high heels sat cock-ended by the sideboard. Keys in the bowl. One earring beside it – the other glittering away on the carpet.

Aye, not the kind of place to be wandering about bare handed.

He pulled his glove back on, working both stubs back into place against the prosthetic extensions, and climbed the stairs. Not touching anything.

At the top, the landing turned into a corridor, stretching away to either side, with a bunch of closed doors to explore.

After all, the paper's new owner could be hurt, right? Lying on the floor unconscious, somewhere. Maybe even dead.

Now *that* would make a great story.

So, he poked his head into each and every room: kid's bedroom that smelled as if they still pished the bed; box room; a semi-furnished bedroom; then the main bedroom with its en suite and walk-in closet. The bed was made, no deid body decomposing beneath the duvet or in the bath.

There wasn't a corpse in the big family bathroom either, which just left the one door, at the far end of the corridor.

It opened on a large home office, lined with bookshelves – though they were empty, except for a couple of Aberdeen guidebooks and a thin layer of dust.

An Apple desktop, laptop, and iPad were perched on the desk in their respective stands, along with what looked like one of those combi fax-scanner-printer jobs. And an answering machine with a flashing red light on it.

Nice: old-school.

And if there was one thing a red-blooded journalist couldn't resist, it was an answering machine.

Colin dug out his phone and pulled up the audio-memo app. Set it recording. Then pressed 'PLAY' on the answering machine.

An electronic voice boomed out into the silent house: 'YOU HAVE ... TWENTY-SIX ... NEW MESSAGES AND ... FOUR ... SAVED MESSAGES.' A click. 'MESSAGE TWENTY-SIX:'

Great, it was one of those stupid ones that played everything in reverse order – newest first.

A posh Glasgow accent replaced the robot. '*Tasha? We still on for Winetastic Friday? I got some serious gossip about* You Know Who *– you're going to just* scream *it's so delicious. OK: love you, bye!*'

'END OF MESSAGE. MESSAGE TWENTY-FIVE:'

'*Erm ... hello?*' It was that stripy-jumpered idiot from the Art Department. '*Miss Agapova? It's Louis Garfield, you asked me to do some redesigns on the masthead and layout and I just sort of wondered if you'd be coming into the office anytime to see—'*

Colin poked '←' a few times, skipping back through the messages.

'MESSAGE NINETEEN:'

A cough spluttered out of the speaker, followed by a man's voice. Stuffed full of forced cheer. *'Hi, Natasha? Hi. It's Frank Abercrombie again, giving you a wee tootle back to see if you'd be interested in doing some sort of feature on* Claire. *I really think this is going to be her year. Today: MSP for Aberdeen South and Kincardineshire, but tomorrow: top cabinet post, or even party leader! And I think your paper is perfectly positioned to give Team Fordyce the momentum it needs to—'*

Poke, poke, poke, poke, poke.

'MESSAGE FOURTEEN:'

A plummy English voice. *'You can't keep avoiding me for ever, Natasha. The lawyers say I'm entitled to two weekends a month: you sent her away to that bloody school in Switzerland on purpose! I want to see my daughter!'*

'END OF MESSAGE. MESSAGE THIRTEEN:'

'Are you embarrassed by the state of your doors and windows? Well, let the Auchterturra Glazing Company—'

Poke, poke, poke, poke, poke, poke, poke.

'MESSAGE SIX:'

This one was a slick tit of a man, full of himself and a bit drunk. *'Hey, Natasha? Hi: it's me. I know it's not cool or anything, calling so soon, but why play games? I really liked spending time with you at the ball tonight and I'm pretty sure you had fun too, my little Cinderella.'* You could almost hear the arsehole waggling his head as he said it. *'So let's do it again yeah? How about this weekend? Did I tell you I have a yacht? How cool is that? Give me a call and we'll take her for a spin – picnic on deck, maybe a little champagne, and see what happens next...?'* Leaving a suggestive wee pause. *'Catch you later.'*

Surprised he didn't throw a *'ciao'* in at the end, there.

'END OF MESSAGE. MESSAGE FIVE:'

A man's voice. Hard. Angry. *'Karma comes in like a hurricane,* Bitch, *and it's going to blow your house of lies right down. See you tonight!'*

'END OF MESSAGE. MESSAGE FOUR:'

Then a little girl on the verge of tears. *'Mum? Mum, pick up, OK? Please? I hate it here – they don't even speak English, and it's—'*

Colin poked the '→' button this time.

'MESSAGE FIVE:'

'Karma comes in like a hurricane, Bitch, *and it's going to blow your house of lies right down. See you tonight!'*

'END OF MESSAGE. MESSAGE—'

He hit pause.

Then sat back and blinked at the machine.

Aye, it *could* be nothing, but it'd be a massive sodding coincidence if his new boss went missing, leaving blood all over her downstairs hall, right after a threatening message appeared on her answering machine.

Colin stopped his phone recording. Puffed out his cheeks. Then dialled nine-nine-nine.

41

Half the lights were off, turning the open-plan office into an abandoned labyrinth of cubicles.

Over in the far corner, someone coughed and hacked away, but other than that? Nightshift had succumbed to the lurgie just like everyone else.

But at least it was quiet.

Logan sat at his desk, surrounded by piles and piles of inherited paperwork, drinking horrible coffee from the machine, and picking away at a report on his steam-and-hamster-powered computer.

So much for going home at ten. It was gone eleven now, and still no—

'What the hell are you still doing here?'

Didn't need to look up. That gravelly voice was its own calling card.

He kept on typing. 'Could ask you the same question.'

'Nicking office supplies.' Steel reached over his cubicle wall and pinched his coffee as well. 'But mostly, because we caught a jumper: Marischal Court, right up on the roof – nineteen floors of straight-down-and-splat. Lost his job, his mum, his dog, and his girlfriend in the space of a week.' She blew on the coffee, as if that would improve it. 'Yours truly talked him down, of course. Which gives one the warm-and-fuzzies, but the paperwork's a pain in the arse.' Taking a sip. 'Gah... This is *disgusting*. You never heard of milk and hazelnut syrup?'

He stuck his hand out. 'Give it *back* then.'

She didn't. 'Might grow on me...' Another sip, another grimace. 'You know your problem? You're suffering from NRDS: New Responsibility Derangement Syndrome.'

'What I'm suffering from is Listening To You Rabbit On When I Should Be Finishing This Report Syndrome.'

'See, you've been made up to acting DCI, and now you think the whole division'll grind to a halt without you. Well, it won't.' Steel leaned on his cubicle wall. 'You're just a *greasy wee cog* in a big rusty machine. It'll no' fall apart if you go home and get some sleep.'

'And you thought *I* was bad at motivational speeches.'

'What *will* fall apart are your cases, when you're too knackered to focus tomorrow, cos you've been here all night like a martyred numpty.' She handed back his hideous coffee. 'Go home.' Then wandered off. 'And treat yourself to a stapler and some packs of Post-it notes on the way out!'

Yeah, she was probably right.

Time to go home.

Could always finish this tomorrow, after all.

Steel had almost reached the door, when a lone PC in the full outdoor kit banged through it at speed. Nodding at her on the way past as he hurpled over to Logan's desk. Breathing hard, like a chain-smoking pervert.

So this couldn't be good news.

Logan gave him a nod anyway. 'Aye, aye, Shandy.'

PC Ian Shand looked as if he'd been made by four-year-olds out of knotted string and old cat hair. And when he opened his mouth, every single one of his teeth pointed in a different direction. 'Guv!' He staggered to a halt. 'Bleeding heck...' Bending over and grabbing his knees. 'Not answering … your Airwave...'

The thing hadn't so much as bleeped.

He picked it off the desk and checked the screen. But it didn't even show a missed call, because the battery was flat.

Should've put it on to charge the moment he got back to the office.

Silly sod.

It was a bit late, but Logan plugged it in anyway.

Steel wandered back, hands in her pockets. 'Come on, Shandy: spill it before you keel over.'

'We've got … we've got a *serious* problem!' Waving his hands about. 'Missing … missing person!'

Logan sat upright. 'Is it a kid?'

'Not … a kid.' Shandy shook his sweaty head. 'No, it's … *way* more complicated … than that...'

Chief Superintendent Pine groaned. *'Oh for goodness' sake – did we not have enough on the go?'*

Twenty to midnight, and Natasha Agapova's house was lit up like a funfair. Not just the internal lighting, the outdoor floods were on too, turning the front garden into an ominous wonderland of trees and shadows.

On the other side of the floor-to-ceiling windows, a lock-block driveway played hostess to a patrol car, the Scenes Transit van, the pool car Logan had rocked up in, and a garish-red BMW.

In here, however, a lone forensic tech zwipped-zwopped across the entrance hall and tried to wrestle a gigantic teddy bear into a body bag. Presumably because there were no evidence bags big enough.

Logan leaned on the balcony handrail, making his Tyvek

crumple and rustle. Hood up. Phone tucked inside the elasticated hem. 'You're right: maybe I should hop in my Tardis, jump back to Monday morning, and ask Ms Agapova *not* to get abducted?'

Yeah...

Maybe that wasn't the best idea when talking to the Divisional head of state?

He cleared his throat. 'Sorry, Boss. Been a long day.'

She left a little pause – probably to make sure he knew his place. *'And we're sure it's an abduction, not a kidnap?'*

'No sign of a ransom demand yet. Her ex-husband's seriously loaded, so it's *possible* the kidnappers are waiting for the right moment, but...?'

'Urgh...' A thumping noise, banged down the line. *'Why did she have to be a bloody* press baron? *The media love talking about themselves, can you imagine what they'll be like when they find out?'*

'Ah. About that.' Logan wandered along the landing, peering in through the open doors. Forensic techs haunted Ms Agapova's home office and main bedroom like crinkly ghosts. Going through her things. 'Someone needs to tell the ex-husband. But he only owns three local radio stations; a podcast company; the *Scottish Daily Post*, the *Yorkshire Clarion*, *Midlands Gazette and Bulletin*, and *London Daily Citizen*; so we're probably OK.'

One of the spare bedrooms had nothing but unassembled flatpack furniture in it. The next was full of packing boxes.

Another thump from Pine's end. Maybe she was banging her head off the desk? *'In the name of ... fuck.'* A strangled sigh. *'Suppose I don't need to tell you this is a top priority.'*

'Along with everything else.'

'Exactly.' Thump. *'Suppose I better go wake the Chief Constable. She's going to* love *me.'*

The third bedroom was a little girl's: full of stuffed animals, rainbows, and unicorns. Not dinosaurs, ninjas, and pirates, like Elizabeth's.

'*Anything happens: I'm in the loop, understand?*'

'Boss.'

She hung up.

Logan puffed out his cheeks. Sagged.

Wait a minute.

There was something ... funky in here. Stinky. The sharp-yellow stench of sunbaked urine.

Weird.

The kid – Brooklyn, going by the nameplate on the door – was meant to be abroad at finishing school. And the bed was made. You wouldn't make a bed if someone had *piddled* in it. And surely, if Brooklyn was old enough for finishing school, she was too old for that kind of thing.

He tiptoed across to the window, eyes fixed on the oatmeal carpet. Nothing.

Maybe...

Hang on. The door lay wide open, but there was something hidden behind it. On the floor, by the wall. And the closer he got, the stronger the smell.

Right.

He marched along the corridor to the main bedroom and stuck his head over the threshold. 'Hello?'

The Scenes tech was on her hands and knees, rummaging about under Natasha's bed. She stopped what she was doing and glowered back at him. 'If you're going to make inappropriate comments about my bum again: *don't*.'

'What?'

Whoever it was, sat back on their haunches. 'Oh, it's *you*, Guv. Nothing. Sorry.'

'OK...' Because that didn't sound suspicious at all. He

hooked a thumb back across the corridor. 'There's what looks like a urine stain in the kid's bedroom. Can we run some sort of test on it?'

'It's your budget. I can test whatever you want, long as someone's paying for it.'

'Thanks.'

That sorted, he headed downstairs again, past the wrestling match – which the teddy bear seemed to be winning – down the corridor, past the lounge, home gym, and cinema room, and into the kind of kitchen they featured in design magazines. Perfect. Elegant. Spotless. As if no one had ever cooked or eaten a meal there.

It looked out over a large back garden, where all the floodlights were on too, revealing a pair of techs in the full Smurf-suit outfit, examining a flowerbed at the far end, by the fence.

Steel and Colin Miller slouched at the breakfast bar, nursing mugs of coffee, presumably from the very swanky machine in the corner, by the double fridge. Colin was in trousers and a T-shirt, but Steel had peeled her SOC suit down to the waist, showing off her Police Scotland top with optional biscuit crumbs.

Logan poked a finger at her. 'Have you been sexually harassing the scene examiners again?'

She grinned. 'How was our fearless leader? Was she in bed, in a low-cut lace nightie? Is she, even now, rushing over here to support the troops with handies and tickle-me-Elmos?'

Urgh…

'I don't even *want* to know what a "Tickle-me-Elmo" is.' He unzipped his Smurf suit and plonked his bum onto a spare seat at the breakfast bar. Didn't bother smothering a jaw-popping yawn. 'And thanks for the offer – I'd love a coffee.'

There was a moment's angry scowling, then Steel rustle-flounced off to fiddle with the machine.

Logan swivelled his seat around to face Colin. 'Want to tell me what you were doing creeping around your new boss's house at quarter to eleven on a Wednesday night?'

'Came to tell her where she could stick her job.' He held up a gloved finger. 'Which doesn't count as "motive" cos *I* was firing *her*. Plus: it was me called this in. And I've got an alibi, so don't even start, OK?' Waiting for a response he didn't get. 'OK.'

'Then why didn't you *call* me?'

'Cos it's "quarter to eleven on a Wednesday night!" Far as I know: you're off-duty, half-cut, and playing hide-the-bagpipe with Ginger-Curls McSexpot.'

Over by the coffee machine, Steel snorted. 'Nah, they did that this morning. *Dirty* monkeys.'

'Her name is *Tara*! What is wrong with you two?'

'Whatever.' Colin pulled out his phone. 'And you should probably hear this,' fiddling with the screen until a small, tinny, electronic voice buzzed its way into the kitchen:

'MESSAGE FIVE:'

Followed by a man – sharp-edged, snarling out the words so every syllable became an offensive weapon. '*Karma comes in like a hurricane,* Bitch, *and it's going to blow your house of lies right down. See you tonight!*'

'END OF MESSAGE. MESSAGE—'

The phone went silent.

Colin put the handset down on the countertop. 'Far as I can tell, Natasha Agapova, forty-eight, got herself a taxi from the SME charity-auction dinner at half eleven on Monday night. Dropped her off here around twelve, didn't see anything suspicious.'

'Hold on,' Logan eyed the phone, 'how did you get that recording?'

'Point is: if you check the call logs, that message was from a withheld number at eleven forty-two. So she was already in the car on her way home.'

Steel looked up from the machine. 'Have you been a naughty wee phone-hacking grubby tabloid scumbag?'

'I was searching the house to make sure she wasn't lying unconscious somewhere, in need of help.' His shoulders bobbed up and down. 'I may have *accidentally* bumped against the answering machine...?'

'Aye, and you just *accidentally* happened to have your wee phone out, recording? My sharny arse.'

'Point is: our guy on the phone has to know she's no' here, right? Otherwise, he calls, it tips her off, she gives you bastards a shout, and the whole abduction-kidnap plan's screwed.'

There was more to the monologue, but Logan sort of tuned it out, because over Colin's shoulder – through the kitchen windows, way down at the end of the garden – one of the ghostly Smurfs was on their feet, waving their arms at the house.

As if they'd *found* something.

He wrenched open the kitchen door, marched through a small utility room, and out onto a big triangle of decking.

One of the forensic team hurried across the grass towards him, holding up a hand. 'Found a couple of *great* footprints. Which is lucky – someone must've watered the garden not long before it happened, cos otherwise it'd be dry as a camel's arse out here and the definition would be for shite.' They turned, pointing back to where they'd come from. 'Our guy hopped the back fence, landed in the flowerbed. Should get a *really* sharp cast from the prints – you find us the shoes, we'll prove it was him.'

Yes!

About time something went their way...

XLII

The sky was murderous black through the crumbling window socket, spread with cold dead stars. A sliver of curved bone shone through the trees, as the full moon clawed its way over the horizon. Turning the world to ice with its uncaring light.

But even though the sun had gone down long, long ago, Natasha's prison remained an oven. Turned up full and left to burn everything to a cinder.

Except for the shit.

That roasted in the cloying heat, its foul brown stink seeping into the dirt and stone walls. Lining the leather mask. Helping it suffocate her...

As the light faded, the bluebottles had settled down for the night.

But DS Davis hadn't.

Rock music pounded out of the static caravan, loud enough to make the metal walls *buzzzz*. Because even when they were asleep you couldn't escape the flies...

Natasha lay on her back, in the dirt, gazing up and out of the window at the cool, indifferent darkness of space.

Waiting to die.

Because that was what she was doing here.

Dying.

The only question was, what would get her first: dehydration or DS Davis?

...

Inflicting his revenge for something she didn't even *do*.

Wasn't *her* fault some violent scumbag tried to burn a bunch of migrants to death, was it? She didn't light the match, no matter what the psychotic bastard said.

All she did was reflect the fears of her readers.

She wasn't the monster here.

SHE WASN'T THE MONSTER.

He breaks into *her* house, attacks her, abducts her, strips her, chains her up in a shitty outhouse, tries to kick her ribs in, and somehow *she's* the monster?

Fuck that.

Bastard's *insane*, that's what he is.

A rabid dog who needs taken behind the wood shed and put out of its misery.

Cos she's not the monster.

It's not her fault.

It's *his*.

The music got even louder, and it wasn't all muffled any more, then a *whump* and it was back to being an insect *buzzzz* again.

Like someone had opened and shut the caravan door.

A bobbing light stabbed in through the gaping window hole, illuminating the far wall for a moment, before disappearing again. Then her prison door squealed and shrieked and clattered open.

And DS Davis stepped inside.

He was wearing one of those head torches, turning himself into a shadow, only half seen as a void where the light bounced off the raw stone walls, carrying a bucket and spade. Like he was on his way to Bondi Fucking Beach.

Only they weren't the kind you gave to little kids, they were full-sized ones. He clanged the bucket down, and scooped up Natasha's shit with a disgusted grunt. *Thunk*ing it into the bucket. Retching as it hit the bottom.

Then, holding the bucket at arm's length, he took the turd and the spade away.

Hope he bloody *choked* on it.

But he was back a couple of minutes later, with a spray bottle of something – squirting it onto the ground, smothering the stench of shit with the bitter-bleach stink of lemon-scented toilet cleaner.

A grunt.

Then he was gone again, leaving the door wide open behind him.

But none of Natasha's limbs worked any more, and even if they did, the anchor wouldn't let her go more than six feet.

So, instead, she closed her eyes.

Natasha blinked up at the grey ceiling.

No idea how long she'd been out for, but the moon had crawled its way across the window's jagged hollow, still low in the sky, skimming along the treetops.

The music had changed too – different singer, different band – but deep down it was the same: pounding drums and guitars, full of bitter chords and angst-fuelled rage.

Burning…

Her throat was made of firebricks.

Couldn't even swallow any more.

Just made her whole head jerk with the effort.

Back when she was five or six, she'd hiked up Redpath Hill, behind Nanna Carter's house. There was a roo, must've died in the bush a couple of weeks before. Magpies had been at it, but they'd barely made a dent, cos he'd been a *big* fella. But that was a long hot summer and the skin had shrunk as the body dried, till the ribs stood out like a bloody xylophone wrapped in leather.

She threw stones at it for a while.

Then went for a dip in Hyland Creek, while there was still some water left.

Christ.

To be back there, floating in the cool clear water, listening to the kookaburra cackle in the trees and the dragonflies hum. While the fat golden sun blazed—

'Bitch.'

The whole world disappeared in a sharp glare of white, driving nails into her eyes.

Natasha screwed her face tight shut as those nails stabbed right out through the back of her head.

A foot nudged her ribs.

DS Davis was back – his voice slurred, and angry. But then he was *always* angry. *'You know, you should thank me.'*

Oh, yeah, cos he'd been such a great host!

'I said, you should thank me.'

There was the sound of boots scuffing on the hard dirt floor, then fireworks exploded across her ribs again.

It got him nothing more than a muffled groan and a desiccated sob.

The bastard could slit her throat right now, and sand would pour out.

'Because I saved you,' his knees popped like gunshots, and a waft of whisky breath seeped through her leather mask, *'from a fate worse than death.'*

Something bounced off her arms and crumpled onto the floor.

Natasha forced her eyes open, narrow slits against the harsh beam of Davis's head torch.

The thing looked like a ski-mask: black, with a jagged smile printed across the mouth in sharp, pointy teeth. The fabric was weird though. Thin. But a bit rigid, like there was something

361

sticky on it. Something that had dried to a rich, dark-brown shine. The smell of raw meat seeped out of the fabric.

DS Davis had a bottle of what looked like whisky, dangling from one hand. He took a swig, wiped his gob. 'This piece of shite was in your house, waiting for you to come home.'

The whisky bottle got propped against the window hole, then Davis held up a flat slab of plastic. Opening it brought a laptop screen to life.

A synthetic-faced young man smouldered out at her, from the backdrop, with carefully manicured eyebrows, a precision-trimmed beard, and veneers whiter than Sydney Opera House.

Davis squatted down beside her again, fiddling with the laptop's trackpad till a video played.

Took a moment, but that was *her* back garden. *Her* house. Filmed in the middle of the night, as some bastard hopped over the fence and broke in through the utility room.

Going from room to room, even Brooklyn's bedroom... Then Natasha's walk-in closet and en suite. Out across the hallway, looking down from the balcony as DS Davis barged into her home and punched her in the face.

Natasha rolled her head away from the screen briefly.

'Yeah.' Davis nodded, voice grim. 'Wait till you see what he does to the others.'

Some more fiddling, then DS Davis placed the laptop in front of her face, another video flickering on the screen.

It was much the same to start with – a secluded rural property, sneaking in through the back door to creep through the house... Only this time the footage ended with screams and rhythmic grunts.

Davis grabbed hold of the mask and forced her face towards the screen. 'You're not *watching*.'

She forced a word from her corpse-dry mouth. 'Water...'

'Not to worry, though – I took care of the perverted wee monster. He won't be raping anyone ever again.'

The head torch's light swept across the ground to find the ski-mask again, with its brittle shiny stains and jagged-tooth grin.

'The question is: what to do about *you*.'

He dug into a pocket and came out with a little half-litre bottle of water. Twisted the cap off. Sniffed. Then spat into it. Before screwing the lid on again and giving the bottle a shake.

'Here.' He tossed it at her head, making the thing bounce off the mask with a *thunk*. Rolling away.

Water.

Oh God…

Natasha wriggled across the dirt floor towards it, fingers fumbling at the condensation-dewed plastic.

It was only when she had the thing clutched in her shackled grip that the truth dawned: he was screwing with her. With the mask's mouth zipped and padlocked shut, she couldn't drink it anyway.

'See, *this* bastard,' Davis pointed at the screen, 'ruined the lives of nineteen women. But *you* – with your lies and your hate and your spite – how many lives have *you* ruined? A hundred? A thousand? How many families have you torn apart?' Looming over her. 'Those poor migrant kids: their dad's dead because you whipped up a racist, flag-shagging, far-right mob. The *Scottish Daily Post* isn't a newspaper, it's a hate crime!'

He dipped into another pocket and produced a key ring, held together with what looked like a rabbit's paw. Or it might've been from a small dog…

Grabbing her face in one hand, he twisted her head around, sneering as he slipped a tiny key into the padlock on her leather mask.

Click.

He pulled the lock free and undid the zip.

Natasha hauled in a great gulp of fresh air.

But Davis didn't let go of her face. Squeezing. Digging his fingers in. 'You can have your water; don't want you to die too quickly.' Running the torchlight over her half-naked skin. 'See all those teeny-tiny pale little flecks, like grass seed? They're fly eggs. Give it two days and they'll hatch. Hundreds of lovely maggots to eat your rancid flesh.' A grin. 'You'll want to stick around for that.'

He gathered up the laptop and the whisky.

'Make *one* sound, Bitch, and the padlock goes back on. And *stays* on.' DS Davis toasted her with the bottle, then took a deep swig. Hissing out fumes, before scuffing his way from the room. 'Sleep tight!'

Soon as the squealing door rattled shut, Natasha opened the water and trembled the bottle to her lips.

Spit or not, it was sweet as nectar.

She allowed herself two mouthfuls *only*, before screwing the top back on. Nice though it'd be to neck the whole bloody lot, God knew when she'd get any more.

And meantime: she had an escape to plan.

— dig a deeper grave —

43

The big fish turned around in the bathtub and looked Logan right in the eye. 'YOU *need* TO *do* SOMETHING *about* THESE *sausages*. THEY'RE *eating* ALL *the* CARPET *in* THE *living* ROOM, *and*—'

Three loud knocks battered at the walls of the world.

'Gnnnnphffff...?' Logan jerked awake. Blinking.

Where the living...

Car.

He was in the pool car; passenger seat fully reclined.

And Sergeant Brookminster was peering in through the window at him, one eyebrow raised.

Logan scrubbed his hands across his face and sat upright, pulling the lever so the seat joined him. Then opened the car door.

Brookminster nodded. 'Chief Inspector.'

'Sergeant.' A yawn popped and crackled free. 'What time is...' Squinting at the dashboard clock – 06:41. 'Sod.' He climbed out of the car.

The sun continued its relentless climb up the crystal-blue sky, blanketing the land in another layer of dusty heat.

Colin Miller's red beamer had disappeared from the driveway outside Natasha Agapova's house, replaced by another patrol car and a Mercedes Benz, black as an undertaker's hearse.

Well, of course it was, how else would Brookminster get here? And where there was a Brookminster, Chief Superintendent Pine was never far away.

Logan straightened his rumpled black Police Scotland T-shirt. Then turned. 'Boss.'

She'd been standing *right* behind him, in the full uniform, be-leafed peaked cap on her head, hands clasped, eyes narrowed. 'Why are you still here?'

He popped his neck. 'Supervising the search of the property, Boss. And our victim's husband lives in Knightsbridge, so I've spent half the night "liaising" with the Metropolitan Police, trying to get them to send someone round to his place. And you know what a production *they* make of everything.' Another yawn shuddered through. 'Went to do some emails in the car, round about sun-up and...' He drooped. 'Next thing I know – here we are.'

A whole two hours' sleep, after a twenty-one-hour shift.

Talk about living the high life.

Pine looked up at Agapova's glass-fronted entrance hall. 'The Chief Constable is spitting *napalm* over this one, Logan. We're facing a massive cluster jobbie, soon as the press finds out.' A sniff. 'Surprised they're not here already.'

'Ah... About that.' Deep breath. 'It was a journalist on the *Aberdeen Examiner* who discovered she was missing, last night. He was the one who called us in. So it'll be all over their morning edition.' Logan checked his watch. 'Which will be hitting the newsstands right about now.'

Her face creased. 'Oh for—'

'But that's just one, *local* paper, right? And they're not going to just give their exclusive away, so none of the others will know about it till it's published.'

Pine glared off into the distance. 'At least that buys us a little time.'

'And I asked the Met to stress: we need Mr Shearsmith to keep all this as quiet as possible; that his ex-wife's safety probably depends on it; and until we get a ransom demand, we don't know what we're dealing with.'

'*Good.* The last thing we need is Natasha Agapova turning up bit-by-bit all over the city.' Pine frowned. 'I worked a case in Clydebank where the family couldn't pay the ransom. Every time the postie came, there was another chunk...' She shuddered. 'Ever see a uterus wrapped in an episode of *The Broons*? Never looked at *The Sunday Post* the same way again. Took us weeks to—'

The rest of her sentence was drowned out by the *whump*ing roar of a helicopter. Only it wasn't a Super Puma – high in the sky, on its way to an oil rig somewhere – it was a small dark-blue number, just above the treetops, with the *BBC News* logo on the side. Circling the house. A gimbal camera, mounted on the nose, swivelled as it passed, giving Logan, Pine, and Brookminster a good lonnnnnnnnnnnnnnnnnng look.

Bloody hell.

The Chief Super's mouth pinched, eyes bulging. 'Thought you told the Met to keep this *quiet*!'

'They promised they'd lean on him! Low key, under the sodding radar. How was—'

A second chopper joined the first, howling over their heads. A big silver one this time, with 'SKY NEWS HD' emblazoned across it. Gimbal camera searching for the best view of the property. A massive, and no doubt *very expensive* upgrade from the drone they'd been flying at all the other crime scenes.

Pine jabbed a hand at the thing, going pink in the face. 'DOES THIS *LOOK* LOW KEY?'

Oh, and it just got *better*:

From up here, on the hill, there was a good view down to the main road, and a chunk of the way back towards

Peterculter. Where a convoy of grubby hatchbacks, estate cars, and Outside Broadcast Units was chuntering its way towards Natasha Agapova's house.

No way they only just found out ten seconds ago. And how long would it take to fly a helicopter up here from London? Three hours? Two-and-a-bit with a tail wind?

Logan gritted his teeth as the BBC made another pass. 'You don't think Adrian Shearsmith hates his ex-wife so much he hired a *publicist*, do you?'

Pine scowled up at the chopper. Then out at the line of approaching media. Took a deep breath. 'Given the level of press interest in this, do you want to remain Senior Investigating Officer?' She raised a hand. 'And there's no judgement if you don't. This one's going to be an absolute buggering nightmare, and I know your dance card's full already.'

If she was volunteering, he wasn't going to stand in her way.

'To be honest, Boss, I'm happy *not* taking the lead on this one.'

Because she was right: it *was* going to be a buggering nightmare; involve a shedload of meetings, briefings, blame, and recriminations; not to mention a one-hundred-percent chance of getting shredded by the media for every *tiny* mistake. And once the press got into the inevitable full-on self-referential feeding frenzy, there'd be no stopping them.

Her face sagged. 'Yeah, thought as much.' Then she stiffened her spine. 'Keep working your existing cases. But if I'm going to be SIO here, when I yell "Frog!" I expect you to jump, understand?'

'Yes, Boss.'

'Get back to the station. This is now our number one priority. I want Natasha Agapova found before the parcels start arriving!'

He hurried back towards the pool car.

Sky News made another pass, so Pine had to shout over the hammering rotors. 'AND YOU'RE AN ACTING DETECTIVE CHIEF INSPECTOR NOW – DRESS LIKE ONE!'

Yeah...

This was going to be a *long* day.

The whole team had turned up in uniform, like a colony of rooks, gathered around the whiteboard wall at the front of the office, listening as Logan played the recording again:

'*Karma comes in like a hurricane,* Bitch, *and it's going to blow your house of lies right down. See you tonight!*'

Doreen clicked the remote and the projector juddered back a couple of PowerPoint slides, swapping a shot of the broken vases and bloodstains for a publicity still of their victim.

Logan looked out across his shrunken congregation. Not quite the full contingent, given another four were off on the sick, and a fifth was standing at the back of the room trying to smother a cough that wouldn't die. 'Smithy?'

A hand went up, attached to a stringy PC with a squint nose, squint chin, Clint-Eastwood-squinty eyes, and a brutal haircut that he must've cut himself. With a lawnmower. 'Sarge.'

'Call was from a withheld number – get on to her phone provider and see if they can help. Same goes for Captain Sleazy and the HMS Loveyacht. I want names and details, OK?' Logan gave the nod and Doreen shut the projector down. 'I don't have to tell you just how much we *didn't* need another massive case to work on right now, but, in the immortal words of Rabbie Burns: "God's an evil bastard and he hates us all."'

There were a few nods at that.

'But it doesn't mean we get to abandon the hunt for Charles MacGarioch. Hands up Operation Iowa?'

About a quarter of the assembled officers put their hands up.

'OK, I'm counting on you guys: let's get this murdering racist wee shite found.' Next up: 'DI Marshall's team?'

Another show of hands. Biohazard sat in the middle of them, bum perched against a desk, arms folded. Looking as if his underwear was eating his rectum with big pointy teeth.

'I know our victim isn't what you'd call a "sympathetic character", but I don't care if he was a rapist or a choirboy – *we* get justice for the missing and the dead. Whoever bashed Andrew Shaw's brains out and chucked him in the river is a *murderer*. We let him get away with it: he'll do it again.'

Determined nods rippled through the team.

'Good.' Logan pointed at Doreen. 'Everyone see DI Taylor for your assignments. Only exceptions are Steel, Barrett, Lund, Harmsworth, and Quirrel: with me.' He marched off, making for the door.

Biohazard intercepted him before he got there. 'Guv? Nightshift say they found Andrew Shaw's car. Peugeot Two Oh Eight, parked three streets from Duthie Park. You want Forensics to give it a once-over?'

'Get it towed to Nelson Street first – don't want the press finding out and making connections that aren't there. Got enough unwanted attention as it is.'

'Guv.'

Soon as Biohazard headed off, Rennie scuffed over. Baggy of eyes and runny of nose. He snorked into a hanky. Then blinked and winced at the light spilling in through the windows. 'Anyone seen my sunglasses?'

Logan backed the *hell* away. 'That better be hayfever, because if it's the lurgie...'

The idiot stifled a cough. 'Donna and Lola got sent home with it, yesterday. But I'm *fine*. Dandy. Sharp as a tack and twice as shiny.' Giving him both thumbs up. Before frowning and patting his pockets. 'Just need to find my shades and we can hit the road, adventure-bound.'

Nope.

'"*We*" aren't hitting anything. You're getting yourself a pool car and going to check on the stakeout at Wallace Tower. *On your own*: no infecting anyone else.'

A bunged-up whine snottered out. 'But Gu-uv, it's just a little summer sniffle. Nothing to be—'

'You heard the doctor:' Logan poked a finger towards the door, 'out! Now! Go!'

Looking like a kicked puppy, Rennie blew his nose one more time, then slouched away, muttering to himself. Coughing and spluttering. Like the diseased horror he was.

The marker pen squeaked its way through every letter as Logan printed the words 'ADRIAN SHEARSMITH' next to 'NATASHA AGAPOVA' on the whiteboard wall.

It was every inch the bland corporate space you'd expect from modern policing – lots of magnolia, with miserable carpet tiles, a flipchart, one of those central tables made up of smaller tables, and a collection of cheap blue office chairs where Lund, Barrett, Harmsworth, and Tufty sat. Taking notes and paying attention.

Steel, on the other hand, had her feet up on the desk, going for a wee rummage in her cleavage. Which wasn't easy in a tight-fitting black T-shirt that was clearly two sizes too small, so she'd had to go in from the bottom, exposing a belly shiny-pale enough to light the fires of Gondor.

It was hard to take your eyes off it.

Like a pasty car crash.

Logan stuck the cap back on his pen. 'Lund, Barrett: I need you to have a *thorough* search through Natasha's life.

Who's she friends with, who's her enemies? There's been a lot of redundancies at the *Aberdeen Examiner* – is anyone's nose far enough out of joint to justify abducting her?' He used the pen as a pointer. 'Harmsworth, Steel: you're on the ex-husband. A media mogul like that's bound to have people out to get him. And given how loaded the guy is, could even be an organised crime thing – can you imagine what kind of ransom he could put together? So, get in touch with SOCT and make a nuisance of yourselves till they tell you who Shearsmith's involved with.'

Harmsworth curled his top lip. 'What's Scene Of Crime got to do with— *Ow!*'

Steel gave him another thump on the back of the head. '"Serious Organised Crime Taskforce", you snudging spudge-walloper.'

He rubbed at his bald patch. 'That really hurt!'

Logan chucked his pen at them. 'Stop arsing about. This is serious!' He gave them all a stern look. 'As half the station's off with The Yuck, until we get some backup from other divisions, Davey: you're now Acting Detective Sergeant Barrett.'

'Sweet.' He grinned at Steel. 'I'm sure we'll work together in a *supportive* and *cooperative* manner, *fellow* sergeant.'

'Hey!' *Not* happy.

'And you're now officially Acting Detective Inspector Steel.' Logan folded his arms. 'I'm *trusting* you, OK? Do not screw this up. I want progress and an interim report on my desk by lunchtime.' He headed for the door. 'Tufty: grab a pool car, we're going out.'

The wee loon scrambled to his feet. 'I has being an side-kick?'

'We'll see.'

'Woot!'

Yeah. He was probably going to regret this.

44

The pool car headed northwest along the Parkway, past ware-houses and car showrooms, joining the trucks and lorries heading to various industrial estates as rush hour in the Bridge of Don set in. Grinding everything to a halt. Tufty behind the wheel, while Logan dozed in the passenger seat. Drifting in and out as the wee loon wittered on:

'...so I went down to the Forensic IT lab, and I said to them, I said: "You does has a *being crap* at this computering malarkey!" And they was all like, "No way, we is the bestest!" And I'm like, "Give me Charles MacGarioch's pooter and I'll crack it like a Tunnock's Tea Cake!"' A pout. 'And *they* said, "No." So I said—'

The first bars of Beethoven's 'Ode To Joy' burst out of Logan's phone, cutting across Tufty's *riveting* anecdote. Oh dear, what a shame.

And it would be rude not to answer it. 'Hello?'

A tired voice grumbled into Logan's ear: *'Dr Drummond.'*

'Sorry, you've got the wrong number. This isn't—'

'No: I'm Dr Drummond. Critical Care Unit, Aberdeen Royal Infirmary? I've got a note here to call a "Logan Mackay" about Spencer Findlater?'

Tufty turned onto Lochside Road, swapping industrial-estate chic for a winding maze of mature trees, wee houses, and bungalows.

'Has he got a visitor?' Sitting up a bit straighter.

'He's actually survived the night, which is a surprise, given his injuries. People don't appreciate the damage a car can do, even at thirty miles an hour. Two tons of metal exerts a force of—'

'Is Spencer going to be OK?'

There was a pause, filled with medical seething. Because if there was one thing people like Dr Drummond hated it was being interrupted. Well, tough – that's what he got for getting Logan's name wrong.

Drummond cleared his throat. *'The* important *thing is he's unlikely to drop dead before teatime, so he's not our problem any more. We've transferred him to the Orthopaedic Trauma Unit. Ward two-twelve, in the Pink Zone.'*

At the end of the entrance road, a huge sign reared out of the bushes with 'LOCHSIDE ROAD' at the top, and 'LEADING TO' followed by a list of fourteen different streets, seven on each side.

Tufty took a right.

'You've turfed him out?' Logan shifted in his seat. 'Is that not a bit—'

'Do you have any idea what kind of bed shortages we're dealing with here? If he's stable, he's someone else's problem.' A humphing noise. *'And now that I've done my bit and called you, is it OK if I get back to all these half-dead folk? Thank you.'*

'Hold on! Hold on.' Before the sarcastic bugger could hang up. 'We left an advisory notice – in case Spencer gets a visitor? It's important.'

A long sigh. *'That what all these stupid posters are about?'*

'Can you make sure the new ward knows he's—'

'Don't you think I've got more important things to do than run around after you? I'm trying to save lives here!' And the line went dead.

Logan puffed out his cheeks. 'I get that the NHS is a

marvel, and we're lucky to have it, and most of the people working there are brilliant, dedicated, selfless individuals, who do their best under *incredibly* difficult circumstances ... but by Christ there's some complete and *utter* arseholes.'

He scowled out the window as the pool car wound deeper into the maze.

Had to admit: it was kind of nice here. Green and leafy, arranged around a wee lochan. Like being in the countryside.

Still, there was no time to enjoy the view, not now that Dr Drummond had made life more difficult.

Logan thumbed out a text to Doreen:

Do me a favour and get on to whoever's at ARI today.

Ward 212 need to call ASAP if Spencer Findlater gets any visitors.

Ward 202 has posters!

SEND.

Tufty took another right, into a nest of branching cul-de-sacs, ending up outside a bungalow with a garage conversion and a brown Volvo on the lock-block driveway.

Stifling a yawn, Logan climbed out.

A white picket fence bordered a flat rectangle of grass featuring an array of garden gnomes, dressed as Darth Vader and his stormtroopers, the alien from *Predator* fishing in a star-shaped pond, and a knee-high concrete AT-AT that doubled as a bird bath.

Not exactly what you'd call classy.

Tufty locked the pool car, then trotted up the drive and rang the bell. Instead of a good, wholesome '*ding-dong*' it launched into the Cantina tune from *Star Wars*. Which was far too jaunty for this time in the morning.

As it tootled out, Tufty gazed at the lawn ornaments with a

wistful sigh. 'See, *this* is what you miss out on when you live in a flat.' He gave Logan a wee sideways glance. 'Sa-arge, I know I is only a lowly sidekick and all that, but … I thought we're meant to be all about the big newspapery abduction today?'

'Try it again.'

Tufty poked the button and *'Doot-da-doot-da-dooda-doo…'* parped out once more.

'We are.' Logan stretched his shoulders and back. 'We've got Steel's lot on background, we've got door-to-doors interviewing the neighbours, we've got search teams out, people reviewing ANPR and CCTV footage, Forensics going over the house with a magnifying glass, and support staff sticking it all into HOLMES. So instead of getting in the way, *we* are multitasking. Someone needs to interview the last of Charles MacGarioch's little friends, and it might as well be us.'

He pointed at the bell, and Tufty did the honours a third time.

'Doot-da-doot-da-dooda-doo…'

'Besides: *Chief Superintendent Pine* is in charge of Operation "Find Natasha Agapova". I've still got everything else to run.' Lucky sod that he was. Another point. 'And again.'

'Doot-da-doot-da-dooda-doo…'

Logan's phone *ding-buzz*ed.

DOREEN:

AAAAAAAAAAAAAARGH!!!!!!

Have I not got enough on my plate?

He poked out a reply while the Cantina theme launched into its fourth encore. Or was it fifth?

Good leadership is about delegation.

And I'm delegating to you.

You're a DI now, remember?

So be a good leader.

(as long as it gets done)

Tufty was reaching for the bell again, when the door finally opened a crack and a bloodshot eye peered out at them.

A rough voice slithered after it, reeking of stale booze. 'Frelling smeg. Have you got *any* idea what time it is?' There was a cough, and a sniff, then a long, sticky moan as whoever it was twigged. 'Oh … *wank*. It's the cops.'

Either the Cunninghams were a *proper* bunch of slobs, or they'd thrown some sort of hedonistic rave last night.

The living room was littered with crumpled beer and lager cans, empty wine and alcopop bottles, and overflowing ashtrays. Making everything smell like a pub carpet from the eighties. In what was probably meant to be an ironically retro touch, the remains of a cheese-and-pineapple hedgehog wilted on a fat dinner plate. The hollow bones of Pringle tubes crushed into the floor. Along with what *might* have been Monster Munch.

Framed film posters adorned the walls – *Close Encounters, Alien, Silent Running, Star Trek II* and *IV, The Empire Strikes Back, The Fifth Element…* – and although there wasn't a single ornament on display, a pair of crossed lightsabers glowed above the fireplace. One red, one blue.

A pair of patio doors were cracked open an inch, letting in the grinding snores of a large man sparked-out in the paddling pool. Lying flat on his back with his arms hanging over the inflatable sides, head dangling towards the house. Greying stubble wrapped around a slightly chubby face.

Going by the flush of angry red spreading across his round,

pale, hairy belly and chest, he'd been snoozing out there in the sun for a while.

Tufty bumbled over to the doors, stood on his tiptoes, and peered into the garden. 'Oooh... They does got a firepit that looks like the *Deathstar*!'

Of course they did.

Logan swept a scattering of popcorn and cigarette papers onto the floor, then whumped down on the couch, making the black leather squeak.

Which had the added bonus of giving him a clear line of sight into the kitchen, to make sure their host wasn't doing a runner.

Alexis Cunningham must have partied *hearty* last night because she shuffled about like a broken banana today. Limp hair hanging over her heavy dark eyebrows, pale washed-out face, dark circles under her eyes, and a large mole on her top lip. Not really dressed for company in a grey 'NOSTROMO MAINTENANCE CREW' T-shirt, pink running shorts, bare legs, and fuzzy Yoda slippers.

She thunked the fridge door shut, cracked the ringpull on a fresh tin of Rampant Gorilla – 'CAFFEINATE TO DOMINATE!' – and took a big long scoof. Before belching, sagging, and slouching back through into the living room.

Alexis blinked her way over to the lightsabers and flicked a hidden switch, killing the glow. Then turned to survey the devastation. 'Urgh... Shazbot.' Another scoof. 'You here about Charlie?'

Logan checked to make sure Tufty was writing this down. 'Let me guess: Orphan Grapevine?'

'Our drums have been pounding in the darkness for days...' She banged a palm against the patio doors. 'GRAHAM, YOU DAFT BUGGER: YOU'LL FRY! COME IN!' More Rampant Gorilla. 'Swear to God, that man can *not* drink tequila.'

'Quite the party last night.'

She pulled her top lip back, exposing little pointy teeth. 'Well, aren't *we* an observant little Samuel Vimes.'

Nope.

No idea what that was supposed to mean.

Tufty looked up from his notepad. 'He's the big detective character in Terry Pratchett's Diskworld novels, Sarge.'

Alexis squinted her bloodshot eyes at the wee loon. 'Don't I know you from somewhere?'

'Any chance we can circle back to Charles MacGarioch?' Logan pointed at the scattered party debris. 'Was he here, last night?'

'*Charlie?* Nah.' She crumpled down into a matching black-leather armchair and put her feet on the coffee table. 'Haven't seen him since that night in The Hare and Parsnip. Friday before last?' Her heavy eyebrows scrunched together. 'Or was it a Wednesday...?' She balanced her energy drink on the arm of the chair and rummaged a small metal tin from beneath a pile of *Empire* magazines – popping it open to reveal a pack of Golden Virginia and a thing of rolling papers. Then turned to look through the patio doors. 'You think it's OK to leave him out there? You know, with melanomas and drowning and that?'

'And does the Orphan Grapevine say anything about where Charlie might be hiding?'

'Hmmm...' She sprinkled a line of tobacco across a Rizla. 'Opinion's split on that one. Some people say, "Talk to the cops, it's for Charlie's own good." Others say, "When does talking to the cops ever help with anything? Fuck 'em!"' Licking the paper, then rolling it up. 'No offence, Elijah Baley.'

Tufty held his pen up, before Logan could ask. 'The homicide detective in Isaac Asimov's Robot series.'

Alexis turned in her seat to examine him. 'Takeshi Lev Kovacs.'

'Richard K. Morgan, *Altered Carbon*, 2002. Come on, try a hard one.'

She tilted her head to one side. 'You *sure* I don't know you?'

Logan cleared his throat. 'Drifting off topic again, people.' Waiting till they were both looking at him. 'We really *are* trying to help Charlie. He could be hurt. And what kind of life's he going to have, on the run for the rest of his days?'

'Why are you after him, Master Li?' Snapping a finger-gun at Tufty. 'And that makes you...?'

'Number Ten Ox.' A shrug. 'Could be worse.'

She seemed pleased with that, because she smiled. Nodded. Then sparked up her handmade fag and blew a pillar of smoke at the ceiling. 'Anyone tell you about Wallace Tower in Seaton Park? Used to squirrel off there when his nan was going all Borg Queen on him.'

Which meant they now had corroboration, and Randolph Hay had been telling the truth.

Alexis tapped a flake of ash into the already crowded ashtray. 'Or you could try Keira's place?'

'Thought his grandmother broke them up?'

'She always was a racist sack of rat shite.' Another puff. 'Charlie wasn't *here* last night, because this wasn't an Orphan Outing – just some of Graham's mates, round for his annual DS9 marathon. Charlie *never* misses an Orphan Outing.' Alexis drained her Rampant Gorilla. 'And I mean you could hack off his leg with a rusty *Bat'leth* and he'd still drag himself along. Some people are just...' Her face scrunched up again, and she pointed at Tufty. 'Were you at Roboticon last year, or something?'

No answer from the wee loon.

Because for *once* he'd paid attention about staying on topic.

Logan checked his watch – 07:59 – better get shifting if they were going to visit the final name on the list, before this stupid

MAPPA meeting. 'OK, well if Charlie gets in touch, will you let me know? Please.'

He produced a business card and held it out across the coffee table.

Alexis didn't take it, just looked at the thing as if he'd offered her a sheet of used toilet paper.

Tufty sighed. Then pointed at the framed posters. 'I was in a sci-fi film once, but the studio binned it before release. Was more profitable to take the tax write-off and pulp every copy.' Pulling up his shoulders, before letting them sag again. 'I played a robot-spider-henchperson thing.'

Her bloodshot eyes widened. 'God, I *knew* it: you worked for Baroness Grimdark! Arachnox! We watched a bootleg DVD. Wow...' She ground out her roll-up and scrambled to her flip-flopped feet. 'Can I get a selfie? God. Wow...' Backing towards the patio doors. 'Don't move! I *gotta* get Graham – he'll kill me if he finds out we had a bona fide film star *right here*, and I didn't wake him up!'

And Tufty beamed like a lighthouse.

Logan lowered the sun visor, cutting the glare. Sitting on his tod in the passenger seat, phone pressed to his ear. 'So other than "we have to buy a piano", what else did we get lumbered with after I left?'

A pair of magpies hopped and cackled across the lawn, then jumped up and down on Darth Vader's little gnomey head.

Tara groaned. *'Her art class is doing an exhibition at the Cowdray Hall in October. We're in for five books of raffle tickets to pay for art supplies.'*

'Lovely... What do we get if we win?'

'One of the kids' paintings. Second prize is two paintings.'

He kept his voice flat and dead. 'You're hilarious, you know that, don't you.'

'Oh, and we met a slightly scary Goth girl who says she knows you?'

A yawn stampeded its way through Logan's body, cracking his jaw wide, followed by a wee burp, a shudder, and a sag. 'Sorry. Long night.'

The door to number thirteen opened and Tufty emerged into the sunlight, followed by Alexis and the guy from the paddling pool – now wearing jogging bottoms and a Stargate T-shirt. All three of them grinning away like idiots.

'Only, apparently, Elizabeth is part of her gang now – like it's prison or something. They'll be getting matching tattoos and wearing colours next... Are you sure we can't afford to send her to private school?'

'Rebecca's a good kid, don't be mean.'

Tufty shook Alexis's hand, then the bloke – Graham, was it? – lifted him off the ground in a great big bear hug. Laughing.

'I'd better go – looks like the wee loon's finished playing Sci-Fi Film Star.'

'Invite him to the barbecue, you miserable old bumfart.'

'Go away and ... confiscate some counterfeit handbags. I've got a killer to catch.' He hung up.

That would teach her.

Probably not.

But it was the thought that counted.

Logan took out the list of Charles MacGarioch's associates, and put a line through Alexis Cunningham's name as Tufty pretty much skipped down the garden path and over to the driver's side.

The wee loon wriggled in behind the wheel, then waved out the window at his brand-new fans. Who both waved back at him.

Tufty started the car. 'Weren't Alexis and her uncle *nice*?'

Maybe, if you liked weirdos.

'And she's promised to help us, now – cos I is a international celebrity of famousness.'

'Drive.' Logan pointed back towards town. 'We've only got an hour to wheech over to Broomhill, interview Marshall Carter, and get back to the station in time for that meeting.'

'Nah.' Tufty tapped the dashboard clock. 'Hour and *ten*, Sarge.'

Logan shot a full-on Paddington across the pool car. 'Those ten minutes are my pee-and-coffee time. Do *not* spoil them.'

'Eeek!'

Tufty drove.

45

Granville Place was a quiet residential street, not far from Broomhill Road, with big grey-granite detached bungalows on one side and big pink-granite semis on the other. Lots of attic conversions and neat little front gardens encased in ankle-high walls, well-trimmed hedges and flowering borders. Where nearly every car was a newish hatchback.

Tufty pulled up outside one of the grey houses, featuring a blue door, a handful of rose bushes, and a water feature. 'It's not my fault we had to stop for petrol, Sarge.'

Logan climbed out into the sticky morning. 'You could've picked a car that wasn't running empty!'

'No I couldn't.' Plipping the locks and following Logan up the path to the front door. 'Everyone plays "How Low Can The Petrol Gauge Go?" these days. You lose ten points if you have to fill it up again. I'm on *minus sixty*.' He scuttled ahead and rang the bell. A wee frown puckered his empty forehead. 'I sometime worry that we work with a bunch of Trouser Grinches.'

And speaking of idiots...

Logan pulled out his phone and texted Rennie:

Where's my update on that ICSO?

SEND.

A deadbolt clunked, then the door swung wide, revealing a young woman in Mr Men pyjama bottoms and a T-shirt emblazoned with 'THE MIGHTY MR RHODODENDRON'. Long nose, glasses, and *huge* amount of dark frizzy hair. A bit like Elizabeth's English teacher, only a lot more suspicious of strangers. She looked them up and down, then pulled her chin in. 'Is something wrong?'

'Good morning, Miss.' Logan checked the list. 'Is Marshall Carter in?'

That produced a grimace. 'She is. And before you say anything – I know, but it's too late to change it now.'

Marshall Carter bustled about with mugs and teabags as the kettle rumbled to a boil. '...and I tried going by "Marsha" for a while, but it just ended up as "Marshy", then "Swampy", then "Swamp Thing". Then I had to move schools because of fighting, and it was easier to go back to "Marshall" again.'

The kitchen wasn't bad, with lots of wood and shiny appliances, and a view out over the well-tended back garden.

She peeked into a biscuit tin. Went, 'Poop.' Then plonked it back down beside a wee pile of post, today's paper, and a couple of flyers for 'RUMPLINGTON BROTHERS' CIRCUS OF DELIGHTS!' – complete with photos of strangely un-miserable clowns, acrobats, and a funfair.

Logan leaned back against the worktop. 'I take it you've heard we're looking for Charles MacGarioch.'

She poured boiling water into all four mugs. 'Word is he torched that migrant hostel.'

Tufty raised his eyebrows.

'Really?' Logan kept his voice nice and neutral. 'Who told you that?'

'The first rule of Orphan Club is: you do not clype on other members of Orphan Club.'

'And you'd be ... OK with him burning the hotel down, with *people* inside? *If* that's what he's done.'

'Course not.' Mashing the teabags with a spoon, working her way down the line.

'But...?'

She dumped the first bag in the sink, then fished out a second. 'It's weird. To start with I hated being called an "orphan". It's such a *heavy* word to tie around a child's neck. "You're an Orphan now, Marshall, and you have to go live with Pappa Carter."'

She put on a child's sing-song voice. '"Mar-shall's an orphan, Mar-shall's an orphan."; "Where's your parents, *orphan* girl? Oh, that's right, you haven't *got* any!"'

A splosh of milk in everyone's tea. 'Sometimes you have to reclaim a word, wear it with pride so the bastards can't use it to hurt you.'

She handed a mug to Logan. 'You've been to see Keira, right? Charlie never stayed at her house overnight, because his nan would freak if he was out of her sight for that long. *Obviously* the world's full of corrupting influences for her nice little *white* boy.' A sad little laugh. 'She'll be throwing a total wobbly now he's missing.'

'So ... you think his grandmother radicalised him? He burned the hotel to please her?'

'Charlie's been shagging the darkest one of his friends to *spite* the old cow.' She passed a mug to Tufty. 'Sorry, that was unfair. There was probably a *bit* of spite involved, but Charlie really does love Keira. The only reason he doesn't have her name tattooed across his chest is his nan would find out.' Marshall rolled her eyes. 'And "Oh, the stress would kill her!" Good sodding riddance.'

Marshall picked Mug Number Three off the worktop. ''Scuse me. Need to take this up to Grandad.' Then off she went, shutting the door behind her.

Tufty had a slurp. 'Sarge: you thinking what I'm thinking?'

'I severely doubt it.' Frowning out at the garden. 'Every single one of Charles MacGarioch's friends *swears* he wasn't racist. Or xenophobic. Or a violent prick. So why the arson attack on a migrant hotel?'

The wee loon put on his old-man-doctor voice again. '"In times like these, my old friend and colleague, Mr Sherlock Holmes, would go back to the very beginning, because it's a very good place to start."'

'If you burst into song, I'm going to wallop you one.'

There had to be *some* sort of reason for all this horror and misery. People didn't just wake up one morning and decide to torch a hotel full of people.

A lovely big ginger cat padded its way across the grass, tail a feather-duster plume against the dark foliage.

A blackbird hurled abuse at it from the branches of a plum tree.

A quartet of bluetits swarmed around a dangly thing of peanuts...

Maybe the wee loon had a point?

'OK, let's *go* back to the very beginning: how did we land on Charles MacGarioch as our suspect? Easy: we got an anonymous tip-off on the Crimestoppers hotline.' Logan took a sip of tea. Bit peely-wally, but not bad. 'Can you bring the call up? Play it?'

'Erm...' Tufty fiddled with his phone. 'Might take a while...'

'So, the informant tells us about some forensic evidence planked in Tillydrone. We go look, and lo-and-behold, there's Charles MacGarioch's fingerprints all over a five-litre petrol can. Tests show that bits of foliage from a hedge next to the hotel got trapped when the lid was screwed back on.' Logan plucked the newspaper from the pile of post by the poopy biscuit tin – that morning's *Aberdeen Examiner*. 'We get a warrant – go in locked-and-loaded – and the next thing you know, we're pulling an ice-cream van out of the river and Charles MacGarioch's disappeared.'

He unfolded the paper: 'NEWSPAPER OWNER ABDUCTED BY SICK WEIRDO' above a photo of Natasha Agapova, with the subheading 'POLICE FUMBLE INVESTIGATION AS WORLD PRESS LOOKS ON'.

Bloody Colin Bloody Miller.

'Oh for...' Logan thumped the front page. 'How can we be *fumbling* it? We only found out last night! Bunch of *bastards*.'

'Bingoroonie.' Tufty pressed something, then held his phone out.

A distorted electronic voice crackled from the wee speaker: '*I GOT SOME INFORMATION FOR YOU ABOUT THE FIRE AT THAT HOTEL, WITH THEM MIGRANTS. IT WAS CHARLES MACGARIOCH WHAT DID IT. HE BURNED THEM OUT GOOD. ... AND I GOT EVIDENCE. LOOK IN THE BIG SHARED BINS AT TILLYDRONE COURT. ... HE'S A DIRTY WEE RACIST BASTARD, WHO HATES IMMIGRANTS AND FOREIGNERS, AND HE DESERVES EVERYTHING HE'S GOT COMING.*'

Tufty lowered his phone. 'That's the lot.'

The door banged open and Marshall stomped in, finger up, mouth open, looking as if she was ready to give them a shouting at.

But instead of having a go, she stopped in the middle of the kitchen, frowning. Turning on the spot. Looking for something. Or someone...

'Oh... Thought I heard Spence.' She shook her head, then helped herself to the last mug of tea. 'Muscle-headed idiot still owes me fifteen quid for his circus tickets.' She froze, frowning back at Logan. 'What?'

He put the paper down. 'You thought you heard "Spence"? Spencer *Findlater*?'

'He's got this stupid app on his phone that does voices. You record a message and play it back as ... I don't know:

Hannibal Lecter, or the Joker, or … whatsit – killer robot thing from that Netflix show with all the explosions.' She pulled a face. 'That one got old *really* quick.' Poking the worktop with an angry finger. 'Well, he'd better show with my money or I'll jam that *hilarious* phone of his right up his wankhole. Bastard *swore* he'd come round yesterday, and did he? Did he *bollocks*.'

Sod.

Yesterday.

And Marshall's house was, what, a ten-minute walk from the Balmain House Hotel, where Spencer Findlater had done a runner? Maybe fifteen, tops. He'd been coming *here*.

Tufty opened his mouth, but Logan cut across him, before he could say anything stupid.

'I'll bet. Boys with their toys, eh?' Taking a swig of tea, nice and casual. 'So: you're all going to the circus? I was thinking of taking the family. We're probably too *late* to get tickets, though. As it's the last night.'

She shrugged one shoulder. 'Probably depends which performance you want to see. I booked ours *weeks* ago for the eight o'clock. Couple of pints in the Queen Vic first, wander up to Westburn Park, catch the show, then hit the funfair.' A smile spread across her face. 'Leave a trail of hotdog-and-candy-floss vomit all the way home.'

Oh, to be young and foolish.

She toasted them with her mug. 'If Spence doesn't turn up with my cash soon, I'll scalp you *his* ticket if you like?'

Ah…

'I'm afraid I've got some bad news about that.' Logan put his tea on the counter. 'You might want to sit down…'

'…and flipping *bazinga!*' Tufty bounced about in the driver's seat, as if dancing to some punk-rock tune only he could hear. 'We does has cracked the case wide open, like an alien chestburster and John Hurt's chest. Only we is definitely the xenomorph in this scenario and not John Hurt, cos his character did wind up dead, whereas *we* has wound up victorious investigators!'

Twit.

Carden Place slid by the pool car's windows, its granite buildings sparkling in the burning sun as Logan poked out a text to Chief Superintendent Pine:

> We think it was Spencer Findlater who put in the anonymous tip-off about Charles MacGarioch.
>
> If Forensic IT can crack his phone, they might find a recording.

His finger hovered over the 'Send' icon.

Yes, but what would getting Forensic IT involved *actually* achieve? And how long would it take them, given their case-load? Never mind the operational costs – did it make any difference if they could prove the guy in intensive care ratted out his mate?

Assuming they ever got their hands on Charles MacGarioch, they could just play him the recording and let him jump to his own conclusions.

Logan deleted that last sentence and replaced it with:

> It's possible they were in on it together.
>
> Can you pressure Forensics for an answer on the accelerants?
>
> Thanks.

Because surely the head of A Division would have more luck shouting 'FROG!' at them than he had.

Worth a go, anyway:

SEND.

Tufty stopped bum-dancing and had a frown instead. 'Do you think Marshall's going to be OK? She took it pretty hard.'

'At least she's got her grandad. And her friends.'

Speaking of which...

He brought up Randolph Hay's last text and fired-off a reply:

> Sorry to be the bearer of bad news, but I wanted you to know that Spencer Findlater has been in a serious accident.
>
> He's in ARI: Ward 212

Knowing the Orphan Grapevine, every one of Spencer's friends would know by lunchtime. With any luck, maybe one of them would even check in on his grandad?

Must remember and ask Pine about that care package...

Tufty sighed. 'It's a shame we can't just be the Happy Police. Nothing but good news and handing out sweeties.'

Yeah. That's how people ended up on the register.

Logan tapped his phone against his chin as the pale spiky mass of a deconsecrated church loomed at the side of the road.

In an ideal world, they'd just head up to ARI and interview Spencer Findlater. But that was a bit tricky, what with him being unconscious and everything.

Just have to find Charles MacGarioch the old-fashioned way.

Still no reply from Rennie about the stakeout, so Logan gave the lazy sod a call. Listening to it ring and ring and ring.

Carden Place turned into Skene Street and one side of the street swapped granite grey for leafy green.

'You have reached the Triple-Five Messaging Service. Please leave a message after the tone.'

Bleeeep.

Logan did: 'Where are you?' Then hung up. 'Rennie's not answering his phone.'

Tufty nodded, as if that were only to be expected of a second-rate ex-sidekick. 'Did I tell you Kate's moving in tonight? Well, *mostly* moving in; she's still got a bunch of stuff at her dad's. But I does officially has a "lovenest"!' Dancing in his seat again.

Logan tried Steel instead – it just rang and rang as well.

A grin from the wee loon. 'Never lived with a woman before. Well, my *mum*, but that doesn't count for the purposes of this narrative.' Looking across the car. 'When did you get your first lovenest Sarge? Was it—'

'The hell do you want?'

Charming as ever.

'Progress report would be nice.'

'Lunchtime, you said: it's not even twenty past nine!'

'Have you guys not done anything *at all*?'

'Course we sodding have, but it'd go quicker without you crawling up my bumhole every five minutes.'

They nipped straight through the lights by Aberdeen Grammar School, just as they changed to amber.

'Rennie's not answering his phone.'

'Then go make his *life miserable instead of* mine*! Gaaaah!'* And with that, she hung up. Because Steel had never really got the hang of being demoted, as if the world should just pretend she still outranked him.

'You know,' Logan popped his phone on the dashboard, 'I'm beginning to regret bumping her up to acting DI again.'

Tufty took them straight across the junction with Rosemount Viaduct, past the Noose & Monkey, and on down the hill – because he clearly wasn't wild and rebellious enough to drive down Schoolhill, violating its pedestrian-and-cycle zone. 'If you're looking for someone to promote, I'm in the market, Sarge. Now that I've got a lovenest to support.'

'Detective Inspector Stewart Quirrel...' He pantomimed out a massive shudder. 'That's a bilious sack of cheese-fuelled nightmares, waiting to happen.'

'But it would make a *great* six-part drama for BBC Two. I could play myself, on account of already being an international-film-star-celebrity-type person!'

Do *not* encourage him.

Logan changed the subject: 'When we get back to the ranch, I want you to come up with a plan that'll get me out of this stupid MAPPA meeting, OK? Some sort of breakthrough, like yesterday.' Hang on... 'Only no more dead bodies! We've got enough crap to wade through as it is.'

46

Forty-five minutes in and still no sign of rescue from Tufty.

Instead, Logan was stuck in the same boring Multi-Agency Public Protection Arrangements meeting, with the same *boring* talking points from the same *boring* people, the same assortment of disappointing biscuits, and the same burnt-plastic-tasting-mouldering-away-in-a-thermos coffee.

Wasn't easy – pretending to pay attention when the air was treacle-thick, after a scant two-hours' sleep in the passenger seat of a manky Vauxhall.

Oliver from Waste and Recycling pointed his clicker at the pull-down projection screen and yet another dull graph loomed across the wall. 'So, we can see that the projected refuse from the event is likely to overspill all bin capacity in the designated area...'

Maybe no one would notice if Logan just shut his eyes for a minute or three. Not as if there was anything worth listening to anyway.

Jessica from the Roads Department swirled the little red dot of her laser pointer across a map of central Aberdeen. '...and unless we limit the *scope* of the march, we're looking at road closures on Holburn Street, Alford Place, Rose Street, Chapel Street, Bon-Accord Terrace—'

'All right, Jessica,' Keith from the Council waved a hand in her direction. 'I think we can all read the slide.'

Her face pinched. '*Excuse me*, Keith, but I don't remember interrupting *your* presentation with passive-aggressive attacks. I am *merely* trying to illustrate the *scale* of the challenge presented by the proposed route.'

To be honest, even another dead body would be welcome at this point...

The air in Conference Room One was now so stale you couldn't even sell it as a roadside-service-station sandwich.

Logan propped his head up with one hand, freeing the other to write the same five words in his notepad, over and over again: 'KILL THEM. KILL THEM ALL!'

Abby from the Ambulance Service scrubbed her hands across her face, making her silver bob quiver. Even the three-pipped epaulettes on her dark-green, short-sleeved shirt were beginning to wilt as she had another go: 'Look, I'm sorry if this is inconveniencing everyone, but there's *limited capacity* and we're already looking at a restricted service due to illness. Add in the fact that we're running out of hospital beds, and this whole thing is a major incident waiting to happen!'

Keith gave her the benefit of a patronising smile. 'I think what Abby is *trying* to say is that while there are *challenges* to overcome, Aberdeen can meet them – with sufficient planning and some smart resource management!'

She curled her hands into claws and bared her teeth at the ceiling tiles. 'That's *not* what I'm saying *at all*! I'm saying this march is the worst possible thing, happening at the worst possible time!'

Logan's pen went to work again: 'KILL THEM. KILL THEM ALL!'

•

Two and a half hours after it started, everyone filed out of the meeting room. Bustling off to make someone else's life miserable for a change.

Logan ripped the incriminating pages from his notebook, crumpled them up and lobbed them overhand at the bin.

Ten points.

Which was the first good thing that'd happened since arriving back at the station.

He stepped into the corridor, and there was Captain Useless, waiting for him with a clipboard.

Logan gave Tufty a glare. 'Where were you, when I needed rescuing in there?'

'First: Sergeant Rennie's been sent home with the Snottery Ague.'

Of course he had.

'So, who's running the surveillance op?'

'Sergeant Moore. He says,' reading from the clipboard, '"Still no sign of MacGarioch. Now bored wankless and regretting decision to become a policeman."' A shrug. 'Sorry, Sarge.' Back to the clipboard. 'Second: you've got a review at one for Operation Hedgehog, two o'clock for Operation Red Dragon, half two for Operation Beholder, three fifteen is Operation Basilisk. Then you've got a break till half four and it's Operation Owlbear, four forty-five: Operation Firedrake, and Professional Standards at five. We shall call that "Operation Necrophidius", which, as we all know, means "Death Worm". And DI Marshall wants a word about Operation Disenchanter, soon as possible.'

Logan stared at him. 'What the utter, goat-buggering *hell* are you talking about?'

'I named all the operations, Sarge, so we know which one we're talking about.'

Unbelievable.

He shook his head, stalking off down the corridor. 'Halfwits. Just ... total...'

Tufty scampered after him. 'Oh, and Operation Gelatinous Cube are waiting for you now.' A little wistful sigh whined free. 'They has got *chips!*'

They pushed through the door at the end, into reception.

Council workers bustled about, buying sandwiches from a man with a cart, or heading out for a sneaky lunchtime pint or three to get them through the day.

Logan scuffed to a halt. 'Gelatinous *what?*'

'Cube, Sarge. It's a ten-foot block of acidic ooze that consumes any organic material it finds in the dungeon. Like—'

'Just... What – is – it: the operation, you ffffff...' Don't say it. Calm. Try not to scream at whatever the buggering *fuck* this was. He scrunched his eyes closed and strangled it down. '*Please,* Tufty, do *not* screw with me right now. I've had nothing to eat, except a couple of manky meeting-room biscuits, since yesterday lunchtime; I've had two hours' sleep; I'm running on caffeine and fumes;' peeling one eye open to glare at the little twit, 'and I will *genuinely* murder you!'

Tufty pulled his chin in. 'Ah... OK: it's Acting DI Steel's team doing background on Natasha Agapova and Adrian Shearsmith.'

'THEN JUST BLOODY SAY SO!'

The lunchtime buzz evaporated, and everyone turned to stare at the shouty police officer.

Deep breath. 'Sorry.' Logan massaged his temples. 'Can we...' pointing at the stairwell. 'Please?'

Going pink from the nape of his neck to the tips of his ears, Tufty scurried over there, unlocked the security door and held it open. 'Sarge.'

He stomped past into the stairwell. '*Thank* you.'

Halfway up the stairs, in strained silence, and here came

Biohazard, clattering his way down towards them. Carnivorous underwear eating his rectum again. Leaving him a little out of breath. 'Guv! Guv! Oh, thank shite for that. There's a—'

'Should you not be elbows-deep in a post mortem right now?'

'Got called out of it. We have a … situation. Complication. *Thing.*'

Was there ever anything else?

Logan headed up the steps again. 'Why me?'

Biohazard hurried after him. 'You know you got them to run tests on a pish stain at that newspaper woman's house, right?'

'If someone wants to whinge about the Forensics budget, tell them to take it up with the Chief Super.'

'No, Guv, it's...' He grabbed Logan's sleeve. 'They got DNA off it and there's a hit in the database.'

'*Finally* something goes right! Who was it?' Turning to shout down the stairs. 'Tufty: get a car, we're off to arrest the bastard and save the day!'

'That's the complication:' Biohazard cleared his throat, then looked off into the distance – not making eye contact. 'DNA matches the guy we pulled out of the river yesterday. It's Andrew Shaw.'

Logan barged into the tiny incident room and the stomach-growling aroma of hot chips and sharp vinegar. *'How?'*

Biohazard slunk in after him. 'Well, I don't know, do I! I got the message: I came to tell you. I'm just the messenger here, I'm not for shooting!'

Contrary to expectations, Steel's team had actually done some work for a change: the whiteboard wall was covered in notes and lines and boxes, the flipchart even had a checklist of steps on it – most of which had been ticked off. And now, they were all sitting about, munching through their chipfest.

Steel popped a chunk of fish in her gob, chewing with her mouth open. 'Aye, aye, it's the Chuckle Brothers. Come to spread a bit of lunchtime cheer?'

Tufty pulled a chair over to the whiteboard wall and climbed up onto it to write 'OPERATION "FIND NATASHA AGAPOVA"' at the top, above all the boxes and squiggles.

'You:' Logan stabbed a finger at Biohazard, 'I need a list of last-known associates, right now.'

An embarrassed cough. 'We're still working on it, and—'

Logan clapped his hands, turning to face the lunch-munching room. 'Everybody – change of plan. I need you to stop whatever you were doing and dig into Andrew Wallace Shaw instead.'

'Urgh...' Harmsworth made a depressed-frog face. 'Didn't I say this was going to bite us on the behind?'

Steel sooked her fingers clean. 'And do you want to tell us *why?*'

'Shaw was in Natasha Agapova's house – he pissed in her daughter's bedroom.'

'Eh?' Barrett blinked. 'So, what, we're saying *he* kidnapped her?'

Lund ripped the end off a mealie pudding. 'Didn't do a very good job of it, though, did he? Ended up dead in the river.'

'Yeah, I know *that*, but I thought he was a rapey wee spud, not a kidnappy one.'

A grimace from Biohazard. 'Oh, he was definitely rapey.'

'Can we all *please*...' Logan pinched the bridge of his nose, but the headache was already beginning to form. 'That's why we need a list of Shaw's associates.'

The silence that followed was only interrupted by the sound of crunching and chewing. Lots of frowns doing the rounds. Hopefully as people *thought* about the implications.

Biohazard was the first to twig. 'Hang on: you think Shaw had a *rape buddy*, right? But there's no mention of him having a partner for any of the other attacks! Not in the witness statements, anyway.' He bit his bottom lip, wrinkles growing between his eyebrows. 'But *maybe*, when Shaw breaks into Agapova's house, he's already decided he won't just rape-and-run – he's going to *abduct* her. Take her somewhere to abuse, for as long as he likes. And *that's* why he needs a rape buddy this time.'

Lund curled her lip. 'Can we not use the words "*Rape Buddy*"? There's nothing jolly-ha-ha about it.'

'But something happens: Shaw and his ...' Biohazard cleared his throat as Lund scowled at him, 'and his *accomplice* fall out. They fight, accomplice kills him, dumps his body, makes off with our victim.'

'Ah...' A raised eyebrow from Harmsworth. 'Didn't want to share the ransom.' He bit into his mock chop, then paused, mouthful unchewed – making the words all muffled. 'Hang on. In that case, why phone the answering machine and leave that "karma hurricane" threat?'

Steel crunched some more. 'The boy's got a point.'

A bit of mock-chop-chewing, then: 'Theatrics? Or maybe it's to throw us off the scent? We're off looking for a lone-gunman-sort-of-revenge-killer when it's really a pair of kidnappers?'

Logan pointed at Biohazard again. 'Does the Chief Super know?'

'Oh no.' Backing away, hands up. 'Just because I'm an acting DI, doesn't mean I've got a death wish. And it'll sound better coming from *you*, right, Guv?'

Steel grinned a greasy grin. 'I'll do it.' Then dipped a lump of battered fish into a big sklodge of mayonnaise – munching away as a dollop fell onto her black T-shirt. 'Don't worry, I'll be gentle with her.'

Yeah, right.

'No thank you, Monica Spewinsky. Things are bad enough, without *you* joining in.'

Come on: there had to be a logical way through this…

Logan paced in front of the whiteboard wall. 'Maybe this kidnap plot didn't just spring out of nowhere – maybe Natasha Agapova and Andrew Shaw's paths crossed somehow?' That made sense, didn't it? Logan grabbed Biohazard by the shoulder and marched him towards the door. 'Shaw worked in a hairdresser; she has hair. Start there. And tell Forensics, Shaw's car is now top priority – could be our abduction vehicle. Strip it down to the bare metal if they have to, but *find* us something!' Pausing on the threshold to point at everyone else. 'The rest of you: less eating, more digging!'

XLVII

Natasha stood as far away from her anchor as the chain would allow, looking out through the crumbling window hole.

The air in her prison was like a giant fist, wrapped around her chest, squeezing every breath as merciless sunlight battered down on the world.

Those bastard flies had multiplied, droning through the sweaty, sticky air. And yeah, she used to shake them off, but what was the point? They just landed again. Feeding on the white tidemarks of salt that crusted her dirty, naked skin.

Mind you, it was hard to tell what was dirt and what was bruising. *Everything* ached as her battered flesh darkened – fresh blossoms of red and purple spreading out where DS Davis tried to break her ribs last night.

And speaking of the bastard...

Those fat *buzzzzzzzzzzzzzz*ing bluebottles weren't the only sound; a diesel growl came from behind the barn, joined by a rattling crack, clank, scrape, and rumble.

And there, just visible through the gap between the barn's concrete wall and the other crappy outbuilding, was a sliver of rusty yellow digger. The excavator arm swung back for another go, gouging a huge clod of earth from the weed-choked field. Lifting it high, then swinging it around to dump onto a growing pile.

You'd think the sonofabitch would be out in his patrol car,

beating up suspects and soliciting bribes, or arresting people for telling the truth on social media, but here he was: digging a hole.

Or, more likely, a not-so-shallow grave.

And no prizes for guessing who *that* was for.

Natasha opened her water and took a small sip. Just enough to wet the inside of her mouth. There was still about a third of it left, but there was only so long you could nurse one tiny little bottle.

She struggled the top back on and placed it on the ground at her bare feet – not easy with both wrists cuffed to this stupid bloody collar – then hauled in a deep breath.

Took hold of the chain.

Braced herself.

And pulled.

And pulled.

And pulled…

But the galvanised bucket was stuck firm, wedged up against that bloody line of buried stone.

She gave it one last haul, legs trembling with the effort, jaw clenched, snarling out a strangled scream as black-and-yellow spots flickered across her prison's bare stone walls.

'BASTARD, WANKING … *FUCK!*'

Natasha let go of the chain and staggered, folding over with the effort, blood *whump-whump-whump*ing in her ears.

God, how great it would be to take a sledgehammer and smash the living *crap* out of the thing, till the concrete shattered and the chain came free and the bin was covered in dents. Then go hunting for DS *Bloody* Davis.

Instead, all she could do was bare her teeth, stick her heel against the bucket's lip and shove.

'Fucking thing!'

Another shove, harder this time.

'AAAAAAAAAAARGGH!'

It rocked back on its base.

Not far, maybe only an inch, before slamming down again with a heavy whump and a puff of dust. But it *moved*.

That was something, right?

Oh, that was more than something.

Right now, that was *everything*.

She peered through the window hole again.

The digger arm swung and gouged. Which meant Davis was probably going to be busy for a while.

Natasha dropped down on her bum, scooting forward till she could place one foot onto the bucket's rim, then tipping over onto her back to get the other foot in place. Like she was lying on a doctor's table, waiting for a smear test.

Another deep breath.

Then she *shoved*. And *strained*. And *swore*...

And the bucket bloody *moved* – slowly tipping backwards as her legs trembled with the effort. Then it was past its tipping point and the thing *thump*ed over onto its side.

Yes!

She rolled over and clambered upright again. Breathing hard as she stood over the felled bucket. Then put her heel against the warm metal and pushed.

It was still bloody heavy, but it rolled.

A couple more and she'd even managed to get it over the buried rock.

By shoving at different points along her anchor, it was easy enough to make the bucket go left or right.

And yeah, it'd be *way* easier if she could push the thing about with her hands, but there was no chance of that while her wrists were attached to this bloody collar round her neck.

It was still a gigantic step forward, compared to ten minutes ago.

Now all she needed was for DS Davis to go walkabout for a few hours, so she could make use of her newfound freedom. Bastard had to go to work sometime, right?

Maybe she'd find a hacksaw, or a file, or a pair of bolt-cutters lying about the place? *Anything* that would break this bloody chain and set her free.

Assuming he wasn't planning to finish digging that grave, then drag her straight out there and bury her alive. Screaming and scratching away inside her coffin. Hidden – deep in the cold dark ground – where no one would *ever* find her...

48

The conference room was *packed*. They'd even had to draft in extra chairs from the council offices. And now the noise was borderline deafening, as the assembled press fidgeted in their seats, shouting to each other, checking their equipment, yelling down the phone because it was so sodding loud.

Oh yes: a fatal arson attack on a migrant hotel, and a murdered body in the river, were sort of newsworthy enough, *in their way*, but a missing Media Tycoon was a STORY!

Logan scanned the room again.

No sign of the Chief Super, but PC Sweeny had taken shelter behind the cluster of flipcharts in the corner, crunching Rennies like they were on special offer, a stack of paper clutched to his chest, and a worried look on his face.

Logan slipped around the edge of the seating area and joined him. 'Where's the Boss?'

'She'll be here.' A look of horror slithered across his face. 'Why? Did someone say she *wouldn't* be? Has something happened?' Juggling his paperwork and dragging out his phone. 'God's sake, no one ever tells me anything...'

'Far as I know, the briefing's still on. I'm just looking for her.'

Sweeny scowled. 'Don't *do* that.' He poked at his screen. 'The one-o'clock feeding frenzy is going to be insane. We've got CNN and Fox News and Al Jazeera and ... some stations from France, Germany, and Italy I can't pronounce. Then there's the Australian broadcasters and New Zealand and Mexico and Canada and I just want to go back to CID and be a proper *policeman* again...'

The door opened and in marched Chief Superintendent Pine.

Some of the less experienced newshounds perked up the moment she appeared – microphones, cameras, and notebooks at the ready – while the more practised hands kept right on doing what they were doing, safe in the knowledge that sod-all would happen till the briefing officially started.

Pine marched across the room to Sweeny's flipchart fortress, and raised an eyebrow at Logan. 'Don't remember shouting "frog".'

Sweeny checked his watch. 'We're going to be late.'

'Been trying to get hold of you, Boss. Didn't reply to any of my texts.'

'Texts?' A frown. 'What texts? Are you sure you...' She produced her phone, flipped the cover open, then sagged. 'Bloody battery's flat.'

So, it wasn't just him.

'That's what I get for never being off the damn thing today.' She narrowed her eyes. 'Thought I told you to dress the part.'

Eh?

Full black uniform, peaked cap under the oxter, shiny black shoes. 'But—'

'You were trying to get hold of me?'

Sweeny made wafting gestures towards the podium, with its covered table and garland of microphones. 'I'm sure whatever DCI McRae has to say, it can wait till *after* the briefing. Can't keep the *world press* waiting!'

'Boss: we have a *complication.*'

'Oh God...' Pine's head fell back, and she winced at the

ceiling. 'I knew it was going to be a crap day the moment I got up...'

For a building that was so Gothic and over-the-top on the outside, Marischal College's quad was strangely antiseptic and austere. There wasn't a single bush or tree or bit of green in evidence. Just grey granite walls and big flat paving slabs.

The only things breaking the monochrome monotony were a line of uncomfortable-looking benches, and one of those stupid paint-a-fibreglass-statue-of-some-random-animal-or-cartoon-character-in-whacky-colours-to-express-your-civic-pride things. A large multicoloured haggis in this case, complete with tammy, bagpipe legs, and massive grin.

Somehow, it just made the bare space seem even more grim.

Logan and Chief Superintendent Pine stood in the sunlight, but Sweeny lurked in the nearest shadow. Like an indigestion-prone Gollum.

'Christ.' Pine covered her face with her hands. 'That went well...'

'Hardly *your* fault, Boss. It's one of their own who's missing – they were always going to turn this into a three-ring-circus of shite.'

'Could've done without Adrian Shearsmith recording a sodding video address "for immediate release".'

Yeah...

That *definitely* hadn't helped.

Buried deep in his trouser pocket, Logan's phone *ding-buzz*ed at him. But he left it where it was, because Chief Superintendents were even worse than teachers when it came to things like that.

Sweeny tapped his watch. 'Hate to rush you, Boss, but you've got a one-on-one with Channel Seven News in fifteen minutes. All the way from Australia.'

It was a bit underhand, but Logan floated the idea anyway: 'Don't suppose we can leak that Shearsmith's putting his ex-wife's life at risk with all this publicity?'

'*No!*' Sweeny reached for the antacids again. 'Can you imagine what would happen if they found out we'd briefed against the victim's family? Absolutely not.'

Pine shrugged. 'Though we *could* have a private word with him? Try to make him see sense. All on the same side; pulling together as a team. Appeal to his conscience.'

'He's a media mogul. They don't have one.' Sweeny checked his watch again. 'Fourteen minutes.'

'I would really appreciate some sort of breakthrough on this one, Logan. A morsel of chum to throw to the sharks?'

Suppose this was her officially shouting 'frog'.

OK.

Logan dug out his notebook. 'We need door-to-doors on the road where Shaw's car was found – canvass the whole area. Maybe he was thick enough to park near where they're hiding Agapova?'

'*Could* be worth a try.' Though she didn't sound convinced. 'But why—'

'*SARGE!*'

Everyone turned, and there was Tufty scampering across the quad like an excited squirrel, while Steel sashayed along behind him – playing it cool, pulling on a pair of massive sunglasses that looked suspiciously like the ones Rennie had 'lost'.

'Sarge, Sarge, Sarge, Sarge, Sarge!' The wee loon skidded to a halt, ogled at Pine for a second, then tugged his forelock. 'Oh, and *Boss*, of course.'

Steel caught up with him, waggling her eyebrows at the Chief Super. 'Hey, Sexy.'

Pine stiffened. 'Are you going to be like this till you retire?'

'Probably worse, if anything.' Big smile. 'But I'm sweetly pretty and come bearing good news, so I'm sure you'll indulge me.' Wink. She turned to Logan. 'Remember that bollocks you were on about: "Shaw worked in a hairdresser, Agapova has hair"? Well—'

'We did find an connection!' Tufty bounced on the spot. 'She was one of his clients! Got a trim and her roots done, last week.'

Steel thumped him one for spoiling her big surprise. 'We're on our way to check the place out, if anyone's interested?'

'Go.' Pine gave Logan the nod. 'See who else is on Shaw's books. And if anyone knows about an accomplice.'

Which sounded like a massive waste of time, but a wise frog did what he was told. 'Boss.'

Steel sidled closer. 'Why don't *you* come, Roslyn? Be a bit crowded in the car, but you could sit on my lap? Wink, wink.' Dropping her voice to a saucy whisper. 'If you like, I can get the wee loon to drive over all the potholes. Bump-bump, jiggle-jiggle...?'

'You do know I can have you suspended?'

'Aye: on full pay.' Adopting a damsel-in-distress pose: one arm out and down, the back of her other hand to her forehead. 'Lawd have *mercy* – how *ever* will ah cope?'

Sweeny showed everyone his watch. 'Twelve minutes. Look, it really *would* help to meet the reporter and crew first. Establish a rapport before they start filming? *Please?*'

Right: it was time for someone to take charge.

Logan poked a finger at Steel. 'You: put your wrinkly libido back in its box.' Then Tufty. 'You: get a car.' Then Sweeny. 'You: you're a *police* officer! Stop whining and grow a truncheon.' Then Pine. 'And you...' He lowered his pointing finger. Cleared his throat. 'We'll get right on that. Boss.'

•

Biohazard's voice whined out of Logan's phone, as the pool car drifted up Union Street. *'Oh, in the name of pish! How? I've got three more work-shy bastards signed off on the sick since yesterday – barely coping as it is...'*

To be honest, Aberdeen's main street was a bit depressing these days, dressed in all its boarded-up-and-To-Let-/-May-Sell finery, where charity shops and mobile phone places rubbed shoulders with vape stores, bookies, and the occasional chain outlet. A few local businesses had bucked the trend, but it was nothing like it used to be.

Tufty – doing the driving – was probably too young and teuchtery to remember it in its glory days, and Steel – parked in the back, like Lady Muck – was too demob-happy to care.

'Come on, Guv: where am I supposed to find extra bodies for door-to-doors?'

'That's why they pay you the big bucks, Acting Detective Inspector Marshall. And you'd better PNC check everyone living in a two-street radius as well. Never know your luck...?'

The Doric-columned pomp of the Music Hall went by on the right, draped with banners for the Aberdeen International Book Festival.

On the other side of the road, a busker wanged away on her guitar outside Burger King, singing about how meat is murder and the monarchy are all a bunch of chinless parasites anyway.

'Still there?'

Biohazard groaned. *'Being a DI sucks balls.'* He hissed out a long breath, then: *'I'll see what I can do.'*

'Good lad.' Logan hung up.

Probably wouldn't do any good, but at least it would look as if they were doing something. And with some investigations that was half the battle – making sure no one noticed you were just keeping busy until a lucky break popped up.

And who knew, maybe Andrew Shaw really *had* been thick enough to park his Peugeot outside wherever it was they were keeping Natasha Agapova?

This whole thing could be solved by teatime.

'Sa-arge?' Tufty waved across the car at him. 'Do you think I should have a housewarming, Sarge? Well, another one. I mean I *did* has one when I moved into the flat, but—'

'Ha!' Steel reached through from the back and thumped him one. 'A forty-eight-hour *Dungeons and Dragons* marathon *isn't* a party. A party has booze, nipples, nibbles, and car keys in a bowl.'

Logan scowled at her in the rear-view. 'Do you have to?'

'You're just jealous.'

'I am *not*. I just don't see why you've got to get randier and lechier with every passing day.'

Ding-buzz.

COLIN MILLER:

> Your boss had a well crappy press conference.
>
> Looked like someone jammed a half-defrosted jobbie up her arse.
>
> Terrible liar too.

Steel stroked her chin. 'It's impending retirement that does it. Thirty years I've given this job. *Thirty sodding years.* I've got a lot of repressed angst to get rid of.'

Straight across at the lights, where Waterstones and Ottakar's used to be – replaced by a New-York-style eatery and a Pret A Manger respectively. Because that was 'progress'.

Ding-buzz.

COLIN MILLER:

Something's happened, hasn't it?

Given I tipped you numpties off about this whole thing –
think you owe me an update on any developments!

Cheeky bastard. As if he and his stupid newspaper hadn't
made everything worse.

'Aye, wait, did I say "repressed angst"? I meant "mischief".'
Steel flashed an evil grin. 'Soon as I'm retired, who am I going
to wind up: Susan? She doesn't deserve that.'

'But *we* do?'

'Trust me, Laz: you're gonna miss me when I'm gone.'

'Like a peptic ulcer.'

The car drove past more boarded-up units and estate-
agents' signs. Then a bit of a highlight with Gilcomston
Church – all pointy and fancy, shining in the afternoon sun. A
couple of homeless gentlemen sat on the steps outside: Oliver
Sharples, scoofing tins of Special Brew; while his associate,
Eddy Dunn polished off a two-litre bottle of Strongbow, in
contravention of Aberdeen City Council Bylaws 2009. They
toasted the pool car as it pottered along.

Logan thumbed out a reply to Colin's text:

You didn't 'tip us off' you cried for help. NOT the same thing.

And after your 'fumbling the investigation' story you get sod
all!

That would teach him.

The wee loon slowed for the junction ahead, smiling away
to himself. 'You'd've been very proud, of Old Romantic Tufty,
Sarge. Have I telled you the tale of how I did go down on one
knee and gived Kate a wee jewellery box with her very own
flat key in it?' Wriggling in his seat. 'It was an *special* key off

the interwebs, what you can has cut at a Timpsons or the like, with a happy Totoro on it!'

Nope.

Logan looked over his shoulder. 'Do you have *any* clue what he's on about?'

'To be honest, you kinda tune it out after a while. It's sort of soothing in a way. Like white noise. Or geeky whale song.'

They stopped at the lights, alongside a bus full of school-kids, who all looked as if someone had just told them Peppa Pig was off down the abattoir to be made into sausages.

Ding-buzz.

Colin Miller:

> OK, how's this: the Aberdeen Examiner's official position is 100% BASH THE COPS.
>
> If you're OK with that – don't speak to me.

Great.

The lights changed and Tufty hooked a right, abandoning Union Street for the delights of Chapel Street, where take-aways faced off against boutique stores. 'Ooh, nearly forgot, Kate wants to know: should we bring anything for the barbecue on Sunday?'

'Nooooooo...' Steel wrapped her arms around her head. 'Tell me you didn't invite *him*!'

'Tara insisted.'

'Ooh, ooh: how about mac-'n'-cheese, Sarge? Or pasta salad? Or a *really* big bag of oven chips? Everyone likes chips.' He pulled into a parking space, across the road from a hair-dresser's with pink-and-purple signage: 'Brenda's Hair & Beauty Palace ~ We Do That Voodoo To Your Go-To Hairdo!'

The whole front of the shop was glazed, so passers-by could

watch people getting their hair cut – though all the chairs were empty right now. A trio of posters were taped on the inside of the glass: one offering a loyalty programme, 'SIGN UP FOR MONTHLY HAIR-COLOURING AND GET FORTNIGHTLY ROOT-TOUCH-UPS FOR FREE!'; one advertising that circus in Westburn Park; and one for a 'CHARITY HEN NIGHT!!!', whatever *that* was, at the Hilton DoubleTree.

Logan climbed out into the scalding sunlight. 'No one likes pasta salad, it's like "yuck" mixed with "blah" in a bin-bag full of "meh…"' And that was being polite.

A pair of seagulls screeched at each other from the top of adjoining communal bins, though it was hard to tell which one was winning: Landfill or Mixed-Recycling.

Tufty waited for Steel to slouch out from the back, then locked the car. 'OK, but everyone loves macaroni-cheese, right?'

'Long as you don't put tomatoes in it.'

Steel fiddled with her uniform. 'We have fried onions and bacon bits in ours.' Digging at the crotch of her black Police Scotland trousers. 'But then we're *very* sophisticated.'

Tufty scampered across the road and opened the hairdresser's door for them, with a little bow. Which looked bloody ridiculous in the full stabproof-and-high-vis kit.

Inside, Brenda's Hair & Beauty Palace was … pink. With a pink-and-black tiled floor, pink walls, black work surfaces, and a row of circular mirrors reflecting the pink-and-chrome barber's chairs. Even the sinks were pink. And the whole place had a disturbingly *gynaecological* air.

The usual collection of newspapers and magazines were piled up on a coffee table for the patrons' reading pleasure, while a wall-mounted telly displayed afternoon TV with the sound turned off, so you could really enjoy the piped Bananarama jingling out of the salon's speakers.

A grid of headshots graced the wall above the till – each

one grinning or smouldering for the camera. Andrew Shaw was middle-left, doing his best Blue Steel with that big plastic face of his.

Down here, on the salon floor, a gangly young man was sweeping up a fuzzy drift of brown-and-grey hair, in skin-tight black jeans and a floaty pink shirt. His curly blue locks held back in a bouffant ponytail.

'Welcome to *chez moi*!' A plump middle-aged woman – Brenda, presumably – swept out from behind the desk, all smiles and open arms: pedal-pushers, wedge heels, a pink leopard-print blouse, and *immaculate* hair. She gave all three of them a good look, then wafted a hand in Logan and Tufty's direction. 'Well, I'm not sure even *I* can do anything about you two,' pouncing on Steel to froof her fingers through the rampant chaos of sticky-out grey hair. 'But *this*, I can work with!'

Steel's eyes went wide, flicking from Logan to Brenda and back again. 'Help…?'

No chance.

She was on her own this time.

49

Logan nodded at the wall of photos, above the till. 'Andrew Shaw works here.'

'Andy?' Brenda let go of Steel's mane and grabbed her shoulders instead. Steering her towards a seat. 'Well, *sort of*. He hires a chair. Not been in today, though. Or yesterday, come to that. But it's his money he's wasting, right?' She plonked Steel down and froofed her hair some more. 'Have you ever thought of a bit of colour? I mean, you're *rocking* the grey, but auburn would be nice with your complexion. Ooooooh: or a nice rich chestnut!'

Logan tried again. 'Do you have a list of his clients?'

'Hold on.' Looking over her shoulder. 'EMMA? EMMA SWEETIE, CAN YOU HELP THESE GENTLEMEN WHILE I GLAM UP THIS NICE LADY?'

A young woman emerged from a door at the back of the shop, with blonde hair down to the middle of her back and a wad of chewing gum on the go. All dressed up in pink and black.

Brenda clapped both hands down on Steel's shoulders. 'Now: how do you feel about a curly pixie with shaved sides?'

'Ermm…' Looking a *bit* like a hedgehog caught in the head-lights of an oncoming truck.

Emma slouched up to Logan and Tufty. Gave their haircuts a quick once-over, then rolled her eyes. 'Yup?' Sounding as bored as she looked.

'Hi.' Logan tried a friendly smile. 'We need to see your appointments book, going back about eight wee—'

'Six months would be *great*.' Tufty tilted his head on one side. 'Your hair is *amazing*, by the way. It's like molten gold!'

'Oh.' And she locked right in, giving the wee loon a little hair flip and a giggle. 'Why *thank you*. You're so sweet.' Emma slipped her arm into Tufty's. 'You come with me, and we'll get you logged on to the computer.'

Logan did a slow three-sixty. 'Don't suppose you've got CCTV, do you?'

She pointed with her free hand, lowering her voice to a whisper, even though there was no one else here. 'Cameras are fake.' Then squeezed Tufty's arm. 'Would you like a coffee?' And led him away, back through the door she'd emerged from.

Didn't sodding ask *Logan* if he wanted a coffee though, did she. Just snuck off with the wee loon.

Because women were essentially weird.

Meaning Logan had been abandoned, all alone, in the middle of the salon.

Pfff...

He wandered over to the coffee table and had a squint at the newspapers. The *Aberdeen Examiner* blared out its completely unfair 'POLICE FUMBLE INVESTIGATION AS WORLD PRESS LOOKS ON' nonsense, but because they'd scooped everyone on the Natasha Agapova story, none of the other publications were covering it. Yet. Instead, most of the tabloids hawked some variant of 'SOAP STAR SIGOURNEY'S COCAINE SHAME', except for the *Scottish Daily Post* which screamed 'ILLEGAL MIGRANTS ROBBING OAP GRAVES'. Because when racists were lobbing Molotov cocktails, why not give them tokens for free petrol?

Bunch of bastards.

Logan abandoned the papers and went for a frown out

through the shop windows at Chapel Street's various comings and goings instead. Which wasn't exactly thrilling.

Worse yet, the shop looked straight into the dining room of the hotel opposite, where a bunch of people were tucking into lunch.

His stomach snarled, like a wee gurgly wolf.

Well, it wasn't as if he was *doing* anything right now.

Might as well make use of this time to achieve something...

Logan emerged from the Chapel Bakery – Est. 1954 – the proud owner of a takeaway coffee and two wee paper bags, promisingly spotted with grease.

Soon as his foot hit pavement he opened one of the bags, shoogling the pie inside upwards, until half of it poked out. Took a bite of mince-and-mealie. Whoopha-whoompha-whoomphing his breath around the blisteringly hot, but delicious mouthful.

Then scuffed his way down the street, munching away, trying not to burn his mouth as the sun battered down from its dusty blue sky.

Probably should've put on sunscreen this morning, because the skin on his cheeks was already starting to tighten.

When he got to the pool car, Logan popped his coffee on the roof and went to do the same with his other paper bag. But some sort of evil seagull radar must've tipped off Landfill and Mixed-Recycling to its contents, because the pair of them stopped screaming at each other and glared across the road with envious eyes.

Well, they could sod *right* off.

He kept a jealous grip on both bags. Munching away, and talking to himself, as he reread the posters in Brenda's shop window. 'What the hell is a "Charity Hen Night"?'

A voice cut through the warm air, almost directly behind

him: *'It's kinda like bring-a-party-to-a-party, only with screaming drunken women, and male strippers.'*

Logan swallowing his bite of pie before turning around.

It was the gangly young guy from the salon.

Mr Blue-Hair had swapped sweeping-up for fiddling with a bicycle-handlebar-sized vape. 'And inflatable willies, of course. Lots and lots and lots of inflatable willies.' Fiddling finished, he took a sook on the thing, puffing out a dragon cloud of fruity steam. 'I worked behind the bar at one. Could've scraped oestrogen off the walls – thick as *cream cheese* it was.'

Logan finished off his pie. 'You been at Brenda's for long?'

'Man and boy.'

'Suppose you know Andrew Shaw?'

'Andy? Yeah. Got a *wicked* touch with the colouring. His cuts need work, but that man can take you from a Three-PB Deepest Espresso Brown to a Ten-B Extra-Light Beige Blonde without even breaking a sweat.' Another gargantuan tutti-frutti cloud puffed into the sky. 'Total respect, like. Dude's game's got *crackle*, you know?'

Nope.

Why did young people have to talk a load of shite these days? When did words stop meaning what they're meant to mean? And how *OLD* had Logan become since Elizabeth was born?

He creaked the lid off his coffee and took a sip. 'Andrew have a lot of friends?'

'Nah. Well, maybe down the gym. But think he kinda mostly keeps himself to himself. If we're off for a cocky-T after work, he's like half-a-lager and goneski.'

'I see.' Logan partially unwrapped Pie Number Two and had a bite. *Mmmm*: chicken curry. 'Are *you* his friend?'

The young bloke chewed on the inside of his cheek for a bit. 'Depends what he's done. You being polis and everything.'

'Ever hear him talk about his female clients?'

'What, in a *pervy* way? Naaaaaahhhhh. Andy isn't like that.' A huge sook on the vape produced a volcanic cloud. 'Only time I ever seen him completely tinfoiled was at the Christmas party. We all pile into The Groove Machine, for drinks-and-dancing after dinner, and he snogs some subsea engineer called Duncan. Said he only did it for a joke, but they were joking *hard*, you know? Tongues and,' miming cupping someone's crotch and giving it a squeeze or two. 'Pretty sure he got noshed-off in the gents, after.'

Logan bit into the crisp pastry and savoury filling. 'Just goes to show: you never know with people.' Munch, munch, munch. 'So, what about you?'

His mouth pinched, chin rising an inch with a sniff. 'Just cos I work in a *hairdresser's*, doesn't make me gay.'

'I meant, "are you Andrew's friend?"'

'And it doesn't make Andy gay, either. He's just ... *flexible*. Besides, all our clients are middle-aged wifies; you've seen the bloke – he must be beating them off with a *stick*.'

Logan scarfed down the last mouthful. 'Oh, you have *no* idea.' He crumpled up his paper bags, scoofed his coffee. Frowned across the road at Brenda's Hair & Beauty Palace. 'What gym did he go to? Where he might have friends.'

'Wellheads Fitness Studio, but you're wasting your time. Wanna know who Andy's best friend in the whole-wide-world is? His mum.'

With Steel keeping the salon's owner occupied, and Tufty off mining Emma for information, Logan retreated to the pool car. Sitting in the passenger seat with the windows rolled down, notebook out in front of him and a worried Biohazard Bob in his ear:

Far as I can tell, *they've all got alibis. And you know how you can always tell when someone's a murdering bastard, but trying to cover it up? Not getting that from any of them.'* A sad little breath grunted down the phone. '*Might be wrong, but I'd put a crate of baked beans on whoever killed Andrew Shaw not being one of his victims. Or their family.'*

'Could've hired someone to do it.'

'*Yeah, if you're an* idiot. *That's perfect blackmail material for life, isn't it. Someone goes out and kills for you: next thing you know, you're putting their kids through private school and buying them a five-berth caravan. Sides: you've still got all that guilt by association.'* Biohazard put on a tortured voice: '*"I'm responsible for this guy getting beaten to death…"'* Then back to normal again. '*Hard for everyday folk to live with something like that.'*

True.

Mixed-Recycling and Landfill must've declared some sort of truce, because the pair of them were sharing a half-eaten Mars Bar at the side of the road.

At least, *hope* it was a Mars Bar…

Probably best not to think about it too closely.

'*You coming back to the ranch anytime soon, Guv? Only the Chief Super's giving me the willies.'*

'As long as they're not inflatable.'

Silence.

'Never mind.' Logan tapped his pen on his notebook, where 'VICTIMS = KILLER(S)?!?' was underlined three times. 'Don't suppose they found any other DNA at Natasha Agapova's house, did they?'

'*Nah, because that would be helpful. Normally, you'd think hot-and-dry weather equals long-lasting DNA, but our kidnap victim was a great believer in humidifiers. We were lucky to get what we got from the pish stain.'*

Now that they'd finished the 'Mars Bar', Landfill and

Mixed-Recycling were at it again – screeching and flapping and screaming at each other.

Of course, maybe they *weren't* fighting? Maybe it was a mating dance? Couldn't be any more ridiculous than snogging a subsea engineer in a nightclub and pretending it was just a 'joke'.

'You still there, Guv?'

'Look: go through the ANPR again – see if anything pops out at you. This bastard's out there somewhere.' Logan flicked back a couple of pages in his notebook, to the scribbles about Andrew Shaw's gym membership. 'And get someone to check out Wellheads Fitness Studio. Our victim was a frequent flyer, might have met his killer and-or kidnapping-accomplice there.'

'Urgh...' As if Logan had just plopped a 'Mars Bar' on Biohazard's desk. *'Guv.'*

Logan hung up. Frowned out the window at the quarrelling/amorous seagulls.

Time to go check on his team.

He buzzed up all the windows, then climbed into the gritty afternoon heat. Jogging across the road between a taxi and a gaily painted florist's van.

Ding-buzz.

Safe on the other pavement, he checked his texts under the baleful eye of Landfill and Mixed-Recycling.

Four messages, waiting and unread. Lined up most recent to last.

BEARDY BEATTIE:
> Dear Acting DCI MacRae, I am in Incident Room B2 for our review meeting about Operation Red Dragon. Will you be much longer?

Oh, bloody hell. When did Tufty say that was meant to start – two o'clock or something?

Bugger.

Didn't change the fact that Beattie was a dick, though…

TARA:

> Talk about peer pressure – The Monitor Lizzard wants to go shopping for ALL BLACK GOTH CLOTHES!?!?!!
>
> She's joined a cult!

THE ICE QUEEN:

> Thank you for inviting Colin to your barbecue.
>
> Post-mortem suggests TOD range between 0000 and 0400.
>
> Cranial trauma most likely COD.
>
> Extensive tissue damage + dislocated fingers confirms possible torture.
>
> Will bring burgers and napkins.

And last, but not least:

DS ROBERTSON:

> Hi Guv
>
> We still on for this review meeting?
>
> Operation Hedgehog FTW!
>
> Cheers
>
> Henry

As that was the oldest message of the four, it meant Logan was very, very late for the meeting indeed.

And unlike Beardy Beattie, Robertson *wasn't* a dick.

He drifted to a halt outside Brenda's Hair & Beauty Palace and thumbed out a quick reply:

Sorry, Henry!

Got caught up on this body-in-the-river thing.

I owe you a bacon butty.

Tufty will reschedule, OK?

SEND.

And while he was at it, might as well get back to Tara as well:

It'll do her good to have some friends at school.

Tell her no painting her face white, though – she'll scare Cthulhu!

SEND.

The reply *ding*ed back before he'd even put his phone away, so clearly, Tara wasn't having a busy day at Trading Standards:

You know how obsessive she gets.

We'll be listening to MISERABLE MUSIC and hoovering BLACK GLITTER out of the carpet for years!

Probably. But that was kids for you.
His thumbs *tick-tick-tick-tickticktick-ticked* across the screen:

Let her find her tribe.

Sometimes children need this stuff.

It's how they learn friendship and responsibility and loyalty.

And that shit was *important* in life.
SEND.

He looked up from his phone, and there was that advert for the 'RUMPLINGTON BROTHERS' CIRCUS OF DELIGHTS!', in

Westburn Park. The poster was a cluttered mélange of puppet animals and real clowns and acrobats, with a big top in the background and a red-clad ringmaster in the middle, posing as if he were the most important man in the world.

And tonight was the last night...

'*...you'll never find anyone more loyal...*'

'*Charlie never misses an Orphan Outing.*'

'*...depends which performance you want to see. I booked ours weeks ago for the eight o'clock.*'

Worth a go, wasn't it?

Logan scrolled through his contacts and called Chief Superintendent Pine.

She answered with a sigh. '*If this is more bad news:* don't, *OK? Just heard McCulloch, Porter, and Pearce are down with the bloody plague. There'll be no one left at this rate!*'

'I've been thinking about—'

'*And the sodding press are all over us like a sticky sneeze. Did you hear the drubbing we got on the lunchtime news? You'd think someone had kidnapped the Dalai Lama, way they're going on about it.*'

'Boss, there's a possibility—'

'*And do you know what happened when I got on to head office for more backup? To help us find Natasha Agapova?*' A bitter laugh. '*Aye, right. Remember all those officers I've been promised from other divisions? Not any more. They can't spare* anyone – *most of them are off on the sick anyway.*' Pine puffed out another long unhappy breath. '*If you've got your heart set on a nation-wide crime spree, now's the perfect time.*'

Well, there was one easy win:

'So, cancel the protest march.'

A groan. '*You know I can't do that.*'

'We didn't have enough staff to start with, but now? It's a public-order disaster waiting to happen. Imagine the headlines if something kicks off and we've got rioting on Union Street.'

'Instead we'll have "Fascist Cops Crush Right To Protest!" Any other civil liberties you'd like to abolish while we're at it?'

Landfill and Mixed-Recycling *scrawk*ed into the air, a squabbling tornado of feathers and malevolence.

'No, but I *would* like to run an undercover op this evening. I know it's short notice for all the oversight, managerial, and risk-assessment stuff, but I think half a dozen plainclothes officers should do it. *Eight* would be better, but six would do.'

The seagulls battered away at each other, then Mixed-Recycling wheeled off to divebomb a woman eating a Cornish pasty outside the dry cleaner's.

Chief Superintendent Pine's voice went all thin and suspicious. *'An undercover operation to achieve* what?'

The woman flailed her arms, but Landfill swooped in to attack from the other side, and that was her pastyless, left with nothing to do but shake her fists and swear at the avian larcenists.

Logan looked back at the poster. 'I was thinking a fun night out at the circus...'

50

Brenda was still wrestling Steel's unruly mop into shape, with a hairdryer and set of curling tongs, when Logan stepped back into the salon.

The Crenellated Horror herself was fast asleep in the barber's chair, and by the look of things, she was in for a bit of a shock when she woke up. Which would be nice.

Tufty stuck his head out through the door at the back and gave Logan a wave. 'Sarge? Got something.' Then disappeared again.

Logan followed the vanishing twit into a cramped space with boxes and boxes and boxes of shampoo and conditioner and colourant and every other kind of hairy malarkey stacked up against the walls, two or three deep in places.

No sign of Emma.

A small desk was wedged in beneath a couple of shelves laden with lever-arch files. And that's where Tufty was sitting, fiddling about with a denture-beige desktop PC. 'I went through every appointment for three-and-a-bit years.'

Logan leaned his bum against a carton of hair gel. 'Thought you said six months?'

'Yes, but then I did *find* things. So I went back further and *keeped* finding things. Till three-and-a-bit years ago, which is when...?' Eyebrows up.

'Let me guess: Andrew Shaw started working here.'

'Not saying he was *definitely* responsible, but in addition to the victims we already knew about, I found eleven more. And that's just the ones who *reported* a sexual assault. Otherwise...' The wee loon puffed out his cheeks. 'I know it's wrong to be glad someone's dead, but Andrew Wallace Shaw was an *utter* shite.' A droop. 'Bad Tufty: pound in the swear jar.'

Eleven more victims...

'Think we'll let you off with that one.' Logan pointed at the computer. 'You got a list of names?'

'Should be sitting in your inbox. But just in case:' he hit three buttons on the keyboard and a teeny, old-fashioned ink-jet printer stuttered into life – screeking back and forth as it slowly clunked out a sheet of A4. 'Don't worry, I'll purge the print queue soon as it's done.' Swivelling his chair from side to side. 'Not sure if Shaw was being careful or not, but they weren't all his clients. He *was* working at least one day when the victim was in here getting their hair cut by someone else, though.'

'Bloody hell.' Logan plucked the printout from the machine, scanning the names. 'How did no one notice the connection?'

'Don't think anyone *looked*, Sarge.' A frown. 'To be fair, when someone's been sexually assaulted and we take their statement, we don't usually start with, "Ooh, where do you get your hair done?"' Tufty poked some more keys and 'DELETING PRINT HISTORY' appeared on the screen. He stood. 'Hope when they bury Horrid Andrew Shaw they plumb his grave up with a flush, because there's going to be a *lot* of people widdling on it.'

Quite right too.

The funeral home wouldn't even need to preserve Shaw's body in formaldehyde: his corpse would be pickled in urine.

Logan pocketed the list. 'Meanwhile: let's go see if we can't achieve something on the Natasha Agapova case. Think the Chief Super could do with a bit of good news today.'

Especially after the email he was about to send her.

As he stepped back out onto the salon floor, Brenda had the wee rectangular mirror out – showing Steel what the back of her own neck looked like – full of hairdressery pride. 'It takes *years* off you.'

Difficult to know if Steel agreed though, because she just sat there, in the pink-and-chrome chair, mouth hanging open, eyes wide, blinking at herself.

Her hair was shorn incredibly short at the sides and back, tapering outwards as it rose, towards a big wedge of curls on the top of her head – swept forwards so they coiled over her right eyebrow. Grey at the nape of her neck, darkening to a rich chocolaty brown.

Had to admit it was a huge improvement. Especially as her barnet normally looked as if someone had stuck a pound of Semtex up a badger.

'Time to go.' Logan handed Brenda a business card. 'Thanks for your cooperation. We'll be in touch if there's anything else.'

Tufty lowered his voice and leaned towards her. 'Word of advice – you might want to take this one down,' pointing at Andrew Shaw's portrait, 'and burn it.'

She looked a bit confused at that, but she'd find out soon enough...

> But looking on the bright side, at least this means we can potentially close out eleven unsolved rape cases and bring a bit of closure to Shaw's victims.

Logan gave his email one last readthrough, then sent it off to Chief Superintendent Pine, with Tufty's list attached.

The windows were down in the pool car, but there was precious little breeze to stir the muggy air as they sat outside Brenda's Hair & Beauty Palace waiting for Steel.

Tufty had his phone propped up against the steering wheel,

scrolling away and reading from the screen. 'So, we've missed the case reviews for Operation "Housebreakings Across Rubislaw"; Operation "Car Thefts"; and unless we break the sound barrier, Operation "Break-ins At Sports Shops" will have to start without you. *But*—'

'Nope. I already solved that one: it was Spencer Findlater. He's been feeding his protein-powder addiction. Evidence is all piled up in his bedroom.'

'Oh. Coolio. Tick that one off the list...' Poke, fiddle, scroll. 'Which means, if we leave *now*, you can still make Operation "Drugs In Lithuanian Teddy Bears", Operation "Camper Vans Stolen To Order", Operation "Food Van Turf War", before talking to Professional Standards about Princess Crumpled-Bum McGrumpy-Lumps.'

Speak of the Devil.

The back door opened, and Steel thumped into her seat, with a scowl on her face and brand-new curls bouncing away on top of her head. 'Better no' be talking about me, you pointy-nosed wee fart!'

Hang on...

Logan turned to Tufty. 'Camper vans? Food vans? No, no, no, no, no: those *aren't* Rutherford's investigations.'

'Yeah.' He bared his top teeth. 'They were DCI McCulloch's, only now he's off on the sick as well, so...?'

'Of course he is.' Sagging back in the passenger seat. 'Yet *more* sodding work.'

Steel checked herself in the rear-view mirror. 'Are you *seriously* going to slog your way through a bunch of sharny review meetings? When we could be out there: catching crooks and showing off my swanky new hairdo?'

'God's sake...' Logan scrubbed a hand across his face. 'I have *responsibilities*. I can't just—'

'You're such an idiot, Laz. Did you no' learn *anything* all

433

the years I was your boss?' Tousling her curls as she preened in the mirror. 'You're an acting *DCI* now – you don't do your own case reviews! You pick some hapless halfwit DI and you make *them* do it. And if they whinge, you say it's a "career-path development opportunity" and you're doing them a favour.' Waving a hand as if it was all settled. 'Tell them they have to produce a one-page summary for each meeting – in case some tosser further up the tree asks you about it – and everyone's happy.'

Actually, that wasn't a bad idea.

'Know what? I'm going to take your advice and palm my case reviews off on a hapless DI.' He pointed at her primping reflection. 'Here's a "career-path development opportunity" for you, *Acting* DI Steel.'

'Aye, nice try. Doesn't work if the victim knows what you're up to.' Steel clicked her seatbelt on. 'So: where we going?'

Ah well, it'd been worth a try.

'Altens. Time to have a rummage through our missing newspaper tycoon's work-life.'

The patrol car drifted south along Great Southern Road – which was a very grand name for a tooty-wee stretch of dual carriageway strung between two roundabouts.

Duthie Park was almost invisible behind a granite wall and bank of trees on the left, but a veritable henge of headstones popped above the eight-foot-high enclosure on the other side of the road. Which was, hopefully, tall enough to keep all the dead folk from breaking out of Allenvale Cemetery anytime soon.

Steel had moved on from admiring herself in the rear-view mirror to taking puckered-lips selfies, like a teenager.

Tufty nodded along to whatever song was playing in his hollow little head.

While Logan had a quick peek at his phone's screen to make sure the call hadn't been disconnected.

Doreen finally found her voice again: '*Are you* sure, *Guv?*'

'Think of it as a reward for all the sweaty searching. Plus, it's a great career-path development opportunity: shows the bosses you're ready to step up to DI full-time, if a vacancy opens up.'

'*Thanks, Guv! I won't let you down.*'

'I know: I trust you. Just make sure you've got those one-page summaries done by close of play, OK? Right, off you go. First meeting's in thirty-eight minutes.'

Logan ended the call and sat back in his seat.

Not feeling guilty about it in the slightest.

Not even a tiny bit.

Nope.

Tufty kept his eyes front, mouth pinched shut, not noggin-dancing any more. Radiating ... *judgement.*

'Well, it *is* a good career opportunity.'

Still nothing.

'Oh ... shut up.'

The park's high boundary wall gave way to more decorative wrought-iron railings, but the cemetery maintained its eight-foot barrier to contain the dangerous dead.

Tufty's stomach broke the judgemental silence with a popping grumble. 'Sarge, after we've been to the newspaper, can we go back to the ranch? I has not had no lunch, and there's still delicious curry in the CID fridge from yesterday.'

Steel stopped taking her own photograph for long enough to grin. 'No there isn't.'

'Sarge!' The wee loon pouted across the car. 'Saaa-aarge: tell her!'

'Don't be such a snidge.' She posed for another snap. 'How was I supposed to know it wasn't free to a good home?'

435

'It had a note on it: "Is Tufty's Lunch! Hands Off Thieving Bumheads!" with three exclamation marks!'

'You know the rules: any food left in the CID fridge overnight is fair game.' A happy sigh. 'And a very nice breakfast it made.'

'Saaaaaaaaa-aaaaaarrrrrrrrge!'

Logan shrugged. 'Sorry, Tufty, but rules is rules. You should've…'

Ding-buzz.

The pool car coasted to a stop at the roundabout onto King George IV Bridge, behind a Fiat Punto that some naughty person had prised the 'P' off and replaced with a 'C'.

Logan brought up his messages.

COLIN MILLER:

Got a hot story about to break.

Want to get your excuses in before it does?

Bloody hell, what *now*?

Whatever it was, it would probably be bad news. Because when was it ever anything else?

He dialled the bugger back anyway.

Colin picked up on the second ring. *'News desk.'*

'What story?'

There was a wee pause.

'Why Acting DCI McRae, how lovely to hear your dulcet tones, and that.'

'Don't be an arse: we were on our way to see you anyway. Well, not you. Thought you'd resigned.' The car inched closer to the roundabout. 'What story, Colin?'

'That guy you got flattened by a truck, yesterday – turns out he's one of Charles MacGarioch's mates. Kind of looks like Police Scotland's deliberately targeting these poor benighted orphans.'

Sod. That was quick.

'"Benighted"? Since when did you use big long words like—'

'Or maybe you mean the story about Iain Grant suing Police Scotland for reckless endangerment, causing psychological distress, and the infliction of life-changing injuries?'

What?

'Who the hell is Iain Grant?'

The swirl of cars paused, and Tufty nipped out onto the roundabout, following that Fiat You-Know-What-O, onto the bridge over the River Dee.

Couldn't be far from here to where they'd found Andrew Shaw's body, but that bit of the riverbank was hidden behind a bend in the river.

'Iain Grant, AKA: Mr FreezyWhip. Owner of that ice-cream van you high-speed chased into the River Don, two days ago.'

'He's *suing* us? I pulled him out the water! I saved his life!'

Ungrateful bastard.

'Or it might be the serial rapist you found floating facedown in the Dee, yesterday. You know the one: Andrew Wallace Shaw. With his head bashed in. Ring any bells?'

Logan clamped a hand over his eyes. 'Who's feeding you this stuff?'

'What can I say: I'm a good listener; people like to tell me things.' You could *hear* the smug smile in his voice. 'So, where d'you want to start: "City Cops' Orphan Vendetta", "'Reckless Police Tried To Kill Me' Says Local Businessman", or "Vigilante Ends Serial Rapist's Vicious Spree"?'

'Colin...' Logan gave his head a squeeze, because it probably wasn't a good idea to tell members of the press where they could stick their bloody newspaper.

'Aye: and what do you mean, you're on your way to see me?'

'Your missing boss. I need access to her work stuff.'

'Ah, you mean: "Clueless Cops Can't Find Missing Mother"?'

'Again with the being a dick.' Deep breath. 'How about "Weegie Reporter Impedes Investigation – Gets Uninvited To Barbecue"?'

Silence.

The pool car crossed the bridge, parting company with the Fiat Rudeness as it took a right – around the roundabout, heading towards Garthdee and the road south – while Tufty took the first exit, following a sign for 'Tullos & Altens Ind. Est.'

Eventually, a sniff came down the line. *'Suppose I could wait till you've been here. But I report without fear or favour, understand?'*

At least it was a start.

'OK.'

'Besides, I've just bought five kilos of steak mince, and four dozen burger buns...'

Logan, Steel and Tufty sat on squeaky plastic chairs, looking up at the dusty atrium as *Dougie In The Aifterneen* burbled away on a hidden radio.

'...cos I ayeways wondered fa it was, deen that. It's a fair scunner fan ye find oot, isn't it? An mind that feel loon fae EastEnders, wie a gammy leg and face like a crackit chuntie? Weil, he's jist released a charity single...'

The *Aberdeen Examiner* had invested as much into its reception area as it had in its journalistic integrity. Which was why the place was a depressing hole, with magnolia walls and a beige soul. The collection of plastic pot plants was on its last legs, and the framed front pages needed dusting, while the brown carpet tiles needed taking out and *burning*.

The only redeeming feature was Glenda: the big smiley round lady, with rainbow-striped hair and a ring through her nose, who'd come out from behind the desk to make everyone coffee and offer them a dip in the Quality Street tub while they waited on Colin Sodding Miller to stop playing the diva and come get them.

Ding-buzz.

SMITHY SMITH:

> Heard back from phone company!
>
> Anonymous threat was from a mobile number.
>
> Bunch of tech-blah about carrier network handshake protocols, but upshot = no ID or number.

Great.

So zero help there, then.

Ding-buzz.

SMITHY SMITH:

> Yacht Bloke also called from a mobile!
>
> PAYG handset on Triple-5.
>
> No name/details registered.
>
> Can get started on warrant for IMEI tracking if you want?

Assuming PAYG was 'Pay As You Go', that meant Captain Sleazy was using a burner phone to proposition women, *probably* behind his wife's back. Might have a hard time convincing the Sheriff that was worth a warrant to trace the scumbag's physical location so they could swoop in and unmask him, though.

Besides, there was an easier way to find out who he was: call him back.

Logan fired off a quick reply:

> Thanks Smithy.
>
> Leave it with me.

SEND.

Glenda threw a pained smile in their direction, phone to her ear as she poked at the switchboard. 'I'm sorry; don't know *what's* keeping Colin.' She clunked the handset back into its hook. 'Still not answering.' Then stood. 'Tell you what, would anyone like another coffee?'

Tufty sat up straight. Eager as a little black Labrador. 'Do you have any *biscuits*, because someone stole my lunch and...'

The door through to the inner sanctum opened and Colin Miller strutted in. He was in grey linen today, with a pastel-blue shirt – top three buttons open to show off a jangle-clank of golden jewellery and some greying chest hair. 'Aye, aye. If it's no' Aberdeen's answer to Cagney and Lacey: Crappy and Lumpy.'

'Colin Archibald Miller!' Glenda poked the reception desk with an indignant finger. 'You apologise to these nice people *right* now.'

And just like that, all of Colin Miller's swagger evaporated and his cheeks flushed bright pink. Those black-gloved fingers curling in front of his chest.

Logan grinned. '"Archibald"? You kept that one quiet.'

'Aye, well...' He cleared his throat. Jerked his chin at the door. 'You better come with me.'

51

'Don't get me wrong – it's nice to see you useless buggers doing some work for a change – but shouldn't you be out knocking heads together and asking questions, like?' Colin Miller twisted a key in the lock, then pushed the door open, revealing a large office with a sacrificial-altar-sized desk that played host to a huge leather office chair and a dour portrait of an overweight man in rolled-up shirtsleeves, waistcoat, and clichéd cigar.

Two, much shorter, far less comfortable chairs sat in front of the desk, so any visitor would be at an automatic disadvantage.

A line of CCTV monitors offered grainy windows onto the Bullpen, Advertising, and Picture Desk, along with four different views of heavy machinery in the print room.

Rows of framed front pages filled the space between the windows – blinds down, casting the room into fusty gloom – while a bank of filing cabinets sat across from a triple-length table with downlighters above it.

Colin yanked on a cord, sending the nearest blind crashing upwards. A beam of light slashed into the room. Making the dust motes glow.

Logan stopped in the middle of the room, doing a slow three-sixty. 'Your new boss: how long's she been here?'

Another blind thundered up. 'Three weeks. Three long, *shitey* weeks.'

'She make any enemies in that time?'

Steel scuffed in, followed by Tufty – the melodramatic wee spud holding his tummy as it popped and gurgled an empty song.

'Other than all the poor twats she fired?' Colin clattered the last blind open, brushing dust off his gloves. 'Oh, aye. This isnae the *Parish Gazette* – we rattle buggers' cages here.'

Logan commandeered the throne behind the desk and snapped on a pair of blue nitriles. 'We're going to need a list.' Testing the first drawer – unlocked, but full of pens and assorted stationery. 'She doesn't show for work, two days running, and no one thinks to go check on her?'

'What, cos we all *love* her *so* much? Natasha Agapova makes friends like Jeffrey Dahmer makes pies.'

Tufty sidled over, leaning in close, keeping his voice low: 'Don't look now, but there's a very nervous-looking burglar waiting outside.'

He wasn't wrong.

A thin bloke in a beard and black-and-white stripy jumper, fidgeted on the threshold, carrying a bunch of black cardboard rectangles under one arm, looking as if he was trying to work up the courage to knock.

Colin rolled his eyes. 'Oh for…'

Mr Stripy shuffled his feet and peered into the office. 'Is Mrs Agapova in?'

'She's *gone missing*, you daft wobbler! Have you no' seen the paper today? We went with it on page one, three, seven and nine!'

Pink flushed above the beardline. 'I … don't always have time to—'

'No' to mention it's all over the TV, and the radio, *and* the internet!'

The feet shuffled some more. 'So, she's not in?'

Colin grimaced at Logan for a moment, then back to Mr Stripy. 'Just stick your mock-ups on the table, OK? I'll see she gets them when or if she ever returns... Assuming she's no' already deid.'

Mr Stripy looked down at his sheets of card, then at the table, then at Colin, then licked his lips, then nodded, and hurried over to the long table – laying out six front-page mock-ups, side-by-side so they were all visible. Then stood back to admire his handiwork.

Colin thumped a hand down on Mr Stripy's shoulder, making him jump. 'Now do us all a favour and sod off, aye?'

The pink flushed darker. 'I've got ... lots to be getting on with.' And away he scurried.

'Next time, read the sodding paper!' Colin hissed out a long breath. Shaking his head as the jittery bloke disappeared. 'Is it like this in the polis? Swear to God they get younger and more clueless with every passing year.'

'Yup.' Steel parked her bum on the table. 'And *whinier* too.'

Logan tried the next desk drawer: a worms' nest of cables and phone chargers. 'Did she mention getting any hate mail, death threats, things like that?'

'I mean, what sort of half-arsed "newspaper" can you put out when you fire all the proper journalists?' Colin worked his way along the filing cabinets, to the bottom left, rattling out the final drawer. 'Think interns could've broken Watergate? Or Partygate? Or all that dodgy shite about right-wingers swimming in Kremlin cash?' He pulled out a cardboard box – just about big enough to keep Gwyneth Paltrow's head in – and clumped it down on the desk. 'There youse go.'

Logan frowned at it. 'What's this?'

'Hate mail.'

Opening the top revealed a massive stash of envelopes and

printouts. Had to be hundreds of them in there. 'How many months' worth is this? I only need the stuff sent to Natasha Agapova.'

'Aye, that's just since she got here. Apparently there's another eight boxes back at her place.'

'Eight...?'

'Told you: we rattle buggers' cages. Her more than most.' Colin plucked a handful of hate mail from the box and sank into one of the visitors' chairs, leaning back to put his feet up on the desk. 'Had an editor once, liked to frame the worst ones and stick them on the wall. "Colin," he says, "Colin, you no' doing your job right if nae bastard hates you."' Turning to the first letter, scrawled in red ink on lined paper. 'Here we go: all in easy-to-read block capitals. "Dear Stupid Bitch, I hope you die a slow, sucking-chest-wound death and dogs rape your dead body and then eat it and shit it out. *Ranger's Football Club* are the best football club in the world and you're too stupid to know it." Not a single bit of punctuation, if you don't count the ... four, five, *six* exclamation marks at the end.'

Logan reached in and pulled out a stack of the things. 'She got all this in *three weeks*?'

Mr Rangers-Are-The-Best was placed facedown on the desk and Colin moved on to the next. 'Ahem: "Fuck you, you fucking..." well, I'm definitely no' gonnae say *that* word with ladies and weans present, "You fucking *bleep*, badgers have more right to life than you do. You're the one spreading *bleeping* diseases, whore." Blah, blah, et cetera. "Kill yourself."' He waggled the letter. 'See, *this* moron didn't just submit their hate via the website, or email it in, they got a sheet of paper, and a green biro and they scrawled it all out by hand, then found an envelope, paid for a stamp, and stuck it in the postbox. *That's* dedication for you.'

Logan stuffed everything back in the box, held it out so

Colin could do the same, then carried the lot over to the long table. 'Constable Quirrel: I need these in date order. We're looking for anything connected with the message on Mrs Agapova's answering machine: "karma", "hurricane", "house of lies", and, or, "bitch".'

'Sarge.' Tufty tidied away Mr Stripy's mock-ups and laid the hate mail across the table, shifting individual letters forward and backwards – tongue poking out the side of his mouth.

Steel sniffed. 'What about all the electronic stuff?'

'Aye: in the box. We print every nasty wee message out – in case we need to give it to you lot. You know: if something like this happens. So you can do sod-all about it.'

A knock rang out from the open door, only it wasn't the weedy bloke in the burglar's top – back for another round of Humiliate Mr Stripy – it was a scruffy-looking woman in hiking gear and a bandana. As if ready to go on an Amazonian hike, or climate protest, at the first toot of a pan pipe.

She had a fat grey laptop clutched in both hands. 'Yo, Colin: I hear you're Interim Editor now.'

A frown. 'Says who?'

'Louis.' She held her laptop out. 'You wanna OK the spread for tomorrow's lifestyle section or not?'

Colin put his head on one side, scrunched his lips into a lump, then nodded. 'What the hell.' Patting the desk as he plonked his short arse in the leather throne. 'Henry, these are the cops. Cops, Henry.'

She gave them a wave, then put the laptop down and opened it, bringing up a photo gallery. Swiping through shots of people at the beach and kids playing in the park; some office workers in bikini tops at lunchtime, lounging beneath the trees; more kids eating candyfloss and gazing in wonder at the circus lights.

Colin reached for the screen with a leather-gloved finger,

445

but nothing happened. 'Sodding hell...' He pulled the glove off, curling the stumps into a truncated fist, out of sight, and tried again. *This* time, the images wheeched past beneath his fingertip. 'OK: this one, this, this, not that, or that, this, nope, nope, nope, that one's OK, and...' He drifted to a halt, then looked up at Logan – looming over the pair of them. 'You after something?'

'Go back a couple.'

Henry took control of the screen again. 'Hold on...' Swipe, swipe. 'This one?'

'Hmmm.' Colin frowned at the photograph. 'Aye: I like the *general composition*, but shoulda gone up a couple of f-stops for a longer exposure and got a bittie *motion* in the dodgems.'

'Can always fix it in post.'

'Shouldn't have to, but.' He reached out to swipe past the image again, but Logan grabbed Colin's hand before he could.

'Get off!' Snatching his naked fingers away.

Steel sauntered over. 'What?'

'Ooh,' Henry pointed, 'like the *hair*! Very swish.'

'This old thing?' Steel had a wee preen.

'No *touching*.' Colin forced his hand back into its black-leather prison.

'Sorry.' Logan leaned in.

The photo showed a pair of grown-ups on the dodgems, each with a toddler strapped-in next to them, as they wheeched around the ring. Everyone smiling; having a wholesome family day out at the circus.

Behind them, the big top's outer wall was in perfect focus: red, white, and blue stripes.

'When was this taken?'

'Last night.' Henry stuck her thumbs in her belt loops. 'Went with Brent and the kids. Westburn Park?'

Thought so.

He opened his phone and scrolled through to the photo hidden away in Charles MacGarioch's bedroom. The dodgem cars were *identical*, and so were the trees off to one side. *And* the stripy red-white-and-blue background. 'How long's the circus been there?'

'Dunno. Week, I think.' Henry's eyes narrowed. *'Why?'*

Ah.

Probably best not to tip the press off.

'No reason.' A nonchalant shrug. 'Just ... thinking of taking the family tonight.' Quick: change the subject. 'Don't suppose you've got any photos from that SME charity-auction-ball thing, do you?'

'Oh. Yeah: we did one of those cheesy "out and about" features. Like anybody gives a toss.'

She fiddled with the laptop, bringing up a different slide-show.

With Colin in the editor's chair, Logan was demoted to one of the short ones in front of the desk, perching on the edge to swipe through the awkwardly posed group shots of various numpties from various oil-sector-support companies, in various posh frocks or nearly identical dinner suits. Fake grins and not-so-fake tans.

There were more photos of people at tables, raising their glasses, pretending to have a good time. Then some of the auction for 'things money can't buy' – because no one would sodding want them – followed by a whole bunch of the dancing afterwards.

Logan swiped back and forth, forehead creased, peering not just at the figures in the foreground, but the ones further back. Searching.

Steel reached over his shoulder and tapped the screen. 'Take it *that's* who you're looking for?'

Natasha Agapova, in an elegant black ballgown, sitting at a

table with a sign on it proclaiming, *'Aberdeen Examiner!'*, and a whole slew of empty wine bottles.

She was trapped between that oversized teddy bear of hers and an earnest, rosy-cheeked, shiny-faced middle-aged man.

He had one hand on a nearly full glass of red wine and the other on Natasha's bare shoulder, leaning in and talking. While she looked like someone trying not to appear as bored as she really was.

Another swipe and there they were again, still sitting at the same table, in the background of another dancing shot. Him telling some sort of *hysterical* anecdote with his arms thrown wide – clutching a whisky this time – while Natasha Agapova pretended to smile, and the bear grinned away.

Wonder if her boring dinner companion was Captain Sleazy of the HMS HumpYacht?

Logan zoomed in. 'We have any idea who the guy is?'

'Hold on.' Henry vanished, leaving her laptop behind.

Tufty waved at them from the long table. 'Sarge? I has a finished.'

Might as well, as they were waiting.

The wee loon had made a neat job of laying all the hate mail out – a mixture of A4 printouts, lined sheets torn from various notepads, and random scraps of paper – some of which now boasted little tabs made of orange Post-it note. Tufty pointed at both ends of the table: 'Oldest to newest. One bit of sticky for each keyword.'

It wasn't hard to spot the sheet of A4 with seven bits of bright orange stuck to it. Must've come through the website, because the printout came complete with a wodge of metadata at the top, with things like the user's IP address, time, date, and referring URL.

Username: Anonymous123

Email: fakename@fakefakefakeGTF.com

Department: Editorial

Subject: Reap the hurricane

Message:

REMEMBER ME, BITCH? YOU BETTER, BECAUSE I AM
GOING TO BE THE LAST THING YOU EVER SEE. YOU
CANT HIDE FROM KARMA, BITCH, AND IT IS COMING FOR
YOU! I WILL BURN YOUR FUCKING HOUSE OF LIES TO
THE GROUND WITH YOU IN IT. YOU ARE DEAD, BITCH.
I BET YOU THOUGHT YOU COULD BURY ME, BUT YOU
CANT. BECAUSE I AM EVERYWHERE. AND YOU WILL BE
SCREAMING FOR MERCY AND FORGIVENESS BEFORE I
AM DONE. SEE YOU SOON.

Tufty poked the page. 'I know "see you soon" wasn't on your keyword list, but I marked it up anyway, cos I has an *initiative*.'

Logan checked the 'DATE SUBMITTED', then scowled at Colin. 'Two weeks ago! And you didn't *tell* us?'

'What, I'm supposed to know the content of everyone's Hate Box, now?'

Henry reappeared, holding an issue of the *Aberdeen Examiner*. 'Got it.'

Colin raised a hand. 'Hoy, Henry, you got anything exciting in your Hate Box?'

'Me? Nah.' She opened her paper and spread it across the desk, displaying a whole heap of those uncomfortable group shots of people in suits and gowns, with a list of names under each photograph. 'My hate mail's the usual boring collection

of misogynists, pricks, and people who want to know why
I made them look "so fat" in that photo about the thing.
Oh, and men who won't take "Sod off, I'm married!" for an
answer. Why?'

'Plod here think we should be intimately familiar with every
piece of hate mail that comes into the building.'

Logan pinched the bridge of his nose. 'All right: that's *not*
what I—'

'Hell with that. Be here all week!' She squinted at the laptop.
'Right, let's see who Mr Pink-And-Sweaty is...' Running a
finger over the paper, one photo at a time.

'What I *meant* is: why don't you report the hate mail?'

'God, you're right!' Colin clapped a hand to his forehead.
'Cos if we did *that*, you guys would rush round here with all
guns blazing and solve the crime! Would you? Really? Course
you sodding wouldn't.'

'Got him.' Henry poked a gathering of numpties in
their charity-ball finery. '*Nick Wilson*, director at NorrelTech
Wellhead Intervention Limited – and before you ask: no. No
idea. They donated a fortnight's timeshare in New Orleans, if
that helps?'

Logan picked up the paper, closed and folded it, then
tucked the thing under his arm. 'OK. Thanks for your help.'
Pointed at Tufty and Steel. Turned. And marched for the door,
taking the Post-it clarted printout with him.

'Hoy!' Colin stood behind his Interim Editor desk. 'Aren't
we forgetting something?'

Sod.

Logan paused on the threshold. 'Off the record? Mr
FreezyWhip is an ungrateful bastard; the OAPs are only
milking it for attention; you might want to soft-pedal on
painting Spencer Findlater and Charles MacGarioch as poor
wee orphans, unless you want to end up looking like a *serious*

twat; and we're still contacting Andrew Shaw's victims, so tread lightly. Going to be hard enough on them as it is.'

Colin's chin came up. 'And *on* the record?'

Good question...

'This shit isn't easy, but we're doing our best.'

52

'Oh noes...' Tufty scuffed his little feet to a standstill, gazing across the car park, bottom lip all a-tremble as a large man in T-shirt-and-shorts locked up a food trailer with 'DORIC DAVE'S DEVOURABLE DELICIOUSNESS!' painted all over it.

The *Aberdeen Examiner*'s exterior was every bit as depressing as the inside had been: a large bland grey warehouse, surrounded by other large bland grey warehouses, in the middle of a large bland grey industrial estate.

A wedge of the North Sea was just visible in the distance – down the hill, between an oilfield-digital-services company and an industrial-equipment supplier – sparkling blue beneath the searing sky. But other than that, pretty much everything was a depressing mix of concrete and steel.

Logan marched over to the pool car, digging his phone out on the way. Scowling through a quick Google search. 'Haven't seen MacGarioch in months, my arse...'

Steel slouched up behind him. 'So: we off to noise-up this Sweaty Wilson prick?'

'Turns out Rennie was right – shock, horror – Keira Longmore has been *lying* to us.' He pressed the 'CALL' button.

They picked up on the third ring: *'The Star-Sprinkled Heavens. How can I help you this lovely afternoon?'*

Logan forced a smile. 'Hi. Is Keira working today?'

There was a small pause, then a pinch of suspicion seasoned the maître d's voice. *'Can I ask who's calling?'*

'Detective Chief Inspector McRae, we met yesterday? Got a couple of follow-up questions I need to ask her. Nothing serious.'

And just like that, the salty edge mellowed. *'I'm afraid Keira's not in till tomorrow night. She's going out with friends.'*

Surprise, surprise.

'OK. No problem. Like I said, it's nothing serious. I'll try again tomorrow. Thanks.' He hung up, tried the passenger door handle.

Locked.

Where the hell was...?

The wee loon was still rooted to the spot, mourning the loss of devourable deliciousness.

'HOY, TUFTY!'

He jerked back to the real world, scurrying across the sticky tarmac to unlock the pool car. 'Sorry, Sarge.' Getting in behind the wheel. 'NorrelTech-Wellhead-Intervention-Limited-ho?'

'No.' Logan yanked his door open. 'Think it's about time we mobbed round to Keira Longmore's address and see what else she's been lying about.'

Most of Gairn Terrace was given over to the kind of pale post-war housing that normally featured south of the border, but *this* end of it played host to a ten-storey tower block on one side, and a big lump of flats on the other.

They clustered together in a sort of flattened horseshoe of large beige-and-breeze-block-coloured buildings – four floors each, with Dutch-barn roofs and communal stairwells. The one calling itself 'Allenvale Court' was partially hidden beneath a skin of scaffolding and tarpaulin, where all the harling had been chipped off the front walls, exposing the breeze blocks underneath.

A pair of guys in bum-crack jeans were busy fitting a new UPVC window to one of the properties.

So at least Keira had been telling the truth about *that*.

Mind you, she didn't know Rennie was listening in, so it didn't count.

Logan strode towards the stairwell door, leaving Tufty to plip the locks and hurry after him while Steel strolled along behind, hands in her pockets.

Up the steps – two at a time. Then one at a time. Then puffing his cheeks out and using the handrail. Getting slower and slower. Because two hours' sleep, in a pool car's passenger seat *really* wasn't enough when stairs were involved.

Meaning Tufty had no problems keeping up now, even weighed down by the full stabproof-and-utility-belt kit.

Not so Acting DI Steel – instead she whistled a jaunty tune from somewhere down below, echoing around the bland concrete stairwell. Apparently unbothered about joining them anytime soon.

On the second floor, outside Flat Fourteen F, Logan crumpled back against the banister. Legs like boiled string. And nodded at the doorbell.

Tufty nodded back and gave it a poke.

A good old-fashioned *dinnnnngggggg-donnnnngggg* sounded inside.

Downstairs, the whistling grew fainter, followed by what sounded like a door closing, then silence. The lazy sod hadn't even bothered climbing the first flight of stairs – just sodded off out the back. No doubt to vape and pose for yet more stupid selfies. Because being demob-happy meant you didn't have to do any bloody work.

Well, she was in for a nasty surprise when they finished up here. Let's see how she liked being demoted, *yet again*.

The wee loon was looking at him. 'You OK, Sarge?'

'Just tired. Give it another go.'

But before Tufty could ring it, clunks came from inside, then the door inched open – brought up short by the chain fixed on the inside.

A small, wrinkly old man, with skin the colour of midnight and hair pale as the moon, squinted out at them. Wearing an AFC replica top, grey joggy-bots, furry slippers, and the kind of Aberdonian accent you could plough fields with. 'Aye, aye, it's the polis. Youse here aboot them minkers doonstairs?'

Logan flashed his warrant card. 'Keira in?'

A wet sigh. 'Aye. Fit's she deen, noo?'

'Can we come in, please?'

'Gie's a mintie.' The door clunked shut, there was a rattle of chain, then it opened again. Only their host was already scuffing off down the hall. 'The quine's in her room.' Before vanishing into the lounge. *'Ah'm nae mackin' tea, mind!'*

The hallway was almost the full depth of the building, with two doors off each side and one at the end.

Wasn't hard to guess which one was Keira's. R&B thrummed out through the slab door, making the glittery stickers and 'TRESPASSERS WILL BE PROSECUTED' sign vibrate.

Logan pulled his shoulders back and gave it the police officer's hard three: knuckles rapping against the trembling wood.

A female voice slashed out from inside. *'I already told you, Nana Kweku: go away! I'm busy!'*

'Police. Open up, Miss Longmore, we need to talk.'

Drums and bass rattled out.

'Miss Longmore?' Logan knocked again. 'You're going to have to come out eventually.'

'Gah…' Sounding every inch the stroppy teenager. *'I'm just out the shower, OK? Can I put my pants on? That all right with you?'*

He did a quick three-sixty.

The door on the far right was the living room, where Keira's grandad had gone, so that left three more.

The one at the end of the hall opened on a linen cupboard. The one next to Keira's was another bedroom – old-fashioned, but nice enough. Number three revealed a compact shower room, with white toilet and sink, a soggy towel on the floor, and a medicine cabinet, all misted-up with steam. It smelled... *familiar* in here. Not just the general post-shower soapy fug, but something distinctly *citrusy*. Like a mandarin shagging a block of sandalwood.

Just the sort of thing a young man would liberally squirt himself with, because the adverts liked to pretend it attracted women like black trousers attract cat hair.

...

Bloody hell.

Logan grabbed Tufty, shoving him towards the front door. 'Go! Back of the building: right now!'

The wee loon legged it, banging out into the stairwell as Logan grabbed the bedroom door handle.

Locked.

'Keira?' Rattling the thing. 'I know he's in there!'

Nothing but R&B.

Not today.

Logan took a step back and slammed his boot into the door, just beneath the lock.

BOOM.

The thing flew open, and he stumbled into a messy pit with clothes on the carpet, and a collection of hairy mugs mouldering away on a kid-sized desk. There was a zoo's-worth of stuffed animals spilled across the floor, as if some sort of massacre had occurred.

A striped flag hung above the unmade bed – one band each

of red, yellow, and green, with a black star in the middle. The sheets were crumpled, the pillows in disarray.

And the whole place reeked of Lynx Africa, sex, cigarettes, and shampoo.

In normal times, the room's only window would've looked out over the parking area at the back of the block, but the rear of the building was clad in scaffolding too, hiding the view behind metal poles, tarps, and scaff-boards.

The window lay wide open; no sign of Keira Longmore.

Bloody hell.

Logan lunged over there and clambered out onto the scaffolding boards.

They'd braced the whole structure against the wall with wooden batons in every other window opening, wedging it into place. One of those orange-plastic-chute things zigzagged down to a rubble-filled skip. A ladder sat off to the right, going up to the top floor and down to the first.

And there was Keira: clambering down it to the next level, wearing a biker jacket and a 'NUCLEAR KILL SYNDROME' T-shirt, a pair of jeans clutched in one hand, a pair of red trainers in the other.

'HOY!'

Her head snapped up and she froze, top half poking up through the gap in the boards.

Logan strode over there. 'There's police officers at the bottom, waiting for you, so you can clamber down the ladder with your pants on show, if you like.' Shrug. 'Might be a *little* more dignified going down the stairs with your trousers on?'

Keira closed her eyes, pressed her forehead against the ladder's rung, and swore and swore and swore and swore...

Logan marched Keira out through the stairwell door at the front of the building – now all glammed-up in trousers, trainers, and this season's must-have accessory: handcuffs – to find Steel waiting for him. Glowering.

Bits of twig and leaves poked out of her nice new hairdo, and she looked even more rumpled than normal. 'Blah!'

He steered Keira towards the pool car. 'Where the hell were you?'

Steel spat out a sliver of greenery. 'Waiting round back, just in case. Cos, unlike you, I *remember* what happened at MacGarioch's flat.'

'Then where is he?'

'Some bugger landed on me! Didn't see anything but a naked hairy arse, and *bang*: I'm facedown in the bloody undergrowth.' She pulled a twig from her curls. 'Then that stupid wee spud's sprinting past, going *"Woo, woo, woo, woo, woo!"* chasing after the bastard.'

Another quality A Division operation...

And speaking of disasters:

Tufty limped back along the road, red-faced and breathing like a leaky space hopper, one hand pressed against his ribs. A weeping red scrape arced across his cheek.

No Charles MacGarioch.

The wee idiot staggered to a halt. 'Couldn't ... couldn't catch ... wasn't...' Wheezing and coughing. 'Got ... away from ... from me! ... Pfff...' He sagged against the car. 'Argh... Puff... Pant... Et cetera.'

Keira stuck her nose in the air. 'Told you: haven't seen Charlie for *ages*.'

'Really?' Logan opened the rear passenger-side door. 'So who was the naked bloke slathered in Lynx Africa in your bedroom, then?'

No answer.

'It was Charles MacGarioch, wasn't it.' Logan put a hand on her head, so she wouldn't brain herself on the door frame, and plonked her into the car. Produced his phone and scrolled through to the secret photograph. 'This was taken at the circus in Westburn Park. And *you*, Miss Longmore, have been lying to us.'

Her eyes narrowed, jaw clenching – making the zits writhe. 'I'm not saying anything else without a lawyer.'

The Police Custody and Security Officer printed the words. 'VERY SARKY!!!' on the little wipe-clean noticeboard mounted to the cell door, then clacked the viewing portal closed. Shutting Keira away.

Twin rows of identical, heavy blue doors sealed off each cell in the custody suite's female wing. Though most of them had things like 'BITES!' and 'SPIT RISK!' written on them.

The Police Custody and Security Officer was broad of shoulder and short of leg, with a no-nonsense haircut going grey at the temples, and thick-soled comfortable shoes. She turned back towards the custody desk. 'She's a cool one, eh? You sure she hasnae got a criminal record?'

Tufty poked at the scabbing scrape across his cheek. 'Clean as a whistle, far as we know.'

'Aye, and my arse squirts finest prosecco.' The PCSO checked her watch. 'You'll be waiting here a while: nearest duty solicitor's in Dundee on a double murder.'

Logan groaned. 'Oh, for...'

'Every bugger's got the lurgie. Entire criminal justice system's dropping like flies.' She rolled her eyes. 'All right, all right. I'll see what I can do.'

'Thanks.' He turned and headed back up the stairs again.

'But you owe me a pie or something!'

Which was fair enough.

The stairwell was every bit as awe-inspiring as a stairwell in a police station *could* be, only less so. Bare breeze-block walls, concrete steps, and a 'motivational' poster hanging on every landing.

Tufty followed him up. 'Do you think our half-naked bloke really *was* Charles MacGarioch, Sarge?'

'If you hadn't *lost* him we wouldn't have to guess.'

The wee loon drooped. 'I got wanged by a *minibus*!' He held up a pair of pinched fingers. 'Came this close to getting squished. And I'm too young to be squished – I has a bidie-in and a lovenest to support.' Poking at his scabs again. 'By the time I'd picked myself up out the bushes, there was no sign of the scrunk-wadger...' Then Tufty scuffed his feet on the bare steps, head hanging. 'Sorry, Sarge. I should've caught him.'

Urgh...

Yeah, well.

Suppose it wasn't *entirely* his fault.

Logan waved it away. 'If there's one thing Charles MacGarioch's good at, it's scarpering.'

And burning poor bastards alive...

53

Back at the station, Logan suppressed a yawn and pushed through the double doors, back into the open-plan office. Normally the place would be humming – reverberating with the clatter of keyboards as people slunk in to do 'completely necessary paperwork activities' in the run-up to home time. But today, Divisional Headquarters had a decidedly *Flying Dutchman* feel to it – with only a cursed skeleton crew left to man the ship while storms and sea monsters battered at the hull...

And even then, one of the dwindling support staff was hacking and coughing and spluttering all over the printer.

No wonder the bloody thing never worked properly.

Tufty poked and fiddled with his phone, walking to heel like a good little sidekick. 'We've got time to grab a coffee, then sit in on the review for Operation "Camper Vans Stolen To Order" if you like?'

'I most certainly *don't* like. Besides: wouldn't want Acting DI Taylor to think we were checking up on her.' Pausing at the coffee machine, he poked the buttons till it whirred and grumbled out a frothy wax-paper cup of burnt-toast-flavoured yuck. Yum, yum, yum.

Logan handed the scalding beverage to Tufty. 'That hate mail from "Anonymous One-Two-Three", can you trace the IP address?' Going in for another poke at the machine.

'Already did, Sarge, while we were waiting on Keira Longmore being processed. It's a VPN node in London.'

Nope.

'Worry not, I has an explaining: it does mean Virtual Private Network – hides who you are, where you're connecting from, and encrypts everything in-between. Mr One-Two-Three am being an *ghostie*.'

'Of course he sodding is.' Logan took a sip of hot brown. Which tasted every bit as awful as it smelled. 'In that case, you'd better get on to Spudgun – see if anything's cooking at Wallace Tower. Now we've raided his girlfriend's boudoir, MacGarioch might go to ground again.'

'Sarge.'

'And if he's *still* unfindable, we've got the Orphan Circus Outing to fall back on. Which means we're going to need *at least* a half-dozen tickets. Assuming the Chief Super actually gives us enough bodies to...'

Bugger.

Sergeant Brookminster entered through the far door, stood there for a moment, looking around, then homed-in on Logan. Striding between the cubicles, with an iPad tucked under his arm as if it were a swagger stick. 'DCI McRae.' He gave Tufty a nod. 'Constable.'

The wee loon stuck his hand out for shaking. '*Greetings* fellow comrade in this Great Fraternity of Sacred Sidekicks!'

Brookminster looked at the hand, eyebrows puckering into a one-up-one-down frown. 'Yes, well ... DCI McRae, the Boss would like a word, if you've got a moment?'

Which *sounded* like an invitation, but clearly wasn't.

Fair enough.

Logan gave Tufty a nudge. 'Constable: put your hand away and go chase-up Sergeant Moore. Then see if you can get your hands on those tickets.'

'Aye-aye, Sarge.' A quick salute and click of the heels, then off he scampered.

'Bizarre...' Brookminster led the way through the desks, towards the Forbidden Corridor, where all the bigwigs' offices lurked. 'Is there a *reason* Constable ... Quirrel, is it? – refers to you as "Sarge"? I mean, he does *know* you're an acting detective chief inspector, doesn't he?'

'I was the boy's first sergeant when he was doing his probation. Up in B Division. When B Division still existed.' Ah: the good old days. Sort of. 'Suppose it's a weird term-of-endearment, slash, nickname.'

The Forbidden Corridor was much nicer than the main bit of the office, with a view out over the old Divisional Headquarters on Queen Street, in all its seven-storey grey-and-black liquorice-allsort-striped glory. Which, presumably, someone would be demolishing soon to make way for an even uglier office block.

The corridor also had a couple of large pot plants that looked suspiciously non-plastic, and instead of standard-issue losing-the-will-to-live motivational posters, there were a handful of nice paintings on the walls.

'Yes...' Brookminster's free hand made spiders in the air. 'He certainly seems a little ... odd.'

'Oh, to a *band* playing.'

They stopped outside the door marked 'CHIEF SUPT. ROSLYN PINE OBE', where Brookminster plucked the nasty coffee from Logan's hand. 'Trust me: it's for the best.' Then knocked. And marched off again, leaving Logan standing there. Coffeeless and blinking.

Kind of got the feeling that today wasn't about to get any better.

Pine's voice barked through the door: *'Come.'*

Back straight.

463

Deep breath.

And in we go…

Her office seemed weirdly out-of-place for a police station: no filing cabinets or whiteboards; no coffee-stained carpet tiles; no ceiling tiles that looked like a map of Europe, painted in dysentery. What she *did* have were some nice bookshelves, a nice desk, a nice big office chair, a couple of nice armchairs, a nice coffee table, a nice view over the Marischal College quad – even if it was all grey and empty – and a nice sideboard thing with a pod-coffee machine gleaming away on top of it.

The head cop for Aberdeenshire and Moray sat behind her desk, flipping through a file. She looked up as Logan stepped inside and closed the door behind him. 'Ah, good. Have you seen the *Aberdeen Examiner*'s latest nonsense?' Grabbing that morning's edition from her in-tray and waving it at him.

'Just been there, actually – got a possible line of inquiry for you.' He took the proffered paper and pointed at her armchairs. 'Can I…?' Then avalanched into one of them, sagged, puffed out his cheeks, and unfolded Colin's hatchet-job handywork.

NEWSPAPER OWNER ABDUCTED BY SICK WEIRDO

POLICE FUMBLE INVESTIGATION AS WORLD PRESS LOOKS ON

Natasha Agapova (48) made her career in print journalism. From humble beginnings, reporting on animal shows and am-dram productions for her local newspaper in Melbourne, she graduated to the Australian national press, working on multiple titles, before making the leap to the UK with her (then) husband, media mogul, Adrian Shearsmith. Here she took the helm of the *Scottish Daily Post*, turning it from a failing weekly with falling circulation to a daily tabloid and one of Scotland's most popular newspapers.

Logan sniffed. 'You can always rely on Colin Miller for a run-on sentence and a buried lead. And "most popular newspapers"? I wouldn't use the *Scottish Daily Post* to line my cat's litter tray.' Skimming the text. 'Blah, blah, blah...'

> ...and even though multiple officers searched the house, it was down to this reporter to find the message left by the monster who abducted the *Aberdeen Examiner*'s new owner, in a violent attack at her modest home, near Peterculter.

Bloody hell.

'"Modest"? It's *massive*. She's got four bedrooms, a home gym, a sauna, *and* a steam room. Plus, he was there before we were! How are we supposed to search a property *before* we know a crime's been committed?'

Then another chunk of melodramatic crap about bloodstains and 'the lonely smile of an abandoned teddy bear' before the boot was landed right into A Division's testicles:

> Which means that yet again we need to ask if Aberdeen police are competent enough to investigate a crime of this magnitude, when they're so clearly out of their depth that no progress has been made in discovering who took plucky Natasha from us, or why.

He slapped the paper shut and thumped it down on Pine's desk. 'Blah, blah, wankity wank, wank...' Then sat up, heat blooming in across his ears. 'Sorry, Boss.'

465

'Hmmmph…' She stood, busying herself with the coffee machine. Setting it whirring. 'I think "wank" is putting it mildly, to be honest. Only upside is no one else got the story in time to make the morning editions. *Tomorrow* it'll be everywhere.' She fiddled with little cups, keeping it casual, but the hope was clear in her voice. 'You said you have a possible lead?'

'Second-last person to see Natasha Agapova – Nick Wilson, director at something called NorrelTech. Sat next to her at the charity-auction, Monday night. You've already spoken to the taxi driver?'

She let loose a long, kind-of-pissed-off sigh, then placed a tiny cup on the desk, in front of Logan. 'Espresso. You look like you could use it.'

'Thanks, Boss.' Taking the teeny cup of evil. 'We *did* speak to the taxi driver, didn't we?'

'Of course we did. He didn't *see* anything, didn't *suspect* anything, didn't *do* anything. And he's still managed to sell his story to "one of Scotland's favourite newspapers".' A grimace. 'Meanwhile that ridiculous "Penny Thistle" woman got interviewed in her bikini for Channel 5 and just about every news outlet south of the equator. *Topless* for the Venezuelans.' Pine yanked the spent pod from the machine and hurled it into the bin. 'This whole thing's a disaster: the First Minister's office called *six times* today, Tulliallan are nipping my head on an hourly basis, and the world press are quite happy to paint this division as a bunch of useless, half-witted, flat-footed, couldn't-find-their-*fat*-arseholes-with-a-compass-and-a-team-of-sherpas *clowns*, because *apparently* we should've found Natasha Agapova by now! We are *dead*, Logan, if we can't catch whoever did it and rescue her, ASA-*frigging*-P!' The Chief Super rammed another pod in the machine, slammed it shut, and set it whirring. 'And quite frankly, we could do without the *Aberdeen Examiner* giving us a kicking too!'

Logan took a sip of espresso, dark and bitter and fruity all at the same time. The effects clearly weren't instant, though, because a massive yawn rattled free. He shivered in his seat then slumped a little further. 'Sorry.' Blink. Blink. 'Maybe we could give them something? A little exclusive to get the buggers onside.'

She frowned down at him. 'When did you last sleep?'

'Think I got ten minutes in the pool car, this afternoon?'

'Right: home. And that's an order. I want you sharp and focussed for tonight's op. We are *not* letting Charles MacGarioch get away again, just because you can't keep your eyes open.' She reached across the desk and confiscated Logan's coffee.

'But I was—'

'Go!' Pointing at the door. 'Get some sleep. And I expect you to be properly dressed when you get back.'

'Eh?' He looked down at his perfectly serviceable uniform. 'But I'm wearing the—'

'Standards *matter*, Logan.' The Chief Super glanced at her watch. 'Briefing's at seven, so you'd better get moving. Longer you sod about here, the less time you've got.'

He abandoned his car in the driveway, plipping the locks over his shoulder as he scuffed to the front door and let himself in. Hung his peaked cap on the newel post and kicked off his boots, padding upstairs in his socks – pulling off his Police Scotland T-shirt on the way.

Bathroom: teeth, quick wee.

Bedroom: close curtains, dump clothes on wicker chair, timber into bed, wriggle under covers.

Swear.

Wriggle out again.

Set alarm on phone for 18:30.

Back under covers.

Swear again.

Text Tara:

> I've got an hour and a half at home to sleep.
>
> I love you both but if you wake me up I WILL DIE!!!!!
>
> And I'm taking everyone with me!

SEND.

Back under covers.

Sleep, sleep, sleep, sleep...

Cthulhu hopped up onto the bed, treadled her way up the duvet, then thumped down on the pillow next to Logan. Reached out a paw – big, fluffy, with a faint biscuity whiff – and placed it against his head. Purring her way to sleep.

A smile tugged at Logan's lips. He sighed, closed his eyes, and joined her.

LIV

The rattle-clank-roar of the JCB's backhoe stuttered to an end, and silence settled over the crappy collection of outbuildings.

But it wasn't really silent, was it: the digger's noise had drowned them out, but now the bluebottles' *buzzzzzzzzzzzzzzzz* filled the hot sticky air again.

Natasha stood beside her mobile anchor – rolled as close to the window hole as she could get it – for a slightly better view of the field.

DS Davis climbed down from the JCB's cab, and brushed the dust off his jeans with his work gloves. Sweat darkening the fabric of his faded 'Blod Høst Døds Ulv' T-shirt.

She flattened herself against the wall, peering around the edge of the hole – keeping as low a profile as possible.

Don't come back here.

Don't come back here…

Shit.

That's exactly what the bastard was doing.

He was going to squeal open that door and stab her, or shoot her, or bash her brains out with a fucking axe or something, then stick her in that bloody hole he'd been digging for hours.

Thing must be halfway to Sydney by now…

Most people: they buried a body, maybe only two or three feet down. There were tell-tale signs, like the ground sagging as the body decomposed, and weird patterns of extra growth where the plants feasted on human compost.

But a hole that deep?

Davis was making sure nothing would *ever* be found.

…

But maybe he wouldn't kill her?

Maybe it wasn't a grave?

That was possible, right?

Maybe he was just doing some … fucking farmwork, or something? Sorting out the drainage in the lower field – that kind of shit.

Oh Christ…

She hopped on one foot, using the other to shove at the anchor, rolling the bucket back towards where it was supposed to be all this time.

Fuck.

DS Davis was in the courtyard already, and she was nowhere near getting everything back the way it should be.

There was a clunk, then a rattling squeal of ancient metal rollers on steel brackets.

But her prison door remained firmly closed.

Natasha closed her eyes and sagged, knees curling, threatening to dump her on the hard-baked dirt.

It wasn't her door.

She took a deep breath, then coaxed the galvanised bin towards the window again as quietly as possible.

The door to the other outbuilding was wide open; no Davis.

He reappeared a lifetime later, dragging something.

A man's body – stripped down to the underwear. Skin thick with bruises and scrapes. Head covered by a heavy leather gimp mask that laced up the back; eyes and mouth, zipped shut. His wrists weren't fixed to a metal collar, though, they were handcuffed behind his back.

Davis had his gloved hands hooked in under the body's arms. Can't have been all that heavy, though – you could see every one of the poor bastard's ribs, and his arms and legs were nothing but battered bones. Like he'd been chained-up in there for a *long*, long time.

His corpse got dumped on a pile of pallets, then Davis unlaced the mask and pulled it off the guy's pummelled head. The face underneath was distorted and swollen, discoloured with purples and yellows and greens. Doubt even his mum would recognise him now.

Davis placed the mask to one side.

Well, these things were probably expensive – wouldn't want it going to waste.

Which kinda made you wonder how many other people had died in the one Natasha now wore...

Davis rolled the dead man off the pallets, and when that tortured body hit the ground it groaned, one skeletal leg twitching as Davis hauled the poor bastard across the make-shift courtyard and out towards the field.

'Fuck me...' Natasha covered her mouth with both hands, *staring*.

He was still alive.

Davis dragged him away, then they disappeared out of sight – hidden by the barn.

Not long after that, Detective Sergeant Davis marched across the gap and clambered up into the JCB's cab again.

The engine sputtered and roared.

The backhoe jerked and swung.

And DS Davis buried the poor bastard alive.

— surrounded by bloody clowns —

55

'Gaaaaaaaaaaaah…' Logan's eyes snapped open as a horrible marimba tune bonk-bong-dwiddled out of his mobile. The phone skittered and vibrated away on the bedside cabinet, as if the tune wasn't irritating enough.

One hand fumbled for the bloody thing, killing the alarm.

Then he sagged back into the mattress, blinking up at the ceiling. Followed by a gargantuan yawn. And a groan.

Oh right – the op.

Cthulhu was snuggled into the gap between his arm and his stomach, her fur warm against the skin as she grunted out little-fuzzy-cat snores.

Logan creaked out of bed, pausing to give Cthulhu a kiss on the head, let another yawn shudder-burp free, then grabbed his dressing gown and slouched away for a pee.

Logan scuffed into the kitchen, pulling a plain grey T-shirt on – tucking it into his jeans and hiding all those puckered ribbons of scar tissue – smothering a yawn. Casting an eye at the kitchen clock as he slumped over to the fridge. Twenty-two minutes to get back to the station and set up some sort of operational briefing.

Tara and Elizabeth sat at the table, watching him. Cup of tea for Tara, 'Evening, sleepyhead.'

While the Elizabomb tucked into mini-hotdogs-and-beans

on toast with a dollop of brown sauce and a glass of milk on the side. Very Heston Blumenthal.

Logan ruffled her hair on the way past.

'Da-ad!'

A disapproving look from the Tea-Drinking Department. 'Tell me you're not going back into work.'

He liberated a slice of plastic cheese. 'Have to. Got a horrible little racist scumbag arsonist to catch; briefing's at seven.' Unwrapping the floppy yellow square. 'We're going to swoop in and arrest him at the circus, which is a first for me… I've arrested people at abattoirs, and film sets, stone circles, and sex dungeons, but never the circus.' A bite of buttery, unchallenging comfort.

'Speaking of which – your protégé, Tufty, called. Apparently the lady at the ticket office thought he was a "cutie", so he's got a dozen complimentary tickets for the eight o'clock show tonight.' She took a sip of tea. 'Which means Lizzasaurus Rex and I will be joining you.'

More cheese. 'Tufty might be a lot of things, but he is *not* my "protégé". He's…' Hang on a minute. 'No – you can't come! That's just … no.'

Elizabeth bounced up onto her knees. 'Oh, come on, Daddy! Can we? Can we, please?' Playing up the lisp. '*Pleeeee eeeeeeeeeeeeeeeeeeeeeeeeeathe?*'

Logan finished off his artificial square of processed dairy product. '*Definitely* not. And it'd be way past your bedtime.'

Tara frowned at him. 'Don't see why.'

'How about because it's an active *murder* investigation?' Unwrapping another slice.

'Going by how you're dressed, this is an undercover op, and I do *hundreds* of those with Trading Standards. Probably way more than *you* have.'

'That's not the—'

'And what looks less suspicious – *you* creeping about the circus on your own, like a pervert, or a man with his wife and child?' She stood and plonked her mug in the sink. 'Besides, it'll be nice not having to pretend Dildo's my husband for a change. I mean, his arse is nice enough, but he's an *awful* kisser.'

Kisser?

Logan blinked at her. 'Wait, *what?*'

Tara tidied away Elizabeth's plate. 'Come on, Lizz-zilla: grab your coat and get your boots on. We're going undercover!'

'But—'

She clapped her hands. 'Move it, people: wheels up in five!'

'I didn't agree to any of—'

'Don't want to be late for the briefing, do you?'

'But...'

'We'll take The Tank; I'm driving.'

And she was out the door, with Elizabeth skipping along behind – singing:

> *'Going to the circus,*
> *Going to the circus...'*

Leaving Logan alone in the kitchen with his flaccid slice of not-quite cheese.

Logan strode into the open-plan office, bang on seven o'clock, to see what sort of crack team of hotshot officers Chief Superintendent Pine had assembled for him.

Which turned out to be Steel, Tufty, Barrett, Biohazard, Doreen, and Sergeant Bernard 'Spudgun' Moore – an unremarkable middle-aged man with mousey hair, a pronounced chin-cleft, and one leg slightly longer than the other.

Suppose some days you just had to work with what you had.

They were all dressed up in the full Police-Scotland-black

outfit – with stabproof vests, utility belts, and high-vis waist-coats standing by – playing a spirited game of 'Fud-or-Fanny', waiting for the briefing to kick off.

'OK,' Biohazard bit his bottom lip and narrowed his eyes, 'Vladimir Putin.'

Doreen didn't even hesitate: 'Fud. Massive, monstrous, *murderous*...' She looked up and saw Logan. 'Guv.'

'Why are you all in uniform?'

Tufty struck a pose. 'Chief Superintendent Pine sent out a memo, remember? We must has a reassuring the public.'

Oh, for God's sake.

'It's an *undercover operation*, you bunch of fermented numpties! How are we supposed to sneak up on Charles MacGarioch with you lot dressed like an episode of *The Bill*? Go: get changed.'

The six of them scarpered.

'And no fighting suits: casual clothes only!'

Halfwits.

LVI

The air was thick with flies and their bone-grinding *buzzzz*...

Natasha stood beside her anchor – now upright again, and back where it was supposed to be – rising up on her tiptoes as she peered out through the window hole.

The JCB had gone from the field, returned to wherever the bastard usually kept it. Off to the right, the door to the other outbuilding still lay wide open, probably airing out now that its resident had ... gone.

No music throbbed through the static caravan's walls.

And there was no sign of the dick himself.

Something went *thunk*.

A door? Maybe that was a car door? Maybe—

Then the engine started. Followed by the pop-crunch-ping of tyres on a rough track, fading away into the distance until only the flies remained.

Was he gone?

Maybe Detective Sergeant Davis was off to work? With any luck the bastard would be on nightshift and not back till tomorrow morning.

Unless it *wasn't* him.

What if someone else lived in the caravan too? Maybe they were the one who'd driven off, and Davis was lurking nearby?

Or maybe this was all a test and he'd just driven down the

479

road a bit, parked up, and right now he was hurrying back on foot to see if she'd try to escape?

Or maybe…

A big lardy bluebottle settled on her arm, feasting on the crust of dirt and sweat.

Maybe it didn't fucking matter, because the bastard was going to kill her anyway. And would she rather be trapped here, starving away till she was little more than a skeleton, begging for every sip of water, so he could drag her out and bury her alive? Or go out *fighting*.

Deep breath.

…

Did you come here to win?

Or did you come here to fuck spiders?

Natasha unscrewed the top off her bottle and drained the final half-mouthful. Then got down on the ground and tipped the galvanised bin over.

The dust was still settling when she struggled upright and shoved at the thing with her filthy feet. Turning and rolling her anchor towards the door.

And yeah: getting the door open wasn't going to be easy – what with her wrists shackled to this bloody collar. But there was no way in hell she'd get her anchor out through the window hole, so it was this or nothing.

As long as Davis hadn't padlocked the door shut, of course…

She put her shoulder against one of the door's wooden struts and pushed. And pushed. Digging her bare feet into the hard-packed dirt … until *finally* the metal rollers squealed in their brackets and the huge slab of wood moved. Not much, maybe just an inch. But she staggered forward, barging her shoulder into the strut, and shoved again – getting up a bit of momentum.

The thing howled and groaned about two more feet, before the chain on her anchor snapped tight.

Which was a *start*, but nowhere near enough to get the galvanised bin through.

She rolled it closer, giving herself a bit of slack to manoeuvre with, and heaved again – which was a hell of a lot easier now she had the stone doorway to brace her feet against and the edge of the door to push. The whole thing rumbled and screeched open.

Yes.

Natasha sagged against the ancient wood, breath whooshing against the leather mask, pulse *whump-whump-whump*ing in her ears, sweat glistening in the sunlight, as her head throbbed inside its own personal hot box.

Took a minute for everything to settle down, but soon as she could breathe again, Natasha rolled her anchor into position and out into the courtyard.

After the stifling heat and *stench* of the outbuilding, it was like stepping into an air-conditioned hotel room. She stood there, elbows raised, so the merest wisp of a breeze could get at her sweaty pits. Bliss...

But not for long, because who knew when the wanker could come back?

Up close, the caravan looked even more decrepit. And so did the barn. And the other outbuilding – the other prison.

Weeds choked the courtyard's edges, creeping inwards across the dirt-and-gravel surface: nettles, thistles, and tall, jagged docken, bindweed strangling great clumps of it with its garotte-thin tendrils.

Temptation was to do a runner, right now.

Well, a lurching stagger.

Roll this bloody anchor ahead of her, one miserable step at a time, and get the hell out of here. But the only road out was the one DS Davis had driven off to work on. So that would be the way he'd come back too.

What the hell was she supposed to do when he caught her, halfway down the track, moving at a snail's pace, with her anchor. 'Ah, yeah, sorry, mate. Just thought I'd take me binful of concrete for a walk.'

And trundling this stupid thing across a field would be hard enough, but getting it over a stone wall or a ditch?

No chance.

To get out of here, she needed rid of her bloody anchor.

Various bits of old building equipment lay about the court-yard: rusty cement mixer; a pallet of slates; another of breeze blocks, with a tatty tarpaulin tied over the top; offcuts of wood; a spare bucket for the JCB; builder's tonne bag of gravel; one of sharp sand; a wheelbarrow with a flat front wheel, that was halfway to transforming itself into a colander...

Even if it wasn't virtually rusted through, it'd be no use with her wrists attached to this stupid metal collar. Suppose she *could* get the heavy bastard, concrete-filled bin up and into the barrow, and the thing didn't collapse, how was she supposed to push it? Couldn't even grab both handles.

Nah: what she *really* needed was a bolt-cutter or a sledge-hammer.

And the most likely place to find those was the barn.

She stuck her foot against the bin and shoved.

57

The trees in Westburn Park were in full-green, but that was nothing compared to the riot of colour hiding just behind them.

The circus had taken over both sides of the park, with the big top towering above a slew of small rides and attractions – a red-white-and-blue-striped monarch ruling over its little kingdom, with a trio of long pennants fluttering from the king pole. The larger rides were grouped on the other side of the access road, waltzers and a small rollercoaster, chairoplanes and one of those Viking-longboat-on-a-swinging-pivot things, a haunted house and a whole heap of food stands.

And it was all festooned with flashing lights and copyright-infringing graphics.

A dozen different fairground tunes vied for supremacy, barking over the dings and wibbles that blared at Logan from every side. Because *nothing* here could be accused of being subtle.

All the rides were absolutely rammed and so was the park. As if half the city had turned up to munch on candyfloss, popcorn, and hotdogs, waiting for their go on 'THE VOMINATOR!' and 'SIR PUKESALOT'S SWIRLING BARFLAND ADVENTURE!'

Logan strolled through the crowds, keeping a firm grip on Elizabeth's hand, as she *oooooh*-ed and *ahhhh*-ed at all the garish stuff. Tara slipped her arm through his, laughing as a fire-juggling hipster sent a plume of yellow flames *fwooosh*ing into the sky.

Then Doreen's voice cracked out of Logan's earpiece: *'All clear on the Western Front.'*

Tara gave his arm a squeeze. 'Told you it'd be fine.'

'Won't be if the Boss finds out you're here.'

'Anyone asks: I just *happened* to have tickets for tonight. Why should *I* cancel *my* plans just because Police Scotland wants to play *Smiley's People* at the circus?'

Biohazard: *'Nothing on the south entrance.'*

'I don't think we're slick enough to be Smiley's—'

Somone tapped him on the shoulder and Logan froze.

It was sodding Chief Superintendent Pine, wasn't it. He'd *summoned* her by accident and jinxed the whole operation.

He forced a smile and turned...

But it wasn't Pine, it was Tufty. All dressed down, in jeans and a red 'WILLY'S BAR DARTS TEAM: THE FLYING POLGARA!' long-sleeved T. The wee loon must've been at the face-painting stall, because he'd turned into a tiger from the neck up. And a disturbingly realistic one, at that.

The Lizz-Ness Monster gazed up at him. 'Coooool...'

At which point, Tufty struck a pose, hunkering down in front of her as he burst into song:

> 'Tiger-Man, Tiger-Man,
> Does some things that a tiger can,
> Has a stripy face, pounces too,
> But he doesn't smell of poo,
> Oh no: he's a very clean Tiger-Man...'

Finishing with a slightly camp clawing gesture. 'Rarrrrr.'

Logan winced. 'You are *so* blissfully free from the burdens of reality. What the hell were you thinking?'

'Sneaky cleverness, Sarge.' Bouncing upright again. 'See,

this way none of Charles MacGarioch's friends will recognise me and raise the alarm, cos I is a *Master of the Disguises!*'

'Master of being an idiot.'

He held up a stack of leaflets. 'And I did get a big pile of flyers to hand out. The circus is off to Huntly next, and no one pays any attention to people handing out flyers.' He handed one to Logan, and ... got to admit the wee loon had a point.

Even if he *was* a weapons-grade twit.

There was a little remote extension attached to Logan's Airwave – cable running from the handset in his inside pocket, all the way down his sleeve. He raised it to his mouth and pressed the button, keeping the thing hidden, as if he were covering a cough. 'DI Steel?'

Silence from the earpiece.

A frown pulled at Tufty's tiger face as he wiggled *his* earpiece too.

Let's have another go: 'Roberta ... *Flipping* Steel, report!'

Scrunch, munch, munch, followed by a muffled, *'Sod off. I'm eating a toffee apple.'*

'Do you want to go back to being Detective Sergeant Non Grata? Because the Logan giveth, and the Logan can taketh away.'

'Bludgering hell...' Crunch, crunch, crunch. 'No sign of target at eastern entrance. Happy now?' Scrunch. 'Still say this is a stupid plan. We should take MacGarioch when he's in the big top: way smaller space to secure than the whole park. Which means less potential for him running away and us looking like clueless twunts.'

Not this *again.*

'We've only got *seven* people, OK? We take him soon as he's takeable. Had enough disasters this week, thank you very much.'

Crunch, crunch, munch. 'Won't be saying that when he's halfway

485

down Craigie Loanings, and we're still stood here with our pants round our ankles.'

A second little-big cat appeared at Tufty's shoulder – every bit as short as he was, with oatcake-blonde hair in a ponytail, quirky smile, and a button nose. In a 'KLINGON BALLET' T-shirt. She'd clearly been at the same face-painting stand, only instead of a tiger, she'd gone full-on leopard. Made extra weird by a pair of glasses over the top.

The wee loon beamed. '*Total* coincidence: Kate had tickets for tonight too! Wink, wink.' He threw in an actual wink, as if saying it hadn't been clear enough. 'So we is joining forces, cos she is both a police-officer-type person and highly skilled ninja thing. And won't charge for the overtime.'

Kate grinned. 'Guv.'

'Oooooh…' Elizabeth bounced on her feet, staring at Tufty's feline bidie-in. 'That is so *cool*!' Grabbing Tara's hand. 'Can we, Mum? Can we? Pleeeeeeeeeeeeeathe? I want to be a dinosaur! *RRRRRRRRAAAAAAAAWRRRR*!'

Was there something in the water? Or was everyone always this daft?

Crunch, crunch, mumble. '*And while we're at it: why can't everyone just shut their sodding yap till something happens?*'

Yeah… There was the distinct possibility that Logan wasn't *entirely* in control of the situation any more.

OK. Take charge.

He pointed off into the funfair. 'Yes. You and Mummy should definitely go do that. Off you go. Daddy has people to arrest.'

'"*Report in!*", "*Report in!*" It's nothing more than an ego trip for snudgewadgers and … scrunknips!*'

Tara stuck her hand out at Logan. 'Tickets.'

'Here you goes.' Tufty passed two over. 'When you get to

the face-painting tent, tell Courtney I did send you and she'll give you mates' rates!'

'*What do you think we're gonna do, if MacGarioch turns up and it's not "report in" time? Keep it a frunking secret?*'

With a happy wave, Tara and Elizabeth disappeared into the crowd – off to be dinosaurised.

'*It's no' as if MacGarioch's even going to show. I could be home with my swanky new haircut, my wife, a DVD of* Colette, *and a jar of Nutella right now. Nothing's happening! It's all a waste of—*'

Barrett: '*Aaaaaand we're on the move. Secondary targets are drinking up and exiting the Queen Vic now.*'

Logan pressed the call button. 'Still no sign of MacGarioch?'

'*Negative.*' A *schrooooomph*ing noise crackled in the earpiece, then: '*Yeah, they're getting in an Uber... Sounds like they're headed your way. Will follow on.*'

'Is excitement time!' Tufty beamed at him, like a disturbing *thing* from the island of Dr Moreau.

Kate rolled her shoulders, as if gearing up to ninja someone.

And all around, the crowd flowed by, like a slow-moving river.

Biohazard: '*We're on, my sticky little friends! That's Randolph Hay entering the park by the south entrance with a group of people. Repeat: south entrance.*'

'Is Charles MacGarioch with them?' Come on...

'*Don't see him. Just a bunch of teenagers and some wee kids.*'

Logan headed for the park's south entrance, not pushing and shoving, moving just fast enough not to draw attention, with Tufty and Kate following in his wake. 'Everyone hold your positions – he might try sneaking in by another entrance.' Letting go of the button to gently thump Tufty on the shoulder. 'Get ready. The bastard doesn't get away this time.'

The crowds thinned out a bit when they reached the access road that bisected Westburn Park, thickening again on the other side as people queued for the more popular rides. Now where was...?

Ah – over there.

Ralph Hay, with a handful of teens from yesterday's barbecue and a bunch of weenies. Who all seemed *super excited* to be here.

No sign of Charles MacGarioch.

He'd be here soon though, right? Performance started in sixteen minutes...

Pfff...

Logan stood in the shadow of the half-arsed 'Haunted' House, that made 'spooky' sounds on a ninety-second loop while a thrash-metal version of Michael Jackson's 'Thriller' battered out, and the barker did her best to whip-up some punters with a bullhorn:

'Dare you brave what lurks in the darkness? Dare you take the Blood Road to the very gates of Hell ... itself?'

Which was a bit over the top, given the haunted house had a 'You Have To Be THIS Tall To Ride →' out front that was slightly shorter than Elizabeth.

And *still* no Charles MacGarioch.

Biohazard: *'Incoming.'*

Maybe this was it?

Marshall Carter, Alexis Cunningham, and Jericho McQueen wandered up the road, all rosy-cheeked and smiling after their 'couple of pints' in Rosemount. Taking in the deafening sights and garish wibbles.

Logan shrunk back against the ride.

The three of them met up with Ralph Hay – all hugs and cheek-kisses and ruffling the weenies' hair. Who didn't seem to appreciate the gesture any more than Elizabeth.

Zero evidence of Charles MacGarioch.

Where the hell *was* he?

Perhaps the legendary loyalty and never-missing-an-orphan-outing had been a bit ... exaggerated?

Or maybe the Orphan Club had got together to persuade MacGarioch to sit this one out, because the police were after him?

Or *maybe*, Logan had just got this whole thing wrong?

It'd hardly be the first time.

Probably wouldn't be the last, either.

He checked his watch – ten minutes till showtime.

Come on, come on, come on, come on...

Logan pressed the button. 'He's going to turn up eventually. Charles MacGarioch *never* misses these things.'

Hopefully.

LVIII

The rusty sledgehammer clanged down against Natasha's chain again, skimming off the metal to *chudddd* into the concrete.

Christ knew how long she'd been banging away with the bloody thing: twenty minutes? An hour? Seven and a half *years*? And all she had to show for it were a few flattened dents on a couple of links, and some flakes chipped off the solid grey lump in the bucket.

Didn't help that she couldn't get a decent swing on the bastard – having to hold it halfway down the shaft in an awkward hand-over-hand grip and do a rapid bow towards her anchor instead. Which made aiming the pockmarked hammer-head almost impossible.

And now her arms burned, and her legs throbbed, and every muscle in her back *ached*.

After the blazing light of the great outdoors, the barn was heavy with gloom. At least it was cooler than her prison, being a lot bigger, and only having a couple of filthy skylights in the corrugated-asbestos roof.

Its far end was stacked with triangular trusses and prefab stud walls for some sort of build-your-own-house kit, but going by the cobwebs, dust, and layers of mouse droppings, they'd been here for a *long*, long time.

The next twenty percent was given over to pallets of bricks

and stuff that could probably have lived outside, and bags of cement that definitely couldn't.

And the final thirty percent had been turned into a workshop, with a table saw and a mitre saw and a bandsaw and a bench press and all that kind of malarkey. But when she tried them, nothing happened. Same with the light switches. So, either everything was knackered, or the power was off.

A bunch of hand tools hung on the wall above a long workbench that looked like it'd been cobbled together from old pallets, but they were furry with rust, and none of them were any good at hacking through bloody *chains*.

The sledgehammer's metal head *spangggg*ed off the links one last time – making not the slightest bit of difference – and Natasha dropped the useless thing, letting it clatter to the concrete floor.

'Piece of *shit*!' Every single word a mix of sandpaper and broken glass as she collapsed back against the workbench, breathing hard. Sweat stinging her eyes. Head pounding away inside this stupid fucking gimp mask.

She hauled in a big shuddering lungful of dusty air and bellowed it out again...

Then sagged all the way down, till her bum rested on the gritty floor.

Slumped sideways.

Keeling over till she was lying on her side at the very end of her chain – mask pressed against the concrete.

Going to die here.

Going to never see her little girl again.

Going to get dragged out and dumped in a shallow grave then buried alive.

Tears mingled with the sweat.

Be better to kill herself and have done with it. Deny the bastard the satisfaction.

Natasha rolled onto her back and blinked up at the metal joists and asbestos roof.

Couldn't hang herself – no way to get up there, not with this sodding anchor chained around her neck.

Couldn't poison herself – no drugs, or water to take them with.

Couldn't drown herself – which was ironic, because if she *did* find a creek, or a billabong, the anchor would drag her down and keep her there. Quick and easy.

...

Could slit her wrists on the rusty bandsaw?

Took a while but eventually her breathing slowed, and the tears stopped. Though that might've been dehydration, more than anything.

'You're not giving up on me yet.' Natasha closed her eyes. 'You're *not*!'

59

Five minutes to go.

The park was still jammed, but a whole bunch of people had peeled off for the big top, where Tufty and Kate stood on either side of the entrance, handing out flyers.

Which turned out to be the perfect cover, because no one looked at them twice, not even with the elaborate face paint.

Logan lurked by the 'Space Killer' stall – where kids tried to knock a jiggling flying saucer down with ping-pong-ball guns – because it had a clear line of sight to both the big top and the road. So he had a perfect view of Charles MacGarioch *not* appearing.

A fanfare boomed out across the park, followed by a distorted, echoing voice: *'Ladies and gentlemen, loons and quines, the eight o'clock performance is about to begin, so have your tickets ready and make your way to the big top!'*

Logan pressed the talk button. 'Anyone?'

Doreen: *'West entrance – nothing doing.'*

Spudgun: *'Massive steaming bucket of sod-all.'*

Biohazard: *'No sign of him.'*

Barrett: *'Negative. Repeat: no eyes on target at this time.'*

Then silence from the earpiece.

And more silence.

Logan sighed. 'Are you *still* eating?'

Steel: *'He's no' here and he's no' coming. I vote we spudge off out of it and go home. All in favour?'*

'No one's going home! He'll be here.'

Maybe.

But given the show was about to start, possibly not.

LX

Natasha closed her eyes and lay there, on the rough concrete floor.

'Come on, you lazy bitch: get up.'

But she didn't.

'Please?'

No.

'OK: count to ten, *then* up.'

Ten came and went. Then another ten. And she was halfway through the third before wriggling over onto her side – ready for the undignified struggle to get back on her feet.

Natasha froze, the hair *crackling* across the back of her neck.

Someone was looking at her.

…

But it wasn't DS Davis.

A pair of dark eyes glittered in the gloom beneath the workbench. And now all the hair on her *arms* crackled too. Even her scalp fizzed inside the mask as Natasha's stomach clenched and her heart doubled the beat. Jaw clamped shut to keep the scream inside.

A rat. It was a bloody *rat*. A nasty hairy-bastard rat.

Thick with diseases, dragging that disgusting naked tail behind it, shitting and pissing on everything. Creeping, whiskery, plague-carrying *vermin*.

She flinched. 'Fuck off, you rodenty bastard!'

It stared back at her.

'GO ON! GET OUT OF IT!'

Twitching its slimy pink nose.

Little shit was just waiting for her to croak – cos she must've looked pretty crook in this getup – so it could burrow into her flesh and eat her from the inside.

There was a stone, not much smaller than a champagne cork, sitting on the concrete, close enough that Natasha could wrap her toes around the thing and pick it up off the floor. She bent her knee, bringing the rock closer, then snapped her leg out – hurling it away into the space beneath the workbench.

OK, so her aim wasn't great, but the stone bounced off the ground, then up against the wood, then down again: *clatter, bang, clatter.* And the noise was enough to make the diseased creepy little bastard scurry away.

'YEAH, YOU BETTER KEEP RUNNING, RUPERT FUCKIN' RAT!'

The stone rattled to a halt against something metal, setting whatever-it-was ringing as it spun around a couple of times then wobbled to a halt.

She narrowed her eyes, then shuffled closer to the bench. Till the chain wouldn't let her go any further.

That metal something was an old Stanley knife, long forgotten and coated in spider webs. You fucking *beauty.*

The gap beneath the bench had to be a good six, seven inches, and while she couldn't exactly reach an arm in there, her legs still worked.

Yeah, but where there's one rat bastard there's always more – first lesson she learned in the newspaper world. Didn't help though, did it: she *still* ended up marrying one.

Natasha gritted her teeth, cos she was having that bloody knife, rats or not.

Deep breath.

She reached her throwing leg into the void. Skiffing the side of her foot along the uneven concrete, through cobwebs and little pebbly lumps of what *had* to be rat shit, until her big toe brushed against the Stanley knife's cool metal body. Setting it rocking.

Took four goes, and a lot of delicate manoeuvring, but eventually she got her foot hooked behind the thing and dragged it towards her.

The knife was *ancient*: the metal gone that kind of furry way that old metal did. And it was probably covered in rat piss. But she writhed and struggled and contorted herself till it was close enough to grab with her shackled hands, then thumbed the button anyway. Shoving the mechanism forward.

The blade didn't exactly slide out: it grated and stuttered, the edge chipped and flecked with rust. Streaked with the memory of the last thing it cut through, before it was lost.

She could do those wrists now.

But first...

Natasha placed the blade's tip against the edge of her mask's mouth hole, wriggling it between the zip's plastic teeth, twisting the knife so the jagged cutting edge pointed away from her face. Then sawed.

Nothing happened to start with, the thing just juddered back-and-forth and back-and-forth and then a sizzling *ripping* sound as the knife carved through leather.

She kept going – hacking away at the gimp mask, cutting up one cheek and around the top of her eyebrows. Didn't matter about the sharp sting of metal slitting heat-swollen flesh, didn't matter about the blood, as long as she got this bastarding thing off.

She sawed her way down the other side, and a big chunk of mask hinged forward to flap wide open.

What was left still covered her ears, and her chin, and most

497

of her head, but for the first time since she woke up yesterday, her face was free.

Natasha wiped her other hand across it – wet and sticky, the fingers and palm covered in bright scarlet.

A laugh jangled free, followed by another one, and another until she was sitting on the floor, rocking, screeching it out. An angry, hysterical, *unhealthy* sound.

Eventually it passed, leaving her sagging against the work-bench, breathing hard, ribs aching like she'd suffered another kicking.

She got to work with the blade again, sawing downwards from the side of her mouth. Hacking through to the bottom of the mask.

Soon as the knife ripped through the last bit of leather, she dropped it and pulled at the mask with both hands, hauling it off and flinging the bastard away.

The unwell laughter burbled away, just beneath the surface.

OK, so her hands weren't free, and she was still chained to this bloody anchor, and she'd probably just given herself tetanus, septicaemia, and all manner of rat-borne diseases, but it was a *start*.

And now she had a weapon.

61

Laughter oozed through the big top's walls, joined by frequent *Oooooh*s of amazement and *Ahhhhh*s of wonder.

Out here, the crowd was thinning out. Probably something to do with the circus not being licensed to sell alcohol – so while the kids headed home to bed, the adults headed off to enjoy Aberdeen's legendary nightlife. AKA: get wankered.

Logan lurked by the Whack-a-Mole stall, which some enterprising soul had customised, so the playing field was a big Mrs Doyle's face out of which hairy moles popped up for the player to wallop. Extra points if you could hit the green melanoma.

Twenty minutes into the last performance of the Rumplington Brothers' Circus of Delights and there was *still* no sign of Charles MacGarioch. All his mates were inside, enjoying the show, but the racist wee shite had finally missed an official Orphan Outing.

Pfff...

Yeah, but he *might* still turn up.

But why would he?

Everyone knew the police were after him – it was all over the newspapers, TV, radio, and internet – even if they didn't know *why* he was a wanted man. But MacGarioch did.

Maybe the boy wasn't as thick as he looked?

Perhaps it would be better to stake-out his grandmother's flat instead? Have her followed. After all, if he couldn't stay the night at Keira Longmore's house because his nan would have a fit, how could he justify being away from home for two-and-a-bit whole days? He'd have to get in touch with her *somehow*, right?

Question was: would the Chief Super approve the manpower and overtime to run another ICSO?

Could divert the team from Seaton Park?

Yeah, but what if he turned up there, soon as they left?

And knowing Logan's luck...

Steel's voice groaned in his earpiece. *'This is a bust.'*

Yeah.

Charles MacGarioch was officially a no-show.

Logan pressed the talk button. 'OK, we're calling it a night. Tufty's got tickets, if anyone wants to catch the rest of the show.'

Can't say they didn't try.

He wandered over to the big top, where Tufty waited, all on his own.

The wee loon handed him a ticket. 'Did our best, Sarge.'

'Don't think the Boss gives out participation trophies.'

Biohazard emerged from the dwindling crowd, dressed like a middle-aged man who thinks he's still got it, but clearly hasn't. He accepted the proffered ticket. 'Look on the bright side: we're still getting paid.'

Then it was Doreen and Barrett's turn – grabbing a ticket from Tufty before slipping in through the entrance.

The world's daftest tiger hooked a thumb at the big top. 'Can I...?'

'Go on then.'

'Woot!' And away he scarpered, into the fun and the lights and the—

'Me and Spudgun are off to the pub. If you promise no' to be a misery-faced old snudge, you can buy the first round.'

Tempting.

He pressed the button. 'Better not. Got Tara and Elizabeth here.'

Steel's voice softened. *'It happens, OK? Sometimes the buggers show, sometimes the buggers don't. We pick ourselves up and we have another go.'*

'Yeah, you're probably right.' A smile. 'And that's two quid in the swear jar.'

'Oh, for...'

Then silence. She'd gone.

Logan stepped through the entrance into a tented foyer festooned with fairy-lights, where a tattooed hipster in a ridiculously tall hat tore Logan's ticket in half and ushered him through a velvet curtain into the Rumplington Brothers' Circus of Delights.

A large semicircle of tiered seating surrounded the central ring, broken into six sections of about eighty seats each. And nearly every one was filled.

High above the audience's heads a trapeze and high wire stretched from one side of the big top to the other, caught in the sweeping beams of spotlights. Down below, clowns worked the crowd, while acrobats tumbled and boinged across the sawdust arena.

Logan moved down the aisle, between two blocks of seats, scanning the faces for Tara and Elizabeth.

Which was a bit more challenging than usual, because of the face-paint. In the end it was easier to spot their clothes than their features – middle tier, on the left. And they'd even saved him a seat.

Logan worked his way over there, excuse-me'd past a handful of people and thumped down beside Tara.

And stared.

Tufty's mate, Courtney, might have turned the wee loon

and his bidie-in into little-big-cats, but Tara had received an elaborate *Día de los Muertos* face-and-neck paint job, made up of swirls and patterns and leaves and dots, and she looked ... *stunning*. Elizabeth, on the other hand, was a full-on kid/velociraptor hybrid – grinning away as a clown whooshed a bucketful of confetti over some poor unsuspecting member of the public.

Tara leaned in, voice raised over the hubbub and laughter. 'No joy?'

He forced a smile. 'Worth a go, though.'

Even if it was a sodding disaster, and he'd have some explaining to do tomorrow. And Charles MacGarioch would still be on the run. And the press would be in raptures of self-righteous indignation. And the top brass would be screaming for results. And Soban Yūsuf would be lying in a mortuary drawer, awaiting Isobel's not-so-tender ministrations...

Wasn't exactly a *great* day's work.

The Ringmaster from the poster strode into the ring, wearing his bright-red faux-military uniform with lots of braiding. Raising his top hat for a bow to the audience. 'And now, ladies and gentlemen, I must insist: *no flash photography*! We cannot risk startling the animals. For who knows *what* might happen...'

He stepped back with a big flourishing gesture, and the rear curtain opened. Spotlights swooped in as a Lion and Tiger slunk into the ring, followed by a huge lumbering Elephant.

They were part puppet, part marionette, part animatronic, and part costume. Life-sized and lifelike.

The audience *Ooooh*-ed and *Ahhhhhh*-ed as the 'animals' launched into the kind of routine most circuses could only dream of.

Logan let his gaze wander around the big top, picking out Tufty and Kate, Barrett and Doreen, and Biohazard sitting all on his own. Then across the sea of faces to where Charles MacGarioch's Orphaned Chums had taken over a chunk of the seating block – second from the far end – with the weenies on the bottom row, then the younger teens, then Jericho and Alexis and Marshall and Ralph. The weenies were agog at the animals, and the teens seemed to be too.

Which was kind of lovely and wholesome, especially after all the horror and suffering.

Looked as if Jericho was cultivating his bad-boy gangsta image by sneaking in some tinnies. And yeah, *technically* Logan could march over there and give him a hard time about it – what with council bylaws and everything – but there was no need to be a dick, as long as he wasn't hurting anyone.

And at least Jericho was trying to be discreet.

He popped his empty in a bag, so no littering, then dug out a fresh six-pack of lager: handing one to Alexis, who passed it to Marshall, who passed it to Ralph, who opened it and had a sneaky drink. The next tin stopped at Marshall. Then it was Alexis's turn.

Finally, Jericho opened one for himself, but instead of drinking it, he put the can down at his feet as everyone burst into applause for the Elephant's latest trick.

Maybe the lad was a bit stoned, because when the Elephant moved onto the next thing, Jericho opened another can and took a sneaky scoof. Laughing and cheering along with the rest of the crowd, as the Tiger and Lion jumped through hoops of artificial fire.

Oh, to be young and stupid...

By the time the animals had finished their set, the Secret Orphan Drinking Club were all passing their empties back to Jericho, who popped them, one by one, into his bag. Then finished his own tinny. It joined the collection.

A wee pause, then he did something *strange*.

Jericho reached down to his feet and picked up that extra beer he'd opened. Only instead of drinking it he gave it a wee shake – as if making sure it was empty – then slipped it into his bag with the others.

Hold on a minute.

OK, it was possible he'd downed two tins in the time it took everyone else to drink one, but...

Another six-pack emerged from Jericho's personal off-licence, and away we go again: one passed all the way along, then a second, and a third, then one for the floor, and one for Jericho.

The sneaky bastard...

Yeah, the tin was placed at Jericho's feet, but what happened after *that* was hidden behind the head and shoulders of the teen sitting in front of him on the next row down.

Logan raised the extension to his mouth and pressed the talk button. 'Anyone still about? I *think* the fox is in the hen house.' He leaned over and kissed Tara – trying not to smudge her face-paint. 'Watch the monster.'

Then shuffled out of his seat, pardon-me-excuse-me-ing along to the steps as the spotlights swirled around to focus on a clown car rattling and banging out from behind the curtain. It was a smaller, pedal-powered version of the one that'd been driving all around town, and before it had even gone half a circuit around the ring a similarly rattle-bang version of a patrol car pedalled out after it – complete with two clowns in high-vis waistcoats and Police Scotland black.

And God knew, Logan had worked with enough of those.

The clown car juddered past a prop speed camera – *FLASH* – and a 'high-speed' chase ensued, complete with lights and sirens.

Tufty: *'Where is he, Sarge?'*

'Right-hand side of the tent, where they've just unrolled a zebra crossing.'

Doreen: *'Not seeing him, Guv.'*

'That's because he's underneath the bleachers.'

Biohazard: *'On it.'*

Off to the left, Biohazard hopped out of his seat and hurried to the end of the row, then disappeared down the side.

Doreen and Barrett, Tufty and Kate scrambled out of their stalls too, all at the same sodding time.

'Try not to make it too obvious, people!'

Luckily, the clowns were in the middle of staging some sort of road traffic accident: where a granny clown tried to get across the zebra crossing with her tartan shopping trolley, only to shy back at the last minute as a life-size puppet Zebra thundered across it on inline skates. Which meant the whole Orphan Crew were laughing at *that*, rather than spotting Logan's merry gang of idiots.

Logan strolled down the steps to ground level, acting all casual as the Zebra made another pass and Granny got a second fright. 'I need someone on the entrance.'

The clown car filled up on 'petrol' and the patrol car filled up on doughnuts, momentarily abandoning their hot-pursuit.

Barrett: *'Entrance secured.'*

And there he was, standing just outside the fairy-lit foyer, pretending to stretch his legs.

The Lion puppet reappeared, also on skates this time, and set off after the Zebra. And after a bit of bumbling and running about, the police piled into their patrol car, pedalling furiously to catch up. Blues-and-twos going.

Tufty and Kate disappeared behind their seating block.

The patrol car almost ran over one of the clown-clowns, leaving him spinning round and around on one leg, so for some inexplicable reason, the clown car wheeched after the patrol car.

Kind of got the feeling logic wasn't really a priority here.

Logan ducked behind the stands.

A heavy curtain of black fabric concealed whatever structure held the seats up. Which had the added bonus of hiding what was going on out *here* from anyone in *there*.

He paused for a moment, letting Tufty, Kate, Doreen, and Biohazard catch up.

Keeping his voice low, just in case. 'OK, they're in the second last block of seating. Kate, Biohazard: you take this side. Doreen: you're in the middle. Tufty: with me.'

A wave of laughter roared through the big top, followed by honking and animal noises and sirens, as the clowns got on with the show. Meaning there was no chance anyone would notice Logan and the wee loon sneaking their way around the back of the stands.

More laughter, and a clatter of applause.

Logan checked Doreen, Biohazard, and Kate were in the right place, then tapped Tufty on the shoulder. Pointing at the heavy fabric blocking off the supports.

Tufty eased the curtain back, exposing a forest of scaffolding poles, with clips and pins and bits wrapped around in yellow-and-black warning tape. The whole structure resting on wooden boards and mud mats – liberally sprinkled with fallen popcorn and spilled peanuts.

Bingo.

A figure lurked near the front of the bleachers, leaning on a post, staring through a gap in the seating and out between someone's legs, watching the performance.

Charles MacGarioch.

A tin of lager dangled from the fingers of one hand as he laughed along with the crowd.

Right: the bastard wasn't getting away *this* time.

Logan eased his way into the scaffold jungle, creeping

closer, the seats above his head getting lower with every tier as he advanced on Clueless Charlie.

Tufty snuck in, staying off to one side.

A quick glance left, and there was Doreen, while Kate tiptoed in from the far corner. And just in case, Biohazard guarded the far edge.

Whatever was going on out there, someone must've been directing the crowd, because they all stamped their feet and clapped in rhythm. Sending dust and yet more popcorn pattering down onto Logan and his team.

MacGarioch tried to join in with the clapping, but it clearly wasn't easy while holding a tin of lager. The thing slipped through his fingers, hit the mud mats, and *spoof*ed up a little jet of foam and golden liquid. 'Shitey wank-fucks...' Scrambling to retrieve it before too much spilled out.

Then he froze.

Before turning to stare at Biohazard. Then Kate. Then Tufty. And finally: Logan, less than a dozen feet away.

'Charles Edward MacGarioch, I am arresting you under section one of the Criminal Justice, Scotland—'

That tin of lager hurled through the ranks of scaffolding poles, heading straight for Logan's head. But before it could smash into his face, it hit one of the uprights, crumpling and spewing supermarket own-brand pilsner everywhere.

MacGarioch went left – presumably, because if he'd gone *right*, he'd have to get past every member of Logan's team to escape – meaning he reached the edge of the seating block before anyone else. Shoulder-charging the black fabric wall.

Which didn't do much more than shudder and bounce him back into an upright with a *clang*.

Logan surged forwards, dodging his way through the metallic-bamboo forest as MacGarioch grabbed handfuls of fabric and yanked, ripping the covering away from its Velcro fastenings.

Then he was away – running towards the ring.

Sod.

Logan ducked out after him, into the aisle between the two seating blocks, skidding on the popcorn-slippy floor. Rushing forwards.

The crowd's cheers and whoops crashed against him like a rugby scrum.

Out here, things had taken a weird turn: now the Lion was chasing the patrol car, which was chasing the Zebra, which was chasing the clown car, which was chasing the old lady, round and round the ring.

The cars were only pedal powered, but they were still going at a fair clip. The Zebra, Lion, and old lady had no problem keeping up on their skates, though. Swirling faster and faster, lights and sirens going, as the crowd roared.

MacGarioch hurdled the wooden blocks that lined the ring, and came within two inches of being run over by the clown car. He legged it for the curtain at the back.

Logan jumped the kerb, jinked between the patrol car and the Zebra. 'STOP! POLICE!'

For some reason, the audience seemed to think this was all part of the show, pointing and hooting as Logan gave chase.

Almost at the other side, MacGarioch glanced back over his shoulder, arms and legs still pumping. Not watching where he was going. Straight into the path of the patrol car.

As car crashes went, it was nowhere near as bad as Spencer Findlater's encounter with a Toyota Hilux, but the impact was still enough to send Charles MacGarioch tumbling over backwards and bring the patrol car to a sudden lurching halt.

Presumably the pedal car had been rigged to fall apart at a later part of the show, because it immediately suffered a rapid unscheduled disassembly. The wings collapsed away from the frame, the headlights pinged out on springs, the doors flew off, and the boot and bonnet both *poing*ed up.

And as they weren't wearing seatbelts, the police clowns jerked forward in their seats – slamming the passenger's head into the dashboard while the driver rocked back, still holding the now-detached steering wheel.

The crowd cheered and applauded.

They did it again two seconds later, when the Lion, still going at full pelt and unable to stop at short notice, slammed straight into the open boot.

The driver stumbled out of the car, holding his detachable steering wheel, blinking at the wreckage. His fellow officer stayed in the passenger seat though, with both hands clutching their big red nose as blood streamed down their smiley make-up.

MacGarioch scrambled upright, leaping the patrol car's open bonnet, just as Logan grabbed at his jacket.

Didn't get a firm enough grip to stop him, but it screwed up the jump, and instead of landing on his feet, ready to scarper, Charles MacGarioch went tumbling down the other side.

The Zebra, old lady, and clown car trundled to a halt. Then the clowns climbed out of their vehicle, looking every bit as dour-faced and murderous as they had driving around town.

Balling their fists, they advanced on Logan.

Either the crash or the botched leap had caused a bit of damage, because MacGarioch hurpled towards the curtain through to the backstage area, like a sawdust-covered Igor.

Only he never got there, because Kate pounced from the other side, catching him in a flying rugby tackle. And down he went again.

A huge roar of approval swept through the crowd, people getting to their feet and cheering-on the little leopard as she struggled to get the *much* bigger MacGarioch in an armlock.

Logan skirted the wreckage and hurried over to help.

Jericho McQueen shot to his feet. 'HEY! LEAVE HIM ALONE, YOU LEOPARD-FACED BITCH!'

And with that, the Orphan Army charged, storming down from their seats and into the ring while the weenies ran around with their hands in the air, screeching and grinning and screeching some more.

Logan grabbed MacGarioch's other arm, before he could land a punch on Kate's head. Twisting it into a wristlock. 'Charles MacGarioch, I'm detaining you under—'

Was as far as he got, because a clown battered straight into Logan's ribs, sending them both thumping to the ground in a tangle of arms and legs and big floppy shoes.

The other clowns piled in, and so did the Lion and the Zebra, *and* the little old lady. Then Tufty, Biohazard, Doreen, and Barrett. Then it was the Orphans, turning what should've been a straightforward arrest into a good old-fashioned circus brawl.

Yeah...

This whole op hadn't exactly gone to plan.

LXII

What sort of bastard didn't keep a decent set of tools in his barn?

Of course there were no bolt-cutters, because that would be helpful. And no hacksaws. And no bloody anything that would get this *bloody* anchor from around her *bloody* neck.

The bench press might've done the trick, if there were any drill bits that would cut metal, and the electricity was on. Which it wasn't.

Could say the same for the table-and-mitre saws, only they'd be a hell of a lot more dangerous. Probably deadly.

Even a crowbar would be an improvement on what Natasha had – which was absolutely *fuck* all – could stick it through a link in the chain and twist till it broke. Assuming the link *would* break. Which, knowing the way this bloody life worked, it probably wouldn't.

Been through this whole bloody barn and all she had to show for it were blisters and scrapes and two-steps closer to taking the Stanley knife to her own wrists.

So now it was the workbench's turn – going through each of the drawers, emptying them out, and examining every single last thing. Which wasn't easy with both wrists manacled to her neck.

And if this didn't work, there were only two options left: figure out a way to get into the caravan, hauling a galvanised bin full of concrete that weighed twice what she did, or try to make a run for it.

A very slow, awkward, *painful* run, rolling this sodding anchor along with every step.

Cos there's no way *that* could end in disaster.

She pulled out the very last drawer and tipped the contents onto the workbench. Rusty screws, rusty bolts, rusty washers, couple of angle brackets, a rubber mallet the mice had been at, and right at the very back: a screwdriver. It was one of those cheap-looking piece-of-shit ones: flat head, about six inches long, with a yellow-and-black handle. The sort of thing you could pick up for a buck fifty in your local supermarket.

Sod-all use for getting rid of her anchor. But maybe...

She turned the thing around in her right hand, so the blade and shank pointed at her throat. Then worked them into the ring that her left wrist was cuffed to. The one fixed to her metal collar.

Natasha pushed the screwdriver about halfway in, then pressed the handle downwards.

It rotated – pivoting against the ring – then stopped. So she shoved harder, pulling her chin up and back. Just in case.

Bastard didn't budge.

She wrenched the thing upwards instead, but it clacked to a halt at much the same angle. Only the other way around.

OK. Time to try something a bit more extreme.

Natasha grabbed what was left of her horrible mask and wrapped a chunk of leather around the screwdriver's blade. Bent her knees, so the screwdriver's handle rested on top of the workbench.

Please God, you heartless, vicious, *cruel* bastard, don't let me impale myself through the bloody throat.

Natasha took a deep breath.

Closed her eyes.

And dropped.

Thunk. Then a muted squeal... and *ping*: she crashed to the concrete floor, forehead smacking against the workbench's leg, setting the world ringing like an old-fashioned telephone.

Took a good minute before she could move again, and when she did, the metal cuff was still firmly locked around her wrist ... but it wasn't attached to the collar any more.

Her right hand was free!

The arm it was attached to had turned into a flopping riot of numbness laced with pins-and-needles though, the tendons in her elbow screaming after being bent like that for the last two and a half days. The useless limb dangled at her side, trembling with teeth-grating fizzy pain as she used her still-shackled left hand to feel for a ragged gash in her throat.

Looked like the mask did its job.

Yeah: the screwdriver was a bit bent, but still in one piece. Meaning once her arm came back to life she could have another go, and get the left one free too.

Soon as *that* happened, she'd finally get a decent grip on the stupid, rusty sledgehammer, batter the chain off her anchor. And get the *hell* out of there before DS Davis returned...

63

Backstage, the Rumplington Brothers' Circus of Delights wasn't quite as magical. Through here, in the space behind the curtain, the walls were wobbly, temporary things, with a tented roof and modular shelving racks for props and the like.

Most of the Zebra and Lion puppets were suspended on frames, next to the Tiger and Elephant. Like art exhibits in a bizarre abattoir. While the wreckage of the patrol car lay piled up in the corner.

The show had started again, and the audience clapped and cheered as the barrel organ pounded out its tunes, and the high-wire troupe went through their routines. But no clowns, because they were all in here.

Police Clown Number One was a large man in slightly smudged make-up and handcuffs. 'Well, how were *we* supposed to know you were cops?'

His mate from the passenger seat, sat on a folding chair, head thrown back, pinching the bridge of his nose with one hand and holding a wodge of paper towels to his bleeding nostrils with the other. Voice a mumbled, bunged-up, growl: 'Leave it, Gerry.'

The Old Lady Clown was in cuffs as well, looking as if she was brewing-up a walloping shiner for tomorrow.

One of the *Clown*-Clowns slouched against the wall, vaping.

While the other nursed a pair of battered testicles with a bag of frozen peas. Which can't have been easy in handcuffs.

Doreen, Barrett, and Biohazard – all looking decidedly rumpled – stood guard, while Logan pulled Charles MacGarioch to his feet.

Unlike the clowns, both his hands were cuffed *behind* his back.

'What were we *supposed* to think?' Gerry scowled. 'Come charging into the ring, beating up some random bloke!' His grazed chin jerked upwards. 'Just cos you right-wing thugs got badges, you think it's OK to brutalise—'

'For fuck's sake, Gerry!' The Old Lady Clown kicked him in the shin. 'Stop making it *worse*!'

'Ow!'

'Serves you right.'

Idiots.

Logan escorted MacGarioch out through the back and into a fenced-off area that bordered the park's three concrete-lined ponds. A bunch of Transit vans and a handful of caravans were crammed in – nowhere near enough to service the whole circus/funfair setup, but enough to keep a presence on site so people wouldn't nick things.

The Orphan Posse loitered by the ponds, under the watchful eye of Tufty and Kate – who both looked a bit scruffy and slightly tattered, with their feline faces all smeared-and-smirched from the fight.

Alexis was in cuffs, and so was Jericho, wincing as Ralph blotted his swollen eye with damp cloth.

Ralph dumped the cloth in a bucket, and waved at Logan, then strolled over. Nodding at the prisoner du jour. 'Hey, Charlie.'

Charles MacGarioch smiled back. 'Hey, Ralph.'

He fell in beside them as Logan marched MacGarioch

towards a waiting patrol car. 'I know it all got a bit "spirited" in there, but they were only trying to defend their friend. And the circus guys thought *they* were being public spirited. You know, intervening in a fight?' A shrug. 'I mean, we're always told that's the mark of a healthy society, aren't we? That good people are ready to intervene when they see an injustice?'

'They assaulted *six* police officers in the process of arresting a wanted man. That's "attempting to defeat the ends of justice", punishable by imprisonment and a dirty-big fine.'

'Yes, and I'm sure they're all really, *really* sorry. But it wasn't intentional, really, was it? And if Alexis gets a criminal record they might throw her off her Uni course: what film or TV company's going to give her a second look then?'

Logan stopped and subjected Ralph Hay to a full-on Paddingtoning.

He just smiled back.

God's sake...

Logan rolled his eyes, then turned to Tufty. 'Constable Quirrel.'

'Sarge?'

'Miss Cunningham bit you.'

The wee loon grinned. 'Yeah, but only because she didn't recognise me with the face paint on. She's absolutely *mortified* now.' Giving his head a swanky wobble. 'Never bitten a *film star* before.'

'Do you want to press charges?'

Tufty curled one side of his face up, then pulled back his sleeve to expose a semicircle of teeth-marks. 'Nah. I'll pop some Savlon on it when I get home.'

Fair enough.

Logan puffed out his cheeks. 'Uncuff her, then. And check with the rest of the team – anyone they *don't* want to prosecute gets off with a caution and a stern talking to. Everyone else spends tonight in the cells.'

'Sarge.' And away he skipped to spread the good tidings: the Get-Out-Of-Jail-Free Fairy.

'Thanks, man.' Ralph Hay nodded at Logan. 'You're one of the good guys.' Magnanimous in victory.

'Ever thought of joining the police? Or the Diplomatic Corps.'

'Nah.' His smile widened. 'Going to be a merchant banker, like my Uncle Pete.'

Strange how quickly you could go off someone.

'Yes, well...' Logan tightened his grip on Charles MacGarioch and marched him over to the patrol car.

'Bye, Charlie. Stay frosty, OK?'

'Bye, Ralph.'

'Mind your head.' Logan squeezed him into the back, did up his seatbelt, then clunked the door shut and got in the other side.

The blue-and-white lights swirled, but because it was only ten minutes since the Great Big-Top Brawl, no one from the press had arrived yet, so there wasn't a swarm of cameras and microphones to fight their way through – just a handful of arseholes who whipped out their phones to film the patrol car as it rolled down the access road, turned left onto Westburn Road, and slipped silently into the traffic.

MacGarioch turned in his seat, craning his neck to capture every last moment of the circus, funfair, and park. 'Do you think they'll let my mates visit me in prison?'

Logan frowned at him. 'Why'd you do it, Charlie?'

The big top disappeared behind the trees, then the edges of the fair vanished, and finally even the trees faded into the distance.

A sigh, then Charles MacGarioch faced front again. 'Dunno.'

One shoulder came up. 'Needed the money. Keira and me are gonna open a B&B in Ireland. Property's never cheap, is it. Then there's your overheads: food and laundry and soap and towels and wee packets of shortbread and teeny pots of jam and tea-and-coffee-making facilities in every room.'

Wow.

Looked as if Ralph Hay had been right about Charlie not winning *Celebrity Mastermind* anytime soon. OK, so he wasn't exactly Lenny from *Of Mice And Men*, but he was no Professor Moriarty either.

'Yeah,' Logan nodded, humouring him, 'all those little expenses soon add...' Swivelling around to stare across the car. 'Hold on: you "needed the *money*"? What money?'

'Spencer says I'm meant to go "no comment" till I get a lawyer.'

'What money, Charlie?'

His brow creased as the wheels inside groaned and squeaked their way around. Until finally: 'No comment.'

Damn.

Still, it'd been worth a go.

LXIV

A loud *SPANNNNGGGGG* rang out as Natasha swung the sledgehammer – double-handed and overhead, now both hands were free – into her chain where it poked out of the concrete.

The links didn't give way. The anchor didn't split open and disgorge the bloody thing, because apparently Detective Sergeant Davis had made sure the bastard ran all the way down to the bottom of the *shitting* bucket.

So far, she'd managed to make a dent in the concrete, but only about the size of a small melon. Digging the slivers out with the bent screwdriver every dozen blows or so. Other than that: nothing had changed, except her legs wobbled more and more, her arms *ached*, every breath rasped its way down her burnt-gravel throat, and a monster-sized headache rampaged through her skull. Howling at her every time the stupid sledgehammer hit.

SPANNNNGGGGG...

She staggered backwards a couple of paces. Clunked the sledgehammer's head down on the barn floor, then sank to her haunches. Then onto her bum. Folding forwards till her thumping forehead rested against the hammer's warm wooden handle.

Maybe it was time to accept this wasn't working.

Try to find some way into the caravan instead.

Might be a phone in there?

Maybe the key to the bloody padlock at the back of her stainless-steel collar?

Or a hacksaw...

Because she'd been at this for *Christ* knew how long, and DS Davis wasn't going to stay at work for ever.

And soon as he got home, she was well and truly fucked.

65

It was a different PCSO behind the desk this time – a neep-faced middle-aged man with a side parting and glasses, squinting away at his clipboard, looking like the kind of person who'd kept a Tamagotchi alive since 1997.

Somewhere deep in the cells, an elderly man launched into a filthy ballad about a nun borrowing Satan's bicycle.

Logan stifled a yawn.

The PCSO turned the page. 'Give us a minute; been mopping up vomit since half seven…' Then a nod. 'Here we go: duty solicitor's in with a Keira Longmore now, so you're in luck. Took us eight hours to find one yesterday.' The clipboard went back on the desk. 'He can see your boy next. Want us to give you a bell when he's ready?'

'Thanks.' Scrubbing some life back into his face. 'Right…' Logan pushed through into the stairwell, with its painted breeze blocks and miserable motivational posters, footsteps echoing back from the concrete floor as he slogged his way upstairs.

He'd almost reached the first landing before his mobile launched into 'Space Oddity'. Slumping against the wall, he checked the screen before answering. 'WELCOME TO TUFTYVILLE!' glowed up at him.

But Logan pressed the button anyway. 'What's gone wrong now?'

'*Sarge? Just wanted you to know that everyone's gone free, so we does has* ring-side tickets *for any time the circus is in town! Which is coolio. But the press turned up with their cameras and microphones and shouty questions, which is definitely* not *coolio. But then word got round that you're doing a media briefing soon, and they all did scurry away – whoosh! So is coolio again.*'

Another yawn juddered free, and Logan let it rip, ending with a sigh and a sag. 'Tell everyone: back to the shop, write up your reports, and sign out for the night.'

You could almost hear the wee loon doing his happy dance. '*We has done good today and did catch the bad guy. That am being the most coolio of all!*'

Had to admit, he had a point.

'Yeah: I suppose you're not *that* bad a sidekick. Now sod off; I've got crap to finish before I go home.' Logan hung up and sagged a little more.

Down in the custody suite, the fabled nun performed a very unwise sexual act with a penguin and a bicycle pump – all belted out in a wobbly baritone.

Then Logan's phone joined in with a *ding-buzz* on the chorus.

SWEENY:

> Where are you?
>
> Press briefing is in 15 minutes!!!
>
> Are you trying to give me a heart attack!?!?!

He let his head *thunk* back against the breeze blocks. 'Come on, Logan, only five more years till you can retire...'

LXVI

Using the screwdriver as an icepick to chip away at the concrete was every bit as laborious and frustrating as battering it with the sledgehammer. Only slightly less exhausting. And even less efficient.

But all this buggering about, in the broiling heat, sweating, and struggling, and worrying, and not having anything to drink for … two days? Three? With nothing but a small bottle of spat-in water, made the whole world thrummmm…

Dehydration.

That would be why her head hurt so much, while her arms had turned into two blocks of solid lead, her legs to overcooked spaghetti, and her tongue was made of burning parchment.

And this *shit* wasn't helping.

Natasha straightened up – back howling in protest – groaned out a gritty wheeze, and dumped the screwdriver on the workbench. Flexing her aching hand.

How long were the shifts police officers did? Eight hours? Or was it twelve, like offshore workers? Either way: the longer she wanked about with this bloody anchor, the sooner Detective Sergeant Davis would rock-up home, bringing his hate and his rage and his digger keys with him.

Time to go.

But she *wasn't* leaving the barn empty handed.

The Stanley knife sat on the workbench, next to the bent screwdriver. She forced the blade back in. Then...

Well, she could hardly stick it in her *pocket*, could she.

And she'd need both hands free to roll the anchor – which had to be easier and quicker than shoving the thing with one foot.

And her pants had been chosen for their might-get-luckiness, rather than their ability to securely hold DIY equipment.

Which left her bra.

The furry metal was *horrible* against her skin – like tinfoil on a filling – but Natasha wedged the Stanley knife into the side of her left cup. Shoving it down till the elasticated lace had a good grip on the rough casing.

Not ideal, but it was that or leave her only weapon behind.

She gritted her teeth and heaved the galvanised bin over onto its side again. It hit the floor with a *bang*, and a chunk of concrete the size of a bowling ball clattered free – coming to rest by the table saw.

Ripper.

She peered inside, but the chain was still firmly held in place. Because no way she could be that lucky today.

Just had to hope there were keys to the padlock at the back of her neck waiting for her in the caravan. Assuming she could get into the bastard.

Natasha bent down and rolled the bin towards the barn doors.

What about the wheelbarrow? Maybe she could make a sort of ramp out of all these bits of wood lying about the place? Then all she'd have to do is load her bucket into the barrow – and now she had both hands free, there was nothing stopping her grabbing the handles – and wheel the fucker up the ramp and in through the caravan door.

Assuming she could wrestle a bin *full* of concrete into the wheelbarrow in the first place, and the rusty bottom didn't just fall out of the thing, and it would still move with a flat tyre…

Natasha rolled her anchor out through the barn doors and into the courtyard again.

The sky had grown a purple tinge while she was inside, fighting with the sledgehammer, the shadows lengthening and turning blue as the sun drifted down towards the treetops. Even the bluebottles had stilled, anticipating night.

She shoved the bucket over to the static caravan.

Up close, there was a strange … *meaty* smell.

Her stomach clenched.

Maybe this wasn't a good idea.

Yeah, but it was this, or try to shoot through.

Natasha reached for the door handle.

Just as her fingers touched the pitted metal, the sound of a car engine swelled in the distance, getting louder as it approached, accompanied by the rattling percussion of tyres on a rough track.

She was too late.

And Davis was back.

67

Journalists packed the conference room, cameras and phones at the ready. Staring at the podium and its Police Scotland backdrop with hungry eyes. As if someone was about to be sacrificed on the table in front of them to appease the Ancient Media Gods...

Logan marched his tired arse down the side of the room and into the little nest of whiteboards and flipcharts, where Chief Superintendent Pine and PC Sweeny were waiting for him.

Well, Sweeny was waiting, Pine was on her phone again.

The Media Liaison Officer closed his eyes and shuddered out a long breath. Knees bending, one hand propping him up against the wall. 'Oh thank Christ for that...'

Pine stuck a finger in her spare ear, swivelling around to face the corner for a modicum of privacy. 'I *know* that, First Minister, this is why we're devoting every available resource to finding Mrs Agapova. ... No, I realise it's—' Her shoulders tightened. 'Yes, First Minister. ... Thank you, First Minister.' She stuck her phone in her pocket and sagged. '*Bloody* politicians.'

'Hey, Sarge.'

Logan turned, and there was Tufty, beaming up at him. 'Why are you—'

'Is everyone ready?' Sweeny pressed a printout into Logan's

hands. 'Finally: some good news to Feed The Beast. Make sure you stick to your prepared statements, OK?'

Pine frowned at hers. 'How did you get these ready so quick?'

'Trick of the trade, Boss.' His swanky swagger wilted beneath Pine's glare. 'Sorry. They covered it in the Media Liaison Officer Training Course: "Always prepare a best-case-scenario briefing as something to work towards." That way, if things actually *do* go well, you're ready for it.'

Which wasn't exactly a vote of confidence in A Division.

Logan peered around the edge of a flipchart. The chatter was fading away as the last sixty seconds ticked down. 'Think they're all here about Charles MacGarioch?'

'Don't care,' Sweeny brushed a knob of fluff off his black T-shirt, 'as long as we come out of this smelling like roses, rather than what they're grown in, it's a win.' Frown. 'But if anyone asks you about anything that isn't on the briefing notes, do *not* engage. *Especially* about Natasha Agapova. Last thing we need is them turning our moment of triumph into a big bag of festering shite.' He checked his watch. 'OK: it's showtime. Let's give these bastards a briefing they'll never forget!' Then strode out into the room and up onto the platform.

Going by the glare Pine directed at Sweeny's back, she hadn't enjoyed that bit about 'festering shite'.

Logan nodded at her private corner. 'Operation "Find Natasha Agapova" not going well?'

'Bloody thing isn't going at all. Our only suspect is lying in the mortuary, Forensics have found precisely zilch, ANPR is useless, nothing on CCTV, and no one saw or heard anything. Other than that? Everything's just sodding *great*.' Pine pulled her shoulders back and marched out after Sweeny.

Tufty patted Logan on the back. 'Break a leg, Sarge.'

'*Why* are you here again?'

'I has a lovenest and a bidie-in to support, so the overtime comes in handy. Plus Kate and me *totally* helped with the arresting, so I does has some basking-in-the-reflected-glory to do.'

Twit.

Logan rolled his eyes, shook his head, then joined Pine and Sweeny onstage.

And the crowd went wild...

LXVIII

Fuck!

The bastard was back, and she was still shackled to this stupid bloody anchor. If she'd made a run for it, she might've reached a nearby farm by now. Called for help...

Probably not, though.

The car's engine growled closer.

Instead, she'd have left a flattened path through the weeds and grass that even a blind corpse could follow. And out in the open like that, in the middle of a field, she'd be shit out of options.

Whereas *here*, she had four.

Number One: Make a run for it *now*. Which was stupid. She wouldn't get more than a few hundred feet before he caught up with her. Then it would be JCB time.

Number Two: Get back to the outbuilding and make like she never left. Wait for the bastard to drink himself to sleep again, like last time, and *then* leg it. Assuming Davis didn't just try to kill her, soon as he got home.

Number Three: FIGHT. Kill the bastard.

Yeah, like she could have a fair go, shackled to a galvanised metal bin full of concrete.

And Number Four: *Hide*.

One and Three were nonstarters.

Number Two was risky. She could hold her wrists up to the

collar, so it looked like they were still shackled there, but all he had to do was look at the bloody mess she'd made of the concrete in her bin, and he'd know *exactly* what she'd been up to.

Which left hiding.

But where? Where was she going to hide, that he couldn't find her in two minutes flat? In the barn? Under the static caravan?

No chance. The thing was surrounded by weeds, which the anchor would flatten – so exactly the same problem as scarpering across the field...

Of course, there was a *fifth* option: stand here, dithering about like a proper whacker, and wait for him to beat the shit out of her again, then get the JCB fired up for a bit of grave-digging.

'Shite...' The word barely made it past her dry, cracked lips.

Number Two it was, then.

But make it *bloody* quick.

Natasha shoved the anchor, rolling the bastard fast as it would go, across the courtyard and in through the door to her stinking manky prison.

Was like running into an *oven*, after the relative cool of the barn.

Soon as she got the thing over the threshold, she hauled at the door – setting those stupid bloody rollers squealing like a ruptured pig.

Please let the bastard still be parking.

Please let his windows be up.

Please let him be playing his horrible music, full volume, so he couldn't hear any of that...

One last yank and the door *clunk*ed into place.

She bowled her anchor back into the middle of the room and heaved it upright again. The concrete inside was ruined – not enough to let go of the bloody chain, but more than enough to get her killed.

So...?

...

Sit on it.

That was fuckin' *genius*!

Her arse would hide the damage.

Natasha clambered onto the bin. Not exactly comfy, but better than the alternative. Then sat there, *listening*.

Outside, the engine noise died. A car door creaked open, then *thunk*ed shut.

Please don't let him have heard any of that.

Footsteps crunched across the dirt outside.

Please, please, please, please, please...

She sat up straight.

Deep breath.

You can *do* this.

The bluebottles must've been disturbed by her charging back in here, because the greasy bloated bodies lumbered into the sticky air again. Circling and *buzzzzzzz*ing.

And now that she was sitting still, the bastards began to settle on her salt-stained arms and legs.

One landed on her cheek.

She brushed it away with a swipe of the hand. A good old-fashioned 'Australian salute', as they used to say, back in the—

Oh fuck...

She could hold her hands in place and pretend they were still cuffed there all she liked, but Detective Sergeant Davis *might* just notice SHE WASN'T WEARING HIS PRECIOUS FUCKING GIMP MASK!

Shit. Shit. Shit. Shit. Shit...

She should've run after all.

69

Whoever invented paperwork could sod right off.

Logan poked away at his keyboard, working his way through the interminable screeds of crap needed to justify every cock-up, mini-triumph, assorted shenanigan, and utter wanking disaster he'd overseen since starting work this morning.

Trying not to stare at the wall clock every two minutes.

The stacks of file folders he'd inherited still littered his desk, but even more of the things had arrived – clogging up his in-tray too. Because in Police Scotland you could never have enough buggering *paperwork*.

He finished off the report on Charles MacGarioch's arrest, hit 'SEND' and slumped back in his chair.

Rubbed at his face.

Groaned.

Looked around at the assorted piles and piles and piles of other people's crap.

Groaned again.

Then heaved the files from his in-tray onto his desk, opening each in turn to have a quick squint at the covering pages inside.

Right at the top was Forensic's preliminary report on Andrew Shaw's Peugeot, which didn't need an entire sheet of A4 – four words would've done it: 'bugger, and indeed, all'. No blood or DNA matching Natasha Agapova, *so far*.

Suppose there was still hope, but you could pretty much guarantee they'd used the accomplice's car in the abduction.

The next one down contained Doreen's summary pages for all the review meetings he'd lumbered her with. But those could wait till tomorrow.

Number Three was a twenty-four-page memo about overtime payments and how to properly account for manpower-spend in relation to operational-budget-overruns and calculate the variance from key-performance-indicator baselines.

That could *definitely* wait.

Then there were a bunch of DCI Porter's cases, and a handful of DCI McCulloch's for good measure. Because the lucky bastards were off with the plague, leaving their crap for the living to wade through.

And right at the bottom: Biohazard's door-to-door-and-PNC-check extravaganza. Which, surprise-surprise, turned out to be a complete waste of sodding—

'*What are you still doing here?*'

Logan looked up, and there was Chief Superintendent Pine, with yet more paperwork tucked under her arm. 'Boss.' He waved a hand at the assorted piles. 'Catching up while we're waiting on Keira Longmore to finish with the duty solicitor, so Charles MacGarioch can have a go. And then we can *finally* interview him.'

Pine perched a buttock on his desk and helped herself to one of his files. 'Are we sure it's wise to let them share a solicitor, given the risk of collusion?' Opening the folder to skim the contents.

'What choice do we have? ... Which is now the *official* motto of A Division.' A yawn crackled free. 'Right now, our pool of duty solicitors contains exactly one person. And we have to share her with Tayside.' He slumped in his chair. 'It wasn't your fault, you know: the media briefing. The buggers had their knives out and sharpened *long* before we got there.'

She kept on reading. 'Aren't *I* the one who's meant to give the motivational speeches?'

'OK, so Natasha Agapova was abducted in the wee small hours of *Tuesday morning*, but we only found out ...' he checked the wall clock again, 'twenty-two and a half hours ago! And we've already identified one suspect and solved over a dozen outstanding rapes. In what screwed-up alternative universe is that "floundering"?'

'The one that sells newspapers.'

Because that was so much more important than the *truth* these days.

'You get anywhere with Nick Wilson?'

A puzzled look. 'Nick...?'

'Second-last person to see Natasha Agapova alive? Captain Sleazy of the Good Ship SexYacht?'

'Oh.' Her brows furrowed. 'Erm ... DS MacDonald's speaking to him. Or *has* spoken. Or at least, he better have.' She cricked her neck. 'Haven't checked my messages yet.' Then grimaced. 'Feel like I've spent the whole sodding day fielding questions and doing interviews. Urgh...' pulling her mouth out and down, like an unhappy bulldog. 'Don't suppose you fancy swapping places and running A Division for a bit, do you?'

'Not even *vaguely*, Boss.'

A sigh. 'Yeah. Me too.' She dumped the file back in his in-tray. 'OK – leave the duty-solicitor thing with me. I'll see if I can't pull a few levers with the local Society of Advocates. Buggers owe me a few favours anyway.' Then hopped down off Logan's desk. 'Go home.'

'But Charles MacGarioch—'

'Isn't going anywhere. That's why we put him in a nice warm cell.' She pointed at the door. 'Home: go.'

Yeah, he wasn't going to argue with that one.

'Thanks, Boss.'

'But for goodness' sake, *properly dressed* tomorrow. Detective Chief Inspectors are expected to set an example.'

Again?

He looked down at his outfit of jeans and a T-shirt. 'We were on an undercover op!'

'I *know* that. When you're back in uniform,' she tapped her epaulettes, then held up a trio of fingers, '*three* pips, not two.' Then marched off. 'And tomorrow we do some spectacular detective work, rescue Natasha Agapova, get lauded in the press, a couple of shiny medals, keys to the city, and a slap-up dinner with champagne and chips.'

Aye, right...

Soon as she'd gone, Logan sagged for a couple of breaths, then stood. Powered down his computer. And sodded off home for the night.

All this pain and suffering and death and horror would still be here in the morning...

LXX

The sky darkened through the ragged window hole, purpling like the bruises spreading across Natasha's ribcage.

And still no sign of Detective Sergeant Davis.

Not that she was looking forward to the bastard coming home, but the waiting was *torture*. Knowing the horror would sweep into the outbuilding with him.

So, she sat on the dirt floor – head throbbing, hands trembling, throat like the bush two days after a fire – with her back against the anchor, forehead resting on her folded arms, propped up on her raised knees. Eyes closed as DS Davis's music barked out of the static caravan, loud enough to make her fillings rattle.

Maybe something had happened?

Maybe that was why he hadn't turned up yet?

Maybe he'd had a bad day at work?

Or maybe he *knew* what she'd been up to, and making her wait was all part of the punishment.

She should've broken into that bloody caravan, smell or no smell. Then at least she could've got a drink of water.

Bet Davis had a fridge in there, with ice, and maybe a chilled bottle of Pinot Gris...

God, she was such a bloody galah.

And now she—

The music got louder and clearer for a moment, then the

clunk of a closing door and it went back to angry muffled noises again, pounding along with the beat.

Oh God.

The waiting was over; it was horror time...

Natasha struggled to her feet, going up on her tiptoes to park her bum on top of the bucket. Concealing the damaged concrete as the heavy wooden door squealed. She jerked her wrists up to her throat, holding them there like they were still cuffed in place – hands over her face to hide the missing mask. Peering out between her fingers. Trying to work up a little spit in her mouth.

Can't talk your way out of *anything* if you can't speak.

The door thudded wide open and the light from Davis's head torch clawed across the broken walls, searching for her.

Then he lurched into the room, bringing with him the bitter smoky stench of second-hand whisky. The bottle was clutched in one hand, but the other held something else. Something that rustled as his shoulder scuffed against the wall, because his legs didn't seem to be working all that well tonight.

Booze smeared his words into each other: 'Where's my favourite girl?'

Oh Christ, not this.

Nah, she'd rather die than have his disgusting body on top of her.

'My favourite, *dirty* girl.'

Wasn't easy, but she croaked out a bit of defiance. 'Go fuck yourself.'

'Hey, look: you're famous!' He hurled his rustling handful at her head.

Halfway there, it turned into three rolled-up newspapers that bounced off her raised arms, one bursting open on its way to the ground, the sheets fluttering as it sloughed apart.

Davis's head torch swivelled down, pinning it to the floor.

'NEWSPAPER OWNER ABDUCTED BY SICK WEIRDO'

Natasha's face smiled back at her from the *Aberdeen Examiner*'s front page. A stupid PR shot, taken years ago at some trade dinner thing she never wanted to go to.

Davis lurched over and nudged the other two with his foot, unfurling them.

It was a copy of the *Evening Express* and the *Glasgow Times*. One had gone for, 'WAS MEDIA MOGUL KIDNAPPED BY TERRORISTS?' the other, 'EX-HUSBAND'S EMOTIONAL PLEA: "BRING BACK MY NATASHA"'. Because there wasn't a single story Adrian couldn't make about himself.

Davis took a swig of whisky. 'Course the pictures don't do you *justice*. Don't capture how *ugly* you are inside. How twisted and hateful and *ugly*.' The head torch's beam swept across the three front pages, then up Natasha's battered body to her face.

And stopped.

Could almost hear the bastard's mouth fall open. 'What... But... Where's your mask?' Air hissed in through his nostrils, to be bellowed out again: 'WHERE'S YOUR FUCKING MASK, BITCH?'

Time to tell the most important lie of her life.

Because if it didn't work, it would be her last.

She kept her wrists at her throat, but turned her fingers into claws. Doing her best to snarl, even if it came out thin and papery instead. 'I *tore it off*. I ripped it to shreds and fed it to the rats.'

With slow, deliberate movements, DS Davis hunkered down and placed his bottle on the floor, by the door. Safe and out of the way. Then stood – taking a lurching step to the side, like the ground had shifted unexpectedly beneath his feet. Straightened himself up. ... And lunged forward, lashing out with a stinging slap that crashed into Natasha's right cheek and hurled her off the anchor, into the dust and eviscerated newspapers.

'HAVE YOU GOT ANY IDEA HOW MUCH THAT COST? YOU UNGRATEFUL BITCH!'

He grabbed her by the shoulders and yanked her around to face him. Not that she could see anything, with his head torch blazing in her eyes, but the hate and booze radiating off the bastard could've lit Melbourne for a year.

Something else glowed with rage, and the hard cold fur of old metal.

Davis coiled a fist. 'I'M GOING TO FUCKING KILL YOU!'

But before he could let it fly, Natasha's right hand slashed out and up, thumb shoving the button on the Stanley knife forward. Not really aiming, just going for anything she could hit.

The jagged blade dug through the bastard's filthy T-shirt, ripping its way up his chest to sever 'BLODHØST' from 'DØDSULV', then out again – soaring free until it slashed into his jaw and across the bastard's cheek.

He shrieked.

Letting go of her, Davis scrabbled backwards, tripping and falling flat on his back, arms flailing.

A sharp glass *clink* and *rattle* as the whisky bottle went flying.

Natasha growled and leapt – as far as the chain would let her – grabbing his leg with her free hand and stabbing the rusty blade into the inside of his thigh over and over again as he screamed and howled.

With any luck she'd sever the bastard's femoral artery.

Blood soaked through Davis's jeans, making the fabric slippery, but she tightened her grip and dragged him closer. Going artery hunting with the Stanley knife again.

'GET OFF ME! GET OFF ME!'

The knife bit into his other leg, inches from his groin, but it'd be infinitely more satisfying to castrate the bastard *before* he died. So the next stab halved the distance.

Davis thrashed and screeched, bawling like a smacked child, writhing hard enough to tear the Stanley knife from her blood-slicked grip and send it clattering off into the darkness.

Fuck.

Unarmed now, she clenched her fist and slammed it right into Davis's balls.

Whoomp – the air and the fight went right out of him with a strangulated whimper. He curled around his battered testicles, moaning.

Strange, you'd think the lacerated thighs would be worse, but that was men and their balls for you.

She ripped the torch from his head and went through his pockets.

Yes!

That foul little dog's paw was in his back pocket, the collection of shiny metal keys dangling from the leg end. The tiny one he'd used to unlock her mouth was still there, as were a bunch of others.

One of these bastards *had* to be for the padlock at the back of her collar, keeping her shackled to this galvanised bin full of bloody concrete.

Leaving him to groan and whimper, she spun the collar around her neck, till the padlock was at the front. A big brass Yale job. And there was only one Yale key dangling from Fido's paw.

Please. After all this…

She skittered the key into the lock and twisted. The *click* of the mechanism as it swung open was *the* most beautiful sound in the world.

Soon as she pulled the lock out of her collar, the whole thing clattered to the ground, chain and all.

She was free.

She was *finally* free!

Now where's the knife, so she can finish the job?

The torch beam swept across the dirty floor and the newspapers and the fallen rocks and big chunks of stone, but the Stanley knife had disappeared.

WHERE THE FUCK WAS HER STANLEY KNIFE?

Davis stopped whining – swapping the self-pitying snivel for a puce-faced hissing rage. Blue jeans turned a deep, glistening shade of claret from waist to shin as he cupped his poor little balls.

Try childbirth, then see what real pain—

His foot lashed out, catching Natasha's left knee, making something inside *pop* as red-hot wires lanced through the joint, twisting and coiling, searing straight out the other side.

Natasha roared as the leg gave way, and she staggered back against her anchor, setting it rocking.

'KILL YOU!' He struggled to his feet. Teeth bared. Spittle frothing out with every Pitbull breath, one hand pressed against his torn, bleeding face. 'I'LL BLOODY KILL YOU!'

And you just *knew* the bastard meant every word.

And he was much bigger than she was.

And standing between her and the open door.

Natasha pulled the head torch on over her matted curls, and scrambled through the window hole. Grunting every time her throbbing knee took any weight, the joint yowling as she tumbled out onto the gravel. She landed with a whump on her back, hard enough to leave her gasping for air.

Lying amongst the weeds, blinking up at the stars and the swirling dots of midges, drawn by the head-torch glow.

Heavy metal *thummm-thummm-thumm*med at the caravan's walls. Angry and jarring. Like her knee.

The bastard had broken something inside it. Or torn the ligaments, or dislocated her kneecap, or *something*.

And he'd do the same to the rest of her, then dump her in a deep pit and bury her, if she didn't move.

Right.

Now.

Natasha fought her way to her feet, and limped towards the caravan. Cos there had to be a phone in there, right? At least, the bastard would have a mobile and even if it was locked, she could still make emergency calls. And once *inside*, she could barricade the door and wait for the bastard to bleed to death. Or pass out. Or she could grab a kitchen knife and finish the—

'BITCH!'

Detective Sergeant Davis hobbled into the courtyard, bloodied legs stiff as a rocking horse. Arms up and out for balance. Glaring at her in the head torch's glow as bright red dripped from his torn face and slashed chest.

Even when her dad was drinking, he didn't look *so* full of rage.

Natasha staggered the last few steps and grabbed the caravan door handle. But it wouldn't even turn.

Locked.

What kind of *bastard* locked the door when he was only going twenty paces?

Keys – where were the keys?

Must've dropped them on the way out the window.

'FUCKING KILL YOU!' Getting closer.

How was she supposed to run away when she could barely *walk*?

Shit. *Shit*, shit, shit.

She abandoned the caravan and limped towards the barn instead, with Davis lumbering along behind her – snarling like a rabid dingo.

The barn door yawned open, with nothing but darkness on the other side. Natasha stumbled through it, the head torch's beam raking the dead machinery and floor. Then lurched around to slam the door in Davis's face.

But he was too close, jamming his foot into the gap before it could fully shut. 'YOU'RE GOING TO SUFFER, BITCH!' Shoulder pressed against the wood. *Shoving.* 'I'M GOING TO SKIN YOU ALIVE!' He reared up then slammed forwards, making the door *boom* and creak. 'I'LL MAKE A NEW MASK OUT YOUR *FUCKING* HIDE!'

Natasha pushed back: good leg braced against the rough concrete floor.

'BITCH!' One last crash and the door flew open, knocking her off her feet, sending her tumbling across the concrete as DS Davis lurched into the barn. 'Going to make you *scream!*'

She scrambled backwards, until her shoulders bumped into the workbench.

He hobbled closer, leaving a trail of blood on the dusty floor. 'Tell you what: why don't I give you the same chance you gave those poor migrants? That would be fair, right?'

'Please – I have money, I have—'

'NOTHING!' Spittle flying, glowing in the torchlight. 'Fast asleep in their beds while some right-wing racist monster SET FIRE TO THEIR HOME!'

She raised her chin. '*You're* the monster.'

'Maybe.' Davis loomed over her. 'But if I *am*, it's because that's what you made me.' Grabbing Natasha by the arms he yanked her to her feet, grinning, eyes wide and pinprick sharp. *Pressing* himself against her. 'I'm the hurricane.'

He wrapped a fist into her hair, holding her head tight as

the other fist curled … then slammed into her face. Snapping her head back.

The world exploded in jagged shades of orange and purple as a choir of arsonists set her skull ablaze.

A second blow turned everything silent and still and dark for a moment, before it all rushed back in a deafening wave.

She probably wouldn't wake up from a third…

And that's when Natasha's searching hand clamped onto the yellow-and-black handle of that crappy buck-fifty screwdriver.

She gripped it tight.

Then rammed the blade and shank right into Davis's side. *Thnk.*

His mouth fell open, fist drooping.

She pulled the screwdriver free – *shkk* – and drove it in again. *Thnk. Shkk.* And again. *Thnk.*

He let go of her hair and staggered back a step. *Shkk.*

This time, the screwdriver stabbed deep into his belly. *Thnk.*

Davis blinked at her.

Natasha tightened her grip on the handle and twisted.

With a normal screwdriver that probably wouldn't do much, but the buck-fifty's shank was all bent from getting her wrists unshackled, so instead of just swivelling around, the blade would be grinding its way through his innards. Causing all sorts of horrible damage.

Good.

Davis swayed back on his good leg, but the other one wouldn't take his weight any more and down he went with a crashing thump.

Left hand clutching his stomach, he tried to claw and push himself away from her, the screwdriver still sticking out of his midriff. Blood-soaked jeans leaving a thick scarlet smear across the concrete floor. Wet and gleaming in the head torch's glow as yet more blood pulsed out of his punctured guts.

The barn swirled around Natasha's head and her working knee gave way, dumping her on her backside against the workbench again. Leaving her swaying. Holding onto the floor to keep herself from falling off as everything danced and spun.

Davis got as far as the table saw.

He was still struggling to escape, but his good leg just slipped on the blood-slicked floor and he didn't seem to have the strength in his arms any more. So eventually he stopped even trying and ... sagged.

Natasha closed her eyes as the waltzing world picked up pace, twirling and reeling. Arms and legs and head and every single breath getting heavier, until everything went...

— an albino crocodile —
on a scarlet lake

71

Sunlight streamed in through the window, making the dusty black flakes sparkle as Logan scraped the burnt bits off his toast, into the sink.

Which turned the low-fat spread a bit grey as he slathered it on. But it was all going in the same place as his mug of tea, so it didn't really matter.

Technically, given he was in full uniform again this morning – complete with a third pip on each epaulette – it should've been coffee and doughnuts for breakfast, but you made do with what you had.

Something folky *high-diddle-de-dee*d out of the radio, to accompany Logan's return trip to the fridge – there to liberate, unwrap, and flop the last slice of plastic cheese onto his hot can't-believe-it's-not-buttery toast.

Crunching away, as the teeny birds mobbed the feeders in the back garden. Like a swarm of itsy-bitsy feathery sharks. All the borders were in bloom, a sea of colour for the bumbling bees. Quite bucolic, for a Friday morning in Aberdeen.

Have to give that grass a mow before the barbecue, though.

The microwave's clock blinked over to 06:18.

Soon be time to get a wriggle on.

And speaking of wriggling: Cthulhu tarted about on the patio, rolling over onto her back and exposing the World's Most Excellent Tummy to the morning light.

The kitchen door opened and in sludged Tara, in a floaty kimono-dressing-gown that showed off a lot of leg, while a yawn showed off a lot of fillings. Hair like Worzel Gummidge in a wind tunnel.

Logan polished off his last corner of toast. 'How come you're up?'

Another yawn. 'Couldn't sleep. Kept having all these *really* weird dreams about clowns and dinosaurs and tigers…' She frowned. 'You weren't there, but I couldn't find my socks. And Tufty kept turning into a penguin.'

'Bet Freud would have a field day.'

'Urgh… That's Friday the thirteenth for you.' She slouched over to the fridge and took a couple of glugs straight from the milk carton, while scratching the back of one calf with her other foot. Very stylish.

Logan downed the last of his tea. 'You've got the table manners of a Labrador, you know that don't you?' Putting the mug in the sink. 'Don't forget to pick up that stuff for Sunday, OK? List's on the noticeboard.'

'I know, I know.' She rummaged through the fridge. 'You want sausages, chicken, pork chops, hotdogs, blah, wankity blah.' Then squinted at him. 'What happened to all the plastic cheese?'

'And go large on the booze: you know what off-duty police and trading standards are like.' He kissed her on the cheek. 'Don't know when I'll be home tonight, depends what happens. And tomorrow's a write-off with this stupid protest.' He drooped against the worktop. 'Really looking forward to a quiet day at home.'

'Good job we've got thirty-one people coming for Sunday lunch then, isn't it?'

'*Thirty-one?* You said it was going to be a "small gathering"! Are you *trying* to kill me, you horrible snudge of a woman?'

The clock hit 06:20.

'Better shoot. Text you later, Fornicator.' He grabbed his peaked cap and marched for the door.

'Hoy: Fart-Fish!'

He turned, halfway out the door, and Tara whipped her kimono open and flashed him. Throwing in a little jiggle for good luck. Then hid it all away again.

Logan groaned.

She grinned. 'See? You love me really.'

True.

But there was no time to do anything about it right now.

'...coming up in a minute, but it's half six, so it's time for the papers. The P-and-J leads with "Search Ongoing For Missing Media Mogul", detailing police efforts to find local press baron, Natasha Agapova.'

Logan cruised along North Deeside Road – with the window down and one arm leaning on the sill – through one of Aberdeen's more affluent bits. The trees offering a bit of cool shade as the sun scorched its way up the sky.

Not a lot of traffic this morning, but then it was still pretty early. A familiar tartan van approached on the other side of the road, with 'AUCHTERTURRA GLAZING COMPANY LTD' down the side. Its battered and dented rear wing held together with duct tape and hope.

'The Scottish Daily Post goes all in on: "Migrant Gang Plot To Kidnap Newspaper Natasha" and there's more coverage on pages three, four, seven, and eight – including an exclusive interview with Natasha Agapova's husband: news tycoon Adrian Shearsmith.'

Who had to be up for a Vindictive Ex-Husband of The Year award by now.

'While the Aberdeen Examiner's gone for "Sicko Sent Hate-Mail Threats To Abducted Editor". Asking: if these threats were *common knowledge* before *she was kidnapped, why didn't the police do anything about it?'*

'Oh for God's sake!' Logan flipped two fingers up at the radio. 'How about because they didn't *tell* us about them till yesterday afternoon!'

Honestly.

The Marcliffe at Pitfodels drifted by on the left, or at least the entrance did, the hotel itself was hidden away behind a riot of trees and assorted greenery.

A bilious man in the full kilt-and-Prince-Charlie outfit stiff-legged it down the drive and out onto the pavement, heading for town. Clearly escaping from whatever wedding he'd attended last night.

Hope he wasn't the groom...

'...and they've also got a big spread on pages four and five that deserves a mention: "City Cops Cause Circus Chaos". And the photos that go with it are well worth a look. Especially if you've never seen an undercover policeman with a clown in a headlock...'

Logan switched the radio off and glowered.

Nothing like spoiling a beautiful morning.

The stale-digestive-biscuit scent of old feet mingled with the sharp cumin-and-chilli whiff of Bombay Bad Boy Pot Noodle, filling Observation Suite Number Two. Three empty cartons in the bin testified to the whiff's provenance, but raised some disturbing questions about who'd been in here last and what they considered a balanced breakfast...

It was a smallish space, with a bench table and a couple of squealy blue plastic chairs, four flatscreen monitors, some push-button microphones, and a worryingly enthusiastic Tufty.

But at least he'd made Logan a mug of instant coffee, rather than fetching something revolting from the machine, so as long as he kept his gusto to himself, that was OK.

The four screens displayed various views of Interview Room Number One – each camera mounted high up, in the corners of the room, and trained on the table where Biohazard and Doreen did their best to get the truth out of Charles MacGarioch. Which was far more difficult than it should've been, thanks to his 'duty solicitor'.

MacGarioch was in grey joggy-bots and a fading blue T-shirt: presumably lent to him by whoever was on the custody desk this morning. While his legal representative wore a suit that probably cost more than his client earned in a year.

Sandy Moir-Farquharson, AKA: Hissing Sid – a tall, thin man who looked as if he'd shrunk a couple of sizes since he last wore that particular Savile Row number. His hair was swept back like a bank of snow, with only a few streaks of grey left amongst the white. But then he had to be in his late seventies now. With a matching silk-tie-and-pocket-square, and a superior tilt to his long nose.

Waiting to strike.

Charles MacGarioch shifted in his seat, looking away with a one-shouldered shrug as the silence stretched on.

Hissing Sid shook his head, as if saddened by having to explain something *blatantly* obvious to someone thick as plasticine. *'My client has already informed you, Acting Detective Inspector Marshall: he is not a racist, does not hold any racist beliefs, and has never discriminated against anyone because of their skin colour or country of birth. Now, can we move on, please?'*

Biohazard leaned forwards. *'Then why burn down a hotel full of migrants, Charlie? Help me understand.'*

MacGarioch just looked at his solicitor.

A smile. *'Perhaps this interview would progress more easily if you took notes as we go? Then you'd be able to see that my client has already denied these baseless allegations.'* Hissing Sid waved a patriarchal arm towards the camera. *'It's not a problem for me,*

*per se – I've got nothing on till lunch with the Lord Provost – but
I understand there's a lot more pressing things that you and your
colleagues could be getting on with?'*

Doreen had a go. *'If you didn't do it, Charlie, how do you
explain the jerry can we found with your fingerprints all over it?
What could've caused that?'*

MacGarioch picked at the tabletop, eyes focussed on the
chipped Formica. *'Dunno.'*

There was a sharp knock on the observation-room door
and Chief Superintendent Pine strode in without waiting.
Frowning at the monitors.

Logan stood. 'Boss.'

'DCI McRae, I need a word.'

On all four monitors, Hissing Sid sighed. *'Surely it's not
illegal for a young man to help a friend in need to* refuel *their car.
Or has that changed since I last practised criminal law?'*

'Yes, Boss.' He thumped Tufty. 'Give the Chief Super your
seat.'

The wee loon scrambled out of his chair and snapped to
attention. Then made seat-offering gestures. Like a creepy
waiter.

Pine sat anyway. 'Thank you.'

*'Or perhaps it's because the petrol can in question was in the bin
for landfill, rather than correctly sorted for recycling? I wasn't aware
Police Scotland were so keen on environmental issues.'*

Logan pointed at the smug git in the sharp suit. 'I know you
said they owed you a favour, Boss, but could you not've asked
for someone a little less … *him*?'

'Mr Moir-Farquharson volunteered. Turns out he's mostly
retired now; does a bit of consulting, one day a week.' A
grimace. 'This is his idea of "keeping his hand in".'

Doreen checked her notes. *'Whose car were you refuelling?'*

'Was Spence, wasn't it. On account of him…' MacGarioch's

mouth clamped shut. That lone shoulder curled its way towards his ear again. *'Running out, like.'*

'Basically, we're screwed.' Logan dumped his pen on the worktop. 'The only way we'll get anything out of MacGarioch now is if he suffers a psychotic brain-fart and spontaneously confesses. And even then, Hissing Sid will walk it back in thirty seconds flat and somehow make out it's all our fault.'

Biohazard leaned in again. *'Were you going to say, "On account of him robbing all those sports shops"? We found enough whey powder in his bedroom to fill a municipal sandpit.'*

'Then perhaps, my dear Acting Detective Inspector, you should be interviewing this "Spence" individual, instead of my client?' Hissing Sid pushed his chair back. *'If you don't mind: I think we should take a brief respite from this wholly unnecessary and unwarranted interrogation, for a comfort break.'*

'We just had one.'

'Sadly, my poor old bladder isn't as young as it used to be. And I'm sure you wouldn't be unsporting enough to continue brow-beating poor Charles in my absence. Would you?'

'God's sake.' Logan folded his arms. 'He just does this to *mess* with us: bet he doesn't even need to go!'

Pine raised an eyebrow at him.

Urgh...

Logan pressed the talk button and leaned into the microphone. 'Let the old fart have his prostate-problem pee break.'

On the screens, Biohazard's shoulders froze for a beat. Then slumped. *'Fine. Interview suspended at oh-eight-thirteen. We'll reconvene in five minutes.'*

A smile. *'Make it ten.'* Smooth and slick, as befitted a serpent.

'Typical.' Logan flicked the switch, killing the speakers. 'Sorry, Boss, you wanted a word?'

'DS MacDonald.'

555

OK... That sounded ominous. Especially given Marky MacDonald's reputation for wandering hands, his two written warnings, and what was going to happen if he *ever* did it again.

Logan glanced at the wee loon. 'Is this something we should be discussing in front of Constable Quirrel?'

'What?' She pulled her chin in, frowning. Then must've finally got the subtext. '*Oh*... No. Nothing like that. I sent him to speak to your Nicholas Wilson, yesterday.'

Nope. No idea.

'The second-last person to see Natasha Agapova? At the ball?' Pine stood.

'Did he find something?'

'No idea.' She stepped out into the corridor and Logan followed, because this was clearly going to be one of those walk-and-talk things 'dynamic managers' were *so* fond of. 'He didn't file a report, and now he's on sick leave.'

Of course he sodding was.

She marched off, leading the way past invigorating motivational posters like: 'You CAN Make A Difference!', 'Integrity Is The BEST Disinfectant!', 'Community Policing ROCKS!', 'Put The "Polite" In Police!', and other such bollocks.

'I'll get someone on it.'

Pine nodded. 'And circulate a memo – all reports *must* be completed before the end of shift. If you can find some way to say "No one else is allowed to come down with this sodding man flu!", without HR getting a wasp in their knickers, that would be lovely too.'

At the end of the corridor Tufty scurried ahead to open the door and hold it for Pine. Brown-nosing little spud that he was.

The open-plan office was nearly deserted, with just the barest *hummmm* of activity going on in the background, because most of dayshift were away trying to find Natasha Agapova. Well, everyone who hadn't come down with The Dreaded Lurgie, anyway.

Temporarily released from their interview trauma, Doreen and Biohazard were slumped at adjoining desks. Doreen scrubbing both hands across her face as a scowling Biohazard crunched his way through a 'MORE TO SHARE!' bag of Chocolate Honeycomb Minis. Though he seemed determined to devour the lot by himself.

The pair of them oblivious to the fact that the head of A Division had just stalked into the room.

Crunch, crunch, crunch. 'Forgot what a *massive* pain in the hoop that tosser is. You could catch Jack the Ripper, red-handed, strangling the Queen Mother, while Hitler cheers him on, and Hissing *Bloody* Sid would still get the bastard off on a technicality.'

Doreen reached for the bag, but Biohazard wheeched it out of her reach. 'Hey! Don't be such a greedy gripe.'

Pine stopped right in front of their desks. 'As you were.'

At which point Doreen flinched, letting out a strangled 'Eeek!' While Biohazard came *very* close to losing his honey-comb.

He scrambled to recover the bag, before its contents went everywhere. '*Boss!* Guv. Erm...' Holding out the almost-spilled sweets. 'Sorry. Charles MacGarioch might as well be a sodding mannequin for all he's contributing in there.'

Everyone helped themselves to a chocolaty treat, even Tufty.

Logan crunched through a cube of salty-sugary goodness. 'Ask him about the money. In the car, on the way back from the circus, he said he did it because he "needed the money".'

Pine peeled the chocolate off her honeycomb, like some sort of serial killer. 'What money?'

'*Exactly*. And don't let Hissing Sid fudge the issue.'

She helped herself to another rattling handful. 'Now that MacGarioch's in custody, I'm sure DI Marshall can tidy everything up here – I need *you* to concentrate on Natasha Agapova and the protest march.' She pointed. 'DI Marshall: keep at him. It's possible he'll let something slip, but I doubt it. We've got enough forensic evidence for a solid case, but I want everything watertight, understand?'

A nod. And a surreptitious lowering of the bag, out of grabbing reach.

'Good. DI Taylor: you're probably better deployed elsewhere. Don't think we need *two* acting detective inspectors in there, twiddling their thumbs.' A sniff. 'Besides, I think DCI McRae wants you to stand in for him at some meetings.'

Logan bit his top lip. 'Ah...'

Busted.

His ears went much hotter than normal.

'Yes, right.' Biohazard gathered up his folders and files. 'Well, we'll ... erm...' and off he scuttled, followed by Doreen – dragging Tufty away with them. Leaving Logan at the mercy of Chief Superintendent Pine.

'You see, Boss, ... I felt ... what with *all the other things* demanding our attention ... and given the *operational* pressures ... besides, it's a valuable *career-path development opportunity* for—'

'I know I said, "delegation is the key to a healthy work-life balance", but you still need to be *fully* across your brief.' Pine stared at him. 'Are you?'

The warmth spread from his ears to his cheeks. 'I get a one-page summary on every meeting she attends.'

Silence.

Pine tilted her head to one side. 'Sounds sensible. And it means you've got nothing distracting you from finding Natasha Agapova. *Today* would be nice. Preferably in time for the lunchtime news.' She turned to go. 'And don't forget to get each of your teams' overtime-budget-and-schedule-variance-against-KPI-baselines calculated. Need that in by the end of the week.'

Striding away to spread her own special brand of joy and delight to some other poor bastard.

End of the week. AKA: *today*.

Logan screwed his eyes shut and sagged.

Friday the thirteenth strikes again...

LXXII

The path winds through the bush, green and glowing as it follows Hyland's Creek.

Been a while since fire's roared through here, and the gum trees are thick and emerald-topped, shedding their bark in great papery blades of grey.

The sun's low in the sky, a faint nip to the air – that'll change as the day warms up, but for now Natasha's breath glows like golden flame as she hikes up Redpath Hill, behind Nanna Carter's house.

It's not a *swanky* house, like on Dad's side, but who needs a view of Sydney Harbour Bridge and the Opera House, when you've got a chunk of bush to call your own?

Somewhere off to the left, a kookaburra cackles like a mad woman. An outback Baba Yaga, calling for children to eat.

Natasha keeps climbing, right on up to the top of the hill.

Can't see very far, cos of the trees, but the sky's a slab of blue opal, with the sun *just* breaking above the gumtops.

Off to her left, a roo freezes, then turns its head to stare at her with those big brown eyes. Face a mix of deer and dog, ears twitching. Then it's off: bounding away between the trees, tail up, the undergrowth pop-and-crackling beneath its spring-loaded paws.

Don't know what's got *him* spooked. Not like she isn't up here every morning.

And then Natasha smells it – a sort of *leathery* scent, with an undercurrent of something bitter and … sticky. Like snags left on the deck for months, drying out in the sun. Attracting flies.

Whatever's dead, it's lying in the scrub just off the path.

She steps closer.

Fat green blowflies drone through the air above a body; hard to tell if it's a bloke or a woman, though. Must've been here a *lonnnnnnnng* time, cos the skin's shrunken tight over the bones, tanned and split open beneath the ribcage, letting the maggots feast.

Poor bastard.

Every now and then, some old codger wanders off from the care home, gets lost in the bush, and karks it. Isn't hunger that gets them – there's plenty to eat, if you know where to look and you ain't squeamish – it's the thirst. Specially in summer, when the thermometer creeps up towards fifty.

Couple of days out here, in the heat? That's you.

Deliria, hallucinations, muscle spasms, then one by one your internal bits-and-pieces pack in and you're a goner.

Weird thing is, this dead bloke's wearing a watch, just like hers. Like the one Mum gave her for her tenth birthday, with 'NEVER LET THE BASTARDS WIN!' engraved on the back, cos of Dad being a total *dill*.

Come to think of it, the bloke's wearing her runners too. And the clump of hair clinging to that wizened skull is the same colour. And—

His eyes snap open and he *roars*.

Only it's not a 'bloke', it's Natasha's own dead face howling back at her.

And the blowflies surge forward, answering the cry—

Natasha flinched, blinking out at the dirty barn with her one working eye. Lying on her side, left arm trapped beneath her, the other reaching out towards the tattered remains of her old mask.

Sunlight flooded in through the open door, stretching halfway across the space between her and Detective Sergeant Davis. Making the pool of blood glisten.

He lay crumpled at the foot of the table saw, skin so pale it looked like he'd painted it with white ochre, an albino crocodile lurking on the edge of a shining scarlet lake.

The air *thrrrrummmmm*ed with the wings of a thousand bluebottles, feasting on all that blood, to a backing track of angry heavy metal – still pounding away inside the caravan.

She coughed. Dry and papery.

Come on, get up.

Get up and get out of here.

The bastard was dead. Couldn't hurt her any more.

All. She. Had. To. Do. Was. Get. *UP.*

Only nothing worked.

Could barely manage more than a twitch.

Her arms and legs were carved from solid granite, her head heavier than a binful of concrete as waves of red-hot nails crashed against the inside of her skull...

At least her knee didn't ache any more, that was something, right? Even if it *had* turned into a swollen watermelon of purple and green.

And the rest of her wasn't much better. Couldn't even open her right eye. Couldn't breathe through her nose. Could barely move her split and bloated lips.

But the only thing that *hurt* was her pounding head.

Which probably wasn't a good sign...

No idea how much time had passed since she killed Davis and passed out on the floor. The barn hadn't heated up yet, so: morning?

Which day, though?

How many days had she gone with just one tiny bottle of spit-laced water to drink?

Because this was one of the final symptoms, wasn't it: the special forces bloke said so, in his doco. Your muscles seize up. And then you die.

All that time and effort spent getting rid of her bloody anchor, and fat lot of good it did her. The caravan was just sitting there, ripe for the taking, and she couldn't even move…

73

The pool car crawled along Auchmill Road, through a forest of orange traffic cones. No idea why they were there though – thousands and thousands of the things: sod-all evidence of anyone doing any work.

Should rechristen them 'Roadnotworks'.

The radio burbled away to itself, but Tufty wasn't boogying along in the driver's seat. Instead, he was making sour-frog faces and doing lots of sighing.

Lounging in the back, Steel was still wearing her peaked cap, kicking the back of his seat every now and then. Scowling away.

Which left Logan in the passenger seat, working through Doreen's one-page reports on all the sharny cases he'd inherited. Blah, blah, blah, blah...

Ding-buzz.

Probably better check that. Never knew: might be important.

And even if it *wasn't* it was better than reading all this boring rubbish.

TARA:
> GOOD NEWS!
>
> Susan says she can get me into Costco on her card.
>
> We're going after work to buy MUCHO FOOD!
>
> AND BOOZE!!!

'Hmmmph.' Steel kicked Tufty's seat again. '*Said* we should've taken the bypass.'

'It's not my fault they has roadworks everywhere!'

Another kick. 'Straight out Hazlehead, get on at the Kingswells junction, and we'd be *there* by now.'

Logan poked out a reply:

> If you see something nice for tea – nab it.
>
> And maybe some corn on the cob?
>
> And a cheap piano wouldn't hurt.
>
> Do they sell pianos?

SEND.

Aaaaand back to the reports.

Tufty raised a finger. 'You know what *I* think?'

Kick. 'You *don't* think, that's the problem.'

Actually:

> Maybe a keyboard would be better?
>
> One with headphones she can plug in, so we don't have to listen to her practising.
>
> I does has a GENIUS!

Hold on a minute.

Logan blinked at the last line. Oh, no, no, no, no, no ... he had *clearly* been spending FAR too much time with Tufty.

He gave himself a shake and deleted that bit.

SEND.

The horrible wee spud had his finger up again: 'I think the press would be happier if something horrible *does* happen to Natasha Agapova. Did you see that thing in the *Scottish Daily Post* this morning? Flipping wingwang!'

And it was back to the reports again. For *real* this time.

He turned to Operation 'Drugs In Lithuanian Teddy Bears', skimming the complete lack of any progress. Glanced at Tufty. 'What about the *Post*?'

'Well…' Cranking up the gossipy vibe. 'They *say* there was this big plot by some of the people-smuggling gangs – joining forces in a League Of Evil Sticky Foreigners – to kidnap Ms Agapova and torture her and send some of her fingers to her husband with a demand for fifteen *million* quids!'

Steel snorted. 'Boll … derdash.' Giving Tufty's seat another kick. 'And who told the *Post* this rubbish: Princess Porkies the *Lie* Fairy?'

'Apparently it's because Ms Agapova's been "*leading the crusade to stop the boats*" and "*save our proud nation*" from "*woke lefty traitors*" who want to "*flood the country with—*" Ow!'

Steel thumped him again. 'Stop making quote bunnies when you're driving!'

The wee loon's bottom lip poked out. 'Only going three miles an hour.' He rubbed at his walloped arm. 'Sa-arge, she's *hitting* me!'

'Aye, well it's for your own good. Says so in the *Highway Code*.'

Logan finished the last page, flipped it over, then back again. Frowning as he rifled through the small stack of paper. 'Where's the summary for Operation … what was it, "Disappointment"?' Digging out his phone to call Doreen.

Tufty sniffed. 'Bet the *Highway Code* says you're not allowed to biff the driver while he's driving!'

'Can if he's a dangerous wee snudgehead.'

'*Boss?*' The sound of clacking boot-heels on a terrazzo floor, rattled from the phone. '*Is it urgent, only I'm bursting for a comfort break and the MAPPA meeting kicks off in ten.*'

'Been going through your cheat sheets and I can't find one for Operation "Find Natasha Agapova".'

'*You mean "Disenchanter"? That's cos I didn't do you one. Thought you were all up to date; otherwise, why leave Biohazard running the MacGarioch interview?*'

'Because you and him are the only trained interviewers on dayshift. Every bugger else is off with The Pestilence.'

Her voice took on a pained whine. '*Guv...?*' Then a groan. '*All right, all right, all right.*' There was a *thunk* and the sound went all echoey. As if Doreen had bustled into some sort of largish tiled space. '*What do you want to know?*'

A smaller *clunk*, and the sound became a bit compressed. As if she was now in a much smaller room. But still strangely echoey.

'If I knew *that*, I wouldn't have to ask.'

An even smaller *clunk* was followed by some rustling. Then: *thump*. '*Hold on...*'

The pool car inched a little further along Auchmill Road, past yet more Roadnotworking cones – some of which wore those jaunty orange blinking lights, so people would be extra vigilant about the workmen who weren't here not doing anything.

Steel pulled her hat on a little tighter. Then kicked Tufty's seat again.

'Stop that! Saa-arge, she's doing it again!'

A sigh of relief slumped into Logan's ear, then: '*OK, let's check the folder... Right: Forensics are having another bash getting DNA from Agapova's house, no joy yet, but they're trying some fancy new technique to amplify samples.*'

At which point, the muffled sound of flushing came down the line.

Urgh...

'Doreen, you better not be on the—'

'*You want this info, or don't you? ... Thought so.*' The gurgling whoosh of a cistern refilling. Or at least *hopefully* that's what the noise was. *'Says here: Biohazard's team is still working their way through Andrew Shaw's associates. Nothing sticks out yet. They even spoke to everyone at the gym he used, but they were sod-all help. And looks like his mum's threatening to sue us for defamation. No way her precious wee angel could* possibly *have raped all those women; rant, rant, rant, rant.'*

Yeah, good luck with that.

'Murder weapon?'

'Probably a hammer, going by the skull fractures. Greedy seagulls didn't help, though. They've bloodied the water by … urgh … eating a bunch of the evidence.'

'No sign of the hammer?'

'We could dredge the River Dee, if you like, or get a scuba team in? Won't be cheap, though.'

Tough one. Maybe adding thousands to the budget would be worth it, *if* they found the thing. Assuming they could get prints or DNA off it after all this time in the water. And assuming it was even *in* the river in the first place. Because if it *wasn't*, the bean-counters at head office would be crawling up his fundament, wanting to know why he'd blown so much money on a dead end.

Logan frowned at the slow-motion creep of traffic along Auchmill Road. 'Better let me clear it with the Boss.' And in the meantime, perhaps there was an opportunity here? Worth a go, anyway. He cleared his throat. 'Speaking of operational budgetary constraints: have you ever calculated overtime variance against KPI baselines? Because if not, I may have a treat for you…'

NorrelTech Wellhead Intervention Limited turned out to be an ugly, two-storey, green-and-white building, wedged in between a logistics-distribution warehouse and a wellhead-service yard. Both of which were surrounded by full-on prison-style jagged metal fencing topped with razor wire, CCTV cameras, and warning notices.

Clearly, NorrelTech was *big* on branding, with far too much signage and liveried vehicles featuring the company logo in shades of green, blue, and yellow. Like a cut-price Bond-villain's lair.

Tufty parked in one of the 'VISITORS ONLY' slots around the front, but there was a bigger area out back full of electric vans and cars, where a white-haired bearded gent was washing the company fleet with a big soggy sponge and not much enthusiasm.

Logan, Steel, and the wee loon climbed out into the blistering sun.

'There.' Tufty plipped the locks. 'That wasn't so bad, was it?'

Steel hit him, then popped on her pilfered shades. 'You're an idiot. Mr Rumpole can drive better than you, and he's a *cat*.'

'Ow! *Saaaaaa-aaarge!*'

Logan pulled on his peaked cap. 'Can we at least *pretend* to be professionals for five minutes?' He jabbed a finger at Tufty. 'You: stay here. And take the bypass next time.' The finger poked in Steel's direction. 'You: stop hitting people.' That got him a scowl. 'Don't care. And when we're inside, you're on taking notes and asking follow-ups. No letching, trouble-making, or being a pain in my hoop – otherwise you can help Doreen with the budget-variance, soon as we get back to the factory, understand?'

She squared her shoulders. 'You remembering I used to be your *boss*, you jumped-up, trouser-faced, wee... Hoy, don't march off while I'm insulting you!'

The reception door *bweep-bwopp*ed as Logan stepped into NorrelTech-logo central. A huge, 3D version dominated one wall. Posters featuring it and various bits of equipment covered most of the other three, while what looked like an old exhibition-display-stand thing stood behind the reception desk, clarted in little NorrelTechs. Even the desk had a big logo on the front.

As if the owners were worried that visitors might forget what they came in for.

A middle-aged blonde woman with a faint horsey air was poised behind the desk, in a black suit, with a NorrelTech neck scarf. Which sort-of gave her the look of a flight attendant. Her name badge said 'MANDY' but her expression was more 'I DON'T GET PAID ENOUGH FOR THIS SHIT'. She forced a smile anyway. 'Can I help you?'

Logan removed his hat. 'Looking for a Nicholas Wilson.'

'Twice in two days? Are you going to arrest him this time?'

Hmmm… '*Should* I?'

The smile warmed a little. 'I'll let him know you're here. Please: take a seat.'

Captain Sleazy, of the Good Ship LustYacht, stood with his back to the room, one buttock perched on the boardroom table, looking out over the storage yard of the drilling services company opposite. Dressed in chinos, deck shoes, and a dark-blue Ralph Lauren shirt. Phone to his ear, head waggling as he talked. 'Yeah. … No, I was thinking of asking you to join me for a weekend's sailing. Pick up a couple of lobsters in Cromarty, and head out for champagne and sunbathing.' Too wrapped up in his call to notice that Mandy had opened the door and ushered Logan and Steel into the room.

Nick Wilson was either cripplingly insecure or in possession of a *towering* ego, because the whole boardroom was plastered with photos of him shaking hands with various local and national bigwigs. He'd even managed to cram in a TV star or six, though most of them barely qualified as D-list.

He threw his head back and laughed, as if he'd just heard the *funniest* joke in the *world*. 'Trust me, Jennifer, you haven't *lived* till you've skinnydipped off a six-berth yacht by moonlight. ... Uh-huh. ... Uh-huh...'

Mandy rapped her knuckles on the door frame, voice raised and sharp as a scythe. 'Nick? That's your *wife* on line one.'

Nick Wilson froze. Then gave a slightly more strangled version of the same laugh. 'What? ... No. No, just someone having a *joke*. You know what we're like at NorrelTech,' turning to glare at the receptionist, 'one big *happy* family...'

His eyes widened as he took in Logan and Steel's Police Scotland uniforms. 'Look, I gotta go, Jennifer. Speak soon, OK? OK. ... Bye.'

Mandy beamed at him. 'And these nice officers are here to see you. Again.' She checked her watch. 'Don't forget you've got Colin from Flarewell coming at ten.' Then swept from the room like a glorious malevolent monster.

Nick Wilson glared after her, but as soon as the door clicked shut, he was all smiles and handshakes. 'Sorry about Mandy, she can be a bit ... *feisty* at times. How can I help you guys?' Waving at the chairs. 'Sit, sit. Can I get you tea? Coffee? Of course I can, hold on.' He leaned over and poked at the starfish-shaped conference-phone in the middle of the table – ignoring the flashing red light. Which was probably 'line one'.

The starfish *bleep*ed.

'Yeah, Mandy? It's Nick in the boardroom – pot of Earl Grey, and a plate of the good biscuits, OK?' Clearly trying to exert his authority after she'd scuppered his chances of getting 'Jennifer' to shiver his timbers.

A sigh hissed out of the speaker. *'Could you not've—'*

'Cheers.' He hung up and rubbed his hands at Logan. 'So...?'

'You appear to have a very *active* social life, Mr Wilson.'

571

'If this is about those outstanding parking tickets, I've had words with the staff. Told them: "The company's not here to pick up your—"'

'Natasha Agapova.'

Nick Wilson bit his lip. Took a little breath. '*Natasha...?* Like I told your coughing colleague yesterday: doesn't ring a bell.' Smile. Shrug. 'Sorry.'

So much for Marky MacDonald's investigative skills.

'Really? Her name's been plastered over every newspaper in the country. On the TV. Radio?'

'Wish I could help you, but—'

'I know what might jog your memory: you sat next to her at the SME charity-auction ball, on Monday night.'

'Did I? ... I meet *so* many people at these things, it's hard to—'

'And then you called her home number using a burner phone – presumably so your wife doesn't find out – and left a message inviting Ms Agapova to a champagne picnic on your yacht.' Logan produced his own phone, holding it up. 'I can play you the call, if you like?'

'Ah...' Nick Wilson licked his lips. Then fiddled with the top button of his shirt. Keeping his eyes on the tabletop. 'You have to understand that Cindy and I have an *arrangement*. I mean, it's not an *open* marriage, but it... What she doesn't know can't hurt her.' He cleared his throat, then tried on that smile of his. 'And what's the point of having a yacht if you can't invite pretty women onboard for a bit of fun, right? It doesn't *mean* anything.'

Steel stared at him, voice flat. 'Oh, you think so, aye?'

Logan gave her a warning look, then turned back to Nick The Prick. 'Where were you, Monday night – *after* the ball. The truth.'

'I ... went home?' He held up his hands. 'Ask Dougie!

See, I knew there'd be drink involved. You know, you have to entertain clients, and no one likes a sober-sides tosser at these things. So I got Dougie to drive me there, wait, and drive me straight home after.'

Silence.

Nick Wilson fiddled with his shirt buttons again. 'Ask him! He's out back, washing the vans.'

Logan let the silence grow.

'OK, OK: maybe not *straight* home. We might've...' An ingratiating smile. 'I know this is going to sound a bit creepy-stalkery, but we followed Natasha's taxi for a bit. Not far! Just... I was, you know, thinking maybe she'd change her mind when she got my message. Ask me in for a nightcap.'

More silence.

'She didn't, all right? And I was tired. So Dougie dropped me off at home. The end.'

Logan didn't even blink.

'Ask him!'

'Oh, don't worry. *We will.*'

74

Logan pulled on his peaked cap and stepped through the door, into the rear car park.

A two-storey block of offices ran down one side, with a spiky fence on the other, to stop any of the NorrelTechies breaking into next-door's warehouse and stealing some logistics. Twin rows of parking bays faced off across the space between, full of company-liveried vans and hatchbacks.

The only vehicle that *wasn't* completely clarted in NorrelTech logos was a swish dark-red BMW i5 – currently getting the soapy-sponge treatment from a short, solid-looking man with close-cropped grey hair and an impressive white beard. Mid-sixties, maybe? The kind of guy who was probably a bit handy if things kicked off.

'Hello?' Logan strolled over there. 'You "Dougie"?'

The man turned, sponge squeezed in one oversized fist. 'I'm not paying anybugger's parking tickets.'

'Nice car.'

A snort. 'Electric bollocks.' He dunked the sponge and slapped a splosh of foam on the bonnet. 'What's wrong with a good old-fashioned petrol engine? The only thing battery power's good for is kids' toys and vibrators.' Washing away. 'And I'm *still* not paying these buggers' parking tickets.'

'You were Nicholas Wilson's driver, Monday night.'

Dougie curled his lip. 'Likes to play the big man. "Turn up

in a chauffeur-driven BMW and 'people' think you're some-body.'"

'He make you wear the hat?'

'Do I *look* like a prick?' Dunk, dunk, splosh. Wash, wash, wash. 'Got to ask: what kinda impression you making, rocking up to an oil-industry bash in an *electric* vehicle? Might as well piss on their shoes.'

A red-white-and-blue Super Puma howled overhead, making for the heliport.

'So, what happened Monday night?'

Dougie froze. 'I need a lawyer?'

'Don't know. *Do* you?'

He frowned. Then dunked his sponge again. 'I pick Nick up at half six in *this* abomination, drive him to the hotel. He tells me to wait for him; so I wait for him.' A grunt. 'Grown man and I'm running round playing nursemaid to a jumped-up...' The BMW's bonnet got an extra hard wash. 'Anyway: there's worse ways to spend a Monday night – few hours peace-and-quiet to read a book without the grandkids crawling all over us. He calls, about half eleven, says to pick him up. And I take him home, same as every other stupid industry dinner.' Dougie hurled his sponge into the bucket, sending a frothy tsunami splooshing out over the side. 'No big deal.'

'You missed a bit.'

Dougie squinted at the car, bending over to the left, then right – surveying the bonnet. 'Where?'

'Where you tailed a woman's taxi.'

'Ah.' He retrieved his sponge and started on the bumpers. 'I drive round from the car park, and there's Nick, sort of hiding behind a potted tree thing, watching the hotel entrance. Which we *all* know means he's on the sniff. Nick gets in the passenger seat, stinking of booze, and says "Follow that taxi!" like something off a Hitchcock film.' Dougie looked away, over the back fence at the fields beyond. 'So we do. Hanging back a couple of cars, just in case, but she doesn't spot us. They never do.' His mouth pinched, making the beard jut out. 'Don't get me wrong, it's not like he ever *does* anything – I wouldn't let him, even if he tried. We just park up outside and watch the house for a bit. Make sure they get home safe.'

Because that didn't sound sketchy *at all*.

Logan folded his arms. 'Safe?'

'Gets himself all hot and bothered, then goes home and gives *his* wife one for a change.'

'How long did you wait this time?'

Splosh, squeeze, scrub. 'Only a couple minutes. He'd had a bucket, and no way I'm cleaning vomit out of leather upholstery.'

Over in the next yard, someone clanged away at a metal pipe with a hammer.

An old ELO track oozed out through a warehouse window.

And Dougie still hadn't made eye contact.

Logan pointed at the BMW. 'Fancy electric car like this must have loads of sensors and cameras.'

'Like Jodrell Sodding Bank. Can't even *fart* without setting off a million dings, bleeps, and flashing lights.'

Excellent.

'Any chance we could take a look?'

LXXV

Sometimes it was OK to give up and just slip away.

Wave goodbye to the pain and the suffering and the struggle.

Like Nanna Carter, in her hospice bed.

Natasha blinked out at the filthy barn.

The air was heavy with flies, making the air *thrummmm* and *buzzzzzzzzzz*. Seemed to be more of them every time she opened her eyes – drawn to the all-you-can-eat buffet of blood. *Gorging.*

Not that DS Davis minded.

A big greasy bluebottle landed on his face, doing a little dance across the ragged scar on his cheek, then onto his top lip. Before disappearing up his nose. Looking for a way to get at those tasty internal organs; somewhere warm and dark to lay a million little eggs that would hatch in a couple of days and—

'Aaaaargh!' His eyes shot open. *'Fuck!'* His right leg jerked and trembled, but the left one – the one she'd turned into a colander with her rusty Stanley knife – stayed dead still.

Davis batted at his ghost-pale face with his right hand a couple of times. Coughing and spluttering. Then a tortured retching noise and he spat the bluebottle out.

It lay on its back in the wide scarlet lake, stuck there, legs twitching.

Davis's left arm hung limp at his side, but he used the right one to shove and swear and cough his way up, till he was half-sitting, half-slumped against the table saw. Breathing hard. Face screwed up in agony.

Good.

Natasha could barely work up a dry, whispery sneer. 'Why can't you just *die*?'

Took a while, but eventually his eyes opened again. 'You don't ... remember me ... do you.'

'Go fuck yourself.'

'Your sort never ... do. You dish out all ... all this *grief* and *hate* ... but ... but there's never any repercussions ... no consequences. ... So you just ... move on to ... next victim.'

She hauled in a deep breath and rasped it out. 'JUST DIE!'

Davis closed his eyes again.

Maybe the bastard had actually done what he'd been told?

But she wasn't that lucky.

He reached into his trouser pocket. 'I could ... save us.' Fumbling a cheap, knock-off iPhone free. He thumbed a button on the side and the screen lit up like Christmas.

The screen was smeared with blood, but he wiped it on the shoulder of his T-shirt and held it out.

Natasha's fingers quivered ... but her arms refused to move.

A smile twisted its way across the bastard's ruined face. 'Don't you ... want it?' Waggling the phone. 'They could save you. ... Not want ... to live?'

'Why are you like this?'

He nodded. 'I'll ... phone the police.'

'YOU ARE THE BLOODY POLICE!'

Squinting one eye shut, Davis poked his thumb against the screen three times. Then held the phone to his ear. 'Hello? ... Is that the police? ... I ... I need an ... an ambulance ... quick.' His voice getting fainter with every word. 'Quick, we're ... we're dying...' Then his arm went limp and his head fell forward.

Now, the only noises were the droning flies and the distant thunder of heavy metal.

'No! Tell them where we are!' The dry words burned through her throat: 'TELL THEM WHERE WE ARE!'

Legs – move your bastard legs.

Get over there.

Get that *fucking* phone.

Get—

Cramp rampaged down the back of her left leg, the muscles tightening like a corkscrew, pulling her foot up and her toes wide, flaying the nerves from her skin. Then her right leg, clamping her jaw shut; arching her back as the cramp rioted along her spine, torturing every muscle on the way.

A scream battered out between her clenched teeth.

Then it was gone, and her body slumped against the dust and rat-piss concrete again. Her head *thunk*ing off the barn floor, setting her ears ringing.

Then a dry sob wracked free.

'Tell them where we are...'

76

Tufty poked and clicked at the borrowed laptop, wheeling a finger round and around the trackpad. Like everything around here, the machine was *festooned* with NorrelTech logos.

A bunch of wires stuck out the side, snaking across the BMW's driver's seat and into a USB port.

Logan huffed out a breath. 'Are you *done* yet?'

'Almost there... Almost there...'

Been saying that for the last five minutes.

Logan turned and parked his bum against the van in the next bay.

And there was Nick Wilson: watching from an upstairs window, chewing away at the fingers on one hand. Probably worrying where all this was going. And how he could spin it so his wife wouldn't get everything in the divorce.

Yeah, good luck with that.

Logan's phone launched into 'Ode To Joy'. Might as well. Just hanging about here anyway. He checked the caller ID, then pressed the green button. 'Spudgun?'

'*Aye, Guv? Yeah, you wanted someone to have a chat with Graeme Anderson, our local Racist In Chief? Scummer says the Anglo Saxon Defence Group has just as much right to march on Saturday as the rest of them. Called me a fascist. Twice.*' A sniff. '*Which was a bit ironic, given his stance on the old democratic process. And invited me to bugger off out of it before he set his swanky-pants lawyers on me for harassment. Only he put it more politely, being a public schoolboy and all that wank.'*

'Think they're going to behave themselves?'

'At the protest?'

Silence.

'Spudgun?'

'Having myself a wee think, Guv. See, pricks like Anderson like to talk the talk, but they like others *to walk it. That way they can take credit if it all goes to plan, and denounce it if it doesn't. So I'm guessing no.'*

'You give him a friendly word to the wise?'

'That's when he threatened us with legal action. But yeah.'

'OK, thanks, Spudgun. Put the word out, though – anyone hears anything about the ASDG, I want to know about it, OK?'

'Guv.' And he was gone.

Logan put his phone away. 'Are you *still* at it?'

'Almost there...'Tufty's wee pink tongue popped out between his teeth as he poked and clicked some more. Then sat back on his haunches, firing finger-guns at the dashboard. *'Peeew! Peeew! And I has blowed up the Deathstar!'* He unplugged the USB cable and handed it back to Dougie. 'Thanks.' Shutting the laptop. 'I'll get this back to you soon as.'

Dougie shrugged. 'No skin off my cock. Not like I use the thing anyway.'

The back door swung open and out scrunched Steel, hat firmly wedged on her head, sipping from an overbranded NorrelTech mug.

She jerked her chin at Dougie. 'Does it no' roast your balls, working for a greasy wee shite like that?'

Logan winced. 'What... Don't! OK? Just...' He turned to Dougie. 'I apologise for my colleague. That was *unprofessional* and *uncalled for*. If you want to make a formal complaint—'

'Nah: she's right. Nick *is* a greasy wee shite. His wife's properly lovely, and there's him shagging his way round every slapper in Aberdeen. "Oooh, come see my yacht, come see my yacht..."' Dougie tossed the cable into the car. 'Getting too old to be running round after arseholes.'

'Aye.' Steel patted his arm. 'Me too.'

Logan's phone launched into 'Ode To Joy' as they headed back towards the pool car, and when he checked the caller ID, there was 'SPUDGUN' glowing away in the middle of the screen.

He poked the button. 'This better be good news.'

Could tell by the pitch of Spudgun's voice that it wasn't. *'Aye, Guv? All hands on deck: we've just had a call...'*

LXXVII

Maybe it *wasn't* too late?

Maybe it didn't matter that Davis hadn't told the police where they were, because the cops could track people's phones now, couldn't they? Triangulate where you're calling from, based on which phone towers the signal pinged off.

Shit, they were probably racing over here *right now*.

Wherever the hell 'here' was...

Course they were.

They were *coming* for her.

Because even though he was a twisted, murdering, violent, bastard – Detective Sergeant Davis was too fond of his miserable hide to die in this shitty barn.

All she had to do was wait.

They'd be here.

It was over.

She was getting out of this shitty hellhole.

...

Davis's eyes flickered open and a little smile tweaked the corner of his mouth. Then he thumbed a button on the side of his phone, making a pre-recorded voice swell out of the speaker, getting louder and louder.

'At the third stroke, the time, sponsored by Triple-Five Mobile, will be nine forty-eight and forty seconds.'

Beep. Beep. Beep.

'*At the third stroke, the time, sponsored by Triple-Five Mobile, will be nine forty-eight and fifty—*'

Davis smashed his phone down against the barn floor, snarling as he hammered it into the concrete:

Once. Twice. Three times. Four.

Until the screen shattered and bits of glass flew off to make ripples in the lake of blood. Followed by a half-dozen chunks of broken electronics.

Disturbed by the sudden violence, bluebottles leapt into the foetid air, performing a slow-motion waltz to the sounds of heavy metal.

Breathing in harsh, shallow gasps, Davis tossed what was left of his phone into the blood. Then his arm fell limp. 'No one's … coming … to save you. … We die here.' An almost-laugh trembled free: '"I turn my body … from the sun."'

Natasha glared at the bastard. 'WHAT THE *FUCK* IS WRONG WITH YOU?'

His voice faltered, getting fainter and fainter. '"For *hate's* sake … I spit my last breath … at…"' There was a hiss of leaking breath, then his head drooped forwards, mouth hanging open. Eyes too.

It took a couple of moments for the bluebottles to pluck up courage, but eventually one fat little bastard landed on Davis's tongue. Then another on his left pupil. And another. And another as the feeding began.

Leaving Natasha to die alone.

78

Aberdeen Royal Infirmary's Orthopaedic Trauma Unit should've been a place of peace and healing, a tranquil space to recover in after serious bone-shattering injury or the kind of violent surgery that still involved saws. Where conversations were held in hushed whispers as life-saving machinery went *ping* and *hissssss*. Instead, a torrent of yelling and howling and shouting and screaming and swearing overflowed into the corridor outside.

Logan shoved through the door, into chaos.

Half a dozen officers in the full uniform, complete with stabproof vests and high-vis, formed a wall outside one of the small, four-bed rooms that lined the ward's outer edges. Shuffling about. Looking as if they were all amped-up to *do* something ... but didn't quite know what.

An equal number of nurses bustled from room to room, doing their best to keep their patients calm and reassured. Which can't have been easy, given all the bellowing going on.

Another three were over by the nurses' station. One sitting on an office chair, with his head thrown back and the front of his scrubs awash with scarlet from a shattered nose, while his colleagues tried to staunch the bleeding.

Logan skidded to a halt on the polished hospital floor. 'What the hell's going on?'

A no-nonsense nurse in the white-trimmed dark-blue top of

a ward sister, stormed over, grey perm quivering as she jabbed a finger into Logan's chest. 'Are you in charge here? Because this is *not* acceptable!'

She ducked as a *crrrrrrrrrssssssshhhhhhhhhhh* of shattering glass turned the four-bed room's window into a mess of spider webs.

Inside, a large, *hairy* young man shook a ward chair at the broken glazing – like a lion tamer, holding the assembled officers at bay. Assuming they allowed half-shaved gorillas in blue jeans and denim jackets to join the circus as staff rather than exhibits.

What was it PC Kent called that look, a Torry Tuxedo?

. . .

Bloody hell, it *was* as well: the guy who'd been lurking outside the burnt-out hotel with a bunch of flowers and a mylar balloon. Darryl Something-Or-Other, whose dad was 'a man of strong opinions'.

Spudgun sidled over. 'We got the call twenty minutes ago, Guv. Your man,' pointing at Mr Hairy, 'shoved his way in here, wanged a member of staff,' pointing at the medical drama bleeding all over itself at the nursing station, 'marched in *there*, and barricaded the door before Security could arrive.'

'Then why are you not booting the door in?'

The Ward Sister poked Logan again. 'Because there are four *extremely* vulnerable patients inside, you idiot!'

God's sake...

'And has anyone actually tried *talking* to him?'

She threw her hands in the air. 'No, we didn't think of that. How very *silly* of us.'

'Won't talk to anyone but you, Guv.'

'*Me?*' Logan pulled his chin in. Violent nutters only ever asked for you by name when everything was about to go horribly wrong. But four vulnerable patients were four vulnerable patients. 'OK...?'

Deep breath and he parted the thin black-and-fluorescent-yellow line, walking forwards till he was just six feet from the shattered window. That would be far enough, wouldn't it? In case anything got hurled through the glass?

Inside, Hairy Darryl lowered the chair and blinked at him.

Logan faked a smile. 'Hey, Darryl. It *is* Darryl, isn't it?'

A nod.

'Right. From the hotel.' Looking around. 'This is all a bit of a mess. Why don't you come out so we can talk about whatever's bothering you?'

His voice was muffled by the glass, but clear enough: 'You were right.' Wiping his nose on his sleeve. 'It's what happens when bastards think it's OK to hate brown people, and Jews, and Muslims, and poofs, and Celtic supporters just cos of who they are, yeah? "You can commit atrocities," you said, "even kill kids."' Then Darryl looked over his shoulder, at the bed in the far corner. 'Not any more.'

Yeah... That didn't sound good.

Logan edged closer, and the names written up on the little whiteboard by the door came into focus: '1: ALBERT HAMILTON ~ 2: MORRIS PEARSON ~ 3: GEORGE MAIR [NBM] ~ 4: SPENCER FINDLATER'.

Sodding hell...

'Darryl?' To hell with flying glass. Logan stepped right up to the broken window, peering through the cracked webs. 'Darryl: what have you done?'

Spencer Findlater lay flat on his back, in the bed furthest from the door. There seemed to be a *lot* of bandages and fibreglass casts keeping his limbs together – so much of it that Spencer might even have looked a little comedic in other circumstances.

He had a pillow draped across his chest and his head tilted back at an unnatural angle. Mouth and eyes wide open.

Not moving.

Not even breathing.

One arm dangled over the edge of the bed, the hand weirdly reminiscent of Adam's – reaching for God on the Sistine Chapel's ceiling. Only, as Spencer was reaching *downward*, probably safe to assume that his appointment was with a slightly more … *subterranean* deity.

It was Sergeant Jeff Downie on the custody desk today, with his hooded eyes and ghostly glow. A man who clearly came from a long line of people who believed in never marrying a stranger when a first cousin would do. Or a sibling.

Word was he had webbed feet and double the usual number of toes.

Logan hung back, by the wall, as a couple of burly PCs led Darryl Merickson away to his cell. Quiet as a headstone. As if he was finally at peace with himself.

Tufty signed Downie's clipboard, acknowledging deposit, then wandered over, hands tucked into the armholes of his stabproof. A frown on his daft wee face 'Not entirely certain how to feel about that one. I mean, we *think* Spencer Findlater maybe helped burn the hotel down, which makes him a horrible, racist, killing-innocent-people person, plus there's all the breaking-in and nicking things, but did he *deserve* what he got?' Making a seesaw gesture with one hand.

'Murder's murder.' Logan made for the stairwell. 'Doesn't matter what your motivation is, or what the victim's done. It's *still* murder.'

'True.' Skipping after him. 'We can has tenses, now?'

'Somehow, I'm not in a celebratory mood.'

The wee lad drooped.

Suppose all this horror wasn't really his fault.

Tufty wasn't the one who'd given Darryl Merickson the excuse he needed to kill someone.

No, *that* was all on Logan.

'Yeah, OK. Off you go.'

'Woot!' The wee loon scampered away, through the doors and up the stairs, like Cthulhu hearing Tara sing.

Logan let a heavy sigh slump out into the custody suite, then tromped after him.

The incident room for Operation 'Find Natasha Agapova' had grown a thick lining of file boxes – piled almost head-high, all bearing varying thicknesses of dust. Towers of paperwork were heaped up against it, along with stacks and stacks of old newspapers. As if Steel and her team had decided to try the hoarding lifestyle.

No idea where the rest of them had got to, but she was the only one here. With her feet up on the desk. Schlurping away at her newly acquired NorrelTech mug, chomping on a bacon roll while she perused an old copy of the *Scottish Daily Post*. Peaked cap still rammed on tight enough to curl the tops of her ears over.

Completely oblivious to the fact Logan had just walked into her grubby lair.

He knocked on the table. '"This what they call working now, is it?"'

She didn't look up. 'Aye.'

Why did he even bother?

Logan had a quick squint at the whiteboards, with their coating of scribbled actions and arrows and photos and notes. 'Have your baboons found anything useful?'

Munch, munch, munch. 'The *reason* I'm reading this right-wing crap-wank, is it's all connected. You think Spencer Findlater and Charles MacGarioch burned that hotel full of migrants for a giggle? Sod-all happens in a vacuum.' Poking the paper. 'These bastards spend their lives shoving hate-and-fear-mongering bollocks down everyone's throats: migrants are stealing your *jobs*, migrants are raping your *women*, migrants are grooming your *kids*. Eating the dogs and the cats of the people who live here...' Slurp. 'And when morons like Spencer Findlater and Charles MacGarioch decide to do something about it, the tabloids clutch their pearls and it's all "violent mobs don't represent British values!" Then they go *right* back to mongering the same shite all over again.'

'She said, cynically.' Logan pointed at the board. 'What about our organised-crime angle? Get anything out of SOCT?'

'Oh aye. Had to do a bit of wheedling, but seems our boy Adrian Shearsmith's been dangling his hook in a *dirty* pond full of Russian sharks. And you know what *nice* people they are.'

Logan lifted the top off a file box – more *Scottish Daily Post*s: 'CIVIL SERVANTS BLOCKING BREXIT BENEFITS', 'MIGRANT INVASION OVERWHELMING NHS', 'EU PLOT TO FLOOD OUR BORDERS WITH MIGRANT CHAOS'.

Lovely.

He put the lid back on. 'So maybe these Russian mobsters kidnapped his ex-wife for a bit of leverage?'

That got a laugh. 'You kidding? Wasn't what you'd call an amicable divorce. Unless your idea of "amicable" is a cage-fight with rusty chainsaws.'

Logan tried another box, flipping through the newspapers inside. All the headlines were much the same: 'Migrants, paedos, crime, crime, murder, migrants, migrants, rape, lefty judges, paedos, migrants, blame the EU, murder, ECHR, migrants, drugs, paedos...' He puffed out his cheeks. 'Why do people read this crap? Is the world not bad enough without some knuckle-dragging "journalist" tit *making-up* stuff to be scared of?'

He tossed the last paper back in the box.

This time the *Scottish Daily Post* had plastered its front page with: 'PAEDO PETER THE SUPPLY TEACHER' above a photo of a youngish bloke in an anorak and glasses – eyes wide, mouth pinched – caught by surprise outside what looked like school gates, with the subheading 'SICKO WORMS HIS WAY INTO CITY SCHOOLS TO BE WITH GIRLS AS YOUNG AS 5'.

Yes, well ... maybe the outrage wasn't *entirely* fabricated.

He parked his bum against the table.

Sighed at the ceiling tiles.

Steel looked up from her paper. 'Do us a favour and sod off somewhere else, eh? You're putting me off my butty.'

He flipped back a copy: 'AULD REEKIE RAPIST IS "FAMILY PRIEST"'. Frowned at the photograph: an avuncular bloke in a dog-collar and cassock, christening someone's baby. 'Wonder how many people she's outed over the years? Agapova. All the sex offenders, politicians, and conmen...'

'Then give her a medal, OK? Just do it somewhere else.'

'Hard to feel sorry for them.' Back to 'Paedo Peter' with his haunted look.

What was it that art teacher at Lizz's new school said about having a painting in the Royal Academy? Something about not everyone enjoying their fifteen minutes of fame?

Hmmm...

Logan pulled out his phone and called Tufty.

The wee sod was doing his pretend old-man voice again, only muffled around a mouthful of something. *'I say, Holmes, is the game afoot? Only, the darndest thing: I've been waylaid by a custard slice!'*

'Got a complicated IT one for you.'

'*Worry not: I have my trusty service revolver and a cup of tea with me. You know, this puts me in mind of the rather* strange *case of—*'

'Just shut up and listen. Is there any way to find out who's been dragged through the mud during Natasha Agapova's time editing the *Scottish Daily Post* and the *Aberdeen Examiner*?'

Silence.

Not even chewing.

He checked the screen, but the call was still connected.

'Tufty?'

'*You're making with the jokey-ha-ha, right?*' Then a groan. '*It'd take* years, *Sarge. We'd have to go through hundreds and hundreds and hundreds of issues, with dozens and dozens of stories in every one. And most of it won't be online, either. You're talking about going to the newspapers' archives and manually searching everything on microfiche! … Years!*'

'Fat lot of use you are.' He gazed up at the tiles again. 'How you getting on with the footage from Nicholas Wilson's BMW?'

'*I is processing as we speak – looking-up every number plate of every car the cameras has recorded, then am running PNC checks on the registered keepers and named drivers, cos I does has a thorough and do specialise in being a* thin *lot of use!*'

'Keep at it.' Logan hung up, then sagged. Then did a three-sixty. Then sagged again.

Steel ignored him – munching away at her butty, when she *should've* been asking what was wrong, offering support and helpful suggestions. Maybe a cup of tea…

He pointed. 'It's rude to wear your hat at the dinner table.'

Chomp, masticate, chew. She put on a robot voice: 'I'm sorry, Roberta isn't in at the moment, please bugger off after the bleep.' Deep breath. '*Bleeeeeeeeeeeeeeeeeeeeeeeeeeeeeeeeeeeeeeeee eeep!*'

At which point, Logan's phone burst into 'Space Oddity'.

Maybe the wee loon had found something?

He hit the green button. 'That was quick.'

Tufty whispered out of the speaker. '*Sarge! I does has an visitor of extreme angriness, who is demanding to speak to the manager! Exclamation mark!*'

Great, *more* work.

Logan had his third and final sag. 'I'll be right there.'

Logan barged into the open-plan office, and there was Detective Inspector Beardy Beattie huffing-and-puffing I'll-blow-your-cubicle-right-downing. Tubby and bearded, his hair was vanishing from the back, as if it'd taken up holy orders and not informed the rest of his head yet. His black Police Scotland T-shirt looked on the verge of splitting its seams, while his belt must've been cutting off circulation north of the border, because his face was turning puce. 'Have you got *any* idea what sort of problem this causes? Well? Answer me, *Constable*!'

Tufty was squirreled back in his chair, looking storm-blown. 'Eeeek...' He looked up and waved. 'Sarge! Sarge: Detective Inspector Beattie thinks—'

'I don't *think*, I *know*!' He glowered over his shoulder at Logan. 'This *creature* claims he's following your orders.'

'Is there a problem?'

The shade of puce darkened. 'Is there a *problem*? Is there a *problem*?' A trembling finger pointed at Tufty. 'He's been running non-stop PNC searches for hours!'

'Well, not *hours*, hours, Sarge. Only since we got back from NorrelTech with the footage?' The wee loon frowned. 'Well, after that thing at the *hospital*. And got we Darryl Merickson squared away. And then I went and got a custard slice for my tenses, but I ate it at my desk being all industrious and multi-tasky. But since then.'

Logan checked his watch. 'So, about fifty-minutes-ish. How many PNC searches can one little PC do in fifty minutes?'

'Four hundred and thirty-seven.'

Beattie stared at him. 'Four hundred and *what*?'

Wow.

Yeah, Beardy Beattie might be a dick, but maybe he had a point this time.

Tufty bounced in his seat. 'See, I ran the footage through an ANPR system and wrote a script to fling the output through…' His mouth clamped shut under Beattie's withering glare. 'Erm… Because of *operational* reasons.' He turned his computer screen to face them, showing off a spreadsheet. 'Everyone's sorted by their line entry from the Police National Computer. But I can re-order it by name, make, registration, or timestamp if you like?'

'It's incomprehensible!' Beattie thumped the cubicle wall. 'Bringing the whole system to its knees!'

'Did you at least *find* something?'

'Mostly parking tickets and speeding offences.' The wee loon clicked about with his mouse and the spreadsheet re-arranged itself into a different order. 'Two with outstanding warrants – one assault, and one not-showing-up-to-court-on-an-indecent-exposure charge. Nine domestic violence. And three sex offenders. Well, two really, cos one was found not guilty.'

'OK: who were they?'

'No, no, no.' Beattie wagged a finger. 'We're losing sight of the *actual* issue here: you can't bombard the Police *National* Computer with rubbish for fun. You have to have "reasonable grounds"! Tulliallan will do their nut; Gartcosh have already been on the phone!'

Logan pointed at the spreadsheet. 'The other two?'

'White Ford Transit: six years for raping his eighty-two-year-old neighbour. Green Honda Civic: interfered with young boys at a juniors' football club. Eight years.'

Just when you thought your faith in humanity couldn't get any lower. 'Order it by timestamp. What's clustered around midnight, when the taxi dropped Natasha Agapova off?'

Beattie stood there quivering, while Tufty poked and clicked. '*Hello?* I'm not yesterday's skirlie here: I want to make a complaint!'

'Closest is the taxi what did take her home. Next up is ...' the wee loon squinted at the screen, 'a grey Vauxhall Astra, but that's our "not guilty".' Click. Scroll. 'One Mr Keith Braithwaite; has a croft round about Durris.'

'Am I talking to myself, here?'

Logan leaned in. 'Not guilty of what?'

'I think it's *highly* unprofessional to be so *disrespectful* when a fellow senior officer is making a complaint.' Beattie stuck his hairy chin out, setting his jowls wobbling. 'Don't think I won't report this to Professional Standards, because I will!' An imperious sniff, and he stomped away. No doubt off clyping to the rubber heelers, like the massive dick he was.

The wee loon opened a new window on his screen, skimming the details with a finger. '*Allegedly*, Mr Braithwaite impersonated a police officer to coerce women to have sex with him. Looks like he mostly preyed on prostitutes and drug users. Only he didn't, because of "not guilty". Allegedly.'

Interesting.

Wonder if *he'd* had his Andy-Warhol-allotted fifteen minutes?

'Search for "Keith Braithwaite" and "the *Scottish Daily Post*".'

Fingers flew across the keyboard. 'Clickity, click, click, pong, aaaaaaannnnd enter.' The screen filled. 'Ooooh... We has a results.' He opened the top link and a newspaper front page appeared, from four years ago: 'FAKE COP PERVERT IS CHARITY SCUMBAG' above the photo of an unremarkable guy in his early forties.

Brown hair, two eyes, two ears...

And that was about all you could say about him.

Pretty much the perfect face for undercover work: bland and forgettable.

Not for his victims though, going by the subheading: 'CHARITY BOSS FORCES VULNERABLE WOMEN TO PERFORM DEPRAVED SEX ACTS'.

Logan thumped a hand down on Tufty's shoulder. 'Print it, then grab a car. We're going to pay Mr Braithwaite a visit.'

79

The pool car pootled along a winding back road in the middle of nowhere, where gorse burned hot-yellow along the sagging drystane dykes and miserable sheep hobbled over sun-baked fields. Definitely the sort of road that you suddenly met tractors coming the other way on. Big ones. That wouldn't even notice if they drove straight over a manky old Vauxhall, squashing it flat.

Which probably explained why Tufty wasn't pelting it, with the blues-and-twos going.

Steel lounged in the back seat, making rancid-fish faces and long-suffering sighs. Still wearing that sodding hat. 'I'm *bored*.'

Logan gave her a Paddingtoning in the rear-view mirror. 'No one asked you to come.'

'Yeah, but Beardy Beattie was being a pain in the patoot, and I'm too Zen to deal with his … plop.' Putting on a terrible Beattie impersonation for: '"Oh, they're all so *mean* to me!", "That Logan McRae's got *ideas* above his *station*!", "*Constable Quirrel* is a useless, impertinent, syntax-mangling, dollop of shite!"'

Tufty joined the Rear-Mirror Frowning Club. 'Hey!' Eyes back on the twisting road. 'Also: pound in the swear jar.'

'Doesn't count if it's a direct quote.'

Actually, once you got past the heat-stroke sheep and

parched fields it was really pretty out here, with plenty of trees and the bracken unfurling in the sunshine.

A teeny clot of seventies bungalows drifted by, complete with sagging sheds and an elderly woman in dungarees grimly chopping firewood for the winter.

Logan went back to his printed-out front page. 'Pfff... Listen to this: "The sign on the door says, 'Wendy's Happy Wishes, Because Every Child Deserves Joy' but twisted charity boss, Keith Braithwaite," brackets, forty-one, "had wishes far darker than any child dying of leukaemia could ever imagine." Talk about melodramatic, sensationalist, *wanky* writing. "The unassuming businessman led a double life – raising money to grant the wishes of suffering children by day, and prowling Glasgow's seedier streets for prostitutes and drug addicts to abuse by night..." Who wrote this?'

He had a wee squint at the byline: 'LEROY McGUIRE'.

Bet the Pulitzer committee kept *his* number on speed dial.

Tufty turned a corner and the trees faded back from the road, replaced by fields awash with clumps of hard green reeds. The buckled remains of a ring feeder lay off to the right, like the ribcage of some huge parasite that had died crawling out of the docken and brambles.

Back to the printout:

'"Braithwaite forged a warrant card for himself, with the fictional name, 'Detective Sergeant Alexander Nairn', which he used to lure women into his battered Ford Focus, where he forced them to perform *lewd* sex acts in exchange for not 'arresting' them."'

'Saaaa-arge?' Tufty scrunched up one side of his face. 'If he was found *not guilty*, how come he didn't sue them?'

Steel sniffed from the back. 'Wee spud's got a point. Some scummer talks poop about *me*, like that? I'm going home with every penny they've got. And their house. And having a big hairy mate of mine break both their frudging legs.'

True.

Off in the middle distance, the grubby fields were punctuated by a series of tumbledown cottages with missing roofs and vacant windows.

Mind you… 'Maybe he did? We've only got the one article, could've taken them for *millions*.'

'Here we is.' Tufty turned left, off the tarmacked road, onto a rough track peppered with potholes. A Mohican of grass ran down the middle and as the car rocked and rolled through the hollows its undercarriage scraped along the raised tufts. Making horrible grinding noises whenever it hit a patch of gravel.

Steel sat forward. 'What if your man decides he's no' wanting to cooperate? *Violently.*'

'Really?' Logan raised an eyebrow. 'Not like you to be all timid. Frightened of messing-up our new hairdo, are we? Can stay in the car, if you like?'

'You looking for a smack? I'm no' "timid", I'm nine weeks from retirement. That's when people in action films get shot, or blown up. Thrown off a train or a building.'

The road hooked around to the left, dropping down a short, steep hill. Gorse rose on either side of the car, tinder-box yellow and ready to ignite in the blazing sun – getting taller as the track dipped, till it towered far above the car's roof.

Tufty peered up at the jagged-green canyon walls. 'She does got a point, Sarge. People with X-weeks left till retirement is *always* dropping like flies.'

At the bottom of the hill the land opened up, revealing a higgledy-piggledy graveyard of rusty old farm equipment. Going by the grass and weeds growing around and up through it, this stuff hadn't moved in months. Maybe years.

Just past the mechanical cemetery, a five-bar metal gate blocked the track ahead.

The wee lad hopped out and scampered over to open it.

Steel poked Logan's shoulder. 'Aye, seriously though: should we no've landed mob-handed? This could go arse-shaped real quick; loads of these teuchter banjo-fuckers have gun licences, and I *don't* fancy a shotgun enema.'

'We'll be *fine*. Besides, we don't even know if this Braithwaite has anything to do with anything.'

'Oh, aye, it's just a *huge* coincidence his car was at Agapova's house the night she disappeared, given her newspaper ruined his life and everything.' Steel scowled as Tufty swung the gate open to *clangggg* against a fencepost. 'Pretty good motive for revenge.'

...

Actually: she had a point.

Tufty hopped back in behind the wheel, drove them through the gateway. Stopped. Scrambled out again, and closed the gate behind them – like a weil-brought-up loon fae the sticks.

'Yeah, you're probably right.' Logan turned in his seat. 'Want to wait for backup?'

Her eyebrows scrunched. 'Might as well take a *wee* look, while we're here. Just in case? Bugger might no' even be in.'

Now that they were Country-Code-compliant, Tufty returned – piloting the pool car past a twisted stand of trees and around another bend.

A small collection of farm buildings loomed ahead: two tumbledown old stone byres; a barn with concrete walls and a corrugated grey roof; and a static caravan in shades of diarrhoea-brown-and-disappointment-beige. A forest of weeds surrounded the place, engulfing piles of building materials, while an ancient JCB backhoe sat off to one side.

Logan knocked on the dashboard. 'OK, listen up: we're on shaky ground here. No one takes *any* risks; no one wanders off on their own – line of sight at all times; no one gets shot, stabbed, beaten-up, their brains bashed in, or killed in any way shape or form. Understood?'

Steel shook her head. 'Aye, remind me to give you a wee training session on motivational speaking, eh?'

Tufty parked the pool car next to a tired grey Vauxhall Astra, and they all climbed out into the stifling motionless air.

Muffled music thudded out of the caravan, heavy metal by the sound of it – the kind that was all screaming and howling and being very, very angry that Daddy didn't buy you a pony.

A pile of pallets lay partially collapsed against one of the outbuildings, woven through with nettles and bramble. The spare bucket for an excavator rusted away, next to a big pile of gravel.

'Aye, aye.' Steel hauled up her trousers and pulled on her stolen shades. 'Sounds like somebody's home.'

Tufty grabbed the Airwave handset mounted on his high-vis, pressing the button and talking towards his nipple. 'Alpha Charlie Eight to Control, we are in situ at Gorseburn Croft, near Durris. Be advised: looking for possible suspect in Natasha Agapova abduction.'

A tinny voice crackled out. *'Roger that, Alpha Charlie Eight.'*

He let go of the button and shrugged. 'Just in case...'

Logan followed a trampled path through the grass and weeds between one of the outbuildings and the barn, into a sort of courtyard.

Then stopped, both arms out, blocking the way for Steel and Tufty.

'What?'

'Shhh…!' He stuck a finger to his lips, then pointed at the trail of blood that spattered between the barn, the caravan, and the far building. Thick and dark. And a hell of a lot more than you'd get with a simple nosebleed.

OK.

Logan pointed at Tufty, then at the outbuilding. Then at Steel, and the caravan. Then at himself, and the barn. Then at both of his own eyes. Which surely everyone would understand?

Tufty nodded, and tiptoed along the side of the courtyard, making for his assigned target.

Good lad.

He peeked in through the ragged window hole. Then shot Logan a worried look, shaking his head and playing an invisible accordion. Whatever the hell that meant.

Steel picked her way across the quad, high-stepping over the trail of blood, to the caravan. Snapped on a pair of blue nitrile gloves and tried the door handle. Pulled a couple of times, before giving up and making a throat-cutting gesture with her thumb.

Locked.

Which left the barn.

The door was ajar, so Logan donned some gloves of his own and gave it a wee push…

Bloody hell.

Two figures lurked inside – one clothed, one half naked – along with a huge pool of blood.

'Call it in: we need the whole circus here, ASAP!'

He stepped over the threshold, into the cool gloom, *technically* compromising the crime scene. But until he checked whether either of them were alive, that was just too bad.

The air stank of butchers' shops and hot dust, full of fat greedy bluebottles that swirled and *buzzzzzzzzzzzz*ed.

Looked as if the bloke, sitting on the floor with his back to the table saw, was dead. What with being pale as a block of lard, sitting in a lake of blood, with a gash right down his face, another across his chest, and a screwdriver poking out of his guts.

Pretty certain he was the man from the *Scottish Daily Post*'s front page: Keith Braithwaite.

Logan squatted down next to him, careful not to step in the scarlet lake, and felt for a pulse anyway. Because there were rules about this kind of thing.

Surprisingly enough: nope.

He stepped around the blood pool, making for the other figure.

Jesus...

Her torso was a map of bruises, her left knee all swollen and red, but her face was awash with dried blood, and a thick line of scabs framing her battered features. Even with the broken nose, black eye, and split lip, Natasha Agapova was easily recognisable.

And she was in her underwear. Never a good sign in situations like this. *Especially* given what Braithwaite had been charged with.

Logan knelt and felt for a pulse. 'Please, please, please, please...' Something trembled beneath his fingertips. 'Ms Agapova? Natasha, can you hear me? It's the police...'

Nothing.

Not even a flicker.

But she was alive.

Barely.

Logan turned, and there were Steel and Tufty – hovering just outside, staring in at the gory tableau. Trying not to mess-up the crime scene any more than he already had. 'I NEED AN AMBULANCE NOW!'

And maybe, if they were lucky, she'd still be alive when it got here.

Today, the circus consisted of a grubby Scenes Transit van, four patrol cars, a handful of crime-scene marquees, and a black Mercedes.

No lions, tigers, or homemade elephants, but lots of hustle-bustle-rustle as techs hurried about in their white Tyvek suits. Taking samples and photographs and videos and fingerprints.

Steel settled back against the pool car, jerking her chin at the static caravan, where Chief Superintendent Pine was deep in conversation with one of the more senior Smurfs. 'You should invite Perky Pine on Sunday. Bet she'd love to sample my lesbian sausages.'

'Definitely not.' Giving her the side eye. 'And what *exactly* is in these "sausages" of yours, or don't I want to know?'

The grin he got in return wasn't exactly reassuring.

Urgh...

She patted him on the back. 'We did good today: rescued the damsel in distress, saved the day.'

'You did *see* the state of Keith Braithwaite, right? Our damsel turned him into a colander. She...' He stood up straight as Pine peeled off from her conversation and strode across the courtyard towards them. 'Here we go.'

Pine nodded. 'Logan, Roberta. I think we...' The rest of that sentence was drowned out as the Sky News chopper howled overhead. Circling the buildings, filming the action on the ground. 'Oh, in the name of God.' Screwing her face into a knot. 'Why do the TV news people get a *helicopter*, but we have to make do with begging Dundee for a drone operator? Who doesn't even turn up, because he's off on the sick!' She glowered at the aerial intrusion for a couple of breaths, then sighed. 'Just heard from ARI – they're trying to stabilise

Natasha Agapova now. Fingers crossed. Maybe.' She kicked the head off a dandelion, sending a puff of teeny-umbrella seeds twirling away into the air. 'What a mess...'

'Erm... *About* that.' Logan pointed at the second outbuilding, the one that didn't contain a puddle of blood, broken whisky bottle, and galvanised bin full of concrete. 'We think there might've been a second victim. And given there's a chunk of the field over there that's recently been dug over...?'

'Oh, that's just *great*.' Pine covered her face with both hands. 'Any other disasters you'd like to coil out on my to-do list?'

'SARGE?' Sounded like Tufty, hollering away some-where behind the barn. *'HELOOOOOOO?'* Getting louder. *'SARGE, SARGE, SARGE, SARGE, SARGE...'* He appeared around the corner. Gave Pine a wee wave. 'Oh, hi, Boss.' Then wiggled his phone at Logan. 'Finally got a signal.'

The thrumming of rotor blades grew again, as Sky News made another pass.

Two white-suited Smurfs emerged from the barn, carrying a blue plastic evidence crate between them.

High in a tree, a pair of magpies screeched defiance, until the helicopter backed off.

And everyone stared at Tufty.

Finally, Logan gave him a poke. *'And?'*

'Oh, yes, I *see*.' The wee twit checked his phone. 'You were bang-on the doodah – one Leroy McGuire, reported missing by his wife six weeks ago. Got an anonymous tip-off on a story, went to check it out, never came home. G Division looked into it, but...' He shrugged, making his stabproof rise up and his neck shrink into the hole. Like a high-vis tortoise.

Logan turned to Pine. 'McGuire was the journalist who broke the story about Keith Braithwaite, Boss. We figure Braithwaite maybe started his revenge tour with him.'

She dropped her hands and stared up into the wild blue

yonder. 'Given the way this week's gone, if we dig up the field and *do* find a body, it'll be someone else entirely.'

'On the plus side: you said, "find Natasha Agapova in time for the lunchtime news," right?'

Just a shame they didn't know if she'd survive or not...

80

Logan ambled through the custody suite with two wax-paper cups of coffee – raising one in salute to Sergeant Downie with his webbed-feet and cave-fish tan on the way past – heading for the cells.

Someone down the end was belting out showtunes, while someone else screamed at them to shut up, over and over and over and over...

Halfway down the line of heavy blue doors, Logan knocked, then lowered the hatch till the safety-screen revealed the interior of Charles MacGarioch's cell and:

'WARNING ~ ↑ HATCH UNSAFE, CLOSE FULLY ↑'

MacGarioch lay on his thin blue plastic mattress, gazing at the advert for Crimestoppers painted on the ceiling.

He sat up.

So, Logan slid the hatch all the way down to 'FULLY OPEN' and balanced one of his wax-paper cups on the little sill. Coffee: milk and three sugars, because apparently that's how MacGarioch liked it. Lukewarm, because Logan wasn't about to have a scalding beverage hurled in his face.

'It's OK, Charlie: you don't have to talk to me. Not without a lawyer. Brought you a coffee.'

MacGarioch unfolded himself from the mattress and slouched to the door. Tall enough that he was only visible from his neck to his chin through the hatch. He took the wax-paper cup and gave it a suspicious sniff.

'I thought you should know that Spencer Findlater died this morning. We notified Ralph Hay, and he's telling the rest of the group, but you're stuck in here, so…'

It took two goes to get the choked words out: 'Spence is *dead*?'

'It wasn't the car crash; they'd transferred him out of Intensive Care. Someone killed him. Took a pillow and just … smothered him.' Logan softened his voice, because even racist dickbags had feelings. 'If it helps, Spencer was on a suitcase-full of sedatives and painkillers, so they don't think he suffered. Probably didn't even know it was happening.'

'Shite…' There was a shaky breath, then MacGarioch *thunk*ed his head against the inside of the cell door. 'He was my mate. Known him since we were *six*.'

'Sorry.' Logan took a sip of canteen coffee – better than the stuff from the machine, but still not great. And at least his one was hot. 'Don't know if this makes things better or worse, but he's the guy who tipped us off about *you* burning the Balmain House Hotel. Told us where to find the petrol can with your fingerprints on it and everything.'

Thunk.

'I think he knew he'd be safe ratting you out, because you're far too loyal to ever break the Orphan Code. Even for someone who's screwing you over, as long as they're a "mate".'

Thunk.

'And *this* way you'd be out of the picture, so he could move in on your girlfriend. Keira said he was one of the "Thirsty Boys", always trying to get in her pants.'

This time the *thunk* was a little harder and came with a growl.

'Something to think about, anyway.' Logan went to close

the hatch, but stopped halfway. Opened it again. 'There's just one thing bugging me: in the car, after we arrested you at the circus – you said you only did it, because you "needed the money". What money?'

Song finished, the bloke in the other cell started in on a medley from *Oklahoma*.

MacGarioch cleared his throat – voice a little strangled, as if he was swallowing tears. 'Thanks … for the coffee.' Then turned and carried his half-cold drink back to his uncomfortable bed.

Logan clacked the hatch shut.

Some people just didn't want to help themselves…

The open-plan office was eerily silent for five past four on a Friday. The only inhabitants: Logan, two support staff, and a PC over by the printer – swearing at the machine between bouts of bowel-rattling coughs.

Logan sat back in his seat and frowned at the computer screen. Deleted his concluding sentences and tried again.

The events at Gorseburn Croft hadn't exactly been straightforward, and the top brass liked everything laid out nice and clearly with as few complications, 'howevers' and 'meanwhiles' as possible. Which made the report on rescuing Natasha Agapova this morning a *massive* pain in the hoop.

Tufty hop-skipped across the room, with a big smile on his pointy wee face and a manila folder tucked under his arm. Throwing in a salute as he clicked to attention in front of Logan's desk. 'World's Greatest Sidekick, reporting for duty, *sah*!' Then plonked his folder in the in-tray. 'I does has a finished.'

Yet another thing to read.

The wee loon made a big ta-daaaa gesture, then shrugged. 'Turns out our abductist – in inverted commas, "Davis" – did sue the *Scottish Daily Post* for every penny it does has. Only the judge told him to go poop in his hat, and awarded the paper costs and stuff.' A sniff. 'No wonder he was on a revenge.'

Logan cricked his neck to one side, making it pop and crackle like bubble-wrap. 'What a sodding day.'

'That's Friday the thirteenth for you.' He raised his eyebrows. 'Though not really, as it's just a case of confirmation bias. Cos people *expect* bad things to happen: they look out for the bad stuff and do go, "Oooh, this bad thingie must be because it's Friday the thirteenth!" But if the same bad something happened on a Tuesday the fourth, they'd be all like, "pooping heck…" and just get on with it.'

Logan had another bash at concluding his report and sent it off. Had a massive stretch, then an equally massive slump. 'Could sleep for a month.'

'Ah, yes, but we did solve the case and rescue Natasha Agapova.' Hoppity-skippity. 'That's successalicious, right?'

True.

Kind of.

If she survives…

He dumped the relevant forms in his out-tray, then reached for the next folder. Which had 'OPERATION FIREDRAKE "FOOD VAN TURF WAR"' printed across it in wonky Sharpie letters. 'Told Charles MacGarioch about his good mate Spence screwing him over. Still wouldn't talk.'

'And now the newspapers will hail us as heroes, and tell everyone how groovy and clever we are, and buy us a extra-nice hat what does say "Brave Clever Person!" on it. In sequins. With an exclamation mark.'

'Wouldn't even tell me how burning a migrant hotel was meant to be a cash earner. I mean, how do you make money doing *that*?'

'Hmmm...?' Tufty raised his eyebrows. 'Can't even make money *running* one, never mind burning it. Look at poor old Mr Murray.'

'Who?'

'Owns the hotel. I did see inside his house when I put him to bed, and he is *totally* skintsville. Looks like he did has to sell all his furniture and stuff.'

Time for more coffee, because if the paperwork for Operation 'Food Van Turf War' was even *half* as boring as the stuff on Operation 'Camper Vans Stolen To Order', he was going to need all the caffeine he could get.

Gathering up all his empty wax-paper coffee cups, Logan dumped them in the bin. Stood. And checked the clock – 16:07. 'Right: soon as the little hand hits five, we're out of here. Got Morning Prayers for this stupid protest at seven tomorrow, and it's going to be a complete...'

Hang on a minute.

He peered at the wee loon. 'This Murray guy's *broke*?'

'I think he kinda drunk the family fortune after his wife and kid died.'

Well, well, well...

'So, a man who's financially screwed, owns a hotel that suddenly catches fire?' Logan grabbed his peaked cap. 'How much do you want to bet there's a dirty-big insurance claim in the offing?' Marching for the door. 'Grab a pool car, we're going to pay "poor old Mr Murray" a house call.'

Logan gave the door three loud, hard knocks, then stepped back.

The dirty granite walls of Mr Murray's house had soaked up so much heat over the last week-and-a-bit that they blared it out like a radiator. Making things even worse as the punishing sun blistered down.

Sweat prickled across Logan's brow, an itch spreading across his shoulders as it clawed its way down to his bones.

Whatever idiot decided to make the Police Scotland uniform all-sodding-black needed a good kick in the unmentionables.

This must be how bread felt when Tara made toast...

Tufty took his cap off and used it to waft himself. But then he was in the full stabproof-and-high-vis getup, so probably on the verge of melting.

Logan tried again: *knock, knock, knock...* 'Don't suppose he's lying in there choking on his own vomit, do you?'

'Totally yes possibles. We should *totes* do a wellness check. Wink, wink.'

'Stop saying "wink, wink", you twit. The "wink, wink" is *implied.*' Looking up at the door lintel. 'Can you see a key?'

'Oh, I can do better than that.' Tufty whirled his hands around in circles, making wiggly finger gestures at the door; then a deep breath and, 'OPEN-SAYS-TUFTEEEEEE!' Like something off *Ali Baba and the Forty Thieves.*

The wee loon turned the handle and pushed.

Then stepped inside. 'Mr Murray? Are you OK?'

What?

Logan followed him into a manky monochrome hallway straight out of a Tim Burton film. 'How did you *do* that?'

'Wasn't locked.' A grin. 'See, a door is either *locked* or it *isn't,* one or the other, so I had a fifty-fifty chance it *wouldn't* be. Worth a punt to look cooltastic, wasn't it?'

Unbelievable.

'You're an idiot.' Logan cupped his hands either side of his mouth. 'MR MURRAY?'

Tufty copied him. 'THIS IS YOUR FOUR O'CLOCK WELLNESS CHECK! ARE YOU OK?' Then stuck his head into the living room. 'MR MUUUUUU-RRAY?'

Logan tried the door at the end of the hall, which opened

on a dusty, gloomy kitchen slowly disappearing under a sea of empty bottles. But no Mr Murray.

Time to search the rest of the house.

Ten minutes, and two floors later, they found him at the very top of the house.

'Mr Murray?' Tufty tiptoed into what looked like a small child's bedroom – still fully furnished and *clean*, unlike the rest of the place – complete with teddy bear and rocking horse. As if the kid was just late home from school. 'Mr Murray, are you OK?'

He was lying on the floor, curled up on the only bit of carpet in the whole building, sobbing quietly, with his face pressed against the tail end of a Mr Man duvet cover.

So not OK.

And from the look of things, he probably never would be again.

Logan stepped over the threshold, blinking as a fug of second-hand booze enveloped him. Sharp and stale and miserable. 'Come on, we'd better get you downstairs.'

Down in the horrible, bottle-filled kitchen, Logan propped Mr Murray up on a rickety kitchen chair, while Tufty went a-rummaging. Banging and clattering his way through the cupboards, looking for supplies to make coffee with.

'Mr Murray?' Logan gave the man's shoulder a squeeze; all friends together. 'Do you want to tell us about Spencer Findlater and Charles MacGarioch?'

He smacked his lips, releasing the stench of too much cheap wine on an empty stomach. 'I used have ... used have dreeeeeeeams, ... know? Dreams.' Waving a hand at the house that festered all around them. 'Not any ... not any more. ... All that's ... all that's *dead*, now. ... Dead, dead, dead.'

'Aha! Sarge: I does has a success.' Tufty clunked a jar of instant down on the worktop. 'Don't you worry, Mr Murray, we've got everything necessary for a good sobering-up cuppa! Except for milk. And sugar. And a clean mug. But other than *that*, we're great.'

'Mr Murray? Why don't we start with how you met Charles MacGarioch and Spencer Findlater?'

The man screwed one eye closed, the other watery and bloodshot as he peered up at Logan. 'S'not ... didn't...' A shudder. 'Wasn't my ... my fault.' Wobbling on his chair as the kettle boiled.

'You *sure* about that?'

'No...' His lips trembled, good eye shimmering as the tears welled up. 'No one was ... no one was meant ... to get *hurr-rrrrt.*' Rubbing at his stomach as the half-word, half-belch dissipated. 'See ... header tank. Header tank!'

'The leak.' The one PC Kent mentioned – the burst pipes that forced the families at the *front* of the hotel to move to the back.

Mr Murray put a finger to his lips. 'Shhhhhhh...! Was meant ... meant to flood all ... should'a ... *all* the bedrooms out. ... But got the pipes ... mixed-up and ... only front ones!' He grabbed the nearest bottle, swirling it in front of his face, as if trying to get the contents in focus. But it was empty, so he chucked it over his shoulder.

It bounced off the tatty wee fridge and smashed against the floor.

'Only *front* flooded. ... Wanted to ... wanted to cancel fire ... but forgot ... to *phone*! ... Forgot to phone.' Grabbing another bottle – empty. 'Too late.' He threw both hands in the air. 'Whoooooosh!'

Smash.

It took a bit of doing, but Logan kept his voice warm and

friendly. 'What made you think the insurance company would fall for it?'

'Ahaaaaa... Cos...' Mr Murray threw Tufty a shifty look, as if he might clype to the authorities. 'Cos everyone knows ... racist pricks ... *everywhere* these days. ... Far-right did it! ... Burning things. ... Thick as pigshit. ... Nazi wankers.' The finger came up to his lips again. 'Shhhhh...! Nobody ever ... will ever know!'

'Yes they sodding well will: on your feet.'

So, it wasn't racism after all.

It was good old-fashioned greed, coupled with incompetence.

Logan produced his handcuffs. 'Craig Murray, I am arresting you under section one of the Criminal Justice, Scotland, Act 2016...'

81

Logan stood on the sun-speckled lawn, arms spread wide as a cool breeze rippled across the back garden. Blessed relief from the relentless baking heat of the last week and a bit.

Birds sang Monteverdi in the treetops, and the moon sparkled like burnished gold, crowning an azure sky.

'*Duran Duran!*' Tara wandered out from the kitchen, carrying a pot of bubbling mince. 'We've got five of Duran Duran's greatest hits, but the song titles have all been scrambled into anagrams. And what *you* need to do is *un*scramble them.'

He bent his knees, and pushed off the green sward.

'"Firing Molls", "I Two Like Lava", "Owls By Id", "Ennui Foot Shaken", and "Eight Flunky Howler".'

Four feet up, Logan swooshed his arms back and his legs together, swimming the breaststroke, higher and higher.

'You get a five-second bonus if you can recite them all in alphabetical order, or ten seconds by date of release, or a whopping *twenty seconds* if you can do it by chart position.'

He soared over the back fence, turning as the sun began to—

A filthy bird flew straight into his mouth, dirty and brown and Logan spluttered, thrashing upright, coughing and gagging. 'Aaaaaaarrgh! What the...?'

616

Steel danced back a couple of steps, wiping a damp digit on her Police Scotland T-shirt. *Grinning.* 'Trust me: you *don't* want to know where this finger's been.' Still wearing her peaked cap.

'Gagh… You *revolting…*' Scrambling out of his chair, making dry spitting sounds, trying to get rid of the taste.

The Critical Care Unit's waiting room was much nicer than the other ones in Aberdeen Royal Infirmary. Probably because anyone stuck in here, killing time till a doctor turned up bearing news of their loved ones, was often about to have the worst day of their lives – and someone thought a bit of soft furnishings would cushion the blow.

So instead of the usual crappy plastic seats, there were half a dozen comfortable armchairs, two couches, assorted coffee tables, a decent-looking plastic pot plant, a water cooler, a vending machine, and a wall-mounted TV screen. Where some stupid quiz show droned away to itself:

'And remember, you can either use any seconds you win to reduce your teammates' sentences in Temporal Prison, *or bank them for extra time in the* Prize Vortex!'

Logan wiped a hand across his tongue. 'What is *wrong* with you?'

'I'm going to miss our happy little workplace interactions.'

'Bloody hell…' He filled a plastic cup with water from the cooler, swilling his mouth out as the gormless-looking bloke on the telly gawped up at the quiz board.

'Ermm… I think I'm gonna… Yeah, sorry guys: I'm going to bank it.'

'You hear about Eddy Dunn?' Steel thumped down into the nearest couch – feet up on a coffee table. 'Poor old sod drowned in that weir thing, out by the Auchmill Golf Course. Full of Special Brew and jellies. Aye, Eddy, no' the weir.'

'Shite… Only saw him yesterday.'

'He was *eight* the first time I arrested him.' She grabbed the TV remote. 'Banged-up his dad dozens of times, and his nan, and his grandad too.' Frowning. 'What chance did Eddy have?'

'*OK, John, it's time to beat The Time Vault! Let's—*'

Steel ponked the button and the quiz show disappeared, replaced by some cheesy drama:

'*Oh, Emily, it's* impossible. *The bridge is out and there's no way to get—*'

Another crappy quiz show:

'*...three more right answers and you can go for the accumulator round! So, for a blue triangle, what's—*'

Reality-TV thing:

'*But what Clive doesn't know is that Hannah's allergic to shell-fish—*'

And the wheel of mindless pap spun on...

Steel sniffed. 'Any news on Agapova?'

'You're disgusting.'

'And *you're* an idiot.' Pointing the finger she'd stuck in his mouth. 'What you doing here, when you should be back at the factory, doing a lap of honour for the cameras? Perky Pine's got the world's press lined up to celebrate us solving the case.'

He dumped his plastic cup in the recycling and sank into his armchair again. 'The preening-glory-hound stuff's never really been my strong suit.' Yawning and stretching. 'Besides, shift's over. This way I get to go *home*.'

'Aye? And how's that working out for you: sat here, waiting for news, like a big gype?'

'Same as it is for you.'

She pursed her lips, frowning as an eighties biopic turned into an American sitcom, then another crappy reality-TV thing, then an ancient film with long-dead stars in it... Her shoulders dipped a bit, followed by a sigh. 'Aye. I'm no' going to miss this bit of the job.' Ancient cop show, scripted reality show, American sitcom, reality show... 'Still: better than waiting in the mortuary! That formaldehyde-and-dead-people stink gets right in your crack.'

Onscreen, the wheel had come full circle. That quiz show must've finished, because an advert for some celebrity property show was playing now. Then the *BBC News* logo pulsed onto the telly like an angry haemorrhoid. Throbbing in time to a techno beat.

Steel hit mute.

A pug-faced newsreader appeared, doing her serious-look-to-camera as she delivered The Headlines, while an inset graphic showed a train crash somewhere down south.

Logan stretched out a bit. 'Can't believe you're *actually* retiring.'

The inset changed to an arson attack on a community library.

'Wee birdy tells me you got a result on the hotel fire?'

He groaned. 'Human beings are bloody awful.'

'Shock, horror. No. Please: say it ain't so.'

'I mean, I used to think people were basically OK, you know? They meant well. Now they're just ... getting stupider and nastier and more and more *selfish*. "Screw the rest of the world, long as *I* get what *I* want – right – sodding – *now!*"'

The fire got swapped for a greasy politician, no doubt caught doing greasy politician things in a greasy political way.

Logan grimaced at the screen. 'Craig Murray's going bankrupt, so he hits on the great idea of burning his hotel down, blaming racist tosspots, and claiming on the insurance. He bumps into Spencer Findlater down the local off-licence, they get chatting, and Spencer agrees to torch the place with a mate of his, for the princely sum of three hundred pounds.

And that's not *each*, that's between the two of them.' Logan's head fell back to stare at the ceiling tiles. 'That's what Soban Yūsuf's life was worth. One-fifty a piece. Jesus...'

Steel shook her head. 'Gotta love people.'

The inset changed to mass protests in some former Soviet country, not keen on the Kremlin wanking about with their elections.

She stuffed a bit of jollity into her voice. 'Can you imagine what my leaving do's going to be like? Booze and strippers *everywhere*.'

'Yeah, but after that it's just golf and gardening and taking the kids to various whatnots for the rest of your days. Sounds...'

Then an aerial shot of Gorseburn Croft filled the screen.

'Hold on.' Waving a hand at her. 'Turn it up, turn it up!'

Steel fiddled with the remote and the newsreader's voice swelled through the speakers:

'*...an isolated farmhouse, twelve miles from the city centre.*'

The picture jumped to the big conference room, where Chief Superintendent Pine and PC Sweeny shared the briefing table with a tanned, tailored, coiffured, middle-aged man. Sort of Indiana Jones meets Crocodile Dundee, in a *very* expensive suit. Adrian Shearsmith: Natasha Agapova's ex-husband.

Bet the chunky gold watch on his wrist cost more than Logan's house.

'Aye, you can tell by looking at him: the boy's an utter bawbag.'

Pine leaned into the nest of microphones. *'Thank you. I can confirm that following an extensive investigation, officers raided a croft in the Durris area and rescued Natasha Agapova at noon today. Ms Agapova was severely dehydrated and had sustained multiple injuries; she was rushed to Aberdeen Royal Infirmary in an Air Ambulance...'*

'*Hello?*' There was a knock at the waiting-room door. A baggy-eyed doctor in pale pink scrubs and purple Crocs slouched across the threshold, most of his face hidden behind an N95 mask. 'You here about Natasha?'

Steel hit mute again and stood, whipping her peaked cap off. Only instead of a carefully styled and curled coiffure, today's hairdo was a flattened mop of hingin' mince. She must've felt him staring. '*What?* I couldn't get it to sit right this morning, OK?'

Dr Pink checked his clipboard. 'The bruising and contusions are fairly superficial, but she's got three broken ribs, and her knee is – please excuse the complicated medical terminology – what our orthopaedic specialists like to call "buggered". If she pulls through, she'll probably want to have her nose reset at some point.' He clutched the clipboard to his chest, like a thin, flat teddy bear. 'The bigger problem is *dehydration*. Go without water for long enough and your body starts to, basically, steal moisture from your internal organs. Leading to kidney damage, multiple organ failure, *brain* damage, and ultimately: death.'

Logan cleared his throat. '"*If* she pulls through"…?'

'The next forty-eight hours will be *extremely* critical, but with a bit of luck?' Dr Pink stopped cuddling his clipboard. 'We're pushing fluids as hard as we can … however: it's going to be a long road. If she can make it to Monday, I'd say we're in with a fighting chance. It's—' A bleeping noise came from his pocket. He pulled out a pager, and squinted at the screen. 'Bugger-fudge. Sorry, got to go.'

And off he clomped, fast as his Crocs would carry him.

Logan slouched back to the seat and retrieved his hat.

On the TV, Pine shuffled her notes and sat down again.

Then Adrian Shearsmith, rose to his feet, pulled his chin up, buttoned his suit jacket, and launched into what looked like a *very* angry rant. Jabbing his finger at Chief Superintendent Pine while she sat there, stony-faced and immobile.

The cameras flashed and flickered as pain crawled its way across Sweeny's face.

And the feeding frenzy began…

— what choice do we have? —

82

The van radio miserabled away in the background, while Barrett and Lund played snap with risqué cards; Harmsworth squinted his way through a dogeared paperback: *PC Munro and the Candlemaker's Bane*; and Tufty tried, yet again, to balance a pen on his pointy nose.

> *'And all the pain that we both owned,*
> *The agony we saved and loaned,*
> *We built it up there, stone by stone,*
> *This grave, this house of burning bones...'*

Everyone was in stabproof vests and high-vis this time, even Logan and Steel – no riot gear though, because apparently that 'sent out the wrong message'.

Probably just as well, though, because the van was sweaty enough without adding in crash helmets, heavy leather gauntlets, and all that extra padding.

They'd parked between the 'ROAD AHEAD CLOSED' and 'ACCESS & EMERGENCY VEHICLES ONLY' signs on Union Terrace Gardens, with the Transit's nose pointing towards Union Street.

Every now and then, a march steward wandered by in their orange high-vis tabard, making sure everything was OK for the impending mob.

'Aye, hang on a minute,' Steel looked up from that morning's edition of the *Aberdeen Examiner* – 'NEWSPAPER TYCOON SLAMS "INCOMPETENT" POLICE AS PLUCKY NATASHA ON BRINK OF DEATH' above a photo of Adrian Shearsmith ranting away at last night's briefing – 'are *we* keeping an eye on the ASDA wanks, or is that Spudgun's idiots?'

'Snap!' Barrett clacked down a topless knave of spades. 'That's a quid in the swear jar.' Gathering up his winnings. 'And it's ASD*G*, the Anglo Saxon Defence "*Group*", not "Association".'

A nod from Lund. 'Well, you can see the supermarket would probably get a bit litigious if they went with "Association". That would be *begging* for a lawsuit. People wouldn't know if they'd popped in to buy a loaf of bread or commit hate crimes against minorities.'

'Oh aye?' Steel glowered at the rear-view mirror. 'One: the swear jar is officially suspended till Monday, and two: shut up. And *three*: are we watching the slithery bum-plukes or aren't we?'

Harmsworth turned the page. 'I heard they weren't coming.'

'Seriously?'

'Yeah, whatshisface, thingy: Graeme Anderson, he's off to the US; gladhanding it with a bunch of right-wing senators and techbros. Wants funding for a political wing.'

'Christ, that's *all* we need. More spunknuggets running for parliament.'

Logan checked the dashboard clock: twenty to nine. Time to make a move. 'All right, everyone, let's keep sharp!' Shoving the passenger door open. 'No hitting people with sticks. No fighting. No swearing. No doing *anything* that makes us look like unprofessional pricks. And especially not on sodding video!'

Steel folded her paper and dumped it on the dashboard. 'Owen: that means no picking your bum in front of the protestors. Let's leave *some* magic and romance, eh?' Drumming her hands on the steering wheel, bongo-style. 'Go, go, go!'

The side door rattled back and Tufty, Harmsworth, Lund, and Barrett piled out. Ready to rock.

Steel grinned across the van at Logan. 'You ready?'

'No. But that's never stopped me before.'

He climbed into the scorching morning sun and clunked the door shut behind him.

Off in the middle distance, the *shreeeep-shreeeep-shreeeep* of whistles and *rat-a-trum-trum* of approaching drums grew louder as the protest made its way along the west end of Union Street. Five, maybe ten minutes away?

'OK.' Logan straightened his peaked cap. 'Let's do this.'

After all, what choice did they have...?

Twenty Years of Logan & Co.

If you'd told me, way back in 2005, that I'd be sitting here, twenty years later, writing a wee note for the back of the fourteenth Logan book, I would've laughed in your face, stolen your hat, and pooped in your soup.

You see, when I finished *Cold Granite*, I had no idea it would be the start of a series. I was working full time in IT in those days, and as the owner of a knackered LaserJet, my dreams of publication entailed getting enough of an advance to buy a new printer. I never thought I'd be lucky enough to do this making-up-lies malarkey for a *living*. And yet...

I first had the idea for Logan McRae while walking up Union Street – halfway across the road between the Sofa Workshop and Starbucks – contemplating the usual format for crime novels. I've always loved them, ever since I was allowed to borrow books from the school library, and most of them followed the same formula: weirdo detective solves crimes while dragging a sidekick around to explain the plot to. The Hero Protagonist is quirky and odd, but the sidekick is usually a much more *normal* kind of person, because they represent us, the readers. The writer needs to show how ingenious H.P. is (and how clever *the writer* is), so the sidekick is there to go, 'By Jove, how the devil did you deduce that?' every time something 'thinky' happens.

But wouldn't it be fun, I thought as I narrowly avoided

being run over by a taxi, to do it the other way around? I'd make *my* detective a normal person, while the people he worked for would be the quirky weirdos. Basically, I would write a crime novel about a sidekick. Only this sidekick would be the one who solved all the crimes.

Oh, and the police officers would act like real people, not ROBOTS FOR JUSTICE. They'd have lives, and make fun of each other, and cock things up, and be jealous and silly and grumpy, and do their best to muddle through. You know, like real people.

Then there were the cops Logan would work for – DI Insch and DI Steel – an angel perched on one shoulder of his fighting suit, and a devil on the other. Though it was never *entirely* clear which was which. And sometimes they swapped.

The setting had to be Aberdeen, of course. At this point in the LongAgo, crime novels could only be written about Edinburgh, Glasgow, or wee Highland villages, by law. The Book Police would arrest you and steal all the vowels from your keyboard if you wrote about anywhere else. But Aberdeen was my hometown, I grew up there, and that made research far easier than setting it somewhere I couldn't walk or drive to in fifteen minutes.

A lot's changed in the past twenty years, both in Aberdeen and the books. It's been a strange old journey, but I'm glad you've been here to share it with me.

Here's to the next twenty...

Stuart MacBride

With Thanks

A book is like a small child (only not as sticky and far less likely to insert jammy slices of toast into your DVD player) in that it needs a village to raise it and teach it how to speak proper and do all that civilised malarkey, so it's ready to go out and face the world.

Here are the inhabitants of *my* village:

Lots of thanks go to my lovely publisher, Francesca Pathak, for putting up with all my nonsense, pernicketiness, and excessive hairiness, ably supported by her excellent sidekick, Emily Sumner. Melissa Bond worked on fixing all my mistakes, while Holly Sheldrake saw the book through production; Linda Joyce was my ever-constant proofreeder (yes, I did that on purpose, just to annoy her). James Annal came up with the lovely cover and art direction stuff; Laura Sherlock is my publicity wunderkind; while Jamie Forrest, Katie Roden, and Claire Bush have marketed up a storm, as have the digital team – Andy Joannou and Alex Hamnet. On the sales front I have been blessed with the superb talents of Christine Jones, Stuart Dwyer, Ellie Kyrke Smith, Richard Green, Gillian Mackay, Charlotte Cross, and Julia Finegan in the UK, with Leanne Williams taking care of international, while Gordon Kemp and Becca Souster do that digital thing. Becky Lloyd is my big noise in the Audio World. And, of course, my hat is off to the excellent Lucy Hale and Joanna Prior for welcoming to the Pan Macmillan family. There are bound to be people I've missed off this list, but even if you're not here, I still think you're lovely!

I *also* want to thank the magnificent Peter James for recommending Pan Macmillan when I was looking for a new home for Logan and the crew. He's a good egg is our Peter. As is m' good friend and colleague Allan Guthrie (né Buchan). Speaking of good eggs, here's a big *hurrah!* to my guide through the uncharted wilderness of Police Scotland (and genuine police hero): Inspector Bruce Crawford.

And, while I'm doling out the thanks, here's to the battalions of librarians and book*sellers* who fight the tide of ignorance and thickness that seems determined to swamp the world. And to you, the person reading this, for taking up arms alongside them!

I'll finish by bigging up Fiona, Gherkin, Onion, and Beetroot – who have helped-and-or-hindered to various degrees (though only one of them brings me tea and biscuits while answering obscure spelling-and-grammatical questions).

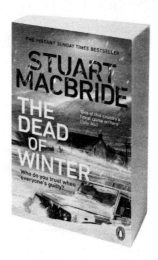

All Detective Constable Edward Reekie had to do was pick up a dying prisoner and deliver him somewhere to live out his last days in peace.

From the outside, Glenfarach looks like a quaint, snow-dusted village, nestled deep in the heart of Cairngorms National Park. But its streets are thick with security cameras and there's a strict nine o'clock curfew, because Glenfarach is the final sanctuary for ex-convicts who can't be safely released into the population.

Edward's new boss, DI Victoria Montgomery-Porter, insists they head back to Aberdeen before they get trapped by the approaching blizzard, but when an ex-cop-turned-gangster is found tortured to death in his bungalow, *someone* needs to take charge.

The weather's closing in, tensions are mounting, and time's running out – something nasty has come to Glenfarach, and Edward is standing right in its way ...

'Written in MacBride's familiar tongue-in-cheek style, it fizzes from every page' *Daily Mail*

'Not your usual crime story, this is a darkly funny Fawlty Towers' *Sun*

'It's a high-wire balancing act, but MacBride never falters' *Scotland on Sunday*

DISCOVER THE WORLD OF STUART MACBRIDE

THE LOGAN McRAE SERIES

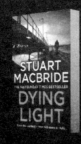

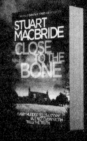

THE ASH HENDERSON NOVELS

STANDALONE THRILLERS

LOOD

both to

non sight now as lefty
constantly about
they try to stop our
rds from protect-
horeline from an
y young men
efs are alien to
ight-thinking

ed officials
ain is full
foreign
her
up a
e is i
n ima
is for h
meron
s owner
. 'I hea
hand too
ing. I
t I four
nt, Paul

Daily

ScottishDailyPost.co.uk

Smu

now filmi
Stornoway

EXCLUSIVE: Behind the scenes with Hamish and Bob

DEER-

Norrel Te
Wellhead Intervention

Nick Wilson Managing D
NorrelTech House
Howe Moss Ter.
Dyce   07700 900 916
Aberdeen 08081 570 388
AB21 1GL N.Wilson@NorrelTech

HEY YOU! **EXCLUSIVE**

We Join Glamorous Natasha Agapo
On A Beach Trip Like No Ot

The media mogul spills the be

juggling a full-on ca
being

• navigating a dif

• co

Ju
to
po
Na
con
Bug
its
corp
again
Sydne
gal's
teame

bein

tak

I LOVE MY LITTLE GIRL BROOKLYN MORE THAN LIFE

GROWING UP DOWN UNDER MEANS I NEVER SKIP SUNSCREEN

AEDO

gusting perve
g around child
l over Glasgow
USIVELY REV
were aware of
but failed to
op him offendin

ot watch every-
ay,' complained
o wanted to
us, 'there are
police on the
number of
register is
' Clearly this
ustice Minis-
ow can we
aedophiles
will?
e country
t we need

sa
th
mak
can.
taken
accept
seem t

commis-
six-part veg-based
cookery show from cheeky Kate,
called 'The Happy Vegan's Guide
to Meat-Free Meals', but are
now 'looking very carefully' at

A Daily Post EXCLUS

The owner of a High
land estate has slamme